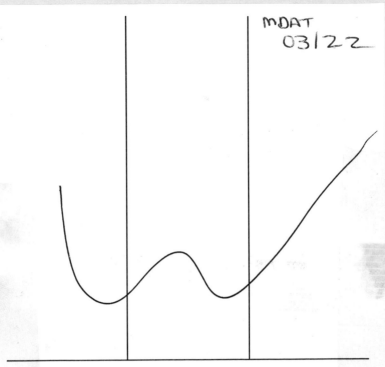

MDAT
03/22

Please return/renew this item by the last date shown. Books may also be renewed by phone or internet.

 www.rbwm.gov.uk/home/leisure-and-culture/libraries

☎ 01628 796969 (library hours)

☎ 0303 123 0035 (24 hours)

www.rbwm.gov.uk

Royal Borough
of Windsor &
Maidenhead

# THE WINTER HOUSE

## P.R. Black

An Aries Book

First published in the UK in 2021 by Head of Zeus Ltd
This paperback edition first published in the UK in 2022 by Head of Zeus Ltd,
part of Bloomsbury Publishing Plc

9 7 5 3 1 2 4 6 8

A CIP catalogue record for this book is available
from the British Library.

ISBN (PB): 9781801102803
ISBN (E): 9781800249370

Cover design © Lisa Brewster

Typeset by Siliconchips Services Ltd UK

Printed and bound in Great Britain by
CPI Group (UK) Ltd, Croydon cr0 4yy

Head of Zeus
5–8 Hardwick Street
London EC1R 4RG

WWW.HEADOFZEUS.COM

For Elaine

# Prologue

They had him – by the arms, the scruff of the neck, and the throat. Dan Grainger had nothing left – no fight, not even a token attempt, and he wheezed as his feet dragged along the front path towards the garden. Before them, the trees waved in the breeze, the branches striped through with the deep blue of a late summer night.

Cramond, the man who held him by the throat, said in a melodious Aberdonian accent: 'I'm a fair person, so I'd appreciate it if you just told me where it is, Dan.'

'Can't breathe,' Grainger croaked.

Cramond let go of his throat, but only a little; the other two on either side of Grainger tensed, taking his weight.

'Thanks,' Grainger said. 'Just wanted to say... you're a bastard. And your dad's a bastard.'

The man with the Scottish accent folded his arms. 'You're right. He was. And I am. That still hurts my feelings, though. I'd really like to hit you for it, Dan. Tell you what I can do, though. Let you look at the place, one last time.'

The two lumps on either side of Grainger turned his head to look at the house. Stolid, red-bricked, with the lights burning in the hallway through the open storm doors. With thick woodland on either side, this sight could have graced the cover of a gentle lifestyle magazine, and gave no hint at the rolling carnival of violence that had ensued earlier, in most of the rooms.

'Had a good look?' asked Cramond. He had a thin face with a cruel mouth, and long straw-coloured hair. From a distance, he might have looked young. 'Hope so. Because that's it. That's the last you'll see. Unless you do the decent thing.'

'You know I won't tell you where it is. Get it over with, Junior.'

Cramond chewed his lower lip, pensively. Then kicked Grainger right in the balls.

'I might have been telling fibs about not hitting you, Dan,' Cramond conceded, as he watched the old man sag. 'No hard feelings, eh? Look... To tell the truth... I *know* you're not going to tell me. So this is the end. You've been straight with me; I'll be straight with you.'

Grainger tried to swear. He only managed a trail of drool. He didn't have the energy to spit into the earth.

'I'll take you on a farewell tour of the place,' Cramond said. 'Some place, right enough. I can see why you picked this spot to go to ground. Imagine having your own woods! Wouldn't mind retiring here myself. In fact, I might even do it!'

He nodded towards the two other men. They dragged Grainger down the path towards the paddock. A long, low building abutted onto an enclosure and an empty field.

Torchlight stabbed through the windows; there was a suggestion of a face at the glass. Horses began to whinny inside.

'They sound nervous,' Cramond said. 'I reckon they're nervous. What do you boys say?'

'I'd say they're nervous,' one of the other two men said.

'Like they might bolt,' Cramond agreed.

Grainger was dragged towards the stables. He saw one horse through the open gate – a chestnut mare he'd insisted they call Molly – and its cries and the panicked dilation of its eyes almost broke him.

Then, when he smelled the petrol, he did break. 'Don't do that, Cramond. You don't have to do that.'

'I do. I'm going to take away what's most precious, before I top you. I just need you to see it and understand before you go.'

'How can you hurt a horse, son? How can you do it?'

'They eat them on the continent. It's like a good barbecue. Decent cut of pork. I wouldn't get sentimental.' Cramond nodded towards someone standing near the stables. The smell of petrol became too strong to bear. Grainger's head swam, and tears obscured his vision.

'It won't get you what you want,' the older man said.

'That depends on you, not me. Something you want to tell me?'

'I already told you. About you. And your father.'

'On that note,' Cramond said, putting a finger to his lips in mock contemplation, 'isn't it strange that when I said "the thing you value the most", you immediately thought about your horses?'

Someone else was dragged into the light. Grainger almost didn't recognise his son; they'd ruined him, criss-crossing his face with what looked like sabre cuts, and taken their time, with it.

'I'm sorry, Dad,' the boy whispered. 'I didn't tell them.'

'That's all right, son. You did well. You did the best you...'

A gunshot brought an end to it. Grainger's son sprawled on his back, his blood gouting and pooling, rich and dark, in the dust and gloom.

The old man mewled like a cat. They held him up – they had to. A hand gripped the white hair above the nape of his neck and held up his head. When he tried to close his eyes, another hand slapped him.

Cramond blew smoke from the barrel of his pistol. He actually touched the metal with his fingertip, recoiling as the heat stung him. 'I can even tell you what's going on the coroner's report,' he said. 'It's going to work out that you and number-one son had a bit of a row. He burned the stables, went a bit mad, blah blah. You'd fallen out recently. A well-known feud – now, that part is true. Some people might have trouble swallowing it. But I'll fix it, the exact same way you fixed it over the years. You're going to kill him... Sorry, you have killed him... with this gun. And then you're going to kill yourself. Your other boy... He's in the woods, decorating a tree. He came upon the scene; didn't stop it. So he despaired. And he did something desperate.'

There was no response from Grainger. Not even a reflection of torchlight in his eyes.

'So, let's crack on,' Cramond said. 'I'll give you something nice to focus on while we do it.'

He nodded towards the figure at the stable doors. The figure struck a match, then leapt back as the air ignited in between him and the stables. There was a rush, and searing white light. The horses screamed.

'Now, we'll just make an adjustment or two, here...'

Grainger fought, for all that. But his hands were prised open – he remembered doing the same with his boy, forty years ago, when he wouldn't let go of something when he was told – and the gun was placed in one hand, and then, as his strength failed, his elbow was bent, his jaw gripped and forced open, and then the warm muzzle burning his tongue and the roof of his mouth, the oily metal taste. He willed himself with every atom to jerk his arm clear and put the gun in the face of Cramond and obliterate it, and losing, and failing, failing, until...

'Lights out, Dan,' Cramond said, and Grainger's own finger tightened on the trigger, and then the white light flared one last time.

# I

Vonny Kouassi woke up slowly. The morning sunshine had stolen a yard or two on her through the skylight, revealing a bright but cold blue pool directly overhead. Vonny smiled at the vision, then instinctively turned to her left and cuddled into Seth.

It had grown cold during the night, but this never seemed to bother Seth, and he'd taken his pyjama top off. She clung to his huge ribcage, imagining the bones of a whale sunk into a beach, expanding and contracting in the sand. He barely stirred when she touched him. However, when the crows landed on the roof, claws scuttling across the bodywork in a shadow play of razor cuts, his eyes flew open.

'Hell is that?' he grunted. 'Pterodactyl, this time?'

'I would say a crow,' Vonny whispered, lips close to his skin.

'How do you know?'

'Quite heavy buggers. That isn't a sparrow. Plus, I saw one land on the skylight. Junior birdwatching badge, St Martha's Junior School. Never leaves you.'

'I just know pigeons,' he said. 'How do you know it's not a falcon or something?'

'Wrong time of year for them. Birds of prey can be quite

dainty. Unless it's, you know, a condor or a golden eagle or something.'

'Kind of thing that would carry a lamb?'

'Or a small child. Yeah.' She giggled at her own joke. Then the claws scuttled over the roof, again, as the bird took flight.

'Sounds like rats,' Seth said, finally. 'I know rats, too.'

'We all know those, darling.'

He sat up and stretched, struggling to fit his elbows in their cramped bed space. He was pale in the strained light of a winter sunrise, with a tuft of reddish hair on his chest, and in his sideburns and stubble, though the long hair on top of his head was black. He had bulked out as he began the long, slow descent into middle age, but had kept his hairline. 'I can't get used to this. My ma's old place in Peckham had a bigger bedroom than this.'

'Just as well it won't be a problem soon.' She watched him get up and kick off his pyjama bottoms.

'At least the water's warm. I like this mini-boiler.' He turned to his right; there was the white door that led to the shower. He pulled the compartment open, and a light blinked on, illuminating a stark white space capsule with a shower head attached. He turned the dial, letting the first few drips tickle his hands, an uncertain expression on his face. 'What there is of it. I guess I won't be too long.'

Vonny lay back on the bed, staring at the blue square of sky above. Not too long, now… That's what they'd said about this place last month, and last week, and even yesterday. Things moved slowly, though. Rubble could pile up, dust could fly, paint pots could be stacked like a child's blocks, but real-time work wasn't like a computer game.

A shadow passed over the top of the skylight, a bird moving too fast to make out in any detail – certainly not a crow, that one – and then, over the top of the shower, came the sound of voices.

'Seth?' she called out. 'What time were they due to arrive?'

'Not for another hour,' he said, through the spray.

'I think they may be keen, then. They're here now.'

'Oh, right.' He shut off the shower. 'Give me two minutes. I'll get dried and go talk to them.'

'I think I can handle it, darling.'

'Better watch. Didn't you say it was a new crew today, to take care of the snagging?'

'Yeah? So?'

'I spoke to the foreman yesterday. When you were out.' He sucked his teeth. 'Builders, pet. You know? Be careful.'

'I think your phone is going.'

Seth frowned, reaching for a towel. 'My phone, did you say? You sure?'

'Yeah. It's the 1970s – they want their attitudes back.'

He grinned. 'Just saying, darlin'. It's the real world, you know? Rough cases, on the building sites. Got to watch your step.'

'I've been managing the site, sweetheart,' she said. 'You know – over here, in the real world. While you were off twiddling knobs and flattering singers almost half your age.'

His only response – the only credible one open to him – was a snorted laugh.

Vonny pulled on her pyjamas, then tied her dressing gown with a savage tug. Her green wellies were beside his on the mat at the front door, a his 'n' hers set of thick rubber boots that struck her as particularly ludicrous. She slid her feet into them, shivering at the feeling of the material slithering up her shins. 'Well. Guess I'd better go and sort the rough cases out.'

She unsnibbed the door and pulled it open.

Seth watched her back as she trotted down the small set of steps outside the ship's cabin-sized door. She was slender and athletic, her daintiness rendering the giant green wellies doubly comical. For all that, she was sure-footed. He chuckled.

Vonny stepped outside the caravan, squinting at the irruption of light. As she came down a short incline into the yard, the frost underneath her feet crackled, but the weather was fine and clear. All around her were the trees, hemming in the entire site. Where the cars and vans had passed was still a little muddy, slashed through with puddles gleaming in the morning light. In the foreground was the house, or what would become the house all too soon. It was on two levels, but enormous. The plastic wrapping had been slashed off the windows just the week before, and she had marvelled at the immense glass features. The roof was flat but sloped, a design that Vonny had stolen from a church she had admired as a child, on the countless journeys to her grandmother's house. What would become the lawn was now something akin to the farmer's field, even down to the smell of soil and interrupted vegetation in the cut earth. The walls on the lower level were white, and, with its hidden garden area pointing south, the structure appeared cut into a diamond shape, a dagger held out towards Vonny as she stomped onto the path.

Still rough, still with lots to do, but now it looked like a house, not a work in progress. The scaffolding had gone; the structure was complete. It had gone from a basic timber frame, to flooring, to grey brickwork, loose wiring and bleached wooden floorboards to something that could almost be called a house, if not yet a home. Sometimes Vonny wrestled with the design, wondering if she should have gone for something simple and square, with brickwork the colour of a fresh-baked loaf. But there was something in the crucible of trees surrounding the house that lent itself well to the glass and whitewashed structure; the hard edges and jutting corners had a certain symmetry and congruity with the bare branches and spiky fingers of the forest.

This was it: a great big house, on the edge of a roughly circular woodland, with a stream running through it and a lake in the middle. On three sides of the property was farmland. The house was maybe two hundred yards away from a twisty A-road, the type you either absolutely loved to drive along, or utterly hated. The path took you through a sturdy set of gates towards the house, looping round to the front. Vonny had planned it all this way. The builders were applying the finishing touches.

There were three men on the site in hard hats, plus another on his phone in the portable cabin set up at the far corner of the site. They all caught sight of Vonny at roughly the same time. They all stopped what they were doing.

And they were all young – horrifically so. They looked like four kids dressed as builders for a Halloween party. Apart from one heavy-set lad with hamster's cheeks stuffed into his hard hat, they were lean and rangy, toolbelts threatening to drag their trousers down.

'Oh,' said the lad in the portable cabin door. He was thin, fresh-faced and utterly startled. In that instant, he reminded Vonny of her young brother being caught raiding the biscuit jar. 'Uh, Mrs, uh…'

'Kouassi. And it's not Mrs. And you can just call me Vonny.'

'Ah right, Vonny, you're Mr Miller's partner, is that right? Apologies if not.' The young man's face was the colour of venison. This happened, of course – had happened, would happen. She'd left Seth in charge of one or two details, to give her a bit of a break. This had been at his insistence, of course. And in calling the snagging crew to finalise their arrival time and other details, he'd somehow forgotten to properly explain the situation. *One job, Seth*, she thought. *One job*.

'I am Mr Miller's wife. In fact, I'm the owner of this site.' She grinned. 'But you're doing fine.'

He slid the mobile phone into his pocket; but the zip was closed, and the phone slithered off his overcoat and onto the well-trampled mud outside the cabin. He scrambled to pick it up, bent double, then jogged forward, wiping his hands on his trousers. 'I'm Devin Marshall, the project manager for the final stage. I think we may have spoken once or twice on the phone, in the early stages. I'm sorry the guys you've been working with couldn't continue – another job came up. I know it's probably not ideal…'

Vonny waved her hand. 'It happens. You're actually the fourth crew I've had out here.'

Devin took a deep breath. 'Anyway, I just want to say, we're so, so sorry.'

Vonny shook his hand, and cocked her head. 'Sorry for…?'

'Waking you up.' Devin glanced very quickly at her dressing gown and Dalmatian-patterned pyjamas, then looked away just as fast. This made Vonny self-conscious that she'd left something unbuttoned or unfastened, but a quick glance showed she was fine. 'We're a bit early,' he stammered. 'I want to make sure the plastering is finished today and we can start to make sure all the connections are clear.'

Vonny wanted to reassure him, but knew if she placed a hand on his shoulder he might take fright, like a colt. 'Early is fine, and getting it finished as close to schedule as possible is double fine. Carry on, we're all grand. Would you like a cup of tea?'

'Oh no, we've got our own tea in the cabin. In fact... shall we make one for you?'

'You're absolutely fine, lads. Carry on.'

'Well.' Devin sighed, hands on his hips. 'Going to be some place, this. Best project I've ever been sent out to.'

'How many have you worked on?' Vonny asked, trying not to smile.

'Three. This is my first big project. I'm totally qualified.'

'I should hope so,' she said, raising her eyebrows.

'I guess, maybe you were expecting, I don't know...'

'Expecting?'

'Someone older.' He swallowed.

'Not at all. You carry on, Devin. I like that you're early. Take care, now. I just came over to warn you – I have someone coming over to take a few pictures of the site, in about an hour's time. For the local paper – what is it, *Brenwood Green Advertiser*? You don't need to be in it, of course.'

'Ah – you selling up? Trying to drum up interest?'

'Absolutely not selling up. This is the dream house. The

forever house. I might drum up some interest in my work, though.' Vonny smiled. 'I won't keep you any longer. Crack on. Give me a shout if you need anything.'

As she turned away, she waited for the punchline – she didn't quite flatter herself that she might be wolf-whistled, but was braced for some sniggering or other foundation-course professional sexism. But nothing came; the four young men picked their way up the path towards the house.

Back in the caravan, Vonny kicked off her wellies and threw herself onto the bed. '"Rough cases," you said. "Watch yourself on building sites," you said. Maybe their dads were rough! Maybe even their grandfathers. Were you having me on? You'll be lucky if they're two years out of school, tops. You knew this, of course.'

Seth grinned, buckling his belt. 'I did know. They phoned me again while you were out exploring yesterday. The boy Devin sounded like he was still at school.'

'Then you were having me on,' she said, sighing.

'I was having you on, yeah. And it totally worked.'

'When they saw a woman, they almost had a heart attack.'

'No wolf whistles? Man, hard times these days when you can't even get that off builders.'

'No wolf whistles.' Vonny sat up, hands braced on the bedcovers. 'Not so much as a raised eyebrow or a smirk. They averted their eyes. I felt like the Pope. Should I be offended? Ask for a discount on the build?'

'I think there's a code of conduct, now. Or laws, or something. Plus, as you say, they're only twelve.'

'Not to be ageist... Are they old enough? They look like they should be playing with blocks, not building houses.'

'Matter of fact, that is quite ageist of you,' Seth said, archly. '"Devin's the best man for the job." That's a quote from the architect. Couldn't speak highly enough of him. Nice lad, too. Kind of lad you'd like your daughter to bring home, you know? And you wouldn't feel bad about bullying him.'

'You saying you want a daughter?'

Seth grinned – and didn't avoid the question, either. 'Why not? Anyway – who cares how old they are? They get the job done quickly, that's all we're worried about. It doesn't fall down, it's all gravy. Money in the bank.'

'So to speak,' Vonny said, eyes narrowing.

'So to speak,' he agreed. 'Anyway, I'm off.'

'You're leaving me here all alone with the wolf pack?'

'Yeah. Got a few things to pick up in town. Plus, I haven't checked out the market square yet. We have to get used to the life of the country squire, m'dear. After this afternoon, the glossy magazines beckon.'

'"Glossy magazines" may be stretching things a bit.'

'I know. The parish blatt is a start, though. We have to establish ourselves, if we're going to be a fixture. And, I've got ideas for the wardrobe department.'

'God help us,' she muttered.

'Relax, you'll love it. Got to look good for your story, pet.'

'Our story.'

'And that's official,' he agreed. 'And totally legally binding.'

'Don't push it, mister.' She kissed him, and watched him tiptoe towards his wellies.

## 2

She hadn't been inside for a few days. She couldn't help herself.

Vonny kicked off her boots at the front step of the house, then slid on the slippers she carried in her hand.

Devin smiled and opened the door. He carried his hard hat in his hand. Vonny felt like the landed gentry, meeting the peasants, and a treacherous part of her liked this.

'You ready?'

'Lead the way, Ms Kouassi.'

Over the threshold. She touched the dark green and gold sign bolted outside; The Glades, it said.

She stepped into a huge, clean white space. She worried about placing a foot on the floorboards, although they were already scuffed with boot marks from that morning.

'As you can see, there's so much light here,' Devin said. 'Really affecting this morning. The kitchen space is absolutely massive, and the skylight really adds to it, I think. The architect really knew what they were doing.'

'I hope so,' Vonny said. 'You're looking at her.'

He blushed, again, and Vonny regretted the remark. 'Oh, I'm so sorry – I was sure it was Beckett-Transom-Hardie.

That's the name on the designs... I consulted with them all the way through.'

'Yeah, they're in charge of the main plans, but the design is mine.'

'That your background? I feel so daft, I didn't know. Everyday sexism, right there.'

'Ach, no. You didn't know. Yes, my background's art and design. I've got the basics, and I knew how I wanted it to look. I'm not an architect, but it interests me. The architect did the hard numbers; I came up with the plan and the penwork.'

'Is it everything you hoped for?' Devin asked, mouth twitching. 'I've been looking in on this project since it arrived. It's quite famous in our offices up and down the country. Kind of place you dream about building. Well, you did actually dream about building it, I suppose.'

She touched him on the shoulder. 'Ah, don't worry, it's better than what I'd hoped. It's exactly what I imagined.' Vonny raised her hand, allowing the morning sunshine to bleed through the gaps in her fingers.

'Lot of rain the past few days, so the drainage system has been put through its paces. It's all working fine – the rainwater drains into the water butts... all tickety-boo. I think the water feature turned out well.'

This latter structure lay beneath the spiral staircase – dry for now. It had a geometrically precise, minimalist fountain, sets of blocks and crystals – organic, but ordered, something in the nature of the Giant's Causeway, black stone blocks shot through with silver strands. Seth had utterly hated this, from its very first charcoal sketch, but Vonny had been insistent. This was her dream; this was what she wanted. 'It's perfect.'

'Regarding snagging and stuff still to be finished – there's a few tweaks we need to make to the special room.' Devin cleared his throat. 'That's not complete yet.'

Vonny nodded absently. 'Not a priority, if it's the place I'm thinking of.'

'No, not a priority,' he said, almost embarrassed. 'But there is a possible issue with flooding. Where it connects to the garden. We'll need to make a couple of adjustments.'

Vonny nodded. 'Let's hope we don't need it between now and then.'

She had said this in jest, but it made Devin jumpy. 'And, eh, the electrician tells me he finished this just last night. Have you seen it yet?'

'I haven't had a chance to play with all the toys, yet, no.'

'Check it out!'

He touched a digital screen set into the wall. A light blue LCD display ignited. Vonny frowned. 'Oh yes. My husband's amendment.'

'It is pretty cool. Check this.' Devin tapped in some details onto the console underneath the blue LCD screen. Then he waved a hand in the air.

Debussy was everywhere, all at once – inside and out, in Vonny's ears, in her throat, in her very veins. *Clair de Lune.* Devin jabbered, trying to make himself heard over the incredible noise that burst from hidden speakers – unsuccessfully. He waved his arms like an inflatable in a football crowd. Eventually, the noise cut out.

'Movement activated, if you're under the sensor; like a theremin.'

Vonny's heart pounded. 'That's effective, I'll say that much for it.'

'Oh yeah. The electrician was really proud of it, state-of-the-art home sound system.'

'I remember my uncle's old ghetto blaster, and thinking it was the pinnacle of hi-fis. And I still think that.'

'Between that and the recording studio, this is state-of-the-art stuff.'

'I get the studio at the top; Seth gets the basement. The soundproofed basement,' she added, smiling. 'That was the deal.'

Vonny strode through the kitchen, and here, finally, was home. An immense space, stone-effect floor, granite tabletops and work surfaces, and a beautiful big table. Then there was the patio, and beyond that...

Vonny's eyes filled up. This was it. The dream house. Just as she'd imagined it. For something to say, in case Devin should notice, she said: 'All these appliances online?'

'Yep, it's all connected up. The plastering should be completed today. We've had the sparks in, the plumbers – you're all connected to the grid...'

'When can we sleep over?'

'Far as I'm concerned, I would say you can move in roughly a week. Maybe less.'

'I'm tempted... There's only so long you can sleep out in a tin can. I feel like baked beans. It's time to spoon me onto the toast.'

'You must be dying to move in. It's some project.'

'I think we might start falling in love with this,' she said, mostly to herself.

'Say again?' Devin blushed.

'I mean, this place. I think I've found it. This is my place.

I had an idea of what my dream house was like, and this is it. Did you ever think that? When you were a kid?'

'You could be talking about a big profit on this plot, I'll say that for nothing.'

Vonny shook her head. 'No, we'll not be making a profit. This is it. Us.'

'A forever house?'

'That's the idea.'

He nodded. 'I get that.'

'How about the pool? There was still some work to be done on that...?'

Devin pointed out towards the garden. Spanish style, slabbed over in places, with a nook where the potted plants would grow. The slabs were still glinting with frost, even with a sliver of low winter sunlight spilling over the back fence. In the middle, of course, was the cyan-tiled pool.

'According to the notes, it's all still to be tested out,' Devin said, 'and it's nowhere near ready to be filled yet... hardly the weather or the time of year, obviously.'

'Ah, you should have seen the communal pool I went to as a kid.' She peered out into the garden site. 'One thing I need to check out with you, right now.'

'Oh. What's that?'

'She with you?' Vonny pointed to a figure striding around the garden paving, hands behind its back, with the air of a colonel carrying out an inspection.

'Who? Oh... No. She's not with us, Vonny.'

Vonny frowned at Devin's sudden diffidence. 'Then would you mind telling me who the hell she is?'

# 3

Devin slid open the patio door and stepped aside. Vonny tugged the door wider still, feeling its weight, the lack of friction. It was perfectly calibrated – it took a little effort to push and pull the sliding door, and a child might find it difficult. But it was a solid mechanism, not the type to be borne away to smithereens on a gust of wind.

The woman in the garden was possibly in her late fifties but could have been a sprightly seventy. She was taller than Vonny, and in her Barbour jacket, olive trousers and green wellington boots she could have been dressed for a day's ride. She was slim and dapper, with a long, thick silver bob that reminded Vonny of a twitchy English teacher who'd made her afraid to speak up in class when she was twelve. This comparison did not help the situation, Vonny realised, as she slipped her own boots back on.

The woman didn't even take in Vonny's approach. She was poised in the centre of the rutted garden space where the roses were to be planted, one hand on her hip, the other pointing. One of the younger lads on Devin's team was lifting up some spare piping that had been allowed to sink in the soil. He was the picture of uncertainty; the newcomer was the polar opposite.

'And when you're done with that, I think you could clear off the garden debris around the edges. That has a habit of hanging around, I find.' The woman's accent was almost exactly as Vonny would have imagined it: a close match to that English teacher of long ago. The woman gave her no consideration as she approached.

'Excuse me?' Vonny said.

'Yes?'

'Can I ask you a couple of questions?'

The woman folded her arms and frowned. 'That depends, dear, on how polite they're going to be.'

'Can I ask... who you are, and what you think you're doing here?'

'I happen to live here, and I'm trying to stop these schoolboys from ruining the plot.'

Vonny spluttered in almost complete astonishment. 'That's weird, because I could have sworn my name was on the title deeds.'

'Ah!' The woman's eyes sprung open. 'Oh, I do beg your pardon. It's just that I saw you have a new crew on the site, and – no offence, young man – youth and inexperience do go hand in hand. I thought they needed some proper supervision. You can't leave inexperienced builders to their own devices, in my experience. They will cost you time and money – and no one has enough of that.'

'Mind telling me how you got in?'

'They let me in,' the woman said, almost incredulous. 'It's all perfectly in order. You needn't trouble yourself. Someone has to look in. You can't let them alone, you see. You have to be on your guard with builders. Keep a close watch. Even the best ones.'

'I think they've done a good enough job. I didn't catch your name, sorry?'

'It's Prill. Short for Priscilla. Prill Fulton. I don't think I've had the pleasure?'

'Vonny.' Vonny took her hand.

'Ronnie?' asked Prill.

'No, Vonny. With a V.'

'Oh, Vonny. That's short for something, I suppose?'

'Yvonne. I never liked it, and I don't think my parents did either, after a while. Always called me Vonny, as long as I can remember.'

'Well, charming, charming. And that accent! Is that a touch of Scots I can hear?'

'I don't think so, though people have told me that before. It's a bit of Irish, in fact. My mum's from Galway, so there's a little bit of the old country in my voice. Dad's from Ghana.'

'Ah, Irish. Well that's charming,' Prill said, in a tone that suggested anything but. 'You're such a young thing to be owning a house like this – and renovating it, too. You must work in the city?'

'No, I'm a graphic designer. Regarding the plot, you could say we got lucky.'

'Inheritance, eh?'

'Not exactly. Luckier than that.'

Prill's eyes sparkled. 'Lottery, then.'

'You could say that.'

'Ah, I knew it. You can tell about some people, you know – born lucky.'

'In actual fact, we won the plot on an auction; £25 stake – we were drawn out of the hat. There was a news article

I saw by complete chance one day. I had a look at the site, made sure it was legit, entered my name – and we won.'

'Auction?' She sounded amazed. 'I didn't hear about that. I'm sure Mainmont, down in the village square, would have told me about that!'

'I think it was done through online channels. Nothing in the local press from what I could see. There was an Instagram campaign. Sign of the times, I suppose. Not exactly hush-hush, just done quickly.'

'Well... hush-hush, that's the phrase. That'd be par for the course for Dan Grainger's family. He was the owner, you know. The man who owned this place.'

'I didn't know anything about the owners – just that the house had burned out and the grounds were derelict. What was he like?'

Prill paused. 'Difficult man to know. Kept himself to himself. Mostly.'

'He died, I think. Is that right?'

'Yes, he died. Still, The Glades, eh? I saw the sign. I like it. It's a good name. You've won a gold mine here, you know. There are some very rich and important people who live in Brenwood Green. Very important people. Present company excepted of course!' Here she broke up into utterly inappropriate, entirely forced laughter. Vonny joined in for politeness's sake.

'You couldn't have picked a better place to make your home, and I mean that most sincerely. And a place to raise children, too. If you want them, of course. Clive and I never did. Perfectly happy on our own. I've seen the big fellow a couple of times – the man of the house, that is. He's your, eh...'

'You mean Seth? My husband, yes.'

Prill nodded, as if this had satisfied something that bothered her. 'You've both made a wonderful job of the site, I have to say. Quite a difference from how it used to be here, of course. When it was Ryefields.'

'The Glades, you mean? That's what it's always been called – the plot, and the woods. I didn't name it. That's what the raffle organisers said, anyway.'

Prill frowned. 'No, there's been some mistake, there. The house and the woods and the meadow are called Ryefields. Not sure any rye's been grown here for about a hundred years, but that's the name. Unless they changed it. I can see why they'd want to.'

'Oh? Why's that?'

'Just a break with tradition, really.' Prill's head snapped up, and she said to one of the builders: 'Goodness, young man – you really must be more careful with that debris. Haven't you got a skip or something to put it all in?'

Devin, who was watching this exchange from the open patio, said: 'We do have some skips around the side. Please don't worry about the waste... in *Vonny's* house.'

Vonny suppressed a smile at the emphasis.

'I'm sure I won't,' Prill said, pointedly, staring at the foreman until he disappeared inside the house. 'Sorry,' she said, turning back to Vonny, 'young men and big projects... I've had experience in these matters. You have to be firm. That'd be my advice to you.'

'So, you're local, then, Prill?'

'Yes, of course – over the road, a hundred yards due east. You might see the sign – *On Pointe*. That's the name of the house. That's a dancing term. Ballet.'

'Is that a fact?' Vonny said, biting the inside of her mouth.

'Yes, I used to do ballet. Long time ago. Clive and I, we've been here a good while. Brenwood Green's not so much of a town, just a collection of houses. We live quietly, here. I'm sure you'll come to appreciate it.'

'Good of you to tell me – Prill, was it?'

'That's right.'

'Well, I'm looking forward to being neighbours, Prill. Perhaps one day I could come over to yours, for coffee?'

The older lady lurched forward and laid a hand on her arm. Vonny flinched; her instincts had told her Prill was going to bite her. 'Oh, do, please do! I'd be delighted to see you. Pop over, day or night. Just mind Archie the dog – it's only taken him six years to get over the postman changing, you know. And some days he'd still like to take a bite out of him.'

'I'm sure I'll be fine. I love dogs.'

Prill's nostrils flared. 'Quite.'

'I hope you'll excuse me, Prill. I have a busy day ahead.' There was a silence; Prill's gaze never moved from Vonny's. She felt every single follicle on the nape of her neck tingle. 'So. You know your way in; I daresay you can find your way out.'

'Yes... Unless you'd like me to supervise these young men for you? It's no trouble. I've got quite a bit of experience in this game, you know. I certainly know builders, though I don't know these ones. Straight out of school, if you ask me.'

'Straight out of school, maybe, but they're employed by an excellent company. Trustworthy, in my book. Was there anything else?'

Ignoring the question and its clear implication, Prill said: 'You must forgive me, young lady, I've taken up quite enough of your time. This project of yours is quite something, I must say. I love the shape of the roof – quite imposing. Though not too imposing. Otherwise I'd have to sue! Ha!'

Here Vonny did laugh, even as Prill disappeared up the path, picking her way carefully through the mud, then disappearing through the side gate.

Vonny signalled to Devin that it was safe to come out. 'What's the deal with the gargoyle, there?' Vonny asked. 'You know her?'

'No. She was walking up and down the road when we drove in. Assumed she lives around here. What did she want?'

'Says she's "concerned".'

'I see.' Devin pinched the bridge of his nose. 'One Who Watches. Your first nosy neighbour, how about that? I'd say she's going to be "concerned" for as long as you live under this roof.'

'I'd say you're right. She mentioned what this place was called before – Ryefields. I'd thought it was always called The Glades?'

'News to me,' Devin said. 'But I can't say I know this place very well.'

'So you haven't heard of the previous owner, then? Dan Grainger?'

Devin shook his head. 'Don't know anything about the place. One of the boys said he had heard the fish and chips are excellent in the town centre, though.'

'I'll bet. You see that door, Devin?'

'Uh, the garden gate? Yeah.'

'Is there something wrong with it?'

Devin looked aghast. 'No, perfectly good, I think. Do you think there's something wrong with it?'

'No, I'm glad to hear that it works fine. So next time – shut it behind you. All right?'

# 4

When Seth pulled up outside the Ellis & Lowe equestrian centre, he felt a sense of childlike excitement that usually only kindled these days in record shops. In its sober red and white livery, set into a long, low-level building, it was every inch the country outfitter's. Seth felt like he was being taken to a toy shop just before Christmas. He indulged the same absurd sense of wonder and glee. It was like being allowed to handle the gold and jewels of an Arabian fantasy, so long as he put them back where he found them. Just to look would be fine.

The car park was busy and there were a number of people inside, most of them wearing the same type of clothes that were visible on the racks. Many of them gave Seth The Look. He always smiled in response, no matter how psychotic-seeming its source, and most of the time, he got a smile in return. Seth had long hair and a nose stud; these people did not.

The place had a garden centre vibe, rack after rack of clothes and equipment – helmets, gloves, jodhpurs, boots, jackets, base layers, fleeces. Saddles, of course, burnished leather with the same finish as the back seat of a Roller, brasses and studs, and then the really kinky stuff – bridles, reins, and God knew what else.

Seth wasn't here for that stuff, although he took his time to drink in the atmosphere, the sense of… well, there was no escaping it, class, that seemed to permeate the room, from the lazy sweep of the brass ceiling fans to the agreeably springy carpeting at his feet. There was no mistaking the horsiness, either – Seth rather suspected that the pneumatic quality of the flooring was to allow the creatures to browse the racks and shelves for themselves. It wouldn't have been the world's biggest surprise to see one leaning over his shoulder to nudge some sturdy cowhide saddlebags, to feel for the quality.

As alien and absurd as much of this seemed, it did not, however, occur to Seth that he might not quite fit into this place. Seth had 'more front than Southend', as his father was fond of telling him.

Equestrian art almost but not quite tempted him – even a painting of red serge, black hats, white jodhpurs and gleaming brass at the Boxing Day Hunt had its charms – as did the garden ornamentation, including some ludicrously sized and priced ornamental carvings of tigers on the prowl – too expensive to be naff, surely. But these weren't what he'd come for.

'Can I help you?' asked a man with the deportment, pointy chin and narrowed eyes of a wary cat, as Seth browsed the racks at another department, tucked near the back of the store.

'Actually, yeah, I think you can.' Then told the cat-like man what he wanted. In return, the little man whooped with laughter.

'That's the first time I've ever been asked that!' the little man said.

'I mean it,' Seth said, though he couldn't help laughing, too. 'No half measures. No quarter asked, and none given, my man. Let's do this!'

A while later, as he was paying for his purchases, the man who'd helped him with his order said: 'So are you a horse-riding man, sir? I never thought to ask, in all that excitement.'

'Not quite, though the thought has crossed my mind. Is it big in this neck of the woods, then? Equestrian, type, horsey-business?'

'Oh, very much so. Good flat countryside around here. In fact, there are a few breeders and trainers in this neck of the woods. There was a place up on Brenwood Green, you know. Place in the woods. Ryefields. Owned by a very strange man. Came to a bad end.'

Seth, who had been accepting a neatly tied parcel of goods – *no plastic bags* here, *my good man* – hesitated for a moment. 'Brenwood Green, did you say? Hey, that's my manor. Or, it is for now. What did you say the name of the place was, again?'

'Ryefields. There was a bit of a to-do last year, a nasty business.'

'What kind of nasty business?'

'Oh, the police were involved... Some grubby family matter that ended badly. All cleared up now. Put it out of your mind. You've moved here recently, did you say?'

'Yeah, we're building a house, in fact. Brenwood Green postcode. The Glades, is the name of the plot.'

'The Glades...' The assistant frowned. 'I'm not sure I

know that one. Well – you've come to the right place. This is one of the best places to live in the country, I can guarantee you that. You'll come back, now, won't you?'

'You bet. I'll bring the other half, next time. She'll love it!'

Seth turned to go, his package tucked under his arm. He'd marvelled at the assistant's old-school dexterity in twining the string around the brown paper package, though he regretted not asking for a bag, whether burlap, sackcloth or bearskin. As he passed, he noticed a tall, stiff-backed man thumbing through a parade of tank tops on the racks, fingers nimble as a croupier's dealing cards. He had a long, angular jaw and a vulpine nose. Straggly white hair poked out the back of a flat cloth cap, the only untidy note in an otherwise well-ordered, almost military ensemble.

Without looking up, the man said to Seth in a loud, clear voice: 'Ryefields is The Glades.'

'Sorry, mate?' Seth stopped, and in doing so the package slithered out from underneath his arm. He swore; he regretted it.

'Let me help you, there – no, it's OK, Benjamin,' the man said, raising a hand as the assistant sprung loose from behind the counter. 'I've got it.'

The newcomer quickly scooped up the package and handed it to Seth, grinning with a pristine set of newish front teeth. 'I do wish they'd sort out some decent bags at this place,' he whispered. 'Don't get me wrong, great customer service – when they actually want you to leave with the stock.'

'Thanks, pal,' Seth said. He carried the package on his

forearms, tucking it in under his chin. 'And, sorry – I think you mentioned The Glades, a minute ago?'

'Yes, that's what you're calling the place now, aren't you? Forgive me – I'm pig-headed at times, my wife will tell you. I'm Clive Fulton – your neighbour, in fact. In Brenwood Green.'

'Ah! Your wife's... Prill. That right? Vonny's met her. Says she's really interested in the plot.'

Clive Fulton didn't quite roll his eyes, but there was no mistaking his exasperation. 'Yes,' he sighed, 'that's her. Extremely interested. In everyone's plots.'

'Oh – right. Well, sounds like she'll keep the builders on their toes, that's for sure. I'm Seth. Pleased to meet you. Wait, hang on a second, I can't shake your hand... There we go, let's do a fist-bump instead.'

Clive complied, grinning, rapping his knuckles off Seth's. 'I'm so sorry I haven't come over to say hello in person – I've seen your wife driving in and out. You might have seen me knocking around the farm across the road. Or out with the dogs.'

'Sorry if I can't place you, pal – I've not been here too much, really – been busy with work. I'm in the music business. Been away in London quite a lot, and had a couple of weeks out in Sweden, too. My wife's in charge of the build, any road up. I'm just a casual observer, there. Nice to meet you – great part of the world, this. And what about this place?'

'Oh, I know, it's a treasure.'

'It's a toy shop for big people.'

'Yes, quite.' Clive chuckled. 'Some toys being more expensive than others, I have to say. Have you seen the garden centre? Excellent selection. There are dedicated centres a few miles' drive up the A-road, but this is a handy little place. Excellent staff. The manager – Benjamin over there's father – he's a class act. Had the place nearly forty years, I understand.'

Seth reflected that it might have been the first time someone had used the word 'quite' in his presence in that context without it coming across as stabbably patronising. 'So, you were saying, sorry – about The Glades?'

'Ah yes. The Glades used to be called Ryefields. Sorry – I'm not usually so nosy, but Benjamin's voice carries, somewhat.'

'Ryefields. That's where the "family difficulty" happened – according to your boy, behind the counter.'

'Something of that nature.'

'Family difficulty meaning someone died?'

'Afraid so. Dan Grainger. The man who owned your property previously. And his two sons. It was a domestic matter, I think.'

'I thought for a minute there you were going to tell me the guy was a serial killer or something. That'd be just my luck.' When Clive didn't answer – as if he *refused* to answer – Seth pressed on: 'How long ago was this... family matter?'

'Oh, about... a year, two years ago? Nothing to worry about. Ancient history. I think every trace of Dan Grainger's house has gone by now. It burned down, you know. Bad business, but it's all been cleared up.'

'Right... Thanks for telling me. I'm glad someone did. I'll check that out. When you say bad business, are we talking... murder?'

'Suicide.' Fulton cleared his throat. It seemed to preclude

Seth's next observation that three people was a lot of suicides. 'You might struggle to find any details about it. People kept things very quiet at the time. Big shock, all the same. I remember seeing the flames. Nothing could be done by the time the police and fire brigade arrived. I take it no one mentioned this to you in the brochures? It didn't feature on any literature about the place?'

'Well, no... It's kind of complicated. We didn't buy The Glades as such. We won it – on an auction, £25 for the whole plot.'

Seth had to take Clive through the story twice before he deigned to believe it. 'My God! I can't believe we didn't know about it. Steal of the century. I would have put in for a couple of tickets myself. How did you hear about it?'

'Advertised online. There was an Instagram campaign, I think... I'm amazed you didn't hear about it. Surely they'd have tried to sell it locally, bad business or not?'

Clive wandered away a little from what Seth was saying. 'Yes... I think if we had acquired Ryefields, we'd have moved our house across the road, expanded our farm a little. Such an amazing plot at Ryefields – sorry, The Glades. I should get that right. Your own woodland – that must be incredible.'

'It is lovely. Though I get a spooky feeling at night. I'm a Croydon boy, you know? I thought I'd love the peace and quiet, but sometimes it gets too quiet. Anyway... I'm sure it'll change once we move out of the caravan and bunk up inside.'

'You've built your own place, is that right?'

'Totally. From scratch. My other half, Vonny – she

designed it, you know. Two levels, skylight, atrium, swimming pool at the back… Going to be some place.'

Clive held open the door for Seth, and followed him outside. 'That's the, eh, dark-skinned girl, yes?'

Seth scanned the man's expression for even the merest hint of anything he didn't like. Finding none, he said: 'That's her. Vonny. Looks like a model, doesn't she? Bit like David Bowie's wife. I know. Don't worry, you can say it. "She looks like Iman." She does. I'm delighted, in case you're wondering. Ever feel like you've won at life? I won at life. Don't actually call her Iman, though, because she does bite.'

Clive was delighted by this. 'I'll be sure to stick to Vonny! Anyway – lovely to meet you, Seth. At some point you should come over, once you're settled – have a glass of sherry with me, have a look around the farm. It's going to be great having you in our community. We could even drop a pint over at the Brown Boar.'

'Dropping a pint – you're speaking my language!'

'Excellent!' They fist-bumped again. Seth watched him climb into a mud-spattered Land Rover – of recent vintage – and nodded as he tooted the horn on the way past.

Once back in his own car, Seth searched 'Brenwood Green' and 'Ryefields' on his phone, cross-referenced.

Nothing came up.

'Now that, my friend, is a puzzler,' he said aloud.

# 5

The day had gone from clear and cold to overcast, and slightly more benevolent. Frost no longer glittered on the lawn and the paths, and the builders had disappeared inside the house to complete some sanding work. This was when Vonny became bored enough to decide she wanted a run.

Her trainers had taken a beating in the few days since she'd moved into the caravan with Seth; they had their own space underneath the steps, where she left them every night, ignoring Seth's warnings about foxes who shit in the night. Dressed in her running bottoms, a training top and a base layer, she bent over to retrieve the shoes. The mud had dried from her yomp of the day before, and she battered the shoes off the caravan steps to dislodge earth from the tessellations of the soles.

She took four or five minutes to head down the path into the woodlands, skirting the spare ground to the west side of The Glades. The debris of the property that had lain here had long been cleared, although the grass seeded into the earth it left behind wouldn't grow until the spring. Even after the rain, the earth had the churned, blackened look of the aftermath of a public bonfire. Vonny had been told a stables and paddock had been on this land, and she could have believed it.

She pushed on into the woodland. The land was flat, barring the odd tree branch, but a carpet of pine needles leavened the hard, pitted earth, leaving a pleasingly springy surface to run on. She'd only stumbled the once on this run previously, and that had been thanks to a grey squirrel who'd made an atrocious decision when it came running out into her path, almost careering right into her before scurrying up a tree. Vonny, for her part, had bee*f*n left to regret reading those James Herbert novels of her father's when she was a girl.

The path was clear enough through a spectral canopy of midwinter oak, sycamore, birch and lime trees, with a foreboding army of Scots pine fringing the far end of the estate. The woods were thick, and while there was a public right of way at the other side, the woods were private. They were also thick and dark, even without any leaf cover at the very start of December, but there were enough gaps to grant a sense of freedom and open space.

On her first run, Vonny had been a little freaked out by the parallax effect as the trees converged, spaced out, and scrolled this way and that as she followed the main path threading from east to west. She wasn't quite frightened of the woods, but the light was fading fast, and there was a sense of isolation, which she wouldn't quite have enjoyed after dark.

On the whole, though, she had the satisfaction of being a landowner, no matter how briefly. *If only dad could see me now*, she thought, as she took a turn off the path and into one of the broader spaces between the trees.

That was when she caught movement behind a twisted oak, which undulated in a bizarre curve in and out of a mound of earth, roots curled among a tangle of bracken-like tentacles.

There was no suggestion of a face; just a hand, resting against a tree branch. This wasn't another of her rodent friends of the forest, or the sudden flight of a startled bird.

She stopped. There was no one there. She was out of breath, and the sweat stung her eyes even as it chilled on her forehead; she tried to focus on the tangle of alder trees where she'd seen the hand clutch the bark.

'Hello?' she said.

Vonny had not expected any response – so the sudden flight of a spindly, dark figure was quite astonishing. Legs and arms pumping, the figure moved deeper into the forest at some pace. Vonny couldn't have caught up with this figure even if she'd wanted to.

'Hey!'

But she was alone again, adrenaline surging through the pain and fatigue. And then Vonny realised that she might be in a horror movie after all.

She turned and ran, the scrolling trees, bristling undergrowth and fluttering birds taking on a new menace until she reached the clearing taking her past the charred stables site and finally the path to her house. No one had followed her.

Devin Marshall caught sight of her from the top floor. Sliding open the patio door at the balcony above, he hailed her as she rested her hands on her thighs, gasping for breath.

'Uh... You OK?' he asked.

'Fine. Got the heart rate up, I suppose. Can I ask – have you seen anyone out in the woods?'

'I haven't seen anyone. I haven't really been out on the paths, to be honest. But I think… You said someone was out there, Stu, didn't you?'

A young man given a Pierrot face thanks to powdered plastering appeared by Devin's side. 'Yeah, some people were out on the path at the back, behind the pines,' Stu said. 'I think there's a public path out there. I was out on my break, like,' he added.

'But no one inside the woods?'

'Nah. That's private,' Stu said.

'Never mind… Probably someone who wandered off the path. I probably scared them more than they scared me. Was there something else you wanted?'

'Someone to see you at the bottom of the drive. She said she'd wait. Her name's Susie. A reporter, I think she said?'

'What?' Vonny checked her watch, and muttered: 'Christ, she's early.'

Vonny had to make her wait, in order to get showered and prepared. Even so, she still caught up with the reporter well ahead of their rendezvous time.

Susie McCracken was leaning against the one fence Vonny really disliked on the property – the one that she thought of as skewed cricket stumps, ready to fall at the slightest contact. And the girl in question was indeed the slightest contact – slim, with pink Doc Martens, jeans and a loose floral top with a long woollen overcoat on top, topped off with long, curly henna-red hair that put her in mind of a Celtic maiden in a storybook. A delicate scarf that was more for decoration than keeping out the chill hung loose over one shoulder, and, Vonny was delighted to see, she clutched a notebook and pen in her hands, rather than a phone. She seemed startled when Vonny approached.

'Hi,' Vonny said, 'I think we spoke on the phone?'

'Hey – you'll be Vonny?' The girl beamed and extended a hand. 'Susie McCracken. I realise I'm super-early. I can come back, if I'm intruding...?'

'Not at all.' Vonny shook hands. 'I'm delighted you could come at all. It's the *Brenwood Green Advertiser*, is that right?'

'Advertiser *and* Chronicle. I think they could have fit a few more names in there, personally. Advertiser, Chronicle and Bugler, maybe.' Susie had the kind of smile you responded to. In close-up, Vonny saw that she was surely no older than nineteen, and even that could be pushing it. Probably not long out of school. Vonny wondered if she was on work experience.

'Is there a photographer on the way?'

The girl held up a smartphone. 'You're looking at her – 108 megapixels. Enough to get me on the front page of the nationals. Now, I don't know how many megapixels is standard, or what that even means, but believe me, 108 sounds a lot.'

Vonny burst out laughing. 'It sounds plenty to me. Come on, it's just down this path, behind the trees. One thing, though – you'll need to take those boots off. There's a lot of white paint on the go in there, and they're just finishing the plastering. I'm talking serious white – like, John-Lennon-video white.'

The girl looked puzzled. 'John Lennon is the guy who managed Celtic, isn't he?'

Vonny paused before speaking, and locked eyes with the girl. 'You're fucking with me,' she decided.

The girl laughed. 'Of course I'm fucking with you! I'll take the boots off, don't you worry.'

'You can take a look around, if you like. Don't worry about the workmen – they definitely don't bite. To be honest, I don't think they bark either.'

The workmen made their excuses and shuffled out of the way, looking doubly embarrassed to be having two women appear within their midst.

'Have you traumatised them?' Susie asked, snapping pictures of the patio, then taking one or two of Vonny. She had changed into a red dress with black dragons stitched into the sides. Seth had been in the mood to complain when she'd told him what she intended wearing to the photoshoot, but he had known better than to actually do so.

'How do you mean?'

'The workmen. They're about the same age as I am. I wasn't expecting workmen to behave like that. I thought I'd be... I don't know, leered at or wolf-whistled. Not that I'm saying I should deserve it, especially, just... it's standard procedure, isn't it?'

'I mentioned this to my man. He said guys on building sites have to sign up to codes of practice. They get sacked if they act like... well, builders. Changed days, they tell me.'

Susie snapped several shots of an alcove that caught the light in sharp angles – Vonny was particularly pleased with this, as the effect mimicked that of the V-shaped balcony above and to the right. 'Weird design – who's the architect?'

'Well, I came up with the base design.'

'No way! You're an architect?' Susie scribbled this detail down on her notepad. She had told Vonny she was recording the conversation on her phone, but chose to record her actual impressions on the pad as she went along.

'Not quite. I studied design when I was younger. I was considering going that way, in time... I worked with the architects on the project, but the main design of it? That's all me.'

'Tell me about the raffle – how did it come about?'

Vonny repeated the story of the chance click on something she'd seen on Instagram. 'My first instinct was scepticism, but I was curious, too. I checked it all out. Sure enough, it was legit. The relatives of the guy who lived here before were offering the entire estate for the price of one raffle ticket. Twenty-five quid. I went for it on a whim, that afternoon. Best of it was, I was skint at the time – it would have taken me onto fumes for the last couple of days of pay.'

'It's weird,' Susie said, 'isn't it?'

'How do you mean?'

'I mean... having your own house. That's weird for a start. A place you can call your own. It's not even rent, or even a mortgage... Just, *yours*. That must mess with your head a bit.'

Trying her hardest not to sound patronising, Vonny said: 'How old are you, can I ask?'

'Eighteen. Just turned eighteen, in fact. At the weekend. Still a bit hung over.'

'I have to be honest with you, Susie, I didn't imagine I'd be owning a house, either. My life hasn't really gone down the job-to-mortgage route. And I'm not sure I'd change anything about it, either – I love what I do. I work freelance, consultancy... But I thought owning a big property was beyond me. But this was just good luck, really. Outrageous fortune, Shakespeare called it. Beyond anyone's wildest dreams.'

'It's not just the house, is it? It's the grounds. I think this is more land than my entire street. Including the football pitches round the back.'

'Are you from around here?'

'Nah, from Norwich. Grew up in Balham, though. That's why my accent's all over the place.'

'I was struggling to pin it down. How did you get to working for the *Brenwood Green Advertiser* and... and whatever the other bit was?'

'Chronicle. First job after school... Which finished in the summer. I did some interning for them. They must have liked me. I was thinking of studying but... I couldn't afford it. Beyond me, you know?'

Vonny smiled. 'I know the feeling. The debt is ridiculous. And I'm not sure there was any point to it, either. "I went to university and all I got was this lousy degree."'

They passed through to the kitchen and dining room, with another massive patio looking onto the garden. Vonny tried the spotlights, and smiled when they lit up the shadows on the corner of the curved room. The long patio doors were draped.

'This is weird,' Susie said, clicking shots of the walls. 'I mean – not weird as in strange, just... unusual. I really like it. It's like there's no straight lines on that wall. That's deliberate – isn't it?'

'Totally – I wanted it that way. I'll tell you a secret – my partner doesn't know this; he'll faint when he hears – I copied the design for the entire house off a toy spaceship my brother had. It was amazing – the front of the house is the prow of the ship, the back is like the engine... I think that's what it was, anyway. Curving outwards.'

'That's superb.' Susie made a lot of notes. 'I'll use that. Out of this world! Did it cost you a lot to put the house together?'

'Yeah... We used some savings here and there. Seth paid for the build. He works in the record industry. Does all right. Not, like millionaire class, but well enough. We were still saving, living in a studio flat. We've sold that, put the profit into this.'

'Still must have cost you a fortune,' Susie remarked.

'Well, it doesn't cost as much to put a house together if you have a decent plot... but it's pricey, for sure.'

'Had've been me, I'd have used a credit card. I think,' Susie said absently. She was still writing down details on her ring-bound pad, riffling over a fresh sheet. She had shorthand; it looked second nature. The speed and skill was fascinating, like watching a potter or a weaver at work.

Vonny hit a switch, and the curtains withdrew with a smooth movement. The garden and the pool came into view – this area had been slabbed and turfed, with immense clay pots at the four corners of the pool. That had been drained, but was still inviting, the mosaic effect of the tiles an intense blue tending towards cyan.

'Oh wow,' Susie said. 'Your own pool! I don't think I'd

stay out of that. I'm a water baby. One of those kids you don't get out of the sea on holiday, you know?'

Then the drapes gathered at the far side of the patio windows – revealing a figure, standing right in the corner, staring into the room.

# 6

Vonny and Susie made almost exactly the same shocked, avian sound. Vonny recovered first, and started giggling.

'You know him?' Susie asked.

'Yep. But I don't know what he's wearing.' Vonny flicked the lock on the patio door and slid it open.

Seth was stood on the pristine patio paving stones. He wore a pair of brown riding boots, buffed to a high sheen, topped off with a pair of tweed trousers, woven in to large, crude squares. Above this was a thick dark green waxed jacket, which might have suited someone with a smaller frame, but on Seth it looked as if a child had attempted to squeeze a baby doll into Barbie's clothes. The jacket was open just enough to display an unspeakable cravat, attempting to escape from collars big enough to cradle Seth's chin. On top of that, a flat cap.

'Hey, darlin',' he said, 'I've been shopping. Who's your friend? Is this the journalist?'

'It is,' Vonny replied. 'Susie, this is Seth, who seems to have chosen the wrong day to go a bit Guy Ritchie on us.'

'Shane Richie might be a better comparison,' Seth said, agreeably. 'Hold on, I'll get these boots off...'

He moved to tug one of the long brown boots off, but Susie ran out to intercept him. 'No – hold on a second there, you look amazing just where you are. Let's have a few shots… Can you move up against the back wall, there? That's perfect.' She clicked a dozen times, from several different angles.

'Oh yeah, no probs… I think this is a better side…' He grinned at Vonny as he turned to the left.

Vonny shook her head. He was such a tart. It might have come across as arrogant or affected, because, as Vonny sometimes took for granted, he was a very good-looking man, whatever he was wearing – but he wore this quality lightly, tending towards self-deprecation. But rarely had she seen him look so self-consciously ludicrous.

'How about pensive? You want me to look pensive?' He reclined on a wickerwork garden bench, elbow rested on his knee, chin resting in his hand, and that's when Vonny stepped in, as Susie flittered around him, taking shots.

'I think that's enough of the garden shots, Seth.'

'Ah, bang on. Hey, glad you could come along. I checked out your newspaper today, in fact – great stuff. Always wanted to be a journalist.'

'I could probably make as much delivering parcels, but I guess it's interesting work,' Susie said. 'Are you from London, too?'

'Bang on. Croydon. How about you, I'm hearing the East Anglian massive in your accent, there. Ipswich, or have I just mortally insulted you?'

'You have mortally insulted me. But I'm a Catholic. I'll forgive you.' Then, as if embarrassed at having struck a rapport, she turned to Vonny. 'Can I have a few shots around the garden, before I head upstairs?'

'Upstairs is out of bounds just now – even for us. They're finishing off the snagging. But feel free to take a few shots around the garden. It's all finished. Don't be tempted to jump in the pool – there's no water in it, though you wouldn't think it to look at the colour of the tiles.'

While she was off trying to capture the bright blue square in the middle of the garden, Vonny tugged at Seth's cravat.

'Leopard skin? A leopard-skin cravat?'

'You should've seen their faces when I walked out the toilets at the coffee shop,' Seth said. 'This little kid cried.'

'It's… going in the paper. Remember that.'

He shrugged. 'A keepsake for future generations. Can get it framed.'

'Where in the name of God did you get that stuff?'

'The horsey shop, about fifteen minutes down the road. Drove past it loads. Went in it once before. I couldn't help it, Vonny. I saw the get-up, and thought: country gent, tweeds, the lot. Next time I'll get a walking stick. I don't want to lean on it. I want to brandish it. You know, like you see guys doing on *Sherlock Holmes?* Leading with it, leaning into it, and back and forward and off we go, you're a toff.'

She kissed him. 'It's time we posed for the joint picture, now that you're here.'

They did so, standing in front of the pool. Over their shoulders was another fringe of pine trees. Susie offered them no instructions, just taking loads of photos. Later, they went into the basement, where Seth had built his rudimentary studio.

'Oh, I was expecting soundproofed booths, control panels, that kind of thing,' Susie said, shooting the computer equipment, the bass guitar and the synthesiser.

'We've got soundproofing – that was one of my big suggestions,' Seth said, tapping the plain white walls.

'Soundproofing was something I was very keen on,' Vonny remarked, drily.

'As for the rest of the gear, it'll come in time. We'll take care of the main stuff in the house, first of all.'

'So, you look like you're into the country way of life,' the reporter asked Seth, 'but you've got all the modern tech downstairs. This is a bit of a, what's the word... juxtaposition?'

'If you say it is, it is.' Seth cackled. 'The country suits me – I was definitely in the mood for a move out of the city. I'd spent some time outside Stockholm, recording with Annika Free... you know her?' When Susie shook her head, Seth stammered, 'She was in the top ten about twenty years ago... I'm producing her comeback record. Dance, you know. High NRG... Well.' Vonny could have cried for him as she watched his cheeks redden. 'Anyway, being over there made me realise what a good decision it was to come to the country. Peace. Quiet. Less of the stress. And if things get *too* quiet, maybe... I don't know.' He caught Vonny's eye, just in time.

'I thought this was a forever house – like you'd be here all your days?'

Vonny squeezed Seth's hand. 'We'll be here for the time being, and beyond that, for sure,' she said.

'Not going to sell the place up and split? I'd be tempted. God knows how much this land is worth. The raffle brought in an utter fortune. You could probably name your price.'

Vonny shook her head. 'This is a dream home. True love. We've had fun doing it up – and we'll stay put.'

'I have to admit...' Susie hesitated. 'I had assumed you'd just punt the place. Had it been me, I'd have sold the plot. But this house you've set up, my God... I wouldn't want to leave! Unless you had bills to pay.'

Vonny laughed. 'Well, we've all got bills to pay, I guess.'

Seth said: 'I do like the place, no question. I never thought for a minute I'd live in a place like this. And the woods, Jesus...'

'Oh – the woods. Can I have a look at those?'

# 7

Susie became more confident when they got out of doors – so much so that her previous poise might well have fluttered away on butterfly wings. She ran her hands across the bark of the trees, letting the whipcord winter branches tickle the top of her head and even, on one occasion, performing a passable pirouette. She had so much energy to burn that Vonny began to find her damned irritating.

She twirled around one birch tree, fingers gliding over the silver bark. It suited the chill so much, it might have just come out of a freezer.

'What a place you've got. How many acres is it, do you know?'

'I should really know that,' said Vonny. 'I'd probably have to look at the survey before I could admit to a figure. It's a lot of land, though, that's for sure. I think some of it's protected.'

'Is this a public right of way? I think I'd like to come through here for a walk in my spare time. Imagine what it's like in spring or summer!'

'No, this is private,' Vonny said. 'There is a public access path at the far end of the estate, running alongside the drystone wall. People can come and go there as they please, but I'm not keen on pointing that out in the report, if you don't mind.'

'It's awesome, though, you have to admit. Like being in your own fairy tale!'

'That's the idea,' Seth said, linking arms with Vonny.

'Are you going to rebuild on that spare ground?' Susie asked, taking a shot of Vonny and Seth as they walked arm in arm through the woods. 'It looks like something used to be there. Like it burned down.'

'We were told that it was a stables. Guy who lived here used to breed racehorses.'

'Yeah? I love racehorses! That'd be amazing if you could do that. God, I think I'll jack the job in and work here.'

'I can see myself owning horses. I think that'd be awesome – not to race them, like. Just to canter around, watch them having a snooze in the hay,' Seth said.

'I can actually see you as a Pop Larkin type,' Vonny said.

'There's a part of me wants to work on the land. The guy across the road? He's a farmer. Don't know if you knew that? He grows pumpkins, rhubarb, wheat and barley. Has the life of Larry over there, it seems.'

'When did you speak to him?' Vonny asked.

'He came right over to say hello, at the equestrian centre. Nice enough bloke.'

'Oh yeah. That'll be his wife I spoke to, earlier on today. She seemed *lovely*.'

Seth noticed the slight stress Vonny laid on the final word of that statement, and raised an eyebrow, just enough for her to notice.

Susie paused. 'So can you see racehorses coming here,

then – what was that you said again about the previous owner?'

'We just heard bits and pieces. I heard today he had racehorses. That's all. Do you know much about it? Truth be told we don't know too much about the property – we haven't had time to look into the history of the place.'

'Not a lot, I have to admit. The story was the auction, really – that's what I'm following up. It might even go national. Lot of coverage for you, anyway. It was a great story at the time. People will be keen to know more about you. And it's an amazing building project.' Susie bent down, changing perspective as she took a shot of the ragged tree canopy.

'Might be interesting to dig into the history of the place. Might even give us some ideas,' Vonny said.

'The treeline is thicker down here – mind if we head through and get some more shots of you both, but in among the trees?' Susie asked. 'I think you'll make an amazing contrast to the foliage.'

'Why not? Haven't had a chance to investigate round the woods, too much,' Seth said. They moved through the forest, on occasion having to bend over to avoid a branch, or get through the tighter space between the trees. Vonny stepped through high weeds, wincing and hoping there was nothing dead hiding down there in the brownish, decaying matter.

'Aw, mate,' Susie said, excitedly, 'check out that spot through there! It looks alive. I mean, alive enough to bite you.'

She pointed towards a space between a tangle of alders, where a jagged knot of brambles formed a formidable, lethal-looking barrier. Vonny instinctively didn't want to stand next to it; the needle-point branches stood as tall as Seth, and Vonny fancied that one of the studded fronds would reach around her neck like a nasty from an ancient B-movie.

'That's perfect,' Susie said, getting one knee on the ground in order to take a new shot. 'That's the one, right there... Hey.' She stood up, frowning.

Vonny spun around, staring into the nettles. 'Not something alive in there, is there?'

'No, it's just... can you see it?'

Vonny and Seth drew closer.

'Bloody hell,' he said. 'I've absolutely no idea what that is.'

'A door, is what it is,' Vonny said. 'Christ. What was that you said about a fairy tale?'

'No way!' Susie bounded ahead. Vonny had a bizarre feeling she wanted to give her a hug, maybe as a means of holding her back. In the tangle of branches ahead of them, there was a regularity where none should have been; a series of pine slats.

'You're not joking, either,' Seth said, snorting. Gently, he took hold of some branches and pulled them back. 'There is a door in the middle of this. Is it... Are we looking at a shed?'

'Who for, a Hobbit?'

'Hold my hugely expensive old man's hat, please,' Seth said, handing Vonny his flat cap. He then unravelled the yellow and black cravat and wrapped it around his hands. Hunkering down, he pulled back more branches, moving closer.

'It's well overgrown, but I reckon there's a shed there,' he said.

'Maybe you should stay away from it,' Vonny said. 'That's my gut feeling. It's there for a reason.'

'Exciting though,' Susie said, taking shot after shot.

'It's hardly going to explode, is it?' Seth said, grinning. Ignoring her, he moved closer into the tunnel. There was a good four or five yards to get into the bushes and brambles. He gave a sharp cry as a thorn tugged at the back of his hand.

'I think I can reach a handle, there,' he said.

'It's padlocked.' Susie had zoomed in on her phone. 'Wow… Someone didn't want people to get in here.'

'It's padlocked, yeah, but it's rusted… Give me a minute. There's loose stone about here.' He backed out and began digging around in the trampled path, where segments of drystone studded the hard earth. Eventually he found a large, flat stone, with a mean-looking edge, and tugged it free. 'Think this was a surgical implement back in the Stone Age. Some livers got removed with this, I reckon.'

'Please leave it, Seth.'

'Aw, where's your sense of adventure? This could be an Aladdin's cave in here.'

'It could be anything. Please, Seth.'

'Nothing's going to happen. Guy who lived here bred horses. It's probably a hay bales store. Been here for years, they forgot about it, and nature takes its course.'

'They call places they keep hay bales "barns", so far as I know, Seth, and that's not a barn.'

'It's cushty. It'll be fine. Trust me.'

'Those sound like famous last words. Whatever this is, someone wanted it hidden.'

'So... You're saying we cover it up and ignore it? No chance. All the more reason to see what's in here, before someone else blames us for it. Look, I'll just snap off the padlock and take a look. We own this now, right?'

Before she could complain, he got back on his haunches and centred himself. His bottom wiggled a little like a rugby player about to take a penalty. She did not see him strike the padlock, but the sound of the rock striking metal was unmistakable.

'Straight off in one,' Seth said, in an awed tone. 'It's just one dinky old padlock – they couldn't have been that bothered about what's in here.'

'Can you open it?' Susie asked. She was practically in there beside him. The light from her phone cast the thorns and branches in an eerie silver among the gloom.

'There's a doorknob here... It's quite stiff...' Seth grunted. 'No, wait, it's coming open fairly easily... Jeez, it smells musty. Maybe something died in here. And... Oh my God!'

'What is it?' Vonny leapt forward. She grabbed him by the only place she could – right on the seat of his tweeds.

Seth yelped. 'Something hanging on the other side of the door. It's... God almighty, it's almost too horrible to describe!'

Even Susie lost a little of her excitement, backing off slightly. 'What have you got?' she said.

'It's... a tarts and vicars charity calendar for the local rugby team.' Seth held up a grimy, moisture-warped calendar, with the faces of the men and women in ridiculous costumes bleached out a little by exposure to water. The year was frozen at 1991, the month of May. The tarts and vicars were apparently playing croquet on a frog-green pristine lawn. A vicar with his tongue protruding between his lips had his hands folded over that of a tart in a basque and suspenders, helping her with her swing on the croquet mallet.

'Ugh, it smells like rats!' Susie said.

'Yeesh, you must be right,' Seth said, hurling the calendar back into the gloom. 'Could you bring the light in? I need to see what's in here...'

'What do you see so far? Is it an actual shed? Can you get in?' Vonny could smell it too; the scent of linen left for too long in a cupboard, or a back room in a shop that had not had a stocktake in a while. It made you automatically want to wash your hands.

'Hang on a minute,' Seth said, 'I'll need to do some walking on the old knees... Good job I've got a pair of action trousers here, eh? Let's go.'

He disappeared inside the door.

Then he cried out. There was a scuffling sound, then a body hitting the ground.

Vonny charged in. 'Seth!'

In the gloom of the shed, something hung from the ceiling; a dark figure, dangling on a rope, the feet suspended off the floor. Seth had collided with it; he'd fallen over, and was scrambling to get back to his feet, and join Vonny at the door. 'There's a body in here!' he gasped.

# 8

It took a second or two for everyone's eyes to adjust in the flood of light, and for the situation to become clear.

'It's not a body,' Vonny said. She began to laugh, the high, piercing sound of incipient hysteria. 'It's just a coat!'

'Hell is that doing there?' Seth said, angrily. 'Idiots, man. Someone's idea of a joke?'

Susie's tittering brought him back.

Vonny approached the coat. It was a branded black waterproof jacket, of uncertain vintage, dangling from a rafter by a coat hanger. It turned slightly as Vonny approached. She touched it, gingerly, as if unsure whether or not the coat was really empty. It spun, slowly, as she prodded a shoulder. 'Spooky. Whoever left this must have known how it would look to people coming in. Maybe it's a warning?'

Seth recovered some poise, and approached the coat. He was six foot three in his socks, and had to stoop a little. 'I've lost a fight with a coat. Today is a day of firsts.' He patted down the pockets, then reached inside. He stopped, face slack with surprise. 'Something in the inside pocket here...'

He pulled out a set of car keys – old keys, too, manual rather than button-controlled central locking.

'How weird,' Vonny said.

Seth pocketed the car keys, then pulled the jacket off its hanger. 'Not much else in here... Best take a look around.' The boards under his feet creaked. He flinched at the kiss of cobwebs on his forehead; something actually scuttled across his neck, and he flailed at it.

'Yuck, man.'

'What is it?' Vonny was at his back, having moved in ahead of Susie.

'The desiccated corpse of a chiiild,' he said, in a disconcertingly accurate impression of Vincent Price's nasal malice. 'Only kidding, a coupla spiders. I'd be careful all the same. Might have to come back with flamethrowers.'

'I don't have too much of a spider problem,' Vonny said. 'So long as I have a fair chance in single combat.'

'You're all good, then.'

Susie held up her phone, the LED light strong. 'This had a promising start, but it's kind of disappointing,' she said.

'Yep. Empty.' Seth sighed. The room was just about bare; ivy leaves left an eerie impression, choked up against the tiny window, off to the left, while a pitted pine desk with a lacquer effect finish appeared to have weathered surprisingly well, apart from a fine mesh of cobwebs. The place had clearly been undisturbed for quite some time, but the roof seemed sound, and there were no obvious signs of damp or leakages despite the musty smell.

Seth fished in the pockets of his wax jacket for his own phone, and soon his own light joined Susie's. Vonny winced at this second light, turning her head away.

'Nothing in the desk?' she asked.

Seth reached for the single drawer, apparent at the front,

then hesitated. 'Odds on a rat or something leaping out on us?'

'Evens,' Vonny said. 'Do it anyway, though.'

'Please,' Susie said, brightly. 'I'm filming this, now.'

Seth's throat clicked as he swallowed. 'All right then. Taking one for the team, here.'

He snatched out the drawer. And exhaled. 'Well,' he said. 'This is a turn-up for the books.'

'What is?' Vonny came forward.

'A turn-up... for the dirty books.' Seth reached in, and lifted out a magazine from the drawer. It was rendered in pure shadow, until Susie's light fell upon the cover.

The two women burst out laughing. 'Oh my God, we've found his stash!' Vonny said. 'Do they even have these things in the modern era?'

Seth grinned. 'You scoff, but these could be collector's items. Might be a rare copy. Some guys, they'll collect anything. Family heirlooms, too – someone's grandmother could be in these pages. This looks as if it's hardly been used, man.'

'Put it down, for God's sake,' Vonny said, still laughing. 'It could be... contaminated!'

'It's been here for a while, pet. Not as long as the tarts 'n' vicars calendar, but definitely "vintage". August '98? Shall we look inside?'

'No, we shall not!'

Seth replaced the magazine. 'That was it. Nothing else in there.' After a moment, he knocked the bottom of the drawer. 'No false bottom, either. Think we should get it to the former owner's family? Might make a nice keepsake.'

'Grim,' Vonny said. 'I have to say, he's gone a long way to keep some blue magazines secret.'

Seth spluttered. 'He's living the dream! Never mind a masturbation station, he's got an entire wank bunker down here.'

'I was hoping for some big secret,' Susie said. 'Well... a bigger secret, anyway.'

'There is the dartboard,' Vonny said.

'Where?' Seth spun around, the light shearing off in an erratic curve until it settled on an ancient, pitted dartboard. The dark sections of the board seemed to have warped, either from neglect or overuse, with white strands poking out through the material. It was fixed to a car tyre, which had been sliced to form a pockmarked buffer zone to absorb wayward shots; it, too, was nailed to the wall. A blackboard was pinned up beside it, with no clear message chalked up; merely the ghost of games from the past. Two darts were stuck in the board, one in the green bed marking double fifteen, the second in the green zone encircling the bullseye, and the third just outside the board, above double top. The flights had the skull and crossbones of the Jolly Roger on them, the whiteness of the skulls almost unbearable to focus on in the concentrated light.

'The last shot,' Seth said. 'Sheesh. This is poignant.' He reached for the arrows.

Vonny felt a plummeting sensation in her guts; her skin tingled on her neck in a current of foreboding. 'Maybe you shouldn't touch those.'

'Don't be daft,' Seth said. 'Not going superstitious on me, are you?'

He took out the darts, and moved back towards the window side of the shed. 'OK. What do I forfeit if I fail to hit... eighty or more with these three darts?'

'Fame and fortune,' Susie said, on the double.

'Fame and fortune it is,' Seth grinned.

'Don't say that,' Vonny said.

Seth ignored her. 'Here we go... the very best of order, ladies and gentlemen. Best of order. Here we go. Drum roll...'

He threw the arrow – it thudded straight into the centre bed of the upper section of the twenty segment.

'Look at that! Still got it, love. Sixty to score. A tall order. Can he do it?'

The second dart landed less than half an inch away from the first dart, its flight tickling that of its predecessor.

'Another twenty! Forty scored... Can he score another forty to take the prize?'

Seth waited. Vonny held her breath, despite herself. Ludicrous, she thought.

He released the last dart. It missed the board, handily, piercing the tyre well ahead of the board.

'Ah, dammit. There goes fame and fortune. I was aiming for the double top. That could have put us over the top. Eighty was a bit of an ask on three arrows, all the same.'

'Silly,' Vonny said. 'Tempting fate like that.'

'It doesn't matter – fame and fortune is in the bag,' Seth said, reaching for the arrows. 'Thanks to our newspaper coverage. Am I right, Susie?'

'Fame, the length and breadth of Brenwood, I would say, and anyone else who's part of our circulation.'

'There you go. Nothing to worry about.' Seth tugged at the dart stuck in the galvanised rubber frame.

As he did so, there was a click, and the board swung out.

'Whoa,' he said, taking a step back.

'What is that?' Vonny asked. 'A safe, or something?'

'Nah... Just a recess, set back in the wall, but there is something there.' His bulk blocked out the sight of what was behind the dartboard for a moment. Vonny crowded in to see.

There, in the light of Seth's phone, was a folded scrap of paper, inside a flimsy plastic wallet – the kind of material Vonny would have used to hand in an essay. 'This is intriguing, wouldn't you say?' Seth lifted the sheath out and emptied the paper into his hand.

It was an A4 sheet of printer refill, folded over twice. Carefully, he straightened it out.

The light of the two phones flooded the square of paper. Squinting, Vonny began to discern what was there.

Susie called it first. 'It's a bloody map!'

# 9

Vonny took it from Seth and held it back from the light. Susie was close enough for her breath to tickle the nape of her neck.

'What's it of?' the younger woman asked.

'I think this is the back wall,' Vonny said. 'Look at the trees; that X is where we are, in relation to the house. It must be. According to the key, the drystone wall is to the south. That looks right.'

Vonny's purple-painted fingernail lightly traced a path along the paper. The surface had a slight texture to it, but was still sturdy enough; whoever had folded it had done so carefully, with a good eye for symmetry, which pleased Vonny instinctively. The map itself was drawn in what could have been black magic marker, or more likely a felt-tip pen. The lines were chunky, but the detail was clear.

'There's the old stables,' Seth said. 'And the house... that's where our house is, now.'

Vonny pointed to another X. 'And that's pointing to something in the middle of the woods.'

All three considered the paper a second. Seth clapped his hands, making Vonny and Susie jump.

'Well then,' Seth said to her. 'We don't have anywhere we need to be right now, do we, darlin?"

'What do you mean?'

'I mean, we're going on a treasure hunt.'

'But it'll be hard to pinpoint. I don't think the map's exactly to scale...' Vonny turned to the map to read some writing, along the outer edge, on the map's west side, a couple of lines of ballpoint in a neat hand. 'Hang on, it says something here. "Mark – go to the delta, stand north, take the bearing. Go straight on till the rough."'

'It's a treasure hunt,' Susie said. 'My God – this could be anything! What if it was actually money or something?'

'Who's Mark – do we know any Marks?' Seth asked.

Vonny shook her head. 'The guy who owned this place was called Dan Grainger. Unless that means anything to you?' She turned to Susie.

Susie shook her head. 'Never heard of him. Sorry. Like I said, I only just got here a few weeks ago – I hardly know anyone. Just my landlady and my boss. And I wouldn't call either of them my friends. That's it.'

'There's no sense of distance. And he says something about a bearing.' Seth sighed. 'We need to sort that out, before we go anywhere. Otherwise we've just got a vague idea of where "X" might be.'

'Well, he said delta,' Vonny said. 'That's where a river meets a lake, if I remember my geography. There's a stream running through this estate. And it pools into a lake, which drains through to the farmer's field.'

'Not marked on the map,' Seth said.

'No – but it's on the deeds. Which I've got downloaded on

my phone.' Vonny soon found the document, then increased the magnification to pick out a blue thread running across the property. 'So, if our map's talking about a delta, then it's... here, I'd say. Where it drains into the pond.'

'Getting warmer,' Seth said, clicking his fingers. 'I can sense it. What about the bearings?'

'That... I'm not sure about.' She studied the paper, but there was no other clue on it. She even held it close to the light, to see if there was anything marked there – perhaps an invisible ink trick, that she'd read about in Nancy Drew mysteries as a girl. 'Is there anything behind the dartboard? Anything at all?'

Seth went in for a closer look. 'Nah. It's all clear. And there was nothing written on the board, was there?'

'There was something on the board,' Susie said. 'The darts. What was the score?'

Vonny brightened. 'I can't remember – but you said you were recording this, weren't you? It'll be on your phone.'

Susie stopped the recording, played it from the start, then scrolled through until the jerky stop-motion-animated Vonny and Seth entered the shed in the woods.

'There,' Vonny said. 'That part in the middle – that's twenty-five, right? And the next one... I can't make that out.'

'Double fifteen – I remember now,' Seth said. 'Thirty. So that's fifty-five scored – the last dart was outside the wire.'

'So we've got fifty-five – or fifty-five degrees,' Vonny said. 'So we go to the delta, stand north, turn fifty-five degrees, then, what was it? "Go on until the rough."'

'Could be a wild goose chase. And it's probably nothing.' Seth sighed – then smiled. 'What are we waiting for?'

# 10

'It's exciting, though. I mean, a proper story.' Susie kept pace with Vonny and Seth as they passed through the trees to the main path bisecting the land. Although it hadn't been maintained so far as Vonny knew, the path was clear enough through a fallow field where pumpkins had once grown. On the other side, the stark treeline.

'Yeah... Hey, you aren't still filming, are you?' Seth asked.

'Not at the moment,' Susie said.

'Did you manage to capture the footage of me, you know... stepping into the unknown?'

'You mean when you got tangled up with the jacket? I don't really know. I'll have to check.' The girl had form, Vonny had to admit; she said it without so much as a blush.

'Hm. Yeah. Just in case it gets uploaded, to... you know, your website.'

'Might get hits,' Vonny mused. 'Might get millions of them.'

Seth brightened. 'Viral. Yeah, you could be right!'

The path ended in a copse, with trees on either side of an unobtrusive wire fence, tightly meshed in silver squares. A slight decline running perpendicular to the path cut underneath it through a pipe, giving way to a narrow stream. This place was overgrown, a tangle of ancient trees, moss and lichen-spotted branches and other detritus that formed a natural dam – one part of which included an ancient car tyre.

Vonny checked her map. 'Beyond this, there's the pond – it's marked as a "lake", here, incidentally, no name attached – so where this part meets is the delta.'

Seth wiped sweat from his brow. 'How do we get to it from here?'

Vonny stepped over the fence and dropped on the other side. Water ran not twelve inches from where she stood, at the top of the decline. 'This is the only path. I hope these new boots of yours are insured, dear.'

The branches closed in on them as they travelled, and the startled flight of an unseen bird almost prompted the same reaction in Seth.

'Let's take a moment,' he said. 'What if we're about to discover, I don't know... bodies or something?'

'Not scared, are you?' Vonny asked. 'You were Mr action and adventure not so long ago.'

Though as she said this, her heart had begun to kick, a noticeable prod in the chest from a very insistent doubt in her head. This was no good. She had known it from the moment they came across the shed in the woods with its ragged crown, like a giant spider poised to spring at them. She did not like this. Bizarrely, she pined for the security of the caravan, for all its close confines and awkward sanitation.

'Just saying. Whoever left the map meant to keep something hidden. So either it's something really valuable, or something... he really doesn't want anyone to find.'

'You're assuming it's a he,' Susie said. 'And I don't think there's anything dangerous or suspect, here. Why would you leave a map leading to it?'

'It was addressed to Mark. Someone was meant to find it. I think Susie's right.' Vonny felt only slightly relieved, though. It might have been valuable, but it still felt like bad news.

Bad news that Susie would doubtlessly put in her feature. It had all been Seth's idea – a great advert for Vonny's skills. Media strategy, he'd said, tapping his forehead. Gotta have one, or you're sunk. Admittedly, the *Brenwood Green Advertiser and Chronicle* wasn't quite *Good Housekeeping* or the *Sunday Times* supplement, but viral things had to start somewhere. Or so Seth had said. Besides, it would be practice for the real thing.

Soon they reached a part where the treeline thinned out, giving way to a clearing marked by a circular pond, maybe forty or fifty feet in diameter. 'Lake' didn't feel like too grandiose a term; in spite of the churned earth and winter-dark dead weed bed hemming the pond in, it was a gorgeous spot. At the far side of the water, a drainpipe allowed the water to escape and continue along the water table as the stream progressed towards the woods beyond. The water had caught the grey afternoon winter light beautifully, reflecting the sky and the fine brushstrokes of cloud in a glassy, perfectly still surface.

'Whoa,' Susie said, as she took multiple shots of the scene. 'Did you know this was here?'

'Didn't get a chance to check it out,' Vonny said. 'I didn't realise the dimensions.'

'It's like your own secret lake!'

'Could go fishing,' Seth mused. 'Looks the job for some fishing. Might dig out my old fishing rod.'

'The delta must be about here, where the stream flows into the pond... or the lake.' Vonny used the compass programme on a stargazing app she didn't consult as much as she'd have liked to. 'So... I think, if we stand here, that's in the direction we've been told. Then we take a bearing...' She fiddled with the digital compass, tutting a couple of times in irritation before turning clockwise, biting her lip in concentration. 'And here we go – it's pointing us at the other side, where the trees are thickest.'

'So we go around the drink?' Seth had already began to move, but Vonny stopped him.

'Nope... we can ford the stream, here. You'll get wet socks at best. I don't want to lose the bearing.'

Grumbling, Seth followed as the two women splashed through the trickling water. Vonny shrieked, annoyed that her socks were wet after choosing the deepest part of the stream. Soon they came to the trees – a thick nightmare of seemingly uniform pine. The scent of the trees was gorgeous, but this part of the estate was all too quiet, and all too dark, with the tall, ancient sentinels standing guard before them.

'We push on. This is the place. Or... we could stop and head back for a cup of tea, maybe come back another time?'

'Nah. We've come too far, don't you think?' Seth grinned. 'This is a big adventure, now. Let's see it through.'

'No, we absolutely have to move on,' Susie said, determinedly. 'This could be the front-page scoop. You'll be the toast of Brenwood if it's treasure or... or something else.'

The latter suggestion seemed to linger in the air as they pushed on through the trees.

It didn't take long for them to spot it.

'That has to be it,' Seth said. 'Look... is that tarpaulin?'

It was. Perhaps grey in its salad days, the material was the same eerie green as the forest in the filtered light. It was stretched tight over something, perhaps shoulder height on Vonny.

'You thinking what I'm thinking?' Seth said, grinning. He started forward.

'No... Hold on, I don't think that's the greatest idea...'

'It's tied down... Hang on, there.' Seth pulled out a pocket knife – he'd surely bought that during his adventure in the village shop – and cut some rope, which was fastened at intervals around the covering. Susie gave him a hand to pull the twine away.

Then he urged them to stand back. 'Camera out for this. This could be the big moment, right here. You ready? Three... two... one!'

It wasn't quite the big reveal he'd planned on – the tarpaulin took an age to slither off the surface of what it concealed. But the effect was stunning, all the same, even for being in slow motion.

'Good God almighty,' Seth yelled. 'Would you take a look at that!'

# 11

It was a car – boxy, sporty and bright yellow. It was a shell-burst in the dull afternoon, its flames licking every shade and tone surrounding it. The car was a coupe, clearly at least forty years old, and upon inspection suffering from patches of rust along the edges of the nuclear paintwork. Two fixed wing mirrors, backed with silver, were only slightly tarnished with grime. The headlights were small, giving the appearance of someone squinting over a pair of spectacles. That was the only grandmotherly quality that could be attached to it. It had a long bonnet and a brawny quality that hinted at some power.

'It's an old Datsun Cherry,' Seth said. He trailed his fingers over the bodywork. 'And hey... what's the odds we've got the key for it, here?' He groped in his pocket for the keys that he had taken from the hanging coat in the shed.

'Wait a second.' Vonny held up a hand. 'Just hold on a minute, here. Let's talk about this. Susie, could you stop filming or taking pictures, or whatever it is you're doing, for a minute or two?'

Susie lowered her smartphone, pressing a key. 'OK, done,' she said, a touch sulkily.

'I think this has gone on far enough, Seth,' Vonny said.

'What do you mean? Don't you want to check this out?'

'No, not really. We should probably call the police, first. Let them handle it, and ask the questions, and find out who this belonged to. It's not for us.'

'It is for us, though,' Seth said, 'because we found it on our land. And this is our land – signed, sealed, and sorted.'

'I don't really care. I reckon we should leave this entire thing, and wait for someone else to check it out. I don't like it, Seth.'

He turned to Susie. 'Tell me, does this car being found on our property make the story less, or more interesting.'

'More, definitely.' Susie had already abandoned Vonny's request, and was taking pictures of the car from every angle. 'Look… those tyres look kind of fresh. Wonder if it'll start?'

'Wonder no more.' Seth dangled the key. Then he slid it into the lock on the driver's side.

The door clicked open.

'There's a reason I'm asking you to stop,' Vonny said. 'It's because things can be hidden in cars.'

'What we saying? Bodies?' Seth grinned, and opened the door. Inside, the leather was mouldy, a fine, grey covering coating the seating like a dusting of cigarette ash. There wasn't much to the bodywork, and no sign of a radio inside either. The head of the gearstick was broken off, leaving a curiously disturbing chrome-plated spear point.

'Don't think I'll take a seat. Nothing inside, bar some kind of fungus. Could be the key to curing cancer or something. You never know.' Nonetheless, Seth reached in and pulled open the glove compartment. 'No documents, nothing.' He craned his neck inside, nostrils twitching. 'Nothing under the seats, that I can see... Smells funny, though. We got plenty of bleach back at the caravan, Von?'

'Best to leave it as it is. Maybe we can get some kind of vintage car dealer to check it?'

'Could do. It isn't in bad shape, all told – should be rustier than it is. It might have been well used, before it was dumped.' He slid the key into the ignition. 'Dare me?' he said, cocking an eyebrow.

'I do not dare you. Seth, please, just leave it...'

Before she could finish the sentence, he had turned the key. There was a dry click, like a nervous man clearing his throat, and nothing. 'Aw shucks. I had to. You know that.'

He grinned at Vonny. 'But we're forgetting the star prize.' He unlocked the boot, tugged it open, sighed, then slammed it back shut before locking it again.

'Nothing,' he said, shrugging his shoulders. 'Still. It's done. I think we'll do as you say, Vonny, and get someone to take it away.'

Susie said: 'Hey, maybe you should both pose in front of the car? It'll be an amazing shot.'

'Nah,' Seth said. 'I don't think we should focus on the car. It's a rust bucket. Let's ignore it. Give me a hand and I'll cover it up with the tarp. I know a guy who works at a scrappie – he might give us a decent price for it. You get some guys who are into the classic cars. They'll maybe pay for the bodywork. Big industry, these days. TV shows and all sorts – people like to see these things restored.'

Vonny frowned at this sudden volte-face by Seth, but she didn't argue. She followed him out of the tangle of trees once they'd pulled the tarp back over the car, and Susie came after.

Vonny whispered in Seth's ear: 'Was there definitely nothing in the boot?'

'Cross my heart. Go and have a look yourself. It was my first thought – that's where the body will be. But no, all clear. Just the usual fluff and stuff you get in a car boot. I'll check the seats as well, before you ask.'

'Weird one, this,' Vonny said.

'For sure.'

Susie called out: 'How about a shot or two out by the lake?'

# 12

Jim Lester kept the taxi for two minutes beyond the regulation five. He had the base call the mobile phone, and he even beeped the horn, before deciding he had a no-show. When he disengaged the handbrake, he grunted along with it, checked over his shoulder, spun the wheel savagely... and that's when the twat appeared at the front of the block of flats.

Student, or someone who wanted to look like one. Tall, one of those rock star haircuts that he was sure had been out of fashion a long time – out of fashion when he was young – and a backpack over his shoulder. Trainers – new ones, as well, would you believe. Legs last seen on a heron, though not quite so elegant. The kicker was the biker's jacket. Biker's jacket! This prick would fall off a tricycle, never mind a motorbike.

He strolled, strolled by God, over to the taxi. Jim Lester bit his lip, hard.

The student grinned and raised a hand. 'Sorry, mate, I was just saying "night night" to your mum.'

'What? What did you just say?'

'I said, I was saying "night night" to my bird.'

'You taking your time, son? Because if you are, you're taking my money.'

A sullen look came into the young guy's face, then. He was pale, with thin slashes for eyebrows. Bereft of any genial expression, the large dark eyes were bloodshot, and might have been difficult to look at if you weren't Jim Lester. Jim Lester saw his hard stare, and raised him.

'Sorry,' the kid said, tugging open the passenger-side door.

'Quite all right. You had the manners to say so. And that's fine. Where we off to?'

'We're doing a pick-up around the corner. At 24 Bournebank Street. Then we're off for a jaunt around the locks.' The kid sat down, resting the backpack beside him, then engaging the seatbelt.

'A jaunt? You didn't order a jaunt when you called the base,' Jim said.

The young guy nodded towards the meter. 'I've got the money, if you've got the time.'

'Well, I've got an airport job at half twelve... but yeah, OK. You're on.'

'My man!' The young guy leaned forward and offered a fist to bump. Jim Lester bit his lip again, and offered a half-hearted bump in return.

Bournebank Street was another dump of a block of flats. The previous pick-up point had been a block on the road down, and had been good at one point. But Bournebank Street had never been a good place. Jim's wires were buzzing the minute he parked up; one of the windows on the lower-ground floor was boarded up, the outer edges blackened with smoke damage. The car ticked into silence as Jim cut the engine. There was no one on the street; no one came to the windows.

'Hope you don't work on the railways,' Jim muttered, checking his watch.

'They're coming now,' the young guy said, tapping something into his phone.

Jim saw some movement in his wing mirror. His jaw dropped as he spotted someone jogging up towards the car. If his wires had buzzed before, they were shrieking now. He caught a glimpse of another figure approaching from behind, this one much thicker-set. He reached for the keys. It was too late; the passenger doors on either side burst open and two figures got in.

Then something prodded Jim in the guts. He turned to the left, and saw the kid with the haircut grinning, and staring straight into his eyes.

He held a hunting knife perhaps twelve inches long from the hilt to the end of the cruel, serrated blade.

Jim's words stuck in his throat.

In the wing mirror, two horribly familiar faces loomed. One was enormous; when he sat down, the left-hand side of the taxi sagged. On the right was a face that matched that of the person sat to his left in the front seat, although his skull was shaved and his neck was tattooed with orange, red and black flames.

'Take us to the locks, please, Jim,' said the kid in the front with the biker's jacket, still smiling, but not blinking. 'In your own time.'

'Christ's sake, lads,' Jim said, his hands quivering as he tried to get a grip on the ignition. 'What's going on here?'

The shaven-headed lad sat forward. 'You know what's

going on here, Jim. But drive to the locks. We'll tell you when to stop.'

The immense man in the left-hand back seat said nothing. He simply glared at Jim, two tiny black eyes in a set of thick eyebrows. Jim saw that he was wearing a white collar and a black tie, loosened about the throat.

The knife stayed at Jim's belly. 'Go on, Jim. I dare you,' the young guy to his left said, and laughed.

Jim's feet quivered on the pedals as the car moved off, heading into greener spaces.

'Won't keep you in suspense,' said the shaven-headed man – Sebastian, obviously the twin brother of the dark-haired lad in the front seat. 'We're here on behalf of Ally. He's indisposed at the moment, you could say, but he sends his regards.'

'How's he getting on?' Jim said. The question, and the querulous tone it was delivered in, made the two brothers laugh, and the massive, twenty-stone man half-smiled.

'He's peachy, Jim. Still a bit sore about that bit of business from a little while ago. It took us a while to track you down. Minicabs, our sources told us. They were right, too. Well, how do you get a hold of a minicab driver, I asked myself?'

'What business is that, Sebastian?' Jim asked, querulously.

'Don't mess us about, Jim.' The shaven-headed young man leaned forward, and the sunlight caught a piercing nestled in his fine, sandy eyebrow. 'Dan Grainger wouldn't tell us anything, and neither did Mark. I respect them for that. We tried to persuade them. Not many people can withstand that kind of persuasion. Can they, Jay?'

'Nah,' said the immense man. 'They usually start screaming, the minute I start on the balls.'

'But fair play to Dan, as I said. A fitting death. You'll have heard he didn't really kill himself, I suppose? And you'll know he'd rather have cut his own hand off than harm a hair on his son's head. Or someone else's hand, more likely.'

'Don't know what you're talking about,' Jim croaked. But he did know. They were getting close to the locks, now, a quiet road running parallel to the canal.

'Some pad he had. No sign of the stuff, mind.' Sebastian scratched his tattooed neck. 'You know what we mean, don't you? The stuff? Our stuff?'

'Lads, take this up with Simmy. He'll tell you – I don't know anything about that.'

'Simmy's dead,' Sebastian said. 'Before he drowned, he agreed with everything we said. He agreed that the deal was ours, and Dan had taken a bit of a liberty. And he told us that you tipped Dan off about the shipment coming in. Places, dates, times… that's what you're good at, apparently.'

'If you've got the money, he's got the time,' his dark-haired brother said from the passenger seat. 'Thing is, it wasn't just any shipment.' He jabbed Jim in the belly with the knife. 'This was the big one. The one that was going to put us over the top. The big ones only come in once in a lifetime, really. That was it. Ally was really, really disappointed when you tipped Dan off, you know. Do you know, lads, he actually cried?'

Jim looked like he wanted to cry, himself. Scenarios flashed through his mind. Crash into the canal; ditch the car; roll out onto the road; take his chances.

Instead, he began to talk. 'Dan set it up from start to

finish. He said he wanted the competition to be put in its place. He said… he said he wanted to see what you'd do.'

'We know all that,' Sebastian said, impatiently. 'We also know the stuff hasn't been moved yet. If it has, it went offshore again, sharpish. But we don't think it did. We think it's still out there. We went to a lot of effort, Jim. I went to a lot of effort, personally. And I know Ally Cramond put everything on the line to get that deal. So, do us a favour. Cut to the chase. Tell us where it is.'

'It's on Dan Grainger's estate. It's somewhere on the grounds.'

'We searched that house, top to bottom. It wasn't in the house. I can tell you that for a fact. It wasn't in any safes, his wife's knicker drawer, anywhere.'

'He hid it somewhere. On the estate. That's all I know.'

'Where?' The kid in the passenger seat increased the pressure on the blade. Now it was starting to hurt, jabbing into Jim's skin, and he shrank from it, belly muscles undulating beneath the fat.

'I don't know.'

'We'll find out if that's true,' Seb said. He gestured over Jim's shoulder, towards an overgrown place hiding a boarded-up industrial unit. Jim knew this used to be an office block, long gone to the rats from the canal, a place even the squatters shunned. 'We'll find out just here. Pull up, Jim. That's it.' He grinned; the slant of his mouth matched the angle of the flames creeping up his neck.

'Honest… I think it was hidden in something, I'm not sure what…' But by then, Jay had disgorged himself from the car with surprising speed, and had already tugged open the driver's side door. A clamp in the form of flesh and five fingers settled on Jim's shoulder; from the other side, the knife went to his throat, right under the chin. Jim whimpered as he was pulled out, as a father might lift a son onto his shoulders. And then his last day truly began.

# 13

On the day the paper went to print, Vonny took a trip to the shops. Seth indulged himself with a lie-in, in the caravan. He dozed, watching the wood pigeons' claws scrape the skylight above.

Then the phone began to buzz on the table next to his head, startling him.

It was his mother, in tears.

'Hey, slow down,' Seth said, heart racing. 'What's going on?'

'It's Jake,' she wheezed. 'We're at hospital. He's being seen to now. He got striped, on his way to school this morning.'

Seth closed his eyes. 'You're joking – Jake? *Our* Jake? How bad?'

'They cut his face. They're putting stitches in now, Seth. They got him across the cheek. He got away, but lost a lot of blood. He won't be the same, Seth.'

Seth's hand tightened on the phone. 'When did this happen? Today?'

'An hour, two hours ago. They spotted him while they were going past on a bus…'

'Who spotted him? Those idiots he's running about with?'

'No. Different ones. He owes them money, Seth. Won't say how much. He needs help. They threatened him before.'

'Then why didn't you tell me this before?'

'You had enough on, with the house and the music and everything. I didn't want to worry you.'

Seth pinched the bridge of his nose. His eyes were tearing up – in fury, as well as sorrow. He tried to picture Jake's face, slashed open. He envisioned blood on the collar of his school shirt.

His baby brother, fourteen years younger. His mother and father's little surprise. The boy who was going to make it; the boy with the GCSEs.

'Tell me everything you know, Mum. Start from the start.'

Vonny triggered the remote control from her car, cursing as she struggled to stop her phone slithering from her grasp. The sensor responded and the gate opened inwards. She was never sure if she had simply imagined a red eye winking at her from the digital display. Once the door had made its ninety-degree turn, she drove the car along the driveway. The gravel crunched underneath the wheels – a sound from a thirty-year-old TV show about yuppies; a sound from a script; a sound she would have never associated with a house she owned, let alone a plot this big – and she knew that the driveway had been laid out properly, so that it didn't spew debris here and there under the wheels. Right kind of gravel, sourced from the right kind of quarry. Sometimes she hated herself.

The workmen were on site when she pulled up close

to the house, and she waved at Devin as he came out to greet her from the balcony. A week of tests had come to an end; they'd even installed the Wi-Fi and changed all their passwords, although the official opening of the cinema room was yet to take place.

One of the workmen appeared as she came out of the car, dragging a bag of shopping with her for the caravan – the youngest-looking one, with his puppy-fat face bulging out from beneath his hard hat like bedding hastily stuffed into a cupboard. 'Nice picture of you and the boss,' he said, proffering a newspaper.

She smiled. 'Who's the boss, then?'

The workman blanched. 'I meant, the big fella. Seth.'

Seeing his terror, Vonny ignored the remark, and unrolled the paper. She already had three copies, of course, hidden among the bags of shopping – for her and Seth, and for their families. It was a weekly, probably facing the same issues as every other print publication these days until they finally disappeared. Its lead story was a council matter on wheelie bin collections. Stuffed in at the bottom right corner – and not as well separated from the lead item as she'd have liked – was a picture of Vonny, Seth and the nuclear yellow Datsun Cherry.

TREASURE TROVE – Brenwood Green couple hit the jackpot again! See pages 3, 4–6

'I'm a page three girl,' Vonny said, listlessly, though the paper visibly quivered between her fingers. The pages were largely taken up with a photoshoot of the new house. It looked wonderful, but there, again, was the Datsun Cherry, a glaring yellow stain, dead centre. 'Hmm. The car's the star. Not how I wanted it to go.'

'Should get a few viewers for the house, eh?' he said to her.

'Not really the intention. Is it OK if I take this?'

'Well sure... I was just heading to the, eh, toilet... In fact you're fine, you're fine,' he said, backing off, and blushing.

She let herself into the caravan, and Seth grunted a greeting.

'Have they shown it to you?' she said.

Seth, who was sat in front of a bowl of cereal at their minuscule fold-down table, nodded. The caravan would have appeared ludicrously cramped to any observer, but over-cosy-to-the-point-of-asphyxia accommodation was nothing new to Vonny and Seth. 'The paper? Yep. The car's the star, after all that,' he muttered. 'You probably warned me that might happen.'

'I'm not sure I did, but, yeah – probably.' She laid the paper down. 'Susie has caught the breakfast bar in the kitchen really well, though, I have to say.'

'She shouldn't have done that. I mean... It's a good story, and all. She used it for a news story on the front page – it's a good lead. We said that. I just...'

Vonny sat down beside him. 'Want to tell me what's bothering you about the car?'

'Exactly what you told me,' he said, without a pause. 'Exactly the thing that bothered you, and that I should have paid more attention to. The possible reasons why someone's buried that car in among a load of thorn bushes and it should probably have stayed there. It could be stolen. It could have been involved in a crime.'

'That being the case – why not burn it?'

Seth drummed his fingers. 'Good question. Anyway. Done now, I suppose.'

'Did you speak to the garage?'

'I did. You were spot on – the guy almost swallowed his phone when I told him what we'd found. Might have to check the licence plate, make sure it's kosher, check the previous owner, but... if it turns out it's ours, he's happy to take it off our hands. Decent enough fee. He was excited about the upholstery, would you believe – not too bothered about the engine being full of mouse shit. He said he'll refit the engine and can sort out the bodywork. There's always a market for these things.'

Vonny noticed he was still tense; that he wouldn't look right at her as he spoke. 'So. What is it, then?'

'What is what?'

'Come on. Want to tell me what else is bothering you?'

He shrugged. 'Nothing. Just... the exposure. I'm all talk in the studio, but I'm a shy boy onstage. Plus... I now realise what a prick I looked in those clothes. It's all to the good, though.'

'Yeah, you said. Good marketing. You looked natty in your Toad of Toad Hall suit, incidentally.'

'Toad of Toad Hall? Really?'

'Sorry... I might have just thought that, but never said it out loud.' Vonny snapped shut the newspaper. 'Did you speak to Devin?'

Seth ate the last of the cereal, careful to fill his spoon with the remaining milk. 'Yep. All systems go to move in on Tuesday.'

'Seriously?'

'Yeah. The house is just about complete, one or two things outstanding, here and there. He mentioned "snagging is never finished", which is true. He said he wants to make a start on the garden next week.'

'You reckon we can get the Christmas tree up?'

He grinned. 'Christmas tree, fairy, the whole lot.'

'Jesus. We've even got our own fire this year.'

'Our own *roaring* fire,' he countered. 'And Jesus is what it's all about.'

She stared at the house's weird lineaments, almost otherworldly from that angle. 'How many lifetimes would we have had to live to be able to buy a place like this?'

'Dozens.' He got up abruptly, clattering the dish into the little sink. He squirted some washing-up liquid and rinsed it out quickly.

She frowned at his broad back. *No. Sorry, love. Good deflection effort, but I'm not leaving it there.* 'Are you sure everything's all right?'

'Yeah, just... Got a couple of things to sort out.'

She laid a hand on his back. He flinched. Vonny got the bigger shock from this exchange. 'Seth... C'mon, darlin'.'

'C'mon what?'

'You're hiding something. Or being economical with the truth. Or lying, just a teensy bit. Which is probably the same thing. You've lost a bit of your sparkle. Nine times out of ten, it's you cracking jokes, and me telling you to shut up. What's wrong?'

'Nothing. Just annoyed at the kid taking those pictures of us. I should learn to close my trap. It was my fault. Mr Comedy with the stupid comments.'

'Don't worry about it. You're right, too – it gets more

attention for us. You had that bit right. Didn't Susie say she'd sell the story to some nationals, or one or two of the agencies?'

'So she says. I just want rid of the bloody car, now. I'm off to get rid of it.' He snatched on his jacket, not meeting her gaze. Vonny folded her arms, not moving out of his way. He towered over her, but she somehow still managed to look down at him, frowning, mouth downturned.

This was hardly ferocious – that face couldn't strike terror into anyone, no matter how hard she tried – but that was all it took for him to fold. The massive shoulders sagged. His head lowered. His voice trembled. 'There's some trouble back home.'

'What kind of trouble?'

'Jake… he's gotten himself into a pickle. Local scumbags. Mum says he's gone wrong.'

Vonny had a picture of Seth's younger brother, sat at a table, wearing the grey flannel trousers and laser-beam-red pullover of his secondary school, still a size too big for him. Books open, pen scuttling over his notes. Beautifully mannered and shy with women. A hilarious dandelion-seed moustache on his upper lip when viewed in profile. But that had been two years ago. 'Jake? I can't believe it.'

'Believe it. He got striped. Twenty-four stitches. Face down to his neck. Could have been…' He passed a hand over his brow. 'I don't know whether to strangle him or hug him. Maybe both. I don't know.'

'What's your dad doing about it?'

'He's said nothing. And he can't do anything. He's angry about it, but… He's a hands-off guy, Von. He's not part of that world. He was never a hard case. That's why we all love him, but… he also knows enough not to call the cops and make it worse.'

'Jesus. Do the police even know? Silly question.' Vonny moved in for a hug and he folded her in his arms. She had meant to comfort him, but it ended up the other way around. Her head against that chest. Safe. Where she liked to be.

'No, don't think the police will be involved much. I don't know the kids involved. I say "kids", it could be grown men…' He swallowed, almost choked. Her own eyes filled with tears at this sound. He was a big man, but soft, so soft – a quality he hid, but a quality she loved. 'He owes money, Vonny. Lots of it.'

She drew back. Now she felt fear, too. 'How much?'

'Tens of thousands. Some sort of deal went wrong… I think they got banged, while moving the stuff. Or carrying out some kind of deal.'

'Stuff. Drugs, you mean?'

'I don't know. My guess would be drugs, but I just don't know. And I can't get him to talk to me. Whatever went wrong, he's been blamed for it. This is what he told my mum. He won't answer my calls. He knows better, I suppose.'

'How has he managed to get in debt for tens of thousands? He's a bloody child! Isn't he studying for his exams? I thought you said he was going to be an astronaut, Seth. Straight-A student. Heading for Oxbridge. How did this happen?'

'Don't know. How does it happen to anyone? Everyone goes a bit wild when they're a teenager. I thought with Jake it would just amount to some dodgy clothes I could take the piss out of when he's older. Some bad records. Christ, a haircut. But he's gone wrong.'

'Taking them or dealing them? Is that another silly question?'

'I don't think he's taking them. He might have tried to deal them. Could have been a one-off. A lot of kids from the right side of the tracks do that. Sometimes they're just passing stuff on. It's an easy way to get kudos. But it makes them a target.' He shook his head, violently, as if trying to physically obliterate what was going on in his head. 'This is my fault. I've got to sort it.'

'Don't be silly. It can't be your fault.' Then, dread. 'How can you sort it out?'

'Leave it with me.'

'You're not going to pay him? We're already up to our necks, Seth.'

At this, he raised his voice. 'Did I say I was going to do that? And I know we're up to our necks. Well aware. Don't forget who kitted the place out. So don't be advising me about money!'

Vonny's chin dropped. 'What? Where did this come from?'

'Look…' Seth said, clenching his jaw. 'I think I need to head on back home. Like, soon. Like, tomorrow. I need to make sure he's OK. I need to make sure Mum and Dad are OK. She's… she sounded old on the phone, darlin'. Really worn out. That was the worst thing. Knowing she's having to deal with this… I can't have it. I've got to go back. I'm sorry. We'll have to delay the grand opening.'

'Seth…'

He fastened his new jacket and closed the door firmly behind him. Vonny sat down, still dumbfounded. On the folding table, on the front page of the local paper, her own grinning face mocked her.

# 14

Vonny surveyed the turf being laid on the front lawn. The gardener she'd hired to do it was older and more experienced than the lads who'd come in to finalise the plastering and the electrics, but seemed no less diffident. He shot her the occasional dirty look as she watched the brown-backed rolls of turf being laid flat on the exposed soil.

'Sorry,' she said, 'I must be putting you off. Watching this is therapeutic, in a way. Like when your windows are being washed.'

The man grunted and got back to work. Vonny, wincing as if she'd made some dreadful faux pas, put her wellies on and went for a walk in the woods.

It was the coldest day on-site yet. A chill mist had risen early, but had left its garlands of frost on every surface. The ground was hard beneath Vonny's feet as she took a direct path through the woods to the stream, oddly wary of the place where they'd discovered the car. It seemed to throb somewhere just over her shoulder.

She had considered sending a drone over the trees while the day was reasonably clear and the branches were bare, to see if there was anything else that might be concealed on the land. Something about the jagged barrier, natural or not, had repelled Vonny on sight. She wished they'd simply ordered the car to be towed away and crushed. She had felt an instinctive dislike for its beaming yellow grin, like a disinterred skull. There was something wrong with that car – though there was nothing inside that pointed to any wrongdoing, she didn't like it one bit. It had been like a bad-taste exhibit, a serial killer's car.

So it was with a sense of some foreboding that she travelled to the east, through the thicker part of the woods. A path still coiled its way around the forest floor, and the terrain was hardly difficult, but it became a lonely place out there, the closer she travelled towards the perimeter of her property. Pooled water had become ice, and it cracked under her feet. She regretted the wellingtons; considered going back for sturdier boots.

A sudden snap in the trees ahead put her senses on alert. Out of pure instinct, she stopped, gazing towards a thicket directly ahead. 'Hello?' she said.

Vonny remembered the impression she'd had earlier of the face in the woods. A fleeting glimpse of a figure, slight, though not well defined enough to be male or female; then it had been gone. There was a sudden crash through the bushes up ahead, and then silence.

Vonny drew back to the thick trunk of an alder tree, peering out towards the scene of the disturbance, maybe forty or so yards away.

There – a dark shadow, blundering through the trees, a slight stirring of low branches, whether in the slipstream of the escaping figure or actually moved aside by it, Vonny could not tell. 'Hey! Where are you going?' Her tone of voice was querulous, not reassuring, as she had intended. She had no wish to follow the figure, wherever it was going.

Up to no good, she thought. Whatever that person was up to, they didn't want to be found.

She stared back instinctively, retracing her steps as quietly as possible. Now, the woods seemed to coalesce behind her, as if a great shining black eye had opened, and focused. Vonny was hyper-aware, now, of every crunch and flex of the foliage, every flicker of every bird. With the treeline as thick as it was, anyone could be stealing behind her now, gaining a few yards every time she returned her gaze to the front.

When she did look in front, she screamed.

'Oh!' Prill said, springing backwards, her hand on her chest. 'I am so, so sorry!'

Vonny staggered towards a tree, resting her hand against the bark, waiting for her heartbeat to slow down. 'Good God... You might have given me some warning!' She laughed – and then started forward when the older woman's face crumpled. 'It's all right, Prill – I'm sorry I startled you. You just gave me a fright. I was sure there was someone up ahead in the trees. I was a little bit freaked out.'

'I was sure you'd seen me – I waved,' Prill said, tears filling her eyes. 'I had no intention to startle you.'

'Oh, you silly sausage!' Vonny opened her arms to hug the older woman, instinctively, and she accepted it awkwardly. At last Vonny drew back, patting her on the shoulder. 'What a pair of prize loons! It's fine. I'm kind of glad I saw you. You can walk me back to the house.'

Prill blew her nose, the sound comically loud, ricocheting off every surface. 'I just came over to say what a wonderful job they did of the house – I saw the pictures in the newspaper. My husband thought they were wonderful, too. And what a surprise when that car was found!'

'Yes,' Vonny said, gazing behind her one last time towards the path, 'that was a real shock to us, too. We asked anyone if they fancied buying it. A couple of classified ads online… A buyer got in touch with us almost immediately. No one would give us any contact details of the family of the previous owner – Mr Grainger.'

'No, I expect his relatives were quite difficult to find. Still – what a thing to have on your land. Like buried treasure!'

Something occurred to Vonny, then. 'This path… it isn't public land, is it? I know there's a path at the drystone wall around the back, which is accessible, but not round here. Would that be right? It isn't that clear on the plans.'

Prill suddenly gripped Vonny's arm, and gazed into her eyes with an eerie intensity. 'I hope you don't mind me coming over here? It's been so long, you know. It's such a beautiful woodland, and people are perfectly welcome to walk through our fields, any time.'

'Well, I'd prefer it if you knocked on my door first – so I could have some company. I think there are paths through here, open to the public – running along the back.' There was a pause after this. *Have to draw a line somewhere.* Vonny had felt relief that she wasn't being stalked – although technically speaking, she was indeed being stalked.

'I hope I wasn't imposing. I thought – how lovely to come around here. So few trees on our property, you know – just around the edges for drainage. And cover, privacy. But none to walk around in. Nothing like this.'

'You're fine to come around for a chat any time, you've got my word. Or to come around and have a cup of tea. We're getting close to official moving-in day, you know. End of the week.'

'Oh splendid, how exciting! You know, my husband was saying, "They'll be selling up as soon as they finish that house. That article in the newspaper was basically a big free advert." I told him, "Nonsense – that's a dream home, not some kind of cut-and-shut enterprise. We don't do that in Brenwood Green, and the house is fit for royalty. That's not the house where people will just put it up and run," I said.'

Vonny smiled kindly. 'We had the luck of the devil winning the raffle. And I do have a bit of inheritance money to use, to get the plot up to scratch. It's a dream home – I helped design it. And it's going to be our home. We're staying put – no intention to sell.'

'Oh, that's wonderful,' Prill said. 'You've no idea how long it's been since we had lovely neighbours. Good company.' She seemed on the verge of saying something else, then nodded, and looked towards the forest floor.

'You know, Prill, if there's something you want to say – feel free. I know I screamed in your face, but I'm not one of those get-off-my-land types. I just wasn't expecting anyone… And I'm still getting used to being a country girl, I suppose. You said you wanted to speak to me about something?'

'Ah. I did.' Prill looked relieved. 'I suppose this makes it easier.'

'Makes what easier?'

'Warning you. About this plot.'

Vonny straightened up. 'If you mean about the suicides…

97

Seth told me. He said your husband told him about them, in fact.'

'It's not just that. It's the entire property. And the people who lived here for the past twenty years.'

Seth was over on the east side, close to the thicket where they'd found the car under the tarp. Two thick tracks were cut into the earth where Devin and the boys had helped Seth roll the car back up to the house, and anchor it until the collector had arrived in his pick-up truck to take it away. The section of ground where the car had been hidden under the tarp was bleached and denuded, even through the encroaching foliage.

He listened to the sound of the stream, and then his own heartbeat, before he made the call.

'Seth,' the other person said on the line, hesitantly. 'I thought you were calling this evening? Interesting text message you dropped me.'

'Hope you're not in the middle of something. I've got stuff on my mind.'

'You're quite right, Seth, quite right. Hold on a second...' The other man said something with his hand over the phone; a woman's voice answered. There was the sound of a door closing, then the voice returned. 'Yeah, I've made some inquiries. Found out some interesting stuff.'

'Go on, Colin. Don't keep me in suspense. I'm in tatters, mate.'

'Hope my Auntie Donna and Uncle Steven are looking after themselves? Because what I heard about my cousin...'

'Don't piss about, Colin,' Seth said, tersely. He grit his teeth, staring into the swaying trees.

'Sorry,' Colin said, genuinely contrite. 'Well, first of all, Jake's problem isn't dealing. He's grifting though, mate. You know he's into computer science, right?'

'I didn't know that, in fact.'

'Bit of a genius, it turns out. Swiped a lot of money off a minicab company based not too far away, is what I heard. I don't think he's the brains behind it, but he's done a lot of the graft. Lot of money's disappeared – the kind you can't see. Numbers in a bank, that kind of thing. Now you see it, now you don't. All done at the touch of a button. Clever dick, your Jake.'

'Jesus,' Seth whispered.

'Yeah. Trouble is, the cab firm, is like... more than a cab firm. It is a cab firm, but it's also a place where things scrub up nicely. Lot of soaps and detergents on the go. Following me?'

'I follow you.'

'And the people who run those type of cab firms aren't too happy about what's happened. They leaned on a few people. Your brother ran into a spot of bother, but it could have been a lot worse. One of those cases of mistaken identity where it worked out for the guy in the receiving end, for once. They thought he was one of your brother's mates. So they gave him a little warning – meant to have been for him, delivered to his mate. Had they known it was your brother, it might have gone worse. So, you could say he was lucky. He's a bit less pretty, but still breathing.'

'How much is he in for, Colin? Do you know?'

'More than you can cover. And more than your brother can cover. He might have helped do the deed, but it's all long gone. Don't know whether they got scammed in return. It's possible. Cash sitting in a bank account in Moscow somewhere, by now, and they don't have a bean to show for it.'

'How much? Ten grand? More?'

'Wallop a zero on it and that's close to what I heard. But it's hard to know.'

'Can you ask for me, Colin? Make some inquiries and find out?'

'I'll try, but he's made it awkward for me. And I don't know any easy way to tell you this… A bit like you, I'm not really a part of that world. Never was. You got into music; I got into business. But I didn't want any ties to the old ways. It's not for me.'

'If you find out, I'll be grateful. I've sent Jake away – paid for him to lie low someplace quiet. Mum and Dad too. The old man, he didn't want to go… I don't think he gets it.'

'He's of the old-old school, that's for sure. Straight shooter. Always admired that about Uncle Steven, man. So. What's next, Seth? I don't envy you, cuz.'

'I don't know.' He closed his eyes for a moment. 'I'm going to get down there and see what's what.'

# 15

'Gangsters?' Vonny's tone was comical. But she wasn't laughing, and neither was Prill.

'In a manner of speaking. He was a businessman, Dan Grainger – legitimate business, anyway. His horses, of course. He bred them around here – plenty of room on the meadow to let them roam. But there were always rumours about him. His elder son, Stuart, he was killed on the street – stabbed. Happened in London. I'm not sure if they ever caught the person who did it. He was coming out of a nightclub, and someone knifed him. I think it was on the news, but not for long. The second son, Mark – he died the same night as Dan. The inquest said it was murder-suicide, that Mark owed Dan money, Dan killed him, then himself. The other son hanged himself.'

'You what?' They were close to the house, now. At the sound of Vonny's voice, carrying across the front lawn, Devin's hard-hatted head shot up from the balcony. 'Killed himself? Where? The woods?'

'I'm not sure which tree,' Prill said, quickly. 'And you've got a few to choose from. Put it out of your mind, Vonny.'

'Jesus. I didn't know this… The raffle was run by an estate agent, but we heard nothing about that stuff. Isn't there a law, that they have to tell you when someone got murdered on the estate?'

'Not that I know of. Maybe in America. But yes, there were rumours that Dan might have been murdered. He had powerful friends. The police turned a blind eye to a lot of things. There were raves, years ago – you remember raves? Hundreds of people on the meadow. Lights and noise all night. I don't know how the horses could stand it. My husband went over to warn them off, and was given short shrift. Now my husband's no shrinking violet, I can tell you that. But he knew when to back off with Dan Grainger, and he did.'

'What was he involved in?'

'There was a rumour he had killed people...' Prill shook her head. 'This is silly. I'm trading gossip. I could attach any rumour to him, and you'd never know the truth. Drugs, of course. He was connected to people in London – that's as much as I heard. I'm inclined to believe it.'

'You said you wanted to give me a warning.'

'It was the car. That's what got me thinking. You know, the one you found, the one in the paper. I think I saw him driving it now and again. Very distinctive colour, and a very distinctive type of car. You saw it around here... He used to speed up and down the road, and his sons after him. It's just that, well... given how the car was hidden...'

Vonny felt like she'd been punched. 'Jesus. I might as well have been putting out an advert.'

'There was nothing in the car, was there? Nothing interesting or unusual?'

Vonny shook her head. 'Pretty sure there wasn't. If there was, it's the vintage car dealer's problem, now.'

'Good. Nothing to worry about, I'm sure. You've got a wonderful house.'

'It's a pretty simple build at its core, for all the cosmetics.' Vonny knew this wasn't quite true, though. There had been ego involved in this project, in getting the house just so. Vonny had ordered and constructed her dream home, using her own inheritance and Seth's funds. It hadn't been simple, it hadn't been cheap, and the results were clear to see. The idea of someone turning it around, as crudely as that, with the décor she'd spent a long time designing torn apart by the new owner, caused her to twitch. *One shot. Chance of a lifetime. And it has to be right.*

'Not at all. It is a grand house. You should be proud. It's something a rock star might live in.'

'And they might, at that! Elton might use it for a country getaway! Hey, if you were worried about raves before…'

Prill laughed, but the sound was remote, and held something in reserve. Vonny realised that she must have actually voiced a fear of her neighbour's. 'Well, so long as it's not The Rolling Stones.'

As she considered the glint of light on the windows of the upper floor, something occurred to Vonny. 'Do you remember the night the old house burned down?'

'Yes,' Prill said quietly. 'We phoned the fire brigade, of course. We didn't want to go onto their land. I wouldn't say we had bad relations with them. They were distant, and that was fine with us. But we knew not to mess. The fire started so quickly… You could see the flames from our house. And then the paddock and stables went up…'

Vonny clamped a hand to her mouth. 'Please tell me the horses weren't killed.'

'No – they were found loose.'

'Thank God.'

'It always struck me as curious that the house was torched. The inquest found that Dan had done it, after he killed Mark. The other son, well, they think he hanged himself out of despair. No one knows why he was there that night. Mark had not long been divorced, if you're wondering. Not the mother of the two sons, she was off the scene before he moved onto the old farm. The new wife, younger than him. Beautiful-looking girl. Maybe not the brightest. Didn't last long. Took a lot of his cash. You can imagine. Older man, younger woman... So anyway, he was on a downward spiral. Taking lots of drugs. He'd become erratic in racing circles, too. Persona non grata, here and there. Given what they say happened to him, some of it added up, but... The second son's suicide never quite made sense, you know. Hanging himself, when the gunfire happened... We'll never know what happened on that night.'

Prill shook her head. 'Anyway. I've said what I came to say. Dan Grainger wasn't a nice man. He died in a terrible way, and his sons are gone, too. I'm sorry you had to find out like this. But you have to be careful. If you find anything strange on the property, anything untoward...'

'We'll tell the police.' Vonny touched the older woman on the shoulder. 'It was kind of you to come over. Why don't we have drinks? You can come around, once the house is finished? You and your husband. The decorations will be up soon. Make it festive. Port, sherry, *all* the calories.'

'That'd be lovely.' She smiled primly. 'Well, I'll be off. I hope you're happy here. I am.' Vonny watched as Prill vanished along the track. Her tone had cooled at the end. Here was the lady Vonny had first seen directing the builders outside the house. Vonny wondered which of the pair of them had said too much.

# 16

Harold Dakins was lost in his work, attempting to fit a new chassis on the car, with the radio blaring in the corner of the garage, so he didn't know he had company until he spotted a pair of shoes somewhere over his shoulder.

With his back resting on a trolley, he wheeled himself out from underneath the car, with only his head visible. 'Hello?'

A young man with thick black hair grown a little too long appeared. He had on a biker's jacket, at least thirty years out of style, and possibly twice as old as its wearer. The boy waved, and smiled brightly. 'Hello there. Sorry to startle you. I was looking for Harold Dakins?'

Harold scrambled to his feet. He was a squat, broad man in his fifties with twin patches of hair clinging on above his ears, which he really should have shaved off long before now. He had on a Blake's 7 T-shirt, bought semi-ironically at first but which was now so worn it looked like the real thing, bought by a real fan. Ancient, oil-stained jeans – which he referred to as his 'working trousers' – completed his look. The yellow Datsun suspended three feet off the floor by a hydraulic lift was a shrieking counterpoint to the brown-toned clutter of the rest of the garage, a riot of ancient car parts long robbed of their shine.

'That's right – Harold Dakins,' he said, wiping his hands on a towel. 'There's a bell on the front, lad – you must have seen it.'

'Ah, sorry, I must have missed it.' The young guy came far too close, his hands on his hips. The boy's biker's jacket reminded Harold of a boy he'd hated at school.

'Then it's polite to knock.'

'In actual fact... Wow. There it is.' The young guy pointed towards the Datsun. 'I read about that, you know. In the papers. I'm a collector.'

'Oh.' Harold brightened a little. 'Yeah, I'm just getting started on that one.'

'It's a beauty isn't it?' The young man cocked his head. 'I mean I just love that colour. Tell me you're going to keep the colour?'

'Yeah, I think I will. You into the Cherry?'

'Cherries are the best, the absolute best.' The boy came forward, gazing at the vehicle in awe. 'I always had a thing for Cherries. I knew a Cherry, at school. Maybe that's the reason. We've all got these hidden motivations. And, my God – it's in great trim as well, wouldn't you say?'

'For sure. Best I've seen. It was kept outdoors, would you believe, but it had been in a garage before that. Not as much rust as you'd think. Cracking piece of work for an E10.'

The young man nodded, ponderously. 'I was just thinking that! I've seen some classy E10s around but this one... This one...' He tutted and stabbed an admonitory finger at the car. 'It's almost naughty how good it looks, eh?'

Harold's smile vanished. 'It's not an E10. It's an F10. Quite clearly – 1977, UK model. I don't even know the

Cherry that well, but I could have told you that from about a hundred yards.'

The young man continued to nod for a few seconds, then chuckled. 'Yep. You got me. I couldn't have told you squat about this car a day ago. That's a useful little nugget you've given me, though. I will bear it in mind. I will file it away for later use. Cherry *is* the name of my favourite girl at school. You never forget a crush, do you?'

'She sounds great.' If Harold was a little bit pleased with himself at having caught someone, *anyone* out, he was more than happy to display this. 'Now. How can I help you?'

'I *am* here about the car. I've got an interest. I mean, I am interested in buying it from you.'

'It's not for sale at the moment.'

'But you do sell cars?'

'Hey, son – the sign's out the front. I *restore* cars. I get them back on the road, and looking good. After that, yes, I sell them. Probably at auction, but I could do a deal before that. I've got one or two potential buyers lined up already. People who love the model. That's who I sell to. People who know an E10 from an F10.'

'So, if I offered you market value, cash in hand, right now, that wouldn't interest you?'

Harold licked his lips. 'I already started the job, so I'll see it through. But yes, I'll listen to any offers. Once it's done, you can take it off my hands, for the right price. Just not today.'

'Whereabouts did the car come from?' The young guy had gone very close to it, now, bending over to inspect the inside, through the window. This made Harold more nervous than anything; proximity to his prize. Physically, the boy was nothing to worry about. Too pretty to be a tough guy. The leather jacket was a prop, a bit like some of them used beards, these days.

'That's none of your business.'

'That's not an answer to my question.'

'Look, son, I've got a lot to do this morning. What to do is, take the number on the sign at the front of the garage, and give me a call in two weeks' time. Or even better, drop me an email. You want to talk business, that's the time to do it.'

The boy looked upset, as if he wanted to cry. He ran both hands through his longish black hair. 'I mean, I just don't get it – the rudeness. This is what I struggle with in people. The *rudeness*. We could sort all this out in two minutes flat, and yet – you're rude. It's a big problem in society. Big, big problem.'

'What did you just say?'

Before the answer could come, Harold's garage was full. Two other men appeared – one with blond hair and a piercing through his eyebrow and orange and red flames inked on his neck, the other a bulky nightmare, a lump of muscle and bone poured into a human mould and squeezed into a suit. The latter's big ball face loomed like a wraith set loose from a cave. They had their hands on him in seconds.

Harold wasn't much of a fighter; but it was only in the following few moments that he clearly understood this. The two newcomers pinned him to the floor. The lad with the black hair placed his boot on the side of Harold's jaw and turned it into the floor with only a little pressure. Breathing hard, sniffing boot polish and dogshit, Harold inhaled some of the dust coating the concrete. He sneezed, so far as the boot would allow.

'Bless you,' said the dark-haired boy. 'Now, where were we? Where did you get the car?'

Harold wasn't much of a stoic, either. Or a bluffer. 'I got it from a guy who found it in the middle of the woods, somewhere. He owns the property. He gave me a call. Asked a fair price.'

'What's the name? What's the house?'

'Guy's name was Seth. Owner's Vonny something. Black girl, it's an African name. French-African, sort of, you know...' he gibbered. 'Kouassi, that was it, Vonny Kouassi.'

'Vonny Kouassi,' the young guy said. 'I will make a note of that. And was there anything unusual in the car? Any bags, boxes... that kind of thing?'

'No, nothing.'

'Definitely?'

'There was nothing.'

A new voice cut in – a pleasant, almost melodic Scottish accent. 'I think Mr Dakins needs a helping hand here, lads. Stick him on that trolley and put him under the car.'

'Hey!'

Harold Dakins might have imagined a scenario like this a hundred times, or a thousand, in his life. He might have modelled it ending in a variety of ways. He might have thought to lift the wrench that was two feet away on top of the toolbox; he might have thrown any number of ridiculous punches or kicks. In actual fact he simply whimpered as they bore him down on the trolley, holding his legs steady, and then wheeling him head first under the car.

'Amazing piece of kit, this,' came the Aberdonian accent. 'Thought you could only get these kind of lifts in garages. This is a kind of a garage, though, I suppose. Controls straightforward, aye?'

The smell of oil and grime were usually pleasant things for Harold Dakins, as was the pungent tang of petrol in the air. Now he only knew fear as the underside of the car remained poised above his head. 'I didn't find anything in the car. It was bare. I swear to it,' he gibbered.

The hydraulic platform grunted. The Cherry rose an inch or two.

'It's responding to my touch,' the Scottish man said, drily. 'Don't mind, mate, do you?'

The platform grunted again. This time, the car descended. Not by much; it seemed a test, more than anything. After one or two further coughs and stutters, the man at the controls had their measure.

He grinned, then began to whistle the bassline to 'Under Pressure'. He punched a button, and the car descended, far too fast, the outer edge of the driver's side door stopping an inch from Harold's chest.

'Christ's sake,' Harold said, openly weeping, 'what do you want from me? I told you I don't know anything about the car. If I did, I'd tell you!'

He couldn't move. Fingers bit into the flesh at his knees and thighs. Someone else held the trolley steady. There was nowhere to go.

One more inch. The metal touched his chest. He gasped, then held his breath.

'Promise?' said the Scottish man.

'Promise! Guy's name was Seth Miller. I remember

now. Seth Miller, Vonny Kouassi. It was at the old house, Brenwood Green, used to be Ryefields. You can take the car, if you want!'

'We'll take a *look* in the car, that's for sure,' said the Scottish man. 'We'll give it a good going over. You can watch, if you like. Share your expertise.'

A quarter inch; no more than the merest touch of the controls. Harold could feel it on his chest, now. The slightest pressure. An inch or two more would crack his chest cavity like a chicken carcass. He turned his head; the stink of rust filled his nostrils.

One of the other two men who had burst in said, in an obscenely excited whisper: 'Shall we just do him in?'

There was a terrible silence. Harold imagined the finger at the button, poised.

'Nah. He's done,' the Scottish man said, at last. 'If this guy knew anything, he'd have told us. Stick the poor bastard in the corner and we'll rip this piece of shit apart, just to be sure. He can tell us all the nooks and crannies. He's got the knowledge. Maybe grab a mop, there, if you would. I think Mr Dakins has had an oil leak of some kind.'

# 17

The funny thing was, before the encounter, Vonny had delighted in the peace.

Even for such a bosky place, calm was unusual. Normally there was the activity of the builders, the odd shout, the tinny treble of their radio. But today was Sunday, and they had the day off. Barring the odd passing traffic on the road behind the trees and the old man's hacking coughs of the magpies, there was nothing to disturb her.

Fears for Seth filled the empty space in her head. He had been somewhat abrupt when she'd asked him to be careful in going back to London to see for himself what kind of hole his brother Jake had managed to dig. That was unlike him, and this worried her; she didn't think he would intervene in whatever his brother was dealing with – he simply wasn't that type of man; he had a softness to him, no one's idea of a hard case. However, he had his moments, usually when under stress, and she knew his background hadn't been idyllic. She didn't want to see him goaded. She could see him being drawn into something, provoked. Even though he gave Jake pelters, it was mostly a front; he was very protective of his little brother.

She didn't let this trouble her. It was another chilly day

outside. Vonny was a perennially busy person, but she knew when it was time to kick back. Besides, she was sick of the caravan, the tight spaces, the inevitable build-up of clutter on its limited spaces, the hair straighteners, the strewn clothes – both equally guilty, here – and the shower cubicle, either a microbiologist's dream, or nightmare. Seth had begun to refer to it as The Tin Coffin, but this wasn't even mildly amusing any more. She had been tempted to spend a night in the house by herself, while Seth was gone. But this seemed somehow more troubling than the idea of sleeping in the caravan alone. Besides, it felt like bad luck, seeing the night in without Seth beside her. Somewhat like spending the night before your wedding with your bride.

That said, she could still enjoy some of the space, at least before the sun went down.

So, after a quick walk into the forest, long enough to get cold and regret the decision, Vonny dug out her tartan blanket and lounged by the empty swimming pool. She pursed her lips at the irony, and even took a selfie.

Although there was no water in the rectangle cut in the earth, the cyan tiles were a fine illusion, and the overhanging branches and huge potted conifers viewed obliquely added to the sense that she was on holiday. Holidays were where it was at. She had to imagine the sea, while she indulged in the rare luxury of being able to disappear into her book. In the cold air, but snug under the blanket, she was alone in her own woollen oasis. The only thing that gave her any pause was the imposing shade of the house. Vonny couldn't help but glance up at the bank of windows every now and again, fearful that a figure might appear there.

A sudden flutter in the grey above startled her; looking up, she noticed the bird of prey.

Vonny was curious about the creatures who lived on her land, although she didn't have any particular mania to know the exact taxonomy and Latin nomenclature attached to each species. However, this one caught her eye, and she became curious.

It wheeled high overhead, not hovering, surely too large to be a kestrel. Although it was difficult to tell beneath the low grey clouds, it appeared smudged, off-white the way a polar bear's fur looked against bleached white ice, wings spread as it wheeled high above the forest. Not a golden eagle, surely. They lived in the highlands, or the steppe, even more accessible places where the rabbits and voles had to look lively. Vonny followed its path as it made its stoop towards a treeline, then halted the dive and returned to the higher air. *Just for a day... To be able to see what it saw,* she thought; *to be aware of even the slightest movement in the twitching trees below. For things to be that sharp, that clear.*

She sat up on the sunlounger and, on impulse, switched her tablet to camera mode. She took a moment or two to train the lens on the dark stripe swooping above, then zoomed in.

It was an owl of some kind. Vonny wouldn't have put her life on the species, thanks to the blurring effect of its flight – as she'd said earlier, she didn't quite have her 'eye in' when it came to the creatures of the woods – but something in the stark hue of the raptor's plumage suggested the phrase 'barn owl' to her. She could see one in her mind's eye, an image from a picture book she'd had as a child, the huge dark eyes, the ruffled neck, the luckless field mouse dangling from its beak. But they were nocturnal, weren't they?

She took several shots, keeping the camera on the bird as it plunged low past the branches. It came past a huge alder tree, surely the biggest in view over the north wall of the house, and then she saw him.

'Oh,' was all Vonny said for a second or two. She dropped the tablet, as if embarrassed on the other person's behalf. Then a mixture of shock and fear took her by the scruff of the neck. She lifted the tablet slowly – not wishing to make any sudden moves, the better not to attract a predator's attention – and zoomed in again.

It took her upwards of twenty seconds to pinpoint him again. Someone in green khaki trousers, perched on a branch. With an actual pair of binoculars. Pointing right at her.

'Bastard,' she said, under her breath. She took several photos of him – a young man with black or dark brown hair, with a pair of hillwalking trainers dangling off the branch, maybe ten or fifteen feet off the ground – and then she got to her feet, hideously self-conscious as she whipped off the blanket, despite being fully clothed down to her shoes. She padded across the chill paving stones towards the patio, got her heavy boots on and was out the front door in two minutes flat.

Having some idea of the topography of the woods and one or two of its byways, Vonny knew enough to be clever about how she approached him. She took the dogleg path to the right, where she'd bumped into Prill, taking care not to glance in the direction of the alder tree. The woods closed in as she made her way along the wall, but occasionally she could see the top of the alder tree – the lumpen, outsized kid in class they made stand at the back of the class photo.

It was stupid, of course, and she tried hard to take deep breaths as her hands worried themselves. Vonny had no clear plan when she caught up with the man in the alder tree, if she actually did catch up with him.

*What should I do? Fire a bloody warning shot?*

It had been a long time since she'd played hide-and-seek. She tried to move as quickly and quietly towards him as she could, always keeping the upper branches of the alder tree in view. She was sweating by this time despite the chill – pure anxiety, not through any exertion – and kept her phone in her hand.

*I'm all alone out here. With him.*

She tried to focus on her indignation. Soon she stepped into a clear space, heading close to the alder tree. Then she saw, as she'd feared, that the tree was empty.

*I'm sure I saw this in a film once.*

As soon as this occurred to her, a branch snapped, over her left shoulder.

Vonny spun around, and there he was.

# 18

He froze, comically, as if preparing his hands to play an invisible piano. 'Deer caught in headlights' was the cliché that came naturally and fit best. He was a boy, Vonny saw, fifteen at the most, of average height but very skinny. He might go on to develop a good jawline and broad shoulders, but for the moment his features hung on him like a bad suit. He had large grey eyes that blinked rapidly, and longish dark hair that draped on either side of his face, parted in the middle. This didn't look like so much of a fashion statement as simple neglect, though the hair was clean enough. Binoculars and a very expensive-looking long-lens camera hung round his neck. His khaki trousers and a dark T-shirt completed the outfit.

Vonny sensed his fear and relaxed accordingly. She held up her hands, as if intimating that she was not armed. 'Hey… It's all right,' she said, softly, as if to an animal. 'You're fine. Please don't run from me.'

'I was just going,' he mumbled, and took a couple of steps. He was tense, ready to run.

'Please, don't run. You're not in any trouble. It's fine. I'm Vonny.'

The boy blushed, and actually looked away from her.

Tears brimmed in his eyes, and Vonny now felt utterly alarmed. 'I'm sorry,' he said. 'I've been tracking the owl. I was trying to see where it nests.'

'Yes – I saw it. A barn owl, was it?'

He nodded. 'That's it. It hunts around these woods, and the farm across the road. The farmer won't let me come onto his land. I've been tracking it, look.'

He started forward. Vonny swallowed, and her heart began to beat out of control.

'Look,' he said, turning the control screen on the back of the camera towards her. 'It quarters over the farmland in daylight. It's rare but some do it. This one's bold.'

Vonny peered forward, making sure she was out of arm's reach. There, indeed, was the owl, in incredible definition. In full flight with its wingspan stretched to the limit, it was far more formidable than the heart-shaped face would have led you to believe. And there was a terrible fixity about the huge, jet-black eyes, lubricious. How many creatures saw their own final struggles reflected in those eyes?

'It is an awesome bird. I saw it from my garden.'

'Sometimes farmers don't like them around, but they're great for getting rid of rats and rabbits, those kinds of things.' He was very polite, with a deep voice long since broken.

The boy flicked through the camera, detailing shot after shot. On one or two of these shots, the house was visible in the background, but never in close-up. Other shots appeared – clearly taken from ground level – showing the greeny-blue sheen of a magpie, a far grander bird in close-up than it seemed from a distance. After that, a dainty little thing in red, brown and black.

'What's that one?' she asked.

'A chaffinch. Lovely little bird. That's from the summer. Seen a few of them around here.' The boy scratched his head, a nervous twitch like a dog flicking its ears.

'You're a… what is it they call it? A twitcher?'

He blushed again. 'I call myself a birder. It's… a weird hobby, I know that. I should get into football or something. That's what I tell my dad, anyway.'

'I think it's awesome – something I always wanted to get into. You live around here?'

'Uh, yeah – few miles up and over the hill.'

'I live here.'

He showed shock. 'What – here? On this land?'

'That's right.'

'You're building the house?'

'It's built.'

'You're related to Dan Grainger?'

'I am happy to tell you that I'm no relation to Dan Grainger whatsoever.'

'That's… kind of a relief.'

'Not a nice man, I'm hearing.'

'No. He chased me off here a couple of times. His eldest son set a dog on me. I started coming back a few weeks ago. I stayed away from the building.' He made eye contact at last. 'I'm really sorry if I've trespassed. My dad told me not to come near the place, but it's such a great site… So many species in these woods and in the farm behind… It's a gold mine for me, it really is.'

'Don't worry about it,' Vonny said. 'You've got my permission to come in and take as many pictures of the birds as you like. It's absolutely fine. The only thing I'd ask is that you stay away from the house. We're still having a bit of work done, and we're going to be pulling down an old shed and one or two other things. I'll warn the crews that you'll be around. But I've no problem with you coming in here and taking shots of the birds... What's your name again?'

'Crispin.'

'Crispin. As I said – I'm Vonny. We're going to be neighbours. It's nice to meet you.'

He looked utterly relieved, though still about ready to kick-start his chicken legs and sprint off into the undergrowth. 'That means an awful lot – I got some incredible shots of a red kite in the summer. You're really lucky to have all this on your doorstep. Dan Grainger and his sons absolutely hated people coming onto his land. They used to fire guns all the time – even if I'd been brave enough to come into the woods, they might have killed me by accident.'

'The more I'm hearing about Dan Grainger, the less I like, to be honest.'

Crispin checked over his shoulder. 'He was a gangster, they say.'

'Is that right?'

'Yeah.' The boy lowered his voice. 'You know it was a murder-suicide, right? I mean... I guess it's creepy and all, but the old house isn't there. Apparently he shot his son, then himself. Then his other son hanged himself. But I heard different.'

'Is that a fact?' She feigned surprise.

'Yeah. My mate Tommy's dad is in the police. You know what he says?'

She shook her head.

'Apparently, he got killed by another gang, who wanted in on his turf. They killed Dan and both sons, then made it look like murder-suicide. Like they'd all lost their minds.'

'Any idea who this gang was?'

'People from out of town. Big players. Local cops know to leave well alone, they say.'

'Well. They're out of the picture now. It was nice to meet you, Crispin. You carry on with your shots. Maybe you can get a print of one of them for me?'

'Sure! Bye now!' Then, bless him, he did actually run off into the forest, binoculars and camera rattling against his chest.

# 19

Most of Seth's life had been an accident, or hit just as hard as one. The bass was only an exception in that it set the tone for every other accident to follow.

He had a Fender bass – a proper one with all the trimmings – but it mostly stayed on its stand, bolted to the wall like a medieval prisoner. He insisted on using the cheapo Fender copy he'd bought for £55 off his mate's uncle when he was fifteen.

The year before that, Seth had entertained dreams of being a singer and guitarist in an indie band. But his progress on guitar had been slow, and, as he'd found to his cost during a practice session attended by girls who had not passed out in a frenzy of lust, but had in fact laughed at him, he could not hold a note to save himself. He'd been asked to take a turn on bass after their original player backed out, and once he'd gotten over himself and practised properly... something had happened.

It had underpinned everything. The singer who'd replaced him in that band – even its name embarrassed Seth, and he never mentioned it in any interviews – had been decent, the guitar player even better, if smug (this was not uncommon, Seth came to discover). And the drummer had been competent, but a year younger than Seth and his friends, meaning he was roundly patronised. So far as Seth knew, the drummer had not gone on to become the George Harrison of the band.

Seth got used to playing bass, enjoying the relative anonymity – or as anonymous as a six-foot-plus teenager could get. Then he had asked Mr Joffrey, the music teacher, what certain buttons on the mixing desk did. Seth had wanted his bass to sound warm, not dirgey. He had found out how to do it. It was alchemy, or pure magic, though Mr Joffrey had called it the production process. From there, Seth had indulged a long-mocked interest in synthesisers and sequencers. Soon, he had resigned from the band – and who knew, this might have been their moment of bad luck. The other four members didn't amount to anything in music, though he always had time for them on social media.

Seth had followed a different path. He produced and co-wrote a track that had been a classic club hit, which had then been sampled by a rapper. Seth was an accidental producer; as a sideline, then as his main bread and butter. Then he was a success, producing singles and then full albums, in several different genres. He had been extremely close to being taken on by a band he hadn't mentioned to anyone but Vonny for fear of not being taken seriously, even after his song had been on top of the charts. This shining glory, and just about all of his savings, had been as a result of Ninjakata's number-one single. It had been composed on that one same old bass with the wobbly tone dial. Royalties were still a beautiful surprise, for work carried out years before, sat on the edge of his and Vonny's bed in their cramped flat in Balham, his studio a laptop computer, headphones drowning out the sound of traffic and sirens outside.

Seth had some experience in LA about six or seven years previously, but the experience had been alienating. He hadn't realised he was a homebody until he had that sterile experience of airports, check-ins, hotels and worse, nightclubs. Since then he was largely confined to work in the UK, but he'd had that experience in Scandinavia, a different way of working... And the studio had been somewhere rural, late summer, golden light, longer shadows, still gorgeous. A bright green explosion went off in his mind. Then came the Great Big Stroke Of Luck.

The music business had been an obvious gateway to bad habits for some, but for Seth it had led to a work ethic, professionalism and ultimately escape. As a young man it had been the first time in his life he'd found something to do, something to work at. A college course had helped; while he was a competent player, he'd never quite mastered the bass the way he would have liked, and his sense of rhythm was to this day something of a joke on the dance floor of weddings and family parties, Seth had mastered computers, the recording of sound, where and at what volume to place certain instruments.

This adherence to a flat 4x4 professional beat had been a fluke. Because Seth's path might have been different. Nowadays, he had no contact with Script, Ross Langley, Hibbo, the Jock, or any of the other guys in his block he'd run around with as a boy, and that was for the best. He'd had a knife in his hands, but never used it. He had, however, used a baseball bat, an heirloom from a hard cousin who had sold it to him way before the other uncle sold him the bass. Specifically, he'd used it on a car, then a face, both in the same incident. It made his name. He knew the disgust of this early.

Seth had always been tall and broad for his age, but he'd never thought of himself as a fighter. Indeed, he'd been beaten up several times in primary school skirmishes; on one less than memorable occasion, his pal Hibbo had challenged kids from another school to a fight on the top deck of a bus, before running and leaving Seth to it when more kids than expected had piled in. Seth had been thrown down the stairs, a seemingly out-of-body experience with his actual body being folded in half; even now he regarded it as a miracle in that he hadn't ended up in a wheelchair. However, 'like drinking or shagging', as Hibbo had remarked, with authority far beyond his age and experience, the more Seth did it, the better he got at violence.

He grew to enjoy the fear he engendered, which only rose the more he hit back. He'd known from before he went to big school how fighting really went – not the morality of TV kung fu, never mind the Marquess of Queensberry, but simply how many friends you had around you at the time, and also being the aggressor, rather than the defender. He'd only badly hurt one or two people – he could remember one kid, hands pressed to his face, bent double, eyes wide in utter shock as the blood ran through his fingers and stained his trainers.

Usually at this point in the story a girl would appear, showing him the error of his ways, but it didn't quite happen like that. There had been two major relationships in his life, both of which had ended badly. He hadn't met anyone who complemented him in the same way Vonny did; someone equally creative, but utterly uncompetitive. The constant had been music, his escape pod, stemming from indie productions and word of mouth and a good teacher and then an indulgent lecturer with a contacts book and a willingness to open it up.

Basslines were the beginning for Seth, the creative impulse from which his songs emerged, and there had been a weird, ugly bassline running through his life, one his fingers couldn't help but pluck. Dirgey, as on the school morning this sound had first irritated him, not warm.

It got louder on the morning Seth took the train back to London. Head full of his own songs, the demos he'd transferred over to DJ Ninjakata, tracks for her full debut album. Seth didn't like sending his material over the internet, no matter what protocols, VPNs or firewalls were in place. Like releasing a movie on streaming, once it was out there, it was out there, for Seth's money. Even so, reviewing it on his phone, his outsize headphones cushioning his head against the train window, he smiled to himself, enjoying the thrum and thump of the bass and drums, knowing every note already. He had a hangar full of riffs, beats, chord structures and sequences in his head, some of them backdated from his teenage days, and these were among his newest, and his catchiest.

Seth's drive was to make DJ Ninjakata a pop artist, rather than a grime artist. She'd used her singing voice in the chorus of their big hit, and everyone's ears had pricked up as a result. On the front cover they'd turned her into a purple and pink tech-noir sci-fi demon, the kind of thing you'd see in anime, flitting along the skyscrapers of a neo-Tokyo. Seth had thought it was an utter mess, but the image had caught on. In this vein Seth had pushed on, producing a poppier sound, something a little more European. He'd even thrown in a chill-out remix of their original single, and this pleased him more than the number-one hit.

So Seth had immediately divined something was wrong when he arrived at her label's head office, and she was flanked by two big men he didn't recognise. Far from a leather-clad demon from five hundred years in the future, now she was just a tiny figure with a black headband across her forehead and tiny shades to hide her eyes.

The executive in the room was younger than Seth, and more abrasive than what Seth was used to. He did all the talking. 'To be straight up with you, Seth, we're not feeling the tracks.'

Back in his teenage years, Seth had been rejected by a girl he'd adored. The claw-fingered clutch he felt in his chest cavity had felt similar. He should have known how this would go, right away. He had subconsciously twigged, the moment he sat down, the moment DJ Ninjakata had taken a quick sip of her takeaway coffee and looked away.

'Not feeling it? What do you think this is, a fucking craft beer tasting session?'

The two big men on either side of the small woman sat forward a little.

'Let's not be rash, Seth. They're good tunes, they're just not what we're looking for...'

'So – who've you signed up, instead?'

'Come on, don't be unreasonable, Seth. We decided to be up front, to tell you to your face.'

'Duly noted. I could have done without my time being

wasted. Got stuff to do, here.' He pointed at the executive. 'Money in the bank by lunchtime, yeah? We'll go over the small print later, then I'll decide whether or not I'm suing.'

And so that same old bassline intruded in his head as he took the tube back home. He was actually white-knuckling it at one point, his fists in his lap, before he snapped back to himself. It was humiliating, painful, like a physical beating – and worse, there was the reputational damage to come. People would find out what had happened to Seth in that executive's lounge. The experience would stain him. It might make him less bankable, less marketable. It might be the end of the good days, his time in the sun. At least they'd gotten it out of the way early. It gave him something to chew on while he got on with the second part of his trip into London. To where his family were hiding, at an aunt's house.

Jake had opened the door. They'd glared at each other, comically, before Seth had broken the silence.

'Mum in?'

Jake shrugged and turned away – tall, now, possibly taller than Seth. Seth blinked, waiting for the doorway to clear. He hadn't known what he'd see, but he would see it forever. His brother's face swaddled in bandages, eye to chin, with that rotten yellow iodine staining. They must have opened him properly, Seth thought.

Jake wouldn't talk to him about it. 'Who?' he'd asked. 'Just a name. Do you know? Who they running with?'

'Nothing you can do, Seth.' Seth hated his brother's poise, the insolence with which he met his gaze. 'Happens, doesn't it? Happens to the bravest. You told me that.'

'Who did it? And how much are you in for?'

There had been more arguing then – fury which their mother had to separate. As Seth grew angrier, his younger brother grew calmer. He might even have smirked once or twice, on the good side of his face.

'No lectures,' Jake had said, as he left – he hadn't even taken his coat off. 'You're out of it. Enjoy your life, mate.'

Seth's feet followed a well-travelled course to the Seal and Trapper.

Tony was still there behind the bar, still with his head shaven right to the quick so that you couldn't tell if he was properly bald, properly greying, or still magically twenty-five years old. He recognised Seth right away, but reacted uneasily. 'Hey stranger, how's it going?'

Lunchtime, but one or two souls in there already. An old man who might have come with the title deeds, smart, starched white collar underneath his raincoat, taking an eternity over his half-pint and his paper. Someone else, bent double, either concentrating hard on what was on their phone or struggling to remain continent.

After dealing with the small talk amiably enough – yes, he was in London for a spot of business, yes, a big project, one he couldn't talk about – he asked Tony: 'Has our Jake been in?'

Tony had been racking up glasses; he moved without pause, all except for his eyes. 'Not sure... Isn't he a bit young?'

'Everybody was a bit young in here, Tony. I think I was fifteen when you first pulled me a pint.'

'You've never been fifteen in your life, Seth.'

'How about some of the boys he knocks around with?

Ryan Cross, the Abbeys' boy? Think he's still knocking around with them.'

The scarcely perceptible shake of the head should have tipped Seth off. But he continued: 'Only asking because, he's had a spot of bother lately.'

Seth didn't hear them approach. Hadn't even known they were in the pub. They might have levitated through the floorboards. Two faces, either side of him, pinched and twitchy. He gripped the bar, resisted the urge to back off.

'Sorry to cut in there, big guy. You mentioned Jake – that Jake Miller, you mean?'

Tony retreated slowly and stopped as close to his poorly stocked gantry as he could get without damaging the optics. He threw the bar towel over his shoulder and actually began to whistle to himself, as if the situation hadn't instantly gone wrong and scary.

'Who's asking?' Seth picked the one who'd spoken; he locked eyes with him. He was young, his hair thick and swept back from his head.

'You Seth Miller? His big brother?'

'Again – who's asking?' He swung round to look at the sidekick, a scrawny runt... but somehow scarier. This one grinned, the whites of his eyes curdled to a baby romper-suit shade of pink. This time Seth did back off, but only a little. He kept his foot on the bar stool.

'Interested parties.' The speaker grinned, teeth like tribal jewellery. 'You let him know he's got a deadline to start paying. You hear?'

'Give me a name, and I'll sort it for you,' Seth said.

'He knows, mate. He knows the name. No need for you

to get involved. Or make inquiries. You seen him lately? Haven't seen him near your mum and dad's for a while. We'll go to your mum's first, though. If he doesn't sort things out.'

'You go near my mum's house, I'll kill you.' No backing out now; the bassline off at a gallop, notes becoming indistinguishable, one long ululating thrum.

A scratch across the floor as the bar stool to his right shifted; then Seth worked on reflex, fast and smooth, his own bar stool in the air, swung hard, with some purchase in the middle, and then the grinning freak to the right was on the floor, bent at the hinge of his hips, holding his face.

The skinny one to the left backing off, reaching into his jacket... and his hand staying there.

'Doing, you doing, out of here, muppet,' were the only words Seth could discern among a jazzy run from Tony's mouth. He didn't wait twice.

'You remember what I said,' he added, for good measure, pointing at the skinny guy who stood, shaking like washing in a high wind. 'If I hear he's been hurt, I'll bury you... Believe it.'

He wanted to run, though he knew he shouldn't. He looked at his hands. Not a mark on them. He couldn't say the same for the stool. Maybe there were some teeth marks in it?

Suddenly he felt nauseous. He paused in an alleyway and shivered, breath steaming up in the air, while fairy lights winked at him from the window of a Chinese takeaway across the road. He felt like he might cry, or laugh. Other thoughts came to him – had the kid he'd smashed died?

Blood clots came to mind, aneurysms, fractures, the blood-brain barrier, convulsions and blackouts.

And then he saw Vonny's face. Her reaction. What if she'd been there? What if she'd seen it? Somehow that was the worst of all, dirty fingers on something immaculate. It had the sense of cheating on her, somehow. It was the summit of his disgrace.

Seth moved as if his legs were pipe cleaners, bypassing the nearest tube station and tapping onto a bus across the river.

A drink, now. And someone to drink with. Hold it in abeyance. Talk it over.

He called Bri, an old friend who worked as a chef in a steakhouse. He was free, and they met up. They soon covered what had happened. There was sympathy at first, but after three pints they were laughing about it. 'Been a while since you smacked someone, Seth. Feel like getting back into it?'

'Christ, no,' Seth said, draining his beer. He held up the glass. Then he put it down and held up his hand. 'Still shaking. Look at that. I must be getting old.'

They talked about the house. Then they moved on to the Datsun Cherry.

'Not being silly or anything, Seth,' Bri asked. 'But did you check the car out?'

'Yeah. No bodies, before you ask. No gear, either.'

'You absolutely sure about that? I mean, it's a vintage car, but it's not totally vintage, you hear what I'm saying? Not like you'd found a Lamborghini Countach or a GTO in there. It didn't make you rich, is what I'm saying. No point hiding it all that way out there for just the car.'

'I promise you – I had the same idea. I looked all over. I felt up the seats, everything. There were no drugs in that car. If there were, they've gone to a classic car dealer, and good luck to him if he ever finds them.'

'Doesn't make sense.' Bri took a quick sip. 'I mean... maybe we've both made the easy assumption.'

'Which is?'

'That the car is the object of the game.'

'I don't follow you.'

'You were sent on a treasure hunt, right? You assume the car is the X on the map. Maybe it isn't. Maybe the car's another clue.'

'You drunk already?' Seth said, as he ordered another.

'Just think about it. Have you looked around about where the car was hidden?'

'Some of the contractors cleared away a load of brambles and stuff... But no...' He wondered at that. They'd only cut some of the prickles away – enough to get the car out without scratching it. Had they checked thoroughly?

The thought wouldn't leave him, even as the train pulled away, three hours later. The bassline wasn't quite so dirgey any more, but the percussion had ramped up in his chest as he considered the number hanging over his brother's head, the woods at the back of his house – dark, now, and frozen – and what they might be hiding.

*Home*, he thought. One single destination, cleaving through everything else. *Home to Vonny. Now.*

He dialled her number.

'What's up?' She was outside; he heard her footsteps, heard the lingering remnants of the autumn leaves crunch beneath her boots. This was a curiously lonely sound, even filtered through a phone while he was sat on a train. Seth didn't want to be away from her any longer.

'Nothing's up. Well, not really. Just letting you know I'm coming home.'

'I thought you'd be away till Sunday?'

'Things have all worked out.' It was almost a joke. He might almost laugh.

'Really? You don't sound too chuffed about it.'

'Well... The DJ Ninjakata thing has fallen flat. I've got one or two other people I can try, but... I wasn't happy about it.'

'Hadn't you signed a contract?'

Seth clenched his teeth. 'Unfortunately, no, I didn't do that.'

Vonny sighed. 'I never liked her anyway, Seth.'

'I definitely don't like her now.'

'What about Jake? Did you see him?'

Seth paused. 'He's going to be OK.'

'But...?'

'Well, he's pretty messed up, going by the dressing on his face. God knows how much blood he lost. I heard how much he might be into them for... I can't pay it off, honey. I don't have it. Not after the house.'

'You shouldn't have to!'

'He's my brother... I have to try and dig him out. He's been messing around with Blockchain, Bitcoin... something dodgy to do with that. I don't pretend to understand it. I've spent the last twenty minutes trying to translate a Wikipedia article on it. Computers, that's what it boils down to. He's pissed off the wrong people. He owes a fortune. They'll kill him for it.' He lowered his voice, aware of one or two stares from people sat a few rows away from him.

'Jesus, Seth. What are you going to do?'

'I dunno. It's going to affect Mum and Dad... They target parents, relatives, you know. Collateral. It's not just you who gets it.'

'Oh my God. The police...?'

'Not a chance. I'd be signing his death warrant.'

'Then what are you going to do?'

'I'll think of something,' he said. And he felt his voice breaking at the end. It felt utterly absurd. When was the last time he had wept? He pinched the bridge of his nose.

'Sweetheart,' she said, her voice cracking. 'Get home. We'll think of something. OK?'

'I know, pet. I'm on my way. I'll be home soon.'

The beer helped, but things melted away a little on the journey back home. The train station was a delight every time he saw it; framed by farmer's fields on either side. Brenwood Green's lines stretched far off into a misty haze, a surreal effect that put Seth in mind of virgin railroads in western movies. The station house had long been converted into an actual house – a trainspotter's paradise, Seth supposed; surely the only reason for buying a place where freight trains could rattle through at all hours of the night, and where an express crashed past like the God of thunder.

Next to the station was a pub, the Basset and Beagle. Everything about this pub, from its whitewashed, Edwardian exterior to its large bay windows and the wonderful, faux olde-worlde sign, also delighted Seth. It was a good forty or fifty minutes' walk from the station to their house, down the winding A-road through the green. Seth decided it was time for another pint.

Not too many people inside; lots of Second World War memorabilia dangled from the ceiling, and a Lancaster bomber lit by tracer fire in an image best suited to the front cover of the *Commando* comic was the subject of a massive painting in a far corner. Good fire, well stocked, nipping the cold in the bud. There were one or two people at tables, including a nervous-looking young couple squashed in beside two massive suitcases, drinking vodka and orange.

It was not exactly the stuff of slow-motion pool balls, stopped clocks and heads swivelling on ball joints – it was a train station pub, after all – but Seth was given a good look by the barman. Nerves still jangling, Seth offered him a stare in return.

'Pint of stout while you're waiting, chief,' he said, with as much amiability as he could find.

The barman said nothing, drawing a pint automatically. Without looking up, he said: 'I should welcome you to your new local.'

'What's that, pal?'

'You're up at the old Grainger place, aren't you? Some plot of land, you have there. And cars hidden in the bushes, too!' The barman nodded at a folded newspaper on the bar top. He still hadn't looked directly at Seth's face.

'Ah, got you. Yes, that's me. I'm Seth, incidentally.' He offered a hand, which was taken, and the barman smiled at long last. 'Sorry. I've been miles away. Family stuff. Anyway, yeah, I'm your new neighbour, I suppose. They count neighbours by how many hectares away they are, out here. Or acres. Something.'

'Heh – hope you've got a car; it's a fair walk back to that plot.'

'Ah, three or four miles? That's no problem. Unless it rains.' Seth took a sip. Very fine; it reminded him of the upmarket taproom where he'd used to live, a pop-up operation that got very serious about craft beer, very quickly, at the very crest of that foamy wave. As he'd got older, Seth appreciated the soupier stuff more, though he couldn't drink an awful lot of it, and he wasn't looking forward to testing his bladder elasticity on a long walk back down the road. 'This is nice – local brew?'

'No, mate – Dark Destroyer. Brewed in London, I think. Your neck of the woods?'

Seth chuckled. 'Here was me thinking I was going rustic!'

'You looking forward to putting down roots here, then?'

'I think I'm tangled up in roots already, mate.'

'And how about the people? Did you know anyone in Brenwood Green?'

Seth shook his head. 'There's a couple across the road from us, who myself and my wife have met, but apart from that… Not really. Just the boys on the site. We've been busy. Vonny's project-managed the lot. It's her game… I've been away a lot. She tells me where to put the nails; I bang them in. It's just about done, now. Been busy from the start – this is the first time I've managed to get a pint in.'

'Ah, you're more than welcome here, son. We like new faces.' And Seth might almost have believed him.

★

Seth did have to go for a pee, of course. A second pint had followed the first, and that treacherous, glowy-friendly feeling began to steal over Seth, until he remembered what he had to discuss with Vonny. Then followed his first walk home from the pub. The weather adopted the same theme as his bladder, and the day grew very dark, and very cool, before the clouds finally burst. Thankful for the heavy jacket buttoned up to his neck, Seth traced an unbroken flat line of green fringed by bracken and ancient, crumbled drystone walls. At one point he was sure he was looking at a golf course, until the land grew more uneven and unruly rhubarb crops left over from summer poked their heads above ground. He had an image of the Triffids for a moment, as he chanced a leak against a wall, cringing both at the idea of a car shrieking past, as well as Vonny's imprecations over hygiene.

Somehow, Seth got lost. The road forked, and he chose the wrong one. He was sure he hadn't gone past a huge barn or grain store on previous drives through, and the signposts pointed to places he didn't know, their distance measured in quaint fractions and whole numbers. 'Three and a half miles to Goldswick,' he mused, as he considered turning on his heels, cutting his losses and going back the way he had come.

He was trudging over a sludgy overgrown patch on a fallow field when the gunshot rang out.

## 20

'Jesus Christ!' Had Seth not emptied his bladder, he might have done so now; he saw a figure emerging from the mist, shotgun raised at its shoulder. Seth sank to one knee, hand raised to ward off another shot.

Something flickered in the gloom over his shoulder, something that quaked and expelled feathers as it followed a distressed arc to the ground. Far enough away, Seth would suppose later, but close enough to make an interesting story. Bloodied feathers and a pink razor-topped saurian claw twitched as the figure strode through the mist.

Clive Fulton ran towards Seth, his nimble frame set hard against the wind. He carried the shotgun across his body, pointing down and away from him. 'Seth?' he said, in a high, terrible note – almost a screech.

'What are you doing, man? Almost had my head off there!' Seth got to his feet, knees unsteady. His head throbbed, close to the feeling of an advance hangover at bedtime.

Even through the steady drizzle, Fulton's face was pale, tending to grey. 'I was aiming for that bloody rook, absolute nuisance of a bird... Wasn't aiming at ground level, not a chance. I would have hit a car, or someone going past. Are you all right?'

He caught up with Seth, taking him by the crook of the arm. Seth steadied himself against the drystone wall where he'd just peed, and allowed himself a laugh halfway through a cough. He waved Fulton away. 'It's all happening here, I've got to tell you. Hardly moved in and someone's tried to shoot me!'

'Honestly, you weren't in any danger.' But now that the situation had changed somewhat, and the only casualty was the knot of feathers at his feet, some steel reasserted itself in Fulton's voice. 'But you were trespassing. How did you get in here?'

'The gap, just past the wall. I was at the station pub, and...' Seth turned towards the wall. The section of it where he'd taken a leak was sheltered, which made it all too clear exactly why he'd been on Fulton's land. 'I had no idea it was your land. I'm sorry.'

Fulton relaxed a little. 'Well, in times of desperate need...' He chuckled. 'Come on. I've got a shed a little bit further down. I was just out checking on the crop – you get some idiots coming through here on quad bikes. I was looking for tracks, believe it or not. I've got a decent malt hiding in there from the missus – take a drink. It's the least I could do.'

'No, mate – I have to be getting back. I'm already a bit late, have to head down to the house. I think all the soft furnishings were being delivered. Vonny wanted to push on...'

Fulton tipped back his cap, and a rill of water fell to the

side, just missing the tip of his long nose. 'In this weather? You sure? You've still got a good way to go.'

Seth considered the downpour, then grinned. 'Come to think of it, a single malt doesn't sound too bad an idea.'


'Now, I thought I had a shed... But *this* is a shed.'

It shouldn't have been a surprise to Seth, given that Fulton seemed posher than Porsche, but his shed was more like a second home. It was twice the size of the caravan. It was furnished. The table and chairs would have looked good in any farmhouse kitchen. It was fully wired and had a bigger fridge than Seth had ever had in any house. A tiny, lacquered cupboard next to the window contained the goods: Lagavulin. The very name had an effect on Seth's taste buds; a DJ he'd worked with in the past had raved about it, and left him a bottle as a present one time. Knowing it was The Good Stuff, Seth had left it in the back of a cupboard, only getting it out when people came around. It was like a nippy sweetie Seth hadn't been sure he liked or not as a kid, but was compelled to eat anyway. That was, until the sweet fire broke out in his tummy.

'Have a seat,' Fulton said. He crossed over to a case mounted on the far wall, unlocked it and placed the shotgun carefully inside, after checking the breech. Seth saw a box with gleaming brass shells in a corner of the cabinet, just before Fulton closed and locked it smartly.

Fulton poured them both a dram. 'Well, here's to property values,' he said, raising a toast.

Seth wasn't sure he liked this, but raised the glass anyway. 'And to good neighbours.'

'Heh.' They let the liquor settle in their veins, listening to the rain patter on the roof. 'Well, once again, let me apologise for giving you a scare. I'm well aware of people passing by on the main road – I never shoot at something that isn't flying through the air.'

'Glad I left my wings at home. For the record, Clive, I'm sorry I pissed on your wall.'

'Consider us even.' They clinked glasses.

'You must be pretty good with it – I didn't even know there was a bird flying out there, until it was spitting lead as well as feathers.'

'You get a knack for it. My dad used to take me clay pigeon shooting.'

'Always fancied that, you know. Looked the business. How do you get a permit for it, or whatever?'

'You need a licence to carry shotguns. It's easier for a farmer, obviously – I need them to get rid of pests, as you've just seen. Sometimes scarecrows don't work. I have a humane deterrent; sets off a charge whenever birds fly near the crops.'

'I've heard that – I did wonder if someone was shooting. Vonny calls it the One O'Clock Gun.'

'Just a harmless charge that goes off. Smoke and mirrors, really. But they're quite effective – except for the corvids. They're some tricky buggers. Something to do with the ratio of brain to body, or something. Encephalization quotient, that's the phrase. Smarter than the average bear, or bird. They'll probably succeed us after the apocalypse, rather than the cockroaches and rats. They understand that the scarecrows are inanimate. Some of them, I swear to you, understand that the sound of the charge isn't actually a threat. That's why I need to bring them down. Not a pleasant business, really,' he said, looking strangely melancholic. 'I used to enjoy it when I was younger. Not now.'

'Not a hunter, then?'

'I've shot for the pot,' he said, frankly. 'I think sometimes you'd be a hypocrite otherwise. You eat something, you should be prepared to kill something, at some point in your life. Otherwise you're just shuffling protein. I don't think that's too controversial, do you?'

'I like a good steak as much as anyone. But I don't fancy taking on a bull in single combat.'

'Very true. A bull might be more of a challenge. I might need the twelve-bore for that. But you see my point. On the other side of the farm I've got sheep, and those lovely spring lambs end up on someone's plate. So I have taken down the odd pheasant, and enjoyed eating them, too. But in my old age, it's not so much of a pleasure. We need the guns to keep dogs away from the flock. I've got some lads help out, and one of them killed a dog, one time. One of Dan Grainger's.'

'Oh yeah?'

'Yes. Curious business.' Fulton took a sip of the whisky, and considered his words carefully. 'I think at one point he bred dogs on his property – your property, now – as well as horses. Ugly things. Fighting dogs. Gangster's dogs, was the term I heard used. This enterprise didn't last long. I think it literally spooked the horses. Plus, there isn't much market for Japanese fighting dogs around here. I don't think there's been any badger baiting for about forty years. This is more of an Irish setters and poodles area. A few people keep guard dogs, but they're genteel, if that makes sense. Not the sort of dog you'd see being led on a string outside a bookmaker's. Anyway, one of them got on our property and disturbed the sheep. The lad, Gordon his name was, did the right thing.'

Seth put an imaginary gun to his head. 'Goodnight, Vienna?'

'Indeed. He put it down. He has a legal right, and he was right to do so. Dan Grainger and his son, the eldest one, paid him a visit when he found out. Gordon left the farm not long after.'

'They put the frighteners on him?'

'That's the right term. Curious thing… they didn't lay a finger on him. But he handed in his notice, then didn't serve it. He would not say a word. I think he works at a butcher's, somewhere in Lincolnshire.'

'They sound like nasty pieces of work.'

'They were.' Fulton drained his glass. 'Another?'

'Sure, why not?'

After Fulton topped them both up, he went on: 'There was a strange aftermath in that. I knew the man's reputation and I wasn't about to go throwing around accusations. He let one of his dogs get loose, and it ended up being shot. It happens out here. More than you'd think. I was angry about Gordon, but considered the matter closed. Grainger came over a day or so afterwards. I was expecting some sort of confrontation. You know…' here he began to laugh '… my other half was the big problem. She advocated taking a shotgun out to the meeting. I had to make sure she was out shopping when I met him. I wasn't duly concerned. Used to box for a while when I was younger.'

Seth believed it. The older man was fit, and confident, that was for sure.

'However, I wasn't the one who brought a shotgun. He did.'

'You're kidding. Jeez.'

'Then, you could say he disarmed me. He was very friendly. Said there had been a misunderstanding. He understood what had happened, though he was upset about it, as it was his prize dog. Called it Gogmagog, in fact. Then he said that the dog was worth a thousand pounds. I told him that my flock was worth tens of thousands of pounds, and he might have put that at risk. He said that our lawyers might argue the toss over that and cost us all many more thousands of pounds. So, he told me, he had a proposition.' Here, Fulton got up, and crossed over to another cabinet, also under lock and key. He selected the right key from the ring in moments and then opened it up. He produced a shotgun much like the one he carried, and laid it on the table in front of Seth.

'What? He *gave* it to you?'

'Yes. For safekeeping, he said.'

'Weird.'

'I wonder if, in his own way, he was making a statement of some kind, as well as making an offer.'

Seth studied the gun. 'It must be red hot.'

'I believe it may have been used for something unpleasant. He said he was loath to part with it, but he needed it off his property for a while. It had some sentimental value. He said that if I could hold on to it, in escrow, then he would consider our dispute settled.'

'I'm not sure I'd have done it,' Seth said. The stock looked pristine, until the light caught the edges and showed places where it had been badly stored, or handled. The staining and the grain of it reminded Seth of looking at his own irises in close-up. The metal was dull, not so well-kept. A working weapon, perhaps. 'It's clearly dodgy. Used in a robbery, or... something else.'

'We're of the same mind,' Fulton said. 'Against my better judgement, I agreed to it. We crossed swords once or twice, particularly over the raves he used to have, back when they were in fashion. But I knew he wasn't a man to cross. His son in particular, the elder one... he was the one to watch. Grainger had something badly missing – you have to understand. He was always perfectly civil, but I was aware this was not a normal man, capable of a normal life. His eldest son was less restrained. They were a bad lot.'

'And he never asked for the gun back?'

'He never really got the chance. About three weeks later, it was all over for them.'

'Murder-suicide, I heard,' Seth said, quietly.

'Indeed. So the police say. I told them about a few things I'd seen and heard around about the farm. People I saw late at night. Cars going past, quietly.'

'You reckon someone did them in?'

'I can't prove anything, and I couldn't really say anything that would count as evidence. The coroner was quite clear about how they both died. Anyway... against my better judgement, I hid the shotgun. I should have tossed it into the tarn, or given it to one of the other farmers I know, but... there it is. There's a box of shells, too.'

Seth didn't pick up on what Fulton was saying until the silence dragged on. 'Are you giving this to me?'

'Not exactly. I want to put it back to where it came from. Your property. You've found a few things on the plot already that were never picked up on the survey, such as the car. You could say you found it, hand it in to the police, then the matter is over.'

'The matter is over for you, you mean,' Seth said, quietly.

'I think it would bring the whole business to a neat conclusion.'

Seth looked out the window. 'Looks like the rain's eased off.'

'Indeed. I was going to call the other half – see if she'd bring round the quad bike and trailer. Take you back to your place in style.'

'Have you got a spare half an hour, mate?'

Fulton frowned. 'For what?'

Seth grinned, nodding towards the shotgun. 'Training. If I've got a weapon like that on my property, I'm thinking I should be able to use it, no?'

Fulton tapped a fingernail against his tumbler. 'I'm not comfortable with that. It's an unlicensed weapon...'

'Which you want to pass on to me to take care of a problem. That's fine. You could consider this your way of providing an incentive.' Seth grinned. 'Totally up to you, though.'

# 21

Vonny put the phone down after her conversation with Seth while he was on the train, and bit her lip in frustration. She could see Seth getting involved, all right. He sounded like he'd had a couple of drinks in him – usually this portended nothing more annoying than a late night with his headphones on. But she hadn't expected him back until Sunday. He'd sounded unusually stressed – even the act of talking on the phone on a busy train carriage seemed utterly incongruous for her husband.

'He's had a row with someone,' she declared. 'Probably with Jake. Idiot.'

As she said this, she noticed a flicker of hi-vis yellow through the window. Devin Marshall's familiar face darted past; she waved, but he didn't respond.

Opening the door, she saw that the boys on the site were all here, utterly mob-handed. The flatbed truck that held them was big enough for heavy plant equipment.

Devin wasn't wearing his hard hat, but he was wearing large, Bono-style sunglasses that didn't suit his face at all. Vonny was reminded of a mad auntie at her friend's wedding who wore gigantic glasses that appeared to be a prank of some kind, until you got up close.

She sensed there was something wrong long before she made out his face. 'Hi... It's your day off today, isn't it? Have I got my diary wrong?'

Devin the foreman cleared his throat. 'I'm afraid there's been a change of plan, Vonny.'

'How do you mean?'

He cleared his throat again. 'I'm afraid we won't be able to complete our contract with you.'

'I don't understand... You only have a few bits and pieces still to do?'

'It's really unusual circumstances, and I can only apologise. We'll give you a discount for the final snagging – if you call the office, we'll go through it and come to a reasonable figure.'

Vonny looked beyond him, to the anxious faces peering out of the flatbed truck's window. The biggest lad – Vonny had referred to him as Butterbean, given his soft, infant-like face and cheeks, on the frame of a gridiron star – didn't quite look the same as he usually did. Vonny made out something brilliant white somewhere in the picture – a plaster cast.

Then she stared hard into Devin's sunglasses.

'Devin... Has something happened?'

'Nothing's happened.'

She came a step or two towards him; he drew back, but not fast enough. Vonny reached forward and plucked the sunglasses off his head. Then she gasped. 'What's going on? Have you guys been in an accident?' Then something more ludicrous still: 'Have you been fighting?'

'No, no fighting,' Devin said. Or the creature that looked like Devin. With the shades off, she could see two horrendous black eyes – two plummy mounds that all but closed both eyes, with swellings up and around the right-hand side. His nose had been broken, and quite high up. Someone had smacked him, hard. 'It's just one of those things.'

'Did it happen here?'

'It's one of those things, I said.'

'Your nose is broken.' For an insane second or two, she almost reached out to touch it. He might have screamed if she did. As it was, he backtracked quickly.

'Please, can I have my sunglasses?'

Vonny handed them back. 'Whatever it is... Is it something to do with us? The house? If there's been an accident, we'll have to speak to insurance. Good God, you could have been *blinded*.'

'No need for any of that,' Devin said. 'I am so, so sorry, Vonny. We're just going to collect some gear we had on site then we're going to clear off. I'm sure you understand.'

'I've got to be totally honest with you – I don't understand, at all. What's going on here?'

'We have to go, Vonny. We'll be in touch about the remainder of the contract. It's being shifted out to another company, one we trust. They'll be back in touch in due course...'

He tried to walk past her as he spoke, not even looking at her. 'Stop! What is this? Has someone attacked you? Here?'

'The other company is a snagging specialist – there's an issue with the special room we need to talk over. There's a flood risk – bad work from your architect, frankly, rather than us. And of course there's the railings to secure, one or two other...'

'Devin! Talk to me – what's happened?'

'And that is all!' Devin bellowed, at last. 'Vonny. Please. We're leaving. That's it. OK?'

She backed away. 'Course. Take as long as you like. This is just a shock, it really is.'

'I understand there are some contractual issues, and we'll happily sort those out.' Devin signalled to the truck; the other two men appeared. 'This has been a great project to work on – thanks so much.'

'But you've hardly been here!'

Devin looked like he wanted to say more. What she could see of his face crumpled for a second or two. Alarmed, she reached out for his shoulder, but he strode off to join his colleagues.

She wanted to sag. Had there been a chair handy she would have collapsed into it. They'd been attacked, surely – something had spooked them. She could sue. They were in clear breach of contract... But that wasn't Vonny's main fear.

Had someone approached them while they were working on the house? Warned them off? But if so, what?

Something to do with Dan Grainger?

Vonny shivered, and looked towards the trees.

Back in the house, she sent Seth a message. 'Any chance of hurrying the train up?'

He was in that not-drunk but definitely over-beered state when he returned. He'd had a few drinks, but not recently, and he was more likely to slump in front of the TV and fall asleep than take another one. Perhaps there was a shot of whisky or two on his breath.

'Well, no moving into the house tonight,' Vonny said, holding him tight. 'But...'

'It might be nicer to get cuddled into the Tin Coffin. Just the two of us.'

'My thoughts exactly.'

They did just that, lying together on top of the bedclothes. Seth hadn't even removed his overcoat. 'Thought it was going to snow, just then,' he said. 'It'll look lovely on the skylight when it lands.'

'And on this little skylight, right here.'

'The magpies can leave footprints. Make little snow angels. Snow birds. Whatever they make. You know, I almost forgot Christmas was just around the corner. Hardly thought about it, until a maniac got on board, a few stops before Brenwood Green. Played his phone at full blast. Christmas songs. Slade. Wizzard. Shakey. Wham. And the beautiful thing was, no one even looked annoyed about it. One or two older gents, you know the type – letter to *The Times* if someone farts. They started singing along to John and Yoko.'

'You sound sad you had to leave.'

'Nice little moment.' There was silence for a moment. Then he raised his head, and gazed at her. 'Something's wrong.'

'Kind of. But something's more wrong with you. So, you first.'

'No, tell me. What's happened. Someone upset you?'

'In a manner of speaking. Devin and the crew...'

'Please tell me they weren't rude. After all that, please tell me they didn't do anything nasty.'

'No. Perfect gentlemen. It's just... they're gone, Seth.' She explained the scene from earlier on in the day.

'Someone must have battered them. That's what it sounds like to me.'

'I thought that,' Vonny said, resting her head on his chest as he lay down again. The jacket was in need of some dry-cleaning, or perhaps a sandblast, but it smelled of him; it was a comfort, in its own roughcast-textured way. 'But maybe it was something else. Maybe they had an accident, something like that, or they made a mistake...'

'Or they battered each other. They look like they wouldn't say boo to a goose, but they're young. That's what happens with young guys.' He swallowed. He saw the kid in the pub, folded neatly, immobile. Had the boy bled? He must have. He couldn't remember if he'd imagined the blood, flowing through the boy's fingers, or not. Had he lost an eye? Lost consciousness? Fractured his skull? Was he dead?

'Whatever it is... Seth. Was it something to do with here?'

'The house. The land. Dan "Don Corleone" Grainger?'

'I doubt it. What would anyone crack down hard on a squad of builders for?' Maybe they wanted to know something, was the answer in his own head. Maybe they wanted to find out if something had been dug up.

Seth remembered his mate's words, in the pub. Maybe X marked the spot, after all.

'Whatever it is... I'm going to get onto the builder. First thing Monday morning. There's still bits of snagging here and there. And they left a flood risk in the special room.'

'How's that?'

'Something to do with the angle of the pipe, or pipework not completed... Won't affect the house. Anyway. That needs sorting out.'

'We can take them to court over this. It's not safe, leaving the job unfinished.'

'They were due to finish up next week, anyway. This is what I don't get.'

Seth listened to the sound of their breathing, in the centre of the Tin Can, the cramped confines melting away in the concealing darkness. 'Tomorrow's the day, eh?'

'Tomorrow's the day.' Her lips were close to his neck. 'But you've stalled long enough. What happened?'

He told her. Sweat broke out on his brow – guilty sweat. Vonny listened. She dabbed her fingers against the moisture above his eyes. 'What else, Seth? What else happened?'

He began to shake, as he told her about the two boys in the pub, and the one that ended up on the floor. 'I had no choice. In that situation, you can't wait for someone else to make a move. You'll be on the floor with two or more of them stomping you in a minute flat. In the time it takes for you to work out your first big kung fu kick, or whether or not you might want to use the bar stool. I had to...'

'He could be dead,' Vonny said, aghast.

'Doubt it. They'd have picked me up by now. Hopefully he just has a souvenir from the occasion.'

She did not like the dark irony in his tone. 'Never get into a situation like that again, Seth. Never. Never even walk into a dodgy pub again. Don't go near it. A bar stool?'

'You weren't there,' he said, quietly. 'You didn't see it.' He began to shake again, hands and voice trembling. She held him, until the quaking stopped.

'What are we going to do?' she said.

'Jake, Mum and Dad can't go back there. I'll get them

moved somewhere else. It'll take just about everything else I've got, but they have to move. Jake can go to another sixth form college. From there, university, if he has any sense. He can have a nice scar to impress the girls. I should have gotten them out of that shitty street years ago, but Dad just wouldn't… He's not tough, but he's stubborn. They have to move out now. The house will be marked. I'll get a removals van, move them out first thing in the morning. Bastards won't get them.'

'What about the people he owes? They won't just let him walk away, will they?'

'I was coming to that. It's a lot.'

'How much is a lot?'

'It's not an exact figure. It's not like a balance sheet at the end of the financial year, or…'

'How much, Seth?'

He told her, and she cried. Seth could not tell her it would be all right. He could not assure her that it would turn out well.

'They'll kill him,' she said. 'He'll have to go into witness protection. He'll have to tell the police.'

'No chance. You can't grass. If he doesn't have a death warrant already, he will have after he does that. You cannot put people like that into prison.'

'It might be his only choice!'

Seth could not argue with this.

Then she covered her face with her hands. 'What if they come for *us*?'

'They won't. No chance.' He wished he felt as confident as he sounded.

She whispered, 'We might have to sell this place. That would cover it. Wouldn't it?'

That's when he came closest to tears. 'Never in a million years. Never. This is the place... This is the dream house.'

'Then what else can we do?'

'What I'm going to do is... make some beats.'

'Is that a joke?'

'I never joke about work. I've already got an idea for a suite of tunes. Title's there already – *Tin Can Opera*. Plus I have a memory card full of new tracks that were meant for DJ PissyPants, don't forget. They need a home. I've got a few more contacts – they always want the good stuff. They're good tracks, darlin'. If they're not for her breakout album, they'll be for someone else's. I've got the contacts. Don't worry. They'll get sold. I'll sort out Jake. We'll be sitting pretty, here, before you know it.'

Seth sounded sure of himself. But the only thing he was certain of was that Vonny wasn't fooled.

## 22

While Vonny slept that night, Seth extricated himself from her, watching a blade of moonlight slip across her face as she turned, grunted, and lay at rest. It was an obscene hour, and he was exhausted, but anxiety and booze had shaken his system, jolted him into consciousness he didn't want. He found the wrong solution. He opened up the tiny kitchen cabinet, and withdrew a bottle.

He had aimed to get petulantly pissed, a childish solution to an adult problem. After two single malts, he'd tried to drown it out with music – quickly irritated by the demos he'd been sent, he retreated into the arms of Stevie Wonder, as usual. 'He's Misstra Know-It-All' got him to thinking about his friend at the bar, who'd calmed him down after he hit the kid with the bar stool.

He snatched off the headphones and closed the computer down.

Vonny did not stir as he crept out.

Five minutes later he had a torch tucked into his big jacket pocket and a shovel in his hand, which he'd meant to retrieve from the garden days ago.

The cold nipped at him. Brutal, top-button-fastened stuff,

frost and ice on the path underfoot, the driveway given a coating of sugar.

Seth had a rough idea where he was going, but in the dark this soon turned treacherous. Semi-tipsy bravado turned a little sour in his gut, when he stared into the mass of pines, like ranks of planted spears. He had to turn back once, cursing himself, when he tried to cut through the trees instead of taking the path like any sensible person would.

'Waste of time,' he grunted to himself. 'Fool's gold.'

He played about a bar of music in his headphones before writing this off as a spectacularly bad idea. Even if the scariest thing in the woods in front of him was a badger, then that was plenty scary for Seth, and so he was on high alert. Soon he came to the place where the shed had been, a pile of stunted planks like the font of a scary movie title. Something about this jagged structure upset him, even when the details of grain, splinter and bent nails were exposed by the torch beam.

He swept the light to the left. That's where the path to the bushes was. This was the moment Seth became truly freaked out, as everything closed in. Squeezing through the trees had seemed such a lark during the daytime, with Vonny and the reporter accompanying him. 'Never again,' he whispered, his breath curling around his nose and mouth, 'will I laugh at a scary film.'

A rearing monster in front of him gave him pause; spiky, the dead brown of dried blood even under bright light. 'That's it,' Seth said, squaring his shoulders after the fright. 'That's what I'm looking for.'

He talked to himself as he scraped the shovel along the branches. He was going to have to go a little further in; this would be like a pilot fish picking at the teeth of a shark for its supper. There was a tunnel of sorts, after the boys had cut back the winter-dead vegetation to clear a path for the Datsun. From there they'd had to push it to the side gate along a straighter path, then back down to the road where a hire truck had been waiting.

'I am not crawling in,' he muttered, bending down at the maw of the beast. He could picture it – the sudden smell of rotten meat and bad breath, the realisation that what he was on his haunches in front of was not a plant given a trick of the light, but an animal. Then the spikes would come down and that'd be it – no more Seth. A belt buckle or the eyelets of his boots surviving inside some unspeakable droppings. 'At least the headphones would live,' he said, and chuckled.

He reached out with the shovel – *don't imagine a hand darting out to snatch it, no absolutely not* – and scraped it along the ground.

The metal struck against stone. There was no mistaking the change in pitch and timbre. This was not earth, even freeze-dried, hard-packed earth. He withdrew the shovel and got close to the ground, his chin about an inch away. There was something there, beneath a pile of pine needles and stones. He cleared it away, his gloved hands slithering over the detritus. He felt something tough even through the material, unyielding like the granite worktop in his new house. He brought the shovel blade back in, stabbing at the edge of this slightly raised pile.

A little work uncovered the stone. Hard and flat – like

slate, rather than concrete, organic-looking. Out of place, but not suspiciously so. Not like a manhole or a trapdoor might have been.

There was no leverage to lift it, and Seth didn't trust his back. He found an edge with the shovel, planted it down until it found the lower edge, and levered it up.

His back hurt anyway. But soon it was clear. The slate wasn't too heavy, and indeed it had split in some places, possibly under the weight of one of the Datsun's wheels.

Underneath was another hard surface, caked with dirt, but recognisable even under torchlight.

A suitcase. A great big one; the kind that you knew would attract a penalty should you attempt to put it on a plane, no dissent offered, no grumbling in the queue. And then there was another one, just as big if not identical.

He felt a childlike excitement, the feeling of opening the door to the front room and seeing that yes, Santa had been. Dread soon followed. Whatever this was, it wasn't good for anyone. He felt that certainty.

But he had already made the proper connections, and, although he couldn't be totally sure, the right conclusions. If this was what he thought it was, then... Then there were possibilities. To do with Jake, first of all. And then other possibilities, for him and Vonny.

These connections had all been fully tested and fitted as standard as Seth got busy with the shovel, then his bare hands, shifting the slabs out of the way. Sweat dripped, and it seemed as if he had created his own mist, his own mini-climate, out there in the dark and the cold.

The padlocks sealing the carbon-fibre suitcases had already rusted. Lovely suitcases, too, Seth thought, as he brought down the shovel head, decapitating the shiny locks with a single swing. Pity to damage them.

He paused before breaking the seals. Bodies were a possibility, here. The X might not have marked treasure, after all. Hell of a way to go to hide something. Very complicated. A careful person had done this, a person who knew how to keep secrets, a person who knew people might come for what he was attempting to hide.

No terrible smell rose from the broken seal, but even so, Seth jumped back as he flipped open the top of the first suitcase. Perhaps he'd expected rats to swarm out, bugs maybe.

Instead, there were only tightly packed plastic-coated bricks. Dozens of them, laid out neatly. Vonny might have packed these, was his absurd thought; Vonny, or someone just like her.

He remembered to breathe. He carried out some calculations, and forgot to breathe again. 'No way... No way on God's earth...' he said, shaking his head. It could not be right. He could not be seeing this.

He pulled out one of the bricks, then nicked at the end with a penknife. He was no expert, but he knew what this was, knew what he was holding, knew what it possibly meant. He turned away from it, blinking, all those lights on now, every connection complete, the circuit in perfect operation.

Knowing it was wrong, Seth knew what to do.

'Vonny,' he said to himself. Always her. Always coming back to her.

But if he told her, he knew what she would say...

He shook his head, and shivered. He could not tell her.

She could not know. The minute he broached it... No. She'd call the police. Jake would still be in trouble. And there was a chance, if he contacted a guy he knew... And he knew just the man. The engineer, Simon. That could be a way through. He'd take a hit, a big percentage, but even so...

He had to handle it. Vonny wouldn't stand for it. And then guilt, over and above everything he'd done of late, including annihilating a teenager with a bar stool, clutched at him. No secrets was the rule. Everyone behaves. No one feels as if they have to hide anything. We keep no secrets. They had agreed, early on. Seth had found that candour refreshing. No game playing. Nothing hidden. Honesty. There was no other way.

'I can't,' he hissed to himself, 'just this once. I can't.'

# 23

The next day was chillier. Before he even put on his clothes the next morning, Seth put on his winter coat, once again. It had lasted three winters, now, and he was getting bored with it. But Vonny had to admit that it had staying power. The lining had frayed a little, but he hadn't bought cheap, and it had more than done its job.

'It's not going to die,' he had remarked, slipping it over his shoulders. 'Not so much as a button loose. I'll have to take it to the charity shop. And someone will buy it. And I swear to God, seeing it on someone else, walking through the street, not even knowing that it used to be mine, my heart will break. It's that serious.'

'You're off out? Where are you off to?'

'Couple of bits and pieces I want to get in town.'

'Are you going to the fancy shop, or the regular supermarket for regular people?'

He shrugged. 'What's the difference?'

'Roughly forty quid per trip.'

Seth smirked. 'Don't you worry. Won't be long. I'm going to get secret stuff, to tell you the truth. For tonight.' He nodded in the direction of the house. 'Surprise stuff. Well, not quite surprise, now.'

'Understood.' She smiled. 'How you getting there, if you don't mind my asking?'

'I was going to borrow your car.'

'Sure you'll be all right to drive?'

'I am sure. Why wouldn't I be?'

'Ah, something to do with these.' She brandished two fingers at him, and not in the Winston Churchill or John and Yoko style, either.

'Eh?'

'The two fingers missing from the bottle of The Good Stuff you had last night, while I was in Zed-Land.'

'Ah. That was just one or two. They'll be out my system by now. It's a short trip, anyway.'

'Just one or two, on top of the several you'd had throughout the day. Be careful. I don't just mean the odds of you getting breathalysed.' Seth, a Londoner to his bones, hadn't long learned to drive, at what most people would recognise as an advanced age. He combined lack of experience at the wheel with a certain recklessness, which had already resulted in a £600 bill from a bodywork shop that had been delighted to see them, after a scuffle with a drystone wall, on their first day looking at the plot. Inauspicious, Vonny had thought at the time. The A-roads seemed to demand higher speeds, as evidenced by the screaming passage of the boy racers Vonny sometimes heard in the night.

'You know me. Careful is my middle name.'

'Yeah. Double-barrelled with Reckless. Keys are in my jacket…'

'Right-hand side?'

'That's it.'

Vonny waited until she heard the gate clank behind the car. Then she sprang into action.

Seth had timed it well, if unwittingly. The parcels arrived a few minutes after he left. The delivery driver was a regular, and he knew to drop the boxes off at the caravan, rather than up at the house. She had refrained from cutting open the tape, preferring to wait until... Well.

She checked out the champagne in the fridge; already a lovely new skin of condensation. She trailed a finger along its contours, admiring the liquid sheen on the green glass beneath the trail.

Vonny reckoned she had half an hour, minimum, whatever Seth was planning. She grinned. She came into her element.

She heaved the box inside the new house and closed the door. The sound of the door shutting echoed. A rattly detonation unique to unfurnished houses, sound ricocheting merrily off the flat surfaces and wide open spaces. Soon see to that, she thought.

The front room's sofas were installed – an argillaceous brown that reminded Vonny of a picture in her grandmother's house – although the television and its tentacular wiring had yet to appear from storage. Vonny chose the perfect spot for the tree – a false one, but a good false one – and in three satisfying clicks and twists, she had it erected, branches pulled out, sub-branches perfectly spaced.

And now, the glee of the box of decorations. All brand new, bright white fairy lights, some with a flicker control, some not. She soon had the tree garlanded with lights, though it took a couple of test ignitions before she was happy with the spacing. Next, the baubles, red and gold, with the same colour of tinsel. To look at Vonny in a speeded-up film, an observer might have marvelled at her certainty, her sure placement. This was a talent, to be sure. She visualised it; she made it happen.

It wouldn't be right to say that she had done the same with Seth. When it came to relationships, most of these had exactly gone to plan. Vonny's studies and her work had taken her from place to place, in the days when home working was something that was openly sneered at in businesses and offices. A stint in Manchester after university; another three desperately unhappy years in London, not unconnected to a party boy named Erik who had conned her six ways from Sunday despite seeming utterly genuine; a couple of lost years in Glasgow that had nonetheless given her a name and a reputation in interior design thanks to a newspaper column where her looks, seldom admitted to but always a factor, had worked well in her favour.

And so she had come to the party, where she'd designed the sleeves of a vinyl release for a friend of hers, a jazz singer given an unexpected burst of success. And... well, there he was. The producer no one wanted to talk to. Though he hadn't been making a huge effort in this respect, himself. Although Vonny had appeared once or twice on a home makeover show on television, where everyone assured her she had come across as a natural, she hated the spotlight and was ill at ease with the attention. Her mother had been very strict about not going looking for it, perhaps knowing that with her height, her looks, her stature, she would get it regardless. All the same, Vonny sometimes retreated into the corners at such events. In one such corner she'd met Seth.

He had mentioned straight up that he'd produced the

record for her friend, then went a long way to sabotaging any notion of Vonny being impressed by this with his goofy humour. It wasn't desperate stuff – she'd sensed he was nervous, particularly when he had been seized by his hand by an executive and congratulated on a job well done, when he had clearly had no idea who he was speaking to.

It had seemed the most normal thing in the world to give him her number. And they'd picked up where they left off, that same weekend. And had been together ever since. She'd found someone who matched her drive, who understood what it meant to push yourself. Saturday nights could be spent with him plunking around on the bass, staring into the gulfs of space with his headphones clamped to his skull, while she was hunched over the easel at the far end of the studio flat – used as intended, for once – and it wouldn't be a chore; they hadn't lost out, and at the end of the sessions, there'd be wine, crisps, Graham Norton, God help them.

London had kept them well for a while, as his career went from strength to strength. She had landed a job designing wallpaper, which she hated, but which paid well. One or two media roles had come along; she'd chipped away at that, getting exposure here and there. There had been talk of a spot on a new BBC2 show, looking at reinstating 1970s designs in modern houses, and maybe a one-off special to go onto BBC4. That had been delayed for a year, but the contract had finally been signed. All along, her dream had been to design her own house, and she'd gotten quite far into this fantasy when the ultimate opportunity had come up. She'd haunted forums and property websites and auction houses, searching for that bargain, the one place that would allow her to buy cheap and build the dream house. Then, her cookies had suggested the auction site, a rare example of technology intruding in the right way, for once. She entered the auction, and...

Here she was. She knew to the inch how much wiring she needed, where she wanted the belly of the curve to rest on the walls. Soon she had the lights to match the tinsel and the baubles on the tree, strong and white and red, in among the faux holly and the other ornaments. She had to go on tiptoes to place the golden star at the top. Its waving beams had a pagan look, which she liked. 'Pagan festival after all,' she said to herself, admiring the tree. Big, but not imposing. Tall, but not threatening the roof. In proportion. Perfect. She was tying more lights around the banisters and had almost reached the top level above the water feature when the iron railings slightly gave way.

It didn't fall off – that would have meant a good drop of two-metres-plus onto the water feature below – but there was a screw loose. Vonny chewed her lip, and growled in consternation. She'd have to take that up with the new builders – whoever they might be.

As she tugged the balcony rail back in place, the key sounded in the front door below. Just visible through the door was Seth. He had a plastic bag with a tell-tale clink in his hands, a huge, puffy red and white hat that looked like it belonged on a chef rather than Santa, and an entirely gormless expression on his face as she flew down the stairs to intercept.

Vonny almost tripped and landed flat on her face as she flicked switches, desperately trying to stop Seth from seeing her handiwork. 'Don't... Don't go in the living room!' she yelled, warding him off with a palm. 'I've been busy...'

Seth was in freeze-frame. He'd barely moved an inch since he'd opened the door. 'Well. This is awkward. I wanted to stock the fridge with champagne before we moved in tonight. I thought we could maybe bring the move-in date forward.'

'You aren't supposed to see!' She burst out laughing as she made a star shape, trying to conceal the lights she hadn't quite managed to switch off in time.

'Darlin'... I've seen the lights.' He sniggered. 'They look amazing. I really wish I hadn't bought my own tree for far too much money at the equestrian shop...'

'You didn't!' She came forward to kiss him. 'Never mind. We've got room for two.'

'Communication breakdown. My fault.' He kissed her back, and she linked her hands around his neck. He was cold; the cold air was seeping in, lapping at her shins.

'Baby it's cold outside,' she sang.

'Hey – let's do this properly.'

'Do what? Hey!'

He lifted her off her feet; she shrieked as he backed away – none too steadily. 'Here goes. I'll carry you over the threshold. That's how you're meant to do it. Oh Christ, my back... Wait, you'll have to fold your legs up, or whatever it is you do with them. I need to get you in the door... There you go...'

'I'll carry you next time,' she said, helpless with laughter, as he sagged and deposited her on the floor.

'Thirsty work that. Hey, I brought champagne, and some glasses. Why don't we get cracked into it, and order a diabolically big takeaway?'

'This is our first night? First official night?'

'Yep. You'll notice I built the bed. And put the sheets on.' He waggled his eyebrows, in that way that only he could ever get away with, in a galaxy full of bad jokers and chancers.

'On top of a diabolically big takeaway?' she asked, not completely in jest.

'Ah no. First we work up an appetite.' She kissed him again.

Eventually, they made the top of the stairs. He removed his socks at last, hurling them like grenades towards the balcony, where they hung over the edge. 'Dammit. I was hoping to drop them onto the water feature,' he said.

'Oh, don't touch them! I mean, the railings,' Vonny said, hopping towards their bedroom, one leg of her trousers threatening to hurl her to the floor.

Seth paused, clad only in his underpants and an uncertain expression. 'They're... not really explosive socks.'

'No, but the railing's dodgy.'

'Could have told you that when it was fitted.' He grinned.

'Nah, it's loose; it'll fall away. We'll have to screw it in properly. They've not done it right... Oh look, get in here before you talk me out of it.'

He was in the room in a shot, diving full length onto the bed.

Before she joined him, Vonny turned on the control panel, grinning at its bluish glare – not entirely out of keeping with the galaxy of lights surrounding it. She scrolled to Christmas classics. Slade. Wizzard. Shakey. Wham. Then she joined her husband on the bed.

The door closed over, quietly and efficiently, just the way it had been designed.

# 24

The next morning, Seth had gone into South Brenwood, a much bigger town about sixteen miles away from Brenwood Green. He had pleaded for an afternoon to pick up Christmas gifts – 'Just bits,' he'd explained, 'I've already got your big present.' Outside, low, dark clouds had come in, and with them a definite blast of winter, ice and frost covering the scene outside the windows. Hat, scarf and gloves weather, for sure. She tackled the little pieces of snagging that she felt confident enough to fix. She had planned on tightening the railings on the upper floor, but soon took something of a brainstorm, and decided to head out to the front yard to sort out some of the ragged patches out there.

It was only by pure luck that Vonny heard the bell. Despite the promise of rain in the steel wool clouds above, she had pressed ahead with a plan to strim the edges of the flower beds, irritated by the spiky intrusions out of keeping with the rest of the immaculate lawn as laid down a few days before. She'd had the front garden marked out by a fence, threaded through with privet hedging. It would take the changing seasons to bring out what she had planned for this space.

Soon there would be no fence to be seen at all; the firm she'd hired to lay the turf had been brisk and efficient, and the gentle slope gleamed in the wet. Seeing the spongy turf unravel about a week ago in thick, uniform rolls like plasticine had pleased her, as had the geometric precision of how it had all locked together, cut and dried. The thick beads of rain had remained on the new green fronds in crystal buds, taking a while to be absorbed in the new land, and that had pleased Vonny as well. The stubble around the edges of the flower bed had needed fixing and, despite the grey conditions, she had fixed it. She had stopped at the edge of the last flower bed when she heard the buzzer inside.

They'd tested the security system, but never the front door and camera. She just made it, cursing the wet green-tinged footprints she left on the oak flooring to reach the console.

On screen, a tall, fair man with longish hair stood patiently, staring directly into the camera. This might have been unsettling, except he had a pleasant cast to his young, open face. He was tall and rangy and could have been aged anywhere between his late twenties and forty. He looked like he would have suited a deep tan, a shark-tooth necklace and a surfboard – a beach bum forced into exile in a collar and tie just visible underneath a smart charcoal-grey raincoat. He reached out to press the button one more time. Vonny pressed the intercom before he had the chance to hit the buzzer.

'Hello?'

'Ah, hi there. I wonder if I could speak to the householder?' He had a distinct Scottish accent – maybe from the Highlands, Vonny thought. It had a rasp to it, but there was something sweet, almost melodic to the cadence and rhythm.

'Speaking.'

'I'm Detective Inspector Bell from the Metropolitan Police. I wonder if I could have a quick word with you?'

He presented a warrant card. The details all matched.

'I guess so. Is something wrong?'

'Nothing at all. Just a routine inquiry, really.' He grinned, tucking the card into his inside pocket. Vonny hit the button to admit him through the gate at the bottom of the drive.

He took his shoes off at the front door without being asked, and hung up his raincoat on the stand just inside the front door.

'My goodness, this is some place,' he said, staring at the balcony above the main entrance hall. 'And you won it in a raffle?'

'Guilty as charged on that one,' Vonny said, and then instantly regretted it. 'I always wanted to build a big house from scratch, since I was a little kid. Guess it was our lucky day.'

'You can say that again! Man, you could probably fit every single flat I've ever lived in into the bottom floor alone.'

'Same! It'll take a bit of getting used to.'

'All settled in?'

'Not quite – just got the finishing touches to apply, really.' Vonny gestured over her shoulder. 'I was just taking care of the garden out the front. Just the odd bit of snagging to do, now. The builder is coming back... Well. The builder was meant to be coming back in the next couple of days, but we ran into a problem. I can sort that out in the next couple of days. Plus, there are some bits and pieces I want to change.' She tapped her forehead. 'Perfectionist. Drives my other half mad.'

He smiled and followed her into the lounge. The inspector peered around at the bookcases and CD racks, set into an entire wall space.

'Good Lord, that's a lot of music,' he said. 'I thought my collection was bad! The removal men must have loved you.'

'You should see the vinyl section, being built in the cave downstairs. And the rest of the equipment.'

'He records as well?'

'Oh yeah. It's a whole home studio. Well, that's the idea anyway.'

'What kind of stuff does he do? He's a musician?'

'Yep. Well – a producer, really, but he can turn his hand to anything. Some people might call him a DJ, but he's done a lot of stuff for a lot of different acts. Unfortunately, when it comes to physical media, I can't persuade him to join the early twentieth century. He definitely can't manage the twenty-first. Maybe upgrade to an MP3 player, rather than records. But old habits... you know how they go.'

'Yep. Hard.' He sat down in the leather sofa she indicated, crossing his legs and folding his hands across his flat stomach. 'You have my sympathies. We like our clutter. Gives us a sense of belonging. My younger brother, he's got these Star Wars toys from when we were kids, all lined up on shelves along the wall. Stole half of them off me, the bugger, pardon my French.'

Vonny sat down opposite him in an armchair. For the first time, she felt uncomfortable about the deep-space gaps between humans in this room. She had ordered a rug to close the gap between the sofa, the armchairs and the fireplace, but it hadn't arrived. Again, Vonny had insisted on the best, a vast Afghan rug, meaning the hardest to source. Again, Seth had sucked his teeth and grumbled about the budget, but had agreed eventually. 'That's nothing to my French, when I discovered all the vinyl he'd been hiding from me when we moved out here.'

'Sound system looks great, too,' Inspector Bell said, indicating the porous speaker holes integrated into a white panel set into the wall. 'You'd barely notice the speakers. This house feels like a dream.'

'We've put a lot into it. I remember everything I've ever seen on house renovation shows – don't put too much effort into decorations, fixtures and what have you – stick to the basics. But once we got started, we couldn't help ourselves.'

'You're selling it?'

'Nope. This is the dream house.' She shrugged, almost by way of apology.

'I'm just being nosy. Sorry, I'll get to the point – there was one. I happened to see the newspaper article the other day, about the car being found on your property.'

'Oh yeah. A Datsun, wasn't it? I'm not big into cars, but it got a few folk excited.'

'I'll bet. I think there was a movie about that, wasn't there? Woody Allen?'

Vonny shook her head. 'Before my time. Sorry!'

'*Sleeper*, it was called.' Bell didn't really do uncomfortable; he was smooth and professional, and made no attempt to explain the reference. 'I'm really just asking a couple of questions about the car itself. How you came to find it, first of all?'

'Now, that's the strange thing. The reporter only mentioned a couple of clues in her story, didn't she?'

'That's right.' His grey eyes widened a little, and he sat forward. 'That was a bit of a tease, wasn't it? I imagined there was some mad treasure hunt, or something out of Indiana Jones. Pirate treasure, X marks the spot!'

'You're not wrong,' Vonny said wryly. 'We found these co-ordinates in this grungy old shed out in the woods.'

'A shed, you say?' Bell scratched some notes on a shorthand pad.

'Yeah – it was almost totally obscured by hawthorn trees and nettles. My first thought was "it's a witch's cottage". There'll be a trail of breadcrumbs leading up to it. The chief builder found it, when he was carrying out a deep survey of the place.'

'I might take a look at that, if you don't mind.'

'Sorry – it's in pieces.'

'Pieces?'

'Yeah – we had the builders demolish it. It's going to be a bonfire soon. Sorry.'

'Never mind. So – after that…?'

'When we went out, there was a map behind a dartboard inside the old shed, taking these co-ordinates using what was scored on the board.'

'The actual dartboard? With darts in the board?'

'Yeah, I know. It's bizarre, but… We got the bug, and we went out. The reporter was there with us. We pieced it together, realised it was co-ordinates. I'm not sure who twigged first. There were cryptic clues. So we followed the co-ordinates and it led us to the car, covered under tarp. It was in great condition – didn't look like it had been out there very long, not much sign of rust. Must have been someone's pride and joy, just left out there.'

'Did you attempt to get in touch with the estate?'

'Well… We were told by our solicitor that Dan Grainger had no living heirs. Distant relatives came up with the idea of the raffle. And, with the contract signed, we were advised that everything we discovered on the land was ours. Legally and technically.' She spoke these last words far too quickly and defensively. Bell glanced at her, just for a moment, but continued writing in his pad.

'Legally and technically – that's correct. Can I ask, were you there throughout?'

'For what? The sale?'

'The treasure hunt.'

'Oh! Absolutely. Me, my other half, Seth, and the girl from the paper.'

'Yes, she's next on my list.' He grinned. 'And was there anything else you discovered in the course of this wee adventure?'

'No, the car was astonishing enough for one day. We knew it was a classic car. Plus, we ended up getting cash for the car. There's a collector based not far away. His eyes nearly popped out of his head when he saw the pictures. I get the impression we were ripped off, just a little bit, but it all worked out nicely.'

'Someone went to a lot of trouble to hide it, wouldn't you say?'

'I suppose so.'

'You'll have had a good look around the car?'

'Totally. Wouldn't want to pass on any bodies in the boot to the new owner. I'm guessing that would be an insurance issue.'

'Some of the bangers I've owned in my time – you'd be surprised.' He spoke with the world-weariness of a much older man, which struck Vonny as almost cute. It was a little bit like seeing a child wearing a flat cap or a tweed jacket. 'So you found nothing at all of any interest in the car?'

'Nope. Just dust. Nothing in the glove box. Nothing indicating ownership, either. The weird thing was, according to the licensing agency, the car with those plates was scrapped thirty-two years ago. It had been in a crash, and written off.'

'Now that is interesting,' Bell said. He stared at his own notes for a moment, chewing the side of his mouth. 'Seems strange to go to all that bother to hide a car, wouldn't you say?'

'I wouldn't know what to say.' Vonny fidgeted with the edge of the armrest, realised it made her look nervous, and stopped. 'You'd have to ask the previous owner about that. Though I understand that's difficult.'

'That's for sure. I knew Mr Grainger, you could say. Quite an interesting character.'

'So I believe.'

'Who led you to believe it?'

'Neighbours. Mrs Fulton across the road. The boy who lives on the next farm.'

'What boy is this?'

'Ah, I only recently met him. Truth be told I can't even

remember his name. He loves birdwatching. Comes onto the farm to take a look.'

Bell arched an eyebrow. 'Banned, surely?'

'Banned? Birdwatching?'

'No, I mean, people. Trespassers. There's a right of way at the back of the estate, but not in the main plot or the woods. That's as I understand it. Private land, in other words.'

'Oh, I think he knows that, but I don't mind him coming into the woods. Seems harmless. Quite a good kid.'

'Nevertheless, I'd advise you to be cautious. It doesn't happen too often, but sometimes people target big houses in rural settings. Sometimes in the city there's safety in numbers, but that gets diluted when you move to the countryside. There have been a few horrendous cases... What's your security set-up like?'

'Watertight, I'd say. The camera at the gate works; and the builders set off the alarms to test them. No one's getting in here without us knowing it.'

'What's your security system? A Tanner?'

'It is a Tanner, in fact. Top-of-the-range one. Burst our budget a little bit to get one, but well worth it.'

Bell nodded. 'I have a Tanner myself. Cop, you know? Can't be too careful.'

Vonny nodded. 'I can imagine.'

'And your other half – Seth, is that right? He around?'

'No, he's out doing Christmas shopping.'

'And you said he's in music?'

'Yes. Show business, I guess.' She gestured helplessly.

He grinned. 'This is interesting. Tell me a bit more about the music, if you would.'

'He's a producer. Started off as a DJ, but he got tired

of the lifestyle. He felt it was obscuring the work.' Vonny made a dismissive gesture. 'Load of wank, really, but he was always dedicated to it. He produced DJ Ninjakata – it was at number one for a week.'

'My God, really? He produced that?'

'Yeah – if you speak to him, don't remind him. His ego's big enough as it is.'

'Well, that's amazing. I've got a twelve-year-old daughter. She'd be impressed if she found out I'd spoken to him.'

'He's set up a recording studio in the basement – soundproofed, please note. And he did get his beloved soundproofed listening station downstairs. I got the artist's studio; he got the racket room.'

Bell nodded. 'I am officially jealous. Three kids... I don't get time to do things like that. Listening to music, I mean, not making it. Seth – can I double-check, you said he came with you to the treasure hunt where you found the car?'

'Yeah, he was front and centre. I was...' She had been going to say she was reluctant, but on instinct she moved away from that. 'I was involved, in the hunt if you like. He got into it, though, and pushed through and found the car.'

'Did he find anything in the car?'

That question, again. She was tired of it, and didn't want this to come through in the tone of her response. 'Same thing as me,' she said, shaking her head. 'Fluff and dust.'

He nodded. 'Where is Seth from, can I ask?'

'Croydon.'

'Know it well. Lively.'

If Vonny was supposed to augment this remark or question it, she wasn't tempted. 'You were saying, about finding the car?'

'Yes. There's a reason I ask who was involved and what you found exactly. As you'll be aware, Vonny, the previous owners of this estate were what you would call murky individuals.'

'Murky how?'

The humour dropped from his features. 'Gangsters, in a word. Dan Grainger and his sons ended up dead... Dan killed his son, then set fire to the whole estate, then himself. Somewhere along the way, his younger son killed himself, somewhere else on the estate. Dan and number-one son had fallen out over a business transaction, which showed that Mark wanted to take over all his dad's business affairs. Trouble is, no one told Dan. There are rumours that there are a lot of things buried on the property. Not just fancy cars – but other stuff, as well.'

He allowed a silence to gather pace, before Vonny broke it. 'Other stuff, like...?'

'I'm sure you can imagine. Drugs. Guns. Bodies, maybe.'

She laughed, but there was a timid edge to it. 'Surely they'd have searched the entire property for that?'

'Entire property? I'm sure you would know more than most how much land there is out here, Vonny. Down to the square inch, I imagine. It would take millions upon millions of pounds to search it all, carry out proper surveys, dig up likely spots... They'd maybe do it if they were dealing with a serial killer, and so far as we're aware, Dan Grainger hadn't quite gone that far. I want to tell you that there may be some material on your property that belonged to Dan. The proceeds of crime, cash, drugs for example. If you find them – you'll give me a call, won't you?'

He handed her a card with his name and a mobile number

printed on it. 'Of course I will,' Vonny said. 'Jesus, I'd call you right away. I have to say I didn't know... I mean, *we* didn't know...'

'Guess they didn't make it very clear on the auction site.' He smiled again, disarming her. 'Not to worry. This isn't even the site of the old house, where it all happened... That's up in the clearing in the woods. Not much of the old place left, or the stables. They've done a good job with the place. You've got a good home here, Vonny. Thanks so much for your time.'

He waved at the camera as she buzzed him through the gate. Then she put on the kettle, her phone poised in her hand. *I didn't mention the builders. She couldn't have explained why, either*. She'd wanted to keep that back. She didn't want anything criminal associated with her house, even obliquely.

The house felt stained, now. Murder. Death. Suicide. *Hanging*... Now every corner seemed dark, every shadow wanted to bloat. She didn't want to be alone. She rang Seth. And listened to it ring and divert to answerphone.

Vonny locked every door, made sure the windows were closed – even as the white fairy lights blinked on and off, close enough to her skin to sting.

## 25

Seth scraped up the last of his lasagne, then laid down the fork, with a tinny clash that ricocheted off the walls of the dining area. 'Bit echoey, isn't it?' he said.

Vonny frowned. 'What is?'

'The kitchen. You reckon maybe we should get something in to neutralise it?'

'I don't want to listen to some music, if that's what you're asking me.'

He sighed. 'No, that's not what I was asking you. It's fine. I didn't think I would get used to living in shoeboxes with police sirens all night on a weekend, but there it is. I dunno if it's trauma.'

'You're... not complaining about a big house, are you?'

'No,' he said, a little defensively. 'Just that I'm institutionalised, I suppose. Not used to the wide open space. Same with the great big bedroom upstairs.'

'But you did enjoy christening it.' She had a mischievous little smirk that she knew Seth liked, and deployed it perfectly. But he didn't pay any attention to it.

'Sure. But I meant... having a house that looks onto the woods is going to be weird. You know. No living thing in sight. I wonder if I'll start to think that someone's out there.'

'You've seen too many films, I guess.' She didn't even convince herself. She remembered how the woods had seemed threatening – a frown, gathering on the horizon – after her interview with Inspector Bell. 'And... First of all, there's that security system we paid a lot of money for – your idea, mostly. And remember, it's possible there might be people out there, because there's a public right of way at the back of the house.'

'Granted.'

'Plus... this isn't exactly the crime capital of the country.'

'According to Fulton across the road and his wife, it might well be. Bloody gangsters! Trust us to move out of south London and into some villain's old manor.'

'Speaking of London... Have you spoken to your mum or dad?'

Seth shook his head. 'No. Leaving it for now. There's nothing else to do, there.'

'How about the demos?'

Seth sat back. 'I've farmed them out here and there. Might be something brewing with Morten, at Feisty Duck.'

'I can... pretend to understand that.'

'It's as niche as it sounds, but he's put me in touch with some great singers. And I had a file through from some real throwbacks – early nineties rock, surfers, long hair. Crunchy guitars. About seventeen years old, on average. Something about them. Might go back for another listen. There's always work.'

'Have you decided what you're going to do about Jake?'

Seth's jaw tensed. 'Here's the thing. I had thought about bringing him down here for a bit – get him away from it. Show him something else. He wasn't wearing that. I didn't think he would. Wants to go back to his "manor".' Seth put his face in his hands. 'God help him.'

Vonny got up and placed her hands on his shoulder. 'Let it calm down. That's the best thing to do. It'll calm down eventually. Keep him away from his mates, the places he usually goes. Once it settles, he can move on, then we can move your mum and dad somewhere else. That's the best thing to do, isn't it?'

Possibly she was right. But Seth knew there was another thing to do, something he had discussed with a friend who still had contacts in a different kind of business, even while he'd gone shopping for gifts. And with that one gesture, a little pressure on his shoulder, Seth almost cracked and told her everything. About what he'd found. About his plan.

Except that the buzzer sounded, startling them both.

Seth glanced at his watch. 'We expecting anyone?'

Vonny shook her head. 'I hope it's not the police, again. Inspector Bell said he wanted a chat.'

She crossed to the screen, with Seth glancing over her shoulder. There, cast in night vision by the gates, were Clive and Prill Fulton. Clive's eyes filled the fish-eye-effect lens, a Lovecraftian terror for a moment or two, before he brought up a bottle of wine.

Prill did the talking for him. 'Hi, Vonny, it's only us – from across the way. We couldn't help but see the lights on the past couple of nights, and... Why don't we come over and toast your new home?'


Vonny watched the two men get drunk. Seth, slouched in one of the easy chairs up on the balcony level that the guests had laughed at – a bit too much for Vonny's liking – likening them to egg boxes. Which Seth had found particularly amusing, she noticed.

'Thing is,' Prill said, nursing a generous glass of Chablis that threatened to overflow onto her salt-and-pepper trousers, 'I think it's just marvellous.'

'What is? Sorry, I was listening to my husband trying to pretend he knows about racehorses.'

'Oh, never mind them, my love.' Prill patted Vonny's knee. 'I was just saying, this house, this whole project... Isn't it a triumph? It's like something from the space age. And it tells you something, or it tells other people something. It tells you that anyone from any background can build their own house, absolutely from scratch, follow their dreams, and get the palace that lives in their minds. Isn't that something?'

'Well, we had a very big slice of luck, let's be honest,' Vonny said absently.

Prill wasn't quite sober enough to be deflected. 'I believe that lucky things happen to good people. You might scoff, but I've always found it to be true. People can try to bring you down, but if you're good, and whole-hearted, then I truly believe good things will happen to you. You're young. Young people can be cynical. What's the word? Nihilistic? But as I've got older I've found that good things happen to good people, and the bad never turn out. Though I say this, as I watch my husband attempting to light a cigar.'

'You what? Oh.' Vonny had taken her eyes off Seth for what seemed like mere seconds. Like a toddler, he'd found something incorrigible to do. He was lighting the good cigars his uncle had given them last year as a present, using the tea light candle flames. He didn't seem to be doing too well with this task, and the flickering flames seemed to writhe in mirth as he inhaled at the end of the ridiculously long cigar.

Finally, red taper flames followed their curves along the folds of the tobacco at its tip. 'As Sigmund Freud said, sometimes,' Seth said, trying not to cough, 'a cigar is just... a pain in the arse to light.'

Vonny had indulged the drinking, which started the moment their visitors arrived. Clive and Prill had thrown themselves into it, surprising their hosts. The former, a somewhat austere man in late middle age, but fit and healthy with it – the outdoor life clearly working for him – had been all too eager to sample a "wee shortie", as Seth referred to The Good Stuff. Already depleted by those two stolen fingers from the night before, the bottle took a terrible beating.

Quickly the conversations had split in half as the parties sat on the patio, looking out over the trees, the clear sky and a paintbox patterning of stars up above. It was bitter out, but the newcomers had insisted on sitting out, and Vonny had provided fleeces and tartan blankets, unpacked just that morning.

'Nice smoke, all the same,' Clive said, taking a draw of his own cigar. 'Only, you know you're not meant to inhale, right?'

'Ah, that's a habit that dies hard.' Here Seth winked. Vonny restrained an urge to stop him. New neighbours plus drug references? Not the best idea, she thought, taking a sip of Chablis.

'I wish we had this patio, Clive,' Prill said.

'It's something else,' he agreed, leaning back in the chair. 'Feel like I'm on holiday – and we're just across the road.'

'You're welcome any time,' Vonny said.

'You could fall in love with a house like this.'

'We've fallen in love with the place, that's for sure.'

'But surely your farm's a terrific patch?' Seth asked. 'You guys are in with the bricks here, I'm guessing?'

'You could say that,' Clive answered, considering a plume of smoke as it dissipated into the frigid night air. 'But who's to say we'll stay here forever? Owning the farm is a dream, but I'm getting closer to retirement age. Prill and I don't have any children, you see, so there's no one to take on the work.'

'What do you grow?' Vonny asked.

'All sorts – barley, rhubarb – pumpkins, now there's a crop for you! People have a go at Halloween – being turned into more of an American tradition – but it hasn't half given us a boost, the more popular pumpkins have got.'

'Used to be turnips, didn't it?' Seth mused, boozily. 'They had it in Scotland. I had a Scottish mate who claimed that Halloween was a spooky Scots, Celtic-y type thing. They claim everything, though, the Scots. Tarmacadam, bagpipes, tartan…'

'Oh, I should know,' Clive said. 'Second name Fulton. We've got our own tartan.'

'Whae's like yese?' Seth roared.

Clive only smiled in response, then returned his attention to Vonny. 'So, we do OK, but harvest time gets harder and harder for me… And looking after the sheep and cows is labour-intensive, every day. It's a lot of ground to cover. We'll have to see. Sometimes we dream of a little cottage somewhere, don't we? Maybe even keep a little corner of our land, then sell the rest. What do you think, Prill?'

'News to me,' Prill sniffed. 'They'll carry me out of here in a box. I think we could extend, though. That's a possibility. Well... I think my glass has gotten a little bit damp, Clive, wouldn't you say?'

Clive sighed, and accepted his wife's proffered glass. 'Just as well we brought two bottles, eh?' he said, grinning.

Vonny and Seth shared the briefest look, one only couples could share.

Seth twirled his underpants around the end of his toe, then almost overbalanced as he lobbed them into a corner. 'Good night that, I thought,' he said, similarly struggling to get into a pair of pyjama shorts. 'Nice couple. That Prill's a bit of an odd one. Though I guess she was blazing drunk. Thought we might have to stick her in our wheelbarrow. Even though Clive didn't seem to get drunk, no matter what we poured him.'

'Unlike you,' Vonny said. She was lying in bed with a book open, but struggled to put more than a sentence or two together. It was possible she had overdone it a little. 'So, that little chat you and Clive had, when you thought I wasn't listening... What was that about?'

Seth lay back on the bed and snorted. 'You'll have to give me some details, there?'

'When he talked about how you were "getting on with our new friend?" Like a schoolkid trying to talk in code. What did he mean by that?'

Seth's eyes closed, and his breathing became regular.

'Seth! I'm talking to you.'

But, by God, he actually *had* passed out, his mouth

agape. Vonny, stung for a moment, considered nudging him awake. Then she threw back the covers and stomped off to fetch a glass of water from the en suite. She'd ask him about this, tomorrow.

She liked the en suite, but the ante-room had an unsettling effect in the dark. There was too much glass around, and its edges reflected the moonlight in razor-edge slivers. There was something she disliked about it, robbed of the crude illumination of the light switch, with only the warped light from the frosted windows. As if in a gesture of reassurance, she touched the toasty radiator. At least the heating system worked like a dream; you would never have known about the frost and the freezing fog that had descended outside, unless you opened the window.

When she returned to the bedroom, she gasped. Seth was stood in the middle of the floor, gazing out beyond their balcony towards the jagged treeline, etched against the darkest blue of the sky.

'What is it?'

'Security light came on. Didn't last. Just a bloody fox or something. I didn't think about that, you know. That you might get foxes in every two minutes. Should dismantle it, really.'

'Go back to bed. It's fine. There's no one out here.' Vonny slipped into bed. Fresh, crisp sheets; cool against her face, her neck. One of her favourite things. And plenty of space out here to dry them outside, too. Nothing better than clean sheets dried outside. 'Now I'm worried about the caravan, though.'

'What... you reckon it might get broken into?'

'Or stolen. Maybe we should take it back?'

'We've got too much to do at the moment. Besides, it's coming up to Christmas.' He got in beside her, and his breathing grew more regular. To be fair, his ability to pass out at a few seconds' notice was nothing new. It was an old trick, and one she envied – there had been many nights, tortured by problems both brand new and historical, when she wished she had it. So she got a fright when he said, without opening his eyes or changing his sleeping position: 'We've got the Tin Coffin until the new year. No rush taking it back, no sense piling on the duties. Best we...' He hadn't fallen asleep again; it was a genuine pause.

'Yeah?'

'Nothing. Thought I heard a noise.'

'God's sake!'

'Y'know, I didn't think it would bother me, but it does. The idea that we're all alone out here. Barring the neighbours, half a mile away. There's something weird about it. You say, "There's nothing there", but there is. There's a whole bloody ecosystem. All watching us. Spiders, rats. Wicked witches. Mad murderers with masks on.'

'Shut the curtains, then,' Vonny mumbled.

And she must have fallen asleep, quicker than she gave herself credit for. The next thing she was aware of was shrugging something off her shoulder, and said, 'I'll tell you when I am quite ready. No thank you, no bus for me.'

Then a hand gripped her shoulder, hard, definite, concrete, painful, real. Vonny's eyes flew open.

She was looking into the face of the devil. The actual devil's face, red skin, needle teeth, orange eyes and two obscene horns, curving outward from the head.

'Get up, both of you!' the devil screamed. 'Now!'

## 26

Vonny waved her hands, as if dispersing smoke. But the devil remained. The mask was expensive and horribly detailed, with alternating shades of light and dark red delineating the angles and contours of the face. The devil's eyes were yellow and slit horizontally, like a goat's. Two real, darting human eyes were visible through holes in the mask, just underneath. The mask had long, thin teeth painted into a leer above a classic saturnine beard.

'No,' she said, 'no, wait, wait.'

'Out the fucking bed!' the devil shrieked, tearing off the quilt cover. Vonny cowered, hands clutched to her chest and knees drawn up to her chin. She might have screamed.

Then she saw the machete. The main light had been switched on. The machete looked new. The blade was polished to an almost ceremonial sheen. It was half a metre long or more, and razor-tipped. The devil waved the blade in front of her face. 'Out of the bed! Do it! Run, and I'll take your fucking leg off!'

She got up. The mewling sound came from her own throat. The blade followed her progress and she cringed. She wanted to fold up on the floor. Her bladder had already gone; the wet was cold on her pyjama bottoms.

'Now stand against that wall and don't move or I swear to God, I'll...' The devil's voice rose to an almost unearthly pitch, distorted beyond any rational sense.

Seth bucked and twisted like a cat tossed off a shed roof. Once he'd sprung out of bed and disentangled himself from the inside sheet, a skull loomed in front of him. Again, the mask was detailed, possibly one of a pair alongside the other man's devil covering. Cracks stretched across the dirty white expanse, some of them joined by what looked like sutures, and black hollows surrounded the eye sockets and enhanced the effect of the cheekbones. If the devil's smile was restrained, the skull's mouth gaped in unholy mirth.

The skull carried a samurai sword. The blade was held high, and just far enough away to make a sudden grab for it impossible.

'Fuck is going on man? What's the game here?' Seth stood up on the bed, clutching the under sheet to him – the ludicrous effect of a cartoon elephant shrieking upon sight of a mouse. His jaw literally dropped at what was unfolding in front of him.

'Let's be calm, here.' The man in the skull mask held up his free hand. He had a placatory tone, and sounded much younger than the devil mask man, who was taller and stockier.

The intruders wore black from head to foot. Then Vonny noticed something that made her sob aloud. *Both the intruders wore plastic coverings on their feet.*

'Oh, please don't cry, come on,' Skull Face said, soothingly. 'There is absolutely no need for any unpleasantness. You could treat this as a kind of social call.'

As he said this, the Devil's heavy breathing hissed out

through the slits in the mask. The hand holding the machete towards Vonny trembled.

*Jake. This had to be down to Jake. Something to do with Jake! They found us!*

'It's OK, honey, shhh,' Skull Face said. 'We just want the stuff. Give it to us, and we'll be on our way. Understand me, big guy?'

Seth's lips quivered, but he had recovered some poise. He squared his shoulders. 'I do not know what the fuck you're talking about. Get out of my house, now.'

'Wrong answer,' Skull Face said. He inched closer. 'I think you know exactly what I'm talking about, and exactly where it is. Take us to it, and you both survive. In fact, if you do the right thing, you could both go back to bed, wake up, and pretend this didn't happen.'

'I don't know what you mean,' Seth said again. His eyes watered, and he chewed the inside of his mouth nervously. He dared a look towards Vonny, who still sobbed.

'We just moved here,' she managed to say, 'we just built the house. We don't know anything about it, or anything about Dan Grainger.'

Skull and the Devil shared a glance, at the same moment Vonny and Seth did. Seth jerked his head – whether indicating she should shut up, or a response to something he didn't like, Vonny could not say.

Skull said: 'That's interesting. Dan Grainger, you said? He seems an interesting character. Why don't you tell us about him?'

'We don't know anything,' Vonny stammered. 'We know he lived here before us. We won the plot in a raffle. That's it, that's the only connection. There's no stuff. Whatever it is you're looking for.' She wiped her streaming nose with the back of her hand, like a child.

'You did find the car, though,' Skull said. 'The star prize! Whereabouts did you find it? As a matter of interest, you might say.'

'Near a shed out in the woods,' Vonny said.

'Just stumbled over it, yeah?'

Somehow she found it harder to stare into the illusion of the empty eye sockets in the skull than she did the cartoonish gaze of the Devil, though the latter stood closer. 'Yeah, pretty much.'

'Well. I guess it doesn't matter where and how you found it,' Skull said. 'We think the stuff was in the Datsun. At least, it was, at first. That much we know. I've got a... Well. People we know have access to a sniffer dog, and when we showed it the old Datsun at that guy's lock-up, it just about landed on its back with its feet in the air. Daft thing was on its way back to the sixties. And you know what that means? That means the stuff was in the Datsun at some point. Maybe even in the recent past. Now, I had a word with the guy at the lock-up, the classic cars guy, and he doesn't know anything about any stuff. I believe him. You know why? Either of you can buzz in with the answer, here.'

Seth said nothing. Vonny said, miserably: 'No, we don't know why.'

'Because, after we made it clear we would crush him to death until he told us what we wanted to know, we threatened to take his fingers off.'

'I was going to take his balls off,' the Devil growled. 'That's a bit of motivation for anyone, right there.'

'We need the stuff,' the Skull said. 'Right now.'

The words tumbled out of Vonny's mouth, just about making sense and no more. 'I told you we don't know anything about any stuff! Leave us alone! We have a security system – you'll be plastered all over it. It can dial into the police. Probably has, already. If you leave now, you'll get away.'

Skull and the Devil both laughed. 'Your security system?' said the former. 'You mean the one connected to that little console there, beside the bedside table? That one? The one with the panic button? The one with the little red light? That one?' He jabbed a finger at the panel next to the bed. 'Notice anything odd about it?'

Vonny's breath caught in her throat. The console was dead. No digital figures on the display. No status readout on any of the cameras and sensors. And no red light.

Seth spoke, his voice cracking with strain. 'Look, lads, let's not do anything daft. Right?'

'"Lads,"' sneered the Devil. When he twisted his head to do so, Vonny caught sight of a tattoo at his neck. Flames, red and orange, styled like Hokusai's wave. '"Lads", is it? He's seeing sense now.'

Skull nodded its head vigorously. 'Oh yeah. He wants to be friends. He's making a deal in his head. He really, really wants to. I can sense it.'

'Just make sure you leave her alone. All right? Don't hurt her.'

'You're in no position to seek guarantees,' Skull said. His tone was not so much cold, as completely devoid of emotional content. It might have been a remark about mild weather. 'You're in no position to demand anything. You know what we're talking about. You know what we want. So, take us to it. Right now. Or we'll start hurting her.'

The breath, whistling through the apertures in the Devil mask. The eyes – the true eyes – behind the red and black rubber casing, plotting a haphazard course across several points on Vonny's face and body.

Seth took a long time before he answered.

'It's not in the house.'

## 27

'What stuff?' Vonny screamed. 'There's no stuff!'

Skull chuckled. 'Too late. He's told us there is. Now, here's what we will do. Big guy, you're going to walk very carefully in front of me and keep those hands up in the air when you're doing it. You, sugar tits, will follow behind with my friend the Devil. I don't think I have to explain what's going to happen if either of you decides to do anything unintelligent, do I?'

Vonny glared at Seth, horror taking over as her dominant response now. He had found something. He knew about the stuff, whatever it was. He fucking *knew*.

'Move,' said the Skull. He took two careful steps back, towards the patio door to the balcony, holding the blade above his head. Seth stepped off the bed.

'Can I get my slippers on?'

'Slip your feet into them, my friend. Get yourself comfortable.'

Seth did so, slowly and carefully sliding his feet into the footwear, then walking towards the bedroom door. Skull, watching closely, let him get a couple of steps ahead, then followed up. Vonny gasped as he darted forward and placed the point of the sword between his shoulder blades. Seth's shoulders jerked, and he stopped.

'Just letting you know how quickly I could do it,' Skull said, in that same detached tone. 'Ever had a shish kebab? I love shish kebabs.'

'You've made your point,' Seth said, quietly.

'OK. You seem like a clever fellow. Lead the way.'

When they had both disappeared outside the door, the Devil glared at her and grabbed Vonny by the shoulder. She cried out, as he shoved her roughly in front of him.

There was a minor struggle outside the door. Seth, his weight brought to bear. A grunt, maybe his, maybe Skull's. 'No, don't!' she cried out.

She saw the blade raised towards Seth's neck, a silver spark jumping between two silhouettes. Shadow Seth raised his hands and stepped back, his pyjama top collar caught in Skull's other hand.

'Problem?' The Devil barked, at Vonny's ear.

'No problem,' Skull said. 'Let's keep it polite from now on, yeah? I don't want to have to plunge our genial host here before he tells us what we need to know. Maybe in turn, you could treat the lady nice?'

The intruders paused a moment, and something unreadable passed between them.

The Devil grunted, breaking the tension. 'Sure. I'll be nice. Let's all be nice.'

'Excellent. As you were, then.' Skull lowered the blade and gestured for Seth to move down the stairs.

The procession moved on. But as Vonny stepped through the doorframe, the Devil said in her ear: 'I hope he does something stupid. Your man. Know why?'

Vonny said nothing. Her revulsion at the voice at her ear, and the breath at her neck, straightened her spine. She held her head back and ignored him.

'Yeah. I think you know, all right.' He laughed mirthlessly. 'Need to give you a wash first. Made a mess, haven't you?'

'Surprised you can tell the difference. Fucking pig.' It was as if she'd been possessed, or stolen a voice.

The Devil said nothing at first. But he placed the flat of the machete blade on her shoulder. 'Just remember,' he said. 'Be nice. Be polite.'

They proceeded down the stairs, an awkward train moving as slowly as possible.

'It's outside,' Seth said.

Skull shrugged. 'So? We go outside.'

'It's cold.'

'You can be cold, can't you? Big guy like yourself. Lots of cladding. Lots of insulation.' Now that they were all on a level on the ground floor, Vonny could see that Seth towered over the two intruders – as he did most men. The sense of hope she gained from this was an impostor, she knew. This would not be a time for heroics.

*They might kill us anyway.*

'I'm OK with being cold,' Seth said. 'But it's not fair on her. Let her put her coat on, if we're all going.'

'Which one is your coat, honey?' Skull asked Vonny. He pointed towards the coat and hat stand.

'The waterproof one is fine,' Vonny said.

Mind already several moves ahead, she considered the ultimate treachery – the option of running. *Take to my heels. I know the woods. I could lose them in there.*

Skull patted her jacket down, turning out old till receipts

and half-eaten packets of chewing gum from the pockets. 'Just making sure you've not got any hidden phones in there. Or guns, come to think of it.' Satisfied, he tossed her the jacket, and she was grateful to slip it on over the slim covering of her pyjama top.

'And my shoes,' she said.

The Skull shook its head.

'Christ's sake,' Seth hissed. 'Don't piss about, let her put her shoes on.'

The blow was fast – Vonny didn't even see it land, but she heard it, as well as Seth's cry of shock and pain. From the follow-through, it looked like Skull had backhanded him; Vonny clutched her hand to her mouth, an electric shock of sympathy pain jerking her face.

Seth staggered back against a framed mirror behind him. The mirror wobbled, but didn't fall. Neither did he.

'I told you about being impolite,' Skull said. The blade, which had been held at his side, was now held horizontal. His elbow was bent – ready to send it through Seth's guts. 'No – she's not getting her shoes. I accept it's cruel. But there is some logic to this. I'm going to explain it to you. If she decides to run – and I know it's occurred to both of you – she probably won't get very far in her bare feet. So wherever we're going, you're going to have to brass it out. You, my friend, can stay in your slippers. I don't think you could do much sprinting in them.'

'Do that again and I'll kill you,' Seth said. His voice was strangulated, taut, with a demoniacal, unblinking stare. He was on the verge of an eruption; Vonny had only seen it once or twice in their years together. When it happened, it was never forgotten.

'Shut up,' Skull said, laughing. 'OK. As before. I'll open the door, out we go, in line. You lead, big man. Take us to the stuff.'

He pulled open the door, and gestured for Seth to head out. A pall of moonlight fell across Seth's back and shoulders, casting his retreating form in a pale blue glow.

'How far is it?' the Devil asked, at Vonny's ear.

'You'll see,' Seth said.

Vonny flinched as the new lawn pricked at her bare feet. Cruel; no need to deny her shoes. *They're going to use me as leverage. No question.*

The mist had lifted a little – it was the cold that came with it that presented the bigger problem, rather than visibility. She pulled the coat tighter.

'Don't you worry, pet,' the Devil said. The note of concern he affected was as big an obscenity as anything that had come out of his mouth since the intruders had appeared. His breath steamed up in the air, and despite the near-zero chill outside, it added to the fiendish visage. Steam from the gates of hell. 'I'll see you right. Just give us what we want and we'll be off, don't you worry. You ever done a fire walk? On the coals? I've done it for charity. You just tell yourself it isn't going to hurt, and you walk across the hard bit of ground, and it doesn't hurt. It's amazing. Just try it.'

She ignored him. Seth was taking them towards the new shed, just off the east side of the property, inside the privet-seeded fencing.

Vonny hadn't liked it, but it was a rare instance of Seth putting his foot down and being insistent. It had taken her a while to put her finger on what had irritated her about it – it was, she realised, as if Seth had built it himself, except it had been done professionally, and she knew exactly what it had cost. The builders' mates had done it for a bit of pocket money, but it was just a squat bunkhouse with a low roof, and the staining on the timber was too light – darker would have made for a better contrast with the house. She had been in it once since the final dab of wood stain had been completed. And she had thought she wouldn't be setting foot in it too much in the future. In its narrow confines and the one miserable circular table, she foresaw an unpleasant future involving Seth, his mates, or – even worse – musicians, smoking, drinking, and inevitably, playing cards.

*I'm back in it sooner than I thought.*

The windows inside were dark, and the front of the shed was hidden from the front of the house. 'Wait there by the door,' Skull said. 'Close to the door – close enough for your toes to touch the timber.'

Seth did as he was asked. Skull, keeping the blade within Seth's eyeline, peered into the dark windows for an uncomfortable length of time. At the sound of an animal cry somewhere in the woods, everyone flinched.

'Clear?' the Devil asked.

'Guess so.' Skull turned to Seth. 'OK, big guy. How we getting in?'

'There's a combination,' Seth said. He reached for the heavy padlock and turned the dial. 'Surprised you didn't break in.'

'Nah, non-starter,' Skull said, conversationally. 'We break in, you call the cops… Game's over right away. Plus, we've no idea where the stuff is. Taking you makes sure. Because it is in here, isn't it?'

'Yes.' Seth squinted at the padlock and completed the combination. Everyone heard the soft click.

'We're all going inside,' Skull said. 'Same as before. You and me, then my diabolical friend and your missus. Then you give us what we need, and we'll be on our way.'

'Sure.'

Seth turned on the light – low and well shaded, hanging in the centre of the room above the table, but still bright enough to cause Vonny to flinch. The space was about ten or twelve yards long, with empty shelving and cabinets on either side of the table and chairs. Vonny knew this was meant for a TV and games console, a sound system, of course, and then the indulgence of drinks cabinets. The flooring was boarded over with heavy timber; Seth had planned a rug to cover the floor space, but it hadn't arrived yet.

They filed inside, and the Devil shut the door behind them.

'Stop at the table,' Skull said.

In the sudden quiet, everyone's breathing became apparent. It was most obvious in the two masked men, amplified by the narrow nostril holes in their face coverings. From the rate of breaths taken, they were either on edge, or excited.

'Make it quick,' Skull said. 'I'll be right with you. Point out where it is. Then stand against the far wall.'

'You stay here,' the Devil whispered at Vonny's ear. She felt the lightest kiss of the machete on her shoulder – the blade this time, not the flat edge – and flinched.

Seth took a deep breath. 'It's in the cabinet, right by the space, to your left.'

'Sounds good to me. Let's go for it.' Skull pointed the sword at Seth's stomach.

Seth walked towards the cabinet, the boards at his feet creaking. Despite the cold, Vonny felt sweat prickle her brow; she shifted her weight from one foot to the other to relieve the pressure.

'No lock?' the Devil said, making Vonny flinch.

'It's well hidden,' Seth said, half-turning.

'Show us, then,' Skull intoned.

Carefully, Seth opened the cabinet with an efficient little click. Vonny smelt something then – something that took her back to the clothing shop her mother had dragged her into, a long time ago. Something fibrous and maybe mouldy.

'Carefully,' Skull whispered. 'Very, very carefully. Step back.'

'Sure.' Seth took a step back. Then something blocked him out; a dark red square that utterly swallowed him from view.

'You f...' Skull didn't get to complete the expletive.

The rug that Seth had clearly ordered and had delivered without her knowing unfurled. Skull swung the blade at it; there was a muffled report on impact, but the rug was over his head in an instant. He tugged it off in a second or two and hurled it aside. By that point, Seth was on the move towards the cabinet directly behind him.

'Hey!' The Devil darted forward, raising the machete overhead; but the barrier of the table was awkward to begin with – doubly so as Seth kicked it towards him.

Seth snatched open the door. 'Run, Vonny! Get the fuck out!'

'What are you doing?' was all she could say.

It happened all too quickly – she could only piece it together fully later, like assembling a series of photographs.

The Devil swung wildly at Seth, and he narrowly avoided having his chest sliced to the bone, and perhaps beyond. The blow displaced the air with a thundercrack, but it missed.

Seth reached into the cabinet and grabbed a long, shiny case. By the time his hand closed on it, both Skull and the Devil were onto him.

Blows rained down on Seth – with fists, not with the blades. Seth grunted and fell to the floor, rolling away from the attackers. He raised his hands, protecting his face as the Devil rained down four, five, six fast, brutal punches about his head and body.

'All right! All right! Stop!' Seth yelled.

Vonny jemmied herself between the pistoning shoulders of the two attackers, screaming. 'Leave him!'

Her nostrils filled with the unpleasant chemical stench of the galvanised rubber mask; the Devil's eyes met her own and then she was shoved onto her back, striking her head on the floor. Her tongue clashed with her teeth; light exploded behind her eyes.

The lights swayed above, mesmerising her for a moment, before coalescing into the solid image of the bulb and shade, as the world threatened to spin off its axis. She fought a burbling tide of nausea, and stayed exactly where she was, waiting for equilibrium.

'Can you believe that?' Skull said, breathing hard. 'Big guy went for the home run! And, what have we here?' He raised the case, shaking it at Seth. Seth sat up on the floor, his back to the cabinet he'd tried to raid.

'What is it?' the Devil asked. 'Cutlery set?' Of the two he was the more keyed up, clenching and unclenching his fists, pacing back and forth.

'The case is monogrammed. Check out the brass panel. And... I'll be buggered in the bunting. Look! This is where Dan Grainger kept his rootin', tootin', shootin' iron!'

'What? A gun? You serious, mate?' The Devil hoofed a kick at Seth. He absorbed the shock of it somewhere soft. He cried out and curled up.

'Please.' Vonny wasn't sure if she'd said it or not; if it was drowned in her throat before the sound could escape. 'Please. Don't hurt him. We just want to get out.'

'Afraid that ship's sailed, honey,' Skull sneered. 'Now things are going to get interesting. Meaning we're going to torture you. Then your big hero gets to decide whether or not he knows where the stuff is. I do believe he was threatening violence, you know.' Skull laid the case on the table, stilling the swaying light with his hand. 'I do believe he harboured bad intentions.'

'Can't have that,' growled the Devil.

Seth sat up straight, breathing hard. His eyes glistened with unshed tears. 'You all right?' he said to Vonny.

'Give them what they want,' she said. 'Whatever they want, just give it to them. We've no choice. Don't do anything stupid again.'

'Your lady's very sensible,' Skull said. 'You want to listen to her. You'll go far.' He flipped the catches on the case.

The inside was lined with green baize that shone like fresh pine needles in torchlight. There was a suggestion of a gun inside, the contours of the shotgun perfectly traced, as well as holsters for cartridges. But no gun.

'What's the score here?' Skull said.

'Idiot thought there was a gun in there,' the Devil chuckled. 'It would have been funnier if he'd actually got it open!'

'It's funnier that you fell for it,' Seth said.

He had raised one of the floorboards at his backside without a sound. Then there was a shotgun in his hands. Then he was on one knee, the stock of the rifle against his shoulder. And he pulled the trigger.

# 28

The sound of the blast was colossal in that enclosed space. Vonny flinched and clutched her face, as if she'd been shot herself.

She hadn't been shot. The Devil had been shot. There had been a split second ahead of the discharge of the cartridge, when the Devil hesitated in front of the shotgun barrel, frozen, transfixed. Only his dumb dead yellow eyes, unblinking. The Skull didn't move either.

Vonny must have blinked at the explosion – she wasn't even aware of the Devil falling, or colliding with the cabinet. He was instantly down. His angles – elbows, knees, spine, neck – rearranged themselves into novel shapes. The plastic face was mainly obliterated, as was the face beneath it. There was a divot where the left eye and ear should have been. Inky flames licked at his neck, utterly confusing Vonny for a moment. She didn't see the blood gush or gout, but she was aware of it in the air; she inhaled it, tasted the coppery droplets at the back of her throat, in her nostrils. Living red splashes, bright as lipstick under the lights, streaked the table, which was tipped on its side, and rolled against the same cabinet.

Then Skull was moving, hurling the shotgun case. It betrayed him, flipping open as it travelled through the air, mitigating the blow, but it put Seth off discharging the second barrel. Skull closed on him in moments. His blade was a silver bow in the light, a dance of lightning. Seth twisted; the sword buried itself two inches into the wood near his shoulder and stayed there. The shotgun clattered across the floor, the stock resting inches away from Vonny's hand. Smoke uncoiled lazily from the barrel.

Skull grunted, heaving at the sword. Before it could be retrieved, Seth got to his feet and charged him. He had no strategy beyond obliterating the man with the mask the same shade of white as smoker's teeth and the scorched eyes, and he succeeded in knocking him off his feet through the sheer force of the collision. That might have been enough, had there been enough clearance. But the same lack of space that meant Skull sacrificed the necessary accuracy with the sword also meant Seth couldn't charge him to the floor. Skull's back rebounded against the open cabinet; Seth punched out into his ribs, finding good purchase, and Skull sagged. But only for a second. Then Skull's knee exploded into Seth's groin, and a murderous elbow on the downstroke somehow found its way into the meat of Seth's left shoulder. Seth cried out, and staggered away. Two punches exploded off the top of Seth's head, and he collapsed on the floor, wheezing.

Skull yanked out the sword from the cabinet. And faced Vonny. Who was pointing the shotgun at him.

'Huh,' was all Skull said, before she pulled the trigger.

The explosion blew *her* off her feet, and her head crashed

into the back wall. She dropped the gun; coruscating, pounding, residual echoes, inside and outside her head, the smell of burning plastic and singed flesh.

She saw a blurred Skull lying opposite her, with the mask half-torn off his face. Slick black hair curled out of one side, like a doll's hair, shining under the wan lights. Dead, surely; sat on the floor, knees up, hands by his sides.

But not dead, no. The hands moved. One of them touched the side of Skull's mask, where one eye darted and smoke rose from the hair. On a shelf, a good way above Skull's shoulder, ancient, fusty old vinyl records in a box had been obliterated into lacquered shards, still dripping off onto the floor.

*Missed*, she heard someone say. *You missed! From there! Close, but no cigar!* There was no sound, or all sound, and nothing to be discerned but roaring. For a weird moment she thought: *I'm on fire.* Smoke stole over her like dry ice in a music video; she realised it came from the barrel of the gun, which lay at her side. Vonny's breast hurt, where the stock of the weapon had recoiled into her. Skull got to his feet, eye bulging, as he snatched up the samurai sword. He drew it back over his head. Vonny cringed.

There was a flash of silver, but not from his hand. Despite the ringing in her ears, Vonny did make out the crisp, slapping sound that followed impact. She shut her eyes, instinctively. When she opened them again, she saw Skull stagger forwards. His breath whistled sharply through the mask – a hiss, difficult to tell whether it was inhalation or exhalation. Then he sank to one knee, dropping the sword.

A machete blade was jammed into the side of the mask,

buried from just underneath the blank eyehole right past the jawline and into the neck.

'Your friend dropped something,' Seth wheezed. He was leaning against the cabinet, one hand to his side, breathing hard.

Skull made a desperate sound, one hand flailing, as blood gushed down the white mask. He got up, as if jolted with electricity. And started forward.

Vonny scrambled to get out of his way. Before he reached the door he collapsed, abruptly.

Then Vonny's face was buried in Seth's chest. 'Baby, it's all right, it's all right,' he said, quietly.

'It's not all right!' she shrieked. 'They're dead! They're both dead!'

'They'd have killed us, darlin'.' Seth's voice fluctuated, reaching a weird high pitch, like that of a teenage boy. 'For sure. They were not going to leave us alive. They didn't leave the last guys alive, either.'

'What's this stuff? Drugs? What is going on here?' she wailed. Her head sagged, and she covered it with her hands. In her mind's eye, Skull was still alive, starting forward, the sword held vertical, a model of precise menace.

There was a scraping sound at the door and Seth was back on his feet, gasping.

Skull *was* still alive. Clawing towards the door. He got to his knees, blood still pouring from the angled interface between his head and the machete. The sound Skull emitted was more of a snuffle or a snore than any kind of cry of pain or alarm Vonny had ever heard before – as if there might be a pig's head under that mask.

She watched, stupefied, as he got to his feet, steadying

himself at the door. Then he tugged at the machete in his face. It gave, just a little, a rill of blood running off the edge and pattering onto the floor.

'Mate,' was all Seth said, absurdly conciliatory. He had the shotgun in his hands; he cracked the stock, and the smoking shells flew out.

Skull tugged again, and the machete came out. He gurgled at this, and it was a recognisable quantifiable human sound, all right. He staggered for a moment. Threatened to fall; didn't.

'Get behind me,' Seth said to Vonny. He crouched on the floor, digging for something in the loose floorboard he had prised open earlier. 'Behind the table.'

Vonny didn't wait for an invitation. She was elastic, leaping over the top, then crouching into a ball. She peered out to the side.

Seth was loading the shotgun. Or at least, that's what he intended. One shell slithered through trembling fingers. But the second slid into the breech, snug. Seth snapped the gun closed and cocked it.

Skull grabbed the door handle and snatched it open. He took a faltering step forward, holding on to the doorjamb.

Seth braced the gun against his shoulder and fired. Vonny had prepared herself for it, her fingers in her ears, but the blast was still appallingly loud. She clashed her teeth together, no longer sure in the numbing repercussion if she was sobbing or screaming.

She peered through a haze of smoke. Seth was striding forward. The door to the shed was open. There was no sign of Skull.

Vonny got up and joined him. She babbled, without

thinking, possessed: 'I mean if we call the police we'll have to call them and they can come over; that's what I'll do. I'll get our phone.'

'Quiet,' Seth said, voice taut with tension. He turned out of the doorway, the milky light of the mist illuminating his sweat-slicked skin.

Then Seth's shoulders sagged. He lowered the gun.

Vonny joined him, and they clutched each other as they peered at the figure lying before them on the ground, face down.

The Skull had been blown clean off the man's head, lying a few feet away, still staring at them. The top half was torn away and dripping with blood.

The back of Skull's head was an appalling mess, even in the gloom. It bore no resemblance to a human head. They never would know what his face had looked like.

# 29

Seth carried her out of the shed, and she allowed him to. It seemed to cost him no effort as he made his way up the garden path and back to the house. She clung to him like a little girl, falling into rhythm with each step, lulled by it. Only when he set her down on the floor – collapsed, really – inside the front door did she feel the pain in her feet. The world began to revolve, and her guts with it.

Vonny had heard of people feeling physically sick thanks to something revolting they had experienced as opposed to something they had eaten, but it had never happened to her before that night. Seth was there to pin back her hair while she heaved, miserably, into the en suite.

Even with Seth there, she still didn't want her back to the toilet door, remembering that appalling shock of the light switch bursting into life, and the gleeful, diabolical faces inches away from hers.

'We have to call the police,' she said, breathing hard, after emptying her stomach. 'It's a case of self-defence, simple as that. They invaded our house. They threatened us.'

Seth said nothing. He laid his hand on her back, gently, then he fetched her a glass of water. She gulped it down, rinsed and spat. She took a deep breath, and then the pain hit her from a dozen places; mainly on her back, where she'd collided with various things, and in her shoulders, which were still seemingly cast in steel thanks to the tension.

'They came for us, they hurt us, marched us out...' Vonny wasn't in the strictest sense having a conversation, more rifling through mental index cards, with what had happened on the headings. 'They said it – they were going to kill us.'

'They did say that. Or, one of them did.' Seth's face was swollen around the temple, but he was curiously unmarked about the face, despite the beating. He pulled up his pyjama top, and revealed a massive graze just above his hip, blood from it soaking through the dark material. Vonny cried out when she saw it.

'It's OK,' he said. 'Flesh wound. Ribs aren't broken. I wouldn't have been able to carry you, if it had been any worse than that.'

'You killed them.' Did she think it or say it? Again and again, she heard the thunderclap of the shotgun, the sharp crack of the machete cleaving Skull's mask. She saw him take up a proper firing position, with the stock of the rifle against his shoulder. 'Come to think of it... Where did you get the gun? Where did that come from?'

Seth winced as he sat down. 'Clive Fulton gave it to me. Said it belonged to Dan Grainger.'

And now the shrieking, clanging alarms sounded in Vonny's head. 'And what about the stuff? What is the fucking *stuff*?' Her voice cracked and her face sagged. He tried to hug her, but she backed away. 'Have you got drugs?

You swore. You swore you weren't touching them. You told me half your fucking musicians don't do them any more; they're too professional! What's the stuff?'

'It's nothing to do with me, I swear it. I found it two nights ago. Heroin. Lots of it. I… I wasn't sure what to do.'

'Found it? *Found it?* You don't just find a stash of drugs as if it's a dropped 50p piece in the street! Found them? Explain yourself, now.'

Seth's voice was worryingly flat. He stared, unblinkingly, at a blank white wall, as he spoke. 'I spoke to a mate in London. He told me that if the car didn't have anything dodgy in it, then it might mark the spot where something dodgy was hidden. He was right. The other night, I took a walk over, just to look at the spot where we pulled out the car. Sure enough, there was a heavy stone underneath, and suitcases packed with gear.'

'Why didn't you tell me?'

'I thought… I thought it was a chance to put things right. A windfall. Same as the house. I've got connections.'

'No,' Vonny said, clutching her hair. 'No, no, no. No. This isn't right. You're lying. I can't believe you're lying! You think you can sell drugs? Seriously? There's something more to this. I don't believe you. If this is something you've kept from me, all this time, or something to do with Jake, I swear to God…'

He got up to comfort her, but she turned away, swiping her hands at him. 'Vonny, it's the truth. This is what happened. I am not lying. I don't have anything to do with that world. But if you calm down a minute, and think about it, there's a way through this for all of us – me, you, Jake, everyone.'

'Calm down? In this situation?' Her laughter edged

towards a shriek. 'We have to call the police... Jesus Christ, there are two corpses out there! You killed them! You!'

'You fired the gun at the second one,' he said calmly. 'Forensics will be able to tell who did what. They'll do a simple test, and they'll know you fired the gun, too. And that's the problem with calling the police. There are two guys out there who we... I killed. One of them was shot in the back of the head. That isn't self-defence, is it?'

'We don't have a choice. Let's call them, right now.'

'But we do have a choice. We just have to be calm and think. And we have to act, right now.'

'No,' was all she could say, before she burst into tears.

Still, Seth kept his distance. 'First things first – I'd get showered if I were you.'

'What? Oh. Ugh. *Ugh.*' She could not have been more disgusted had she looked down to see huge, tangerine-jointed tarantulas darting over her pyjamas. The grey fleecy material was flecked with blood. The blood she'd smelled in the air after the Devil had his head blown off. His blood, decorating her.

She tore her clothes off as if they were alive with vermin, and got into the shower, scrubbing every inch of herself. Some of the blood must have been in her hair; it stained the flow of the shower like ichor when she dipped her head. Clotted, it fell away in flakes. Every cut and gash her feet had suffered stung, appallingly. She screamed in frustration and anger, slamming her hands off the tiling.

Seth was still there when she got out of the cubicle, drying herself with a mercifully new, kind towel. He had taken his clothes off, too, and gotten changed into trousers, a fleece and socks. She felt less deranged, but far from calm.

'Did you call the police?'

Seth sighed. Again, his face bore no expression, his eyes dull and blank. She wondered if he was in shock, some sort of trauma-induced fugue state, until he said: 'We're not calling the police, darlin'.'

'What?' she shrieked. 'You have to be joking. You just killed two people tonight. Do you understand? What are you going to do? Act the gangster? Start dealing drugs down at Brenwood Green square?'

He held up a hand and softened his tone. 'Just listen. Please. I killed two people. All anyone is going to take from the crime scene is the truth of what happened. I shot one man in the back, as he was trying to run out. I shot the first guy without any warning. You fired the gun, too. Whether you missed or not is irrelevant. You're part of it.'

'They were going to kill us!'

'Vonny, we don't know that. They might have just taken what they wanted and left us. But I couldn't chance it. I killed them in cold blood, and that's the truth. And that will mean a long time in prison.'

'You don't have a choice – call the police, for God's sake! The neighbours should have done it already!'

'That's reason number one for not calling,' he went on, ignoring what she had said. 'There is another reason.' He sighed and leaned against a radiator, drumming his fingers. 'I could make things disappear for Jake. I could pay what he owes, with a bit on top to make sure he's protected. It's dirty but it could be the difference between life and death.'

'How much of it is there?'

'I haven't weighed it, and I am a long way away from being able to put a figure on a particular weight, but... we are talking kilos of heroin. More than anyone can carry. Packed into bars. I'm not sure of the purity but it's surely worth millions. That's what they were after.' He looked like he actually wanted to laugh. 'Imagine that, hidden here? A million-to-one shot. On top of a million-to-one shot.'

Rage, pure rage coursed through her. She stabbed a finger at his face. 'And you only tell me now? What are you playing at? Are you insane?' Then a deeper horror struck her. 'You were keeping this from me. What was the plan? Sell it and get rich?'

Seth's shoulders began to quiver – anger, now. He bared his teeth; he bit back. 'I was planning on getting Jake out of his mess. Then I was going to make sure we had a nest egg to fall back on. Because let's face it – you said so yourself. The only other choice for us was to sell this place. And there was no guarantee we'd make anything on it, after my investment.'

'The land will be worth a fortune… What are you talking about?' she spoke in a whisper.

'It isn't. I don't know if you checked. I did, the past day or so. They couldn't sell this place for a year. Bad vibes from what happened to Grainger and his sons. Plus, there's a suggestion it's a flood plain. That nice mini-lake? Think about that after a storm. That's why the property barons won't touch it. And then there's planning restrictions around here – wouldn't surprise me if there's an MP lives up the road or something. That's why it can't be sold to developers for homes. We've got a pig in a poke, here, and you know it. And worse, you did everything you were told not to do, by just about anyone who ever watched a bloody property development programme. You built a dream house! You overspent. The features were spectacular enough. All you had to do was put up something basic, kit it out, slap on some magnolia, even. But no – you had to have Unicorn Towers!'

She felt oddly calm in the face of this hostility. 'This is all very interesting, Seth, and I wonder how long you've been storing it up. But we have a bigger problem to sort out, right now. The bodies. What are we going to do?'

'I'm going to handle it, is what's going to happen. You're going to stay right here.'

'I'm calling the police, is what I'm doing...' She made to go past him, but he blocked the doorway.

'You're not.'

'Seth, move out of the way. You know there's no other way to do this.'

'*I'm not going to jail*,' he said, in a glacial tone. 'And neither are you. And I'm not blowing a chance to sort out my brother, and then set us up for life. I'm not talking about a couple of grand, here. I'll be talking about a cut of very, very serious money. Neither of us would have to work again. Think about it.'

'It's insane! That's what I think about it!' She grabbed him then, digging her nails into his shoulders. 'What are you going to do with the drugs? Take them down to the bank? Ask to make a deposit? Get a reasonable rate of interest?'

'I know people,' he said. 'You talk about acting the gangster – but I know people. I have connections. They'll do the hard stuff. And they'll make a cut. As for money, moving that around is the simplest part. There are ways and means in every industry. Especially mine. All you need to do is know the right people. And I do. Big piles of cash come out clean as a whistle. I know people who've walked into some little banks here and there and deposited wads, no questions asked. You've got the money, you sometimes don't need to answer the questions.'

'This is absolute madness.'

'We're not going to jail. Bottom line. They'll throw away the key, pet. Shoot one guy, yeah, you can make an argument. Self-defence, yeah, maybe. Shoot two... I'm going away for six years, minimum. And I'll have to answer questions about having an unlicensed firearm. And whatever lie I tell, they'll see through it. The truth sounds flimsy – a decent lawyer would tear it to shreds, and a jury will applaud him for it.'

'Seth, please...'

'Decision's made,' he said. His face crumpled, and Vonny felt a surge of hope, at rapprochement. But he grit his teeth, shook his head, and said, 'I'm not going to jail. I am going to check every part of this house, then I'm going to deal with it. You lock yourself into the room and wait until I come back. I'll give you this signal.' He gave a combination of knocks on the bathroom door. 'You remember that?'

'I can't go along with this. You can't ask me to do it.' But she no longer sounded sure, even to her own ears. A doubt had taken up residence. A doubt that diverted Vonny from obeying the law towards more pragmatic matters.

'If it all blows up in our face, you're clear. I take full responsibility. I'll say you had no involvement. I did it all. They won't convict you. Please, Vonny. Think about it. I'll be back soon.'

He closed the door firmly behind him.

## 30

Bin bags. Not how he thought the night would go. Not how he thought a mild hangover after a couple of drinks with the neighbours would kick in. Seth swallowed a couple of painkillers, then wondered if he'd already done it, then forgotten. 'Guess it won't kill me,' he muttered, staring at his reflection in the patio window.

He'd checked every door, every window. The security system was buggered – that would have to wait, whether there was a cut wire, a switch pulled or a fuse box bashed somewhere, he didn't know. Surely something. The sensors that he was sure would irritate him every time a sparrow coughed or a badger farted hadn't been activated. The security cameras were dead, as was the alarm system. They must have done it – somehow – right after Seth and Vonny had gone to bed. *They were probably here for hours. Biding their time. Waiting until the right moment in the middle of the night.*

'And look where that got you.' He laughed mirthlessly. With Vonny locked away, his own comments were his only way of sustaining courage. He hurt, now, just about everywhere. Every step he took was painful, from his ankles all the way up to his shins – how did his shins get hurt? Had he been kicked? He must have been – through his torso, all the way up his arms – those grudgingly executed twenty arm curls with the dumbbells every morning hadn't really steeled him for this kind of exercise – and of course his head, which had been buffeted, slapped and punched, but somehow, somehow...

'Still beautiful.' He saw his own lips quiver as he said this; he covered his mouth, instinctively, and his eyes bulged in horror. Here was the image of a frightened child, his own image, too unbearable to look at. He drew in a long, wheezing breath, and wiped his mouth on his hand.

He stuffed the clothes they'd been wearing, including his prized slippers, into one of the bin bags, then shoved it into the backpack, along with the rest of the stuff. He winced as he fixed the straps on his shoulders, then he braved the front door.

The coast was clear. Vonny was safe.

'Decision's made, old son,' Seth muttered to himself, a voice borrowed from his father. 'Got to see it through now. No doubt, my man, no doubt.'

They had a wheelbarrow. He grabbed it from the storage cupboard set into the utility room next to the kitchen, then brought it around to the shed. One of Vonny's purchases, part of a frenzy at a garden centre sale not long after they'd won the raffle. 'I can't wait to put in bedding plants!' she'd said. 'You know how long I've wanted a garden?'

'Some fertiliser you've got, now,' Seth grunted. He turned the corner, and the shed came into view. It looked naked in the moonlight, just a sliver poking through the clouds. Then he gasped aloud.

*Where was Skull's body?*

Seth dropped the wheelbarrow handles then charged forward, yelping in panic. *No... you daft git, Seth, the body is still there of course, face down, same position.* 'No one's coming back from that, dimwit. Even if he was a zombie, he's out the game. One in the head for both of 'em.'

It was absurd, but, looking around, Seth realised the beauty of their situation, relatively speaking – he was up to no good, but he was out in the open, under a huge sky, and not overlooked, with no houses anywhere nearby. Totally secluded.

*Except for anyone they had waiting. A lookout. Did they have a lookout?*

Seth didn't think so. Surely the lookout would have gotten involved once Skull fell out of the door, missing the back of his head. Either that, or he might have run. He wouldn't have been waiting, after all that. In the dark. For Seth to walk through the woods in the middle of the night. Surely.

'Shut up,' he hissed.

He had formulated a plan but hadn't completely thought through the details. First things first: get the bodies moved.

He was loath to touch that lump of flesh that, not too much earlier, had been walking, talking, breathing, and thinking. There was a horrid sense of gravity about the body, as if it had been squashed, or dropped from a height. Like a pressed flower.

Seth winced as he grabbed Skull by the shoulders. He did not look at the ruined face – just a hint that what remained of it was completely covered in blood, a bubble of it breaking on the tip of the nose. As he shifted the body, back straining, the arms crossed over, casually, in a disturbing simulacrum of living, breathing animation. The limbs had begun to stiffen, and a terrible stench told him that the corpse had voided its bowels. He grew angry at the body as he shoved it into the barrow, legs dangling, head on one shoulder. Grimacing, Seth picked up the shredded remnant of the Skull mask, and threw it in on the dead man's lap. Then he covered the body over with bin bags, and carted his load into the woods, the path tricky. Seth was reminded of a wayward shopping trolley that wouldn't behave whichever way he pushed it. He cursed it, regularly, then grew silent as the trees closed in. Low-lying mist threaded through the boughs.

He turned on the head torch. In many ways he wished he hadn't. *If there's a lookout in here, I've practically turned on the Bat-Signal for him.*

And then what?

Seth kicked out at the leg that trailed over the wheelbarrow. 'Dickhead. Your own fault, wasn't it? You had it coming, and you got it.'

The concept rang round Seth's mind as he trundled along the path, with every single stone, pine cone and puddle an added irritant to a tricky journey.

He came to it, soon enough. The remnants of the cabin where they'd found the tarts 'n' vicars calendar, the keys, and the map; pulling it down was one of the last things the builders had done.

*Just leave it there, lads. Pile it in the middle of that clearing. I fancy a bonfire. Always wanted one.*

Vonny had complained, but he'd insisted, and for once, he'd won. *There's no danger*, he'd said. *Probably won't catch light properly. Stink the place out for days. Might blind passing microlight pilots. Serve 'em right.*

The pile of timber was a deeply forbidding shape in the darkness – intersecting beams and planks, old nails and splinters, dead wallpaper and fixtures, as high as his head. Was there a suggestion of the old tarts 'n' vicars calendar, or the girlie magazine – a pattern break in the grain of the wood in that pile? The metal and wiring had been removed; only things that could burn were left behind. It was a scowl in the gloom, an aggressive but carefully crafted pile. The workmen had piled it up so that it would burn well without getting tangled in the thicket or setting the trees alight. They'd even formed a corona for rocks as a firebreak, just in case anything went wrong. The even consistency of the pyre – a macro version of the kindling you might use at the centre of your barbecue coals – also made it easy to shift the timber out of the way.

Seth heaved out a beam or two, then leapt back in fright as something ran out. Something small, furry, and too swift to discern in the darkness.

'Four-legged bastard,' Seth cursed.

Then he giggled. He giggled a lot. He was still giggling as he heaved the body into the gap. Then he began to lift beams and planks back on top.

He had an unsettling view of the Skull mask, staring right at him through the beams.

Seth wheeled the barrow back to the shed and started the process again. He opened the door, tormenting himself with the notion of the Devil leaping out at him. But the Devil was on the floor, stone dead, toes pointing upwards like a cartoon stiff.

'Oh, this bastard's heavy,' Seth said. He grimaced at a

black trail of blood along the floorboards, but that would have to wait until he'd dealt with the main event.

Couldn't worry about forensics, now. Seth had seen all the shows. He knew that a centimetre of cruddy matter – Christ, less than that; less than you could see with the naked eye – would be enough to put him in jail. *For murder, Seth, the big one, not manslaughter, like if you'd called the cops, like Vonny said.* And there was probably acres of evidence available for microscopic scrutiny now, an invisible explosion that would show up under the gaudy UV effect of the black light; spread all over the shed, the lawn, the front of the house, inside the house, and now trailing all the way up to the pile of timber in the woods.

*Take it easy. No one knew these punks were here. Someone asks, deny everything. Worry about it all later. You've got this. Move the stuff in the next couple of days. Get Vonny away from here. Check into a hotel. After that, if need be, put the place up for sale, and fuck off out of it with the cash. Everybody's happy.*

But when he heaved the Devil-faced corpse onto the wheelbarrow, dread overrode reason. When the body tilted backwards, the head slammed against the barrow, and the yellow goat's eyes glared at him, and just like that, Seth began to cry. Huge, big, pathetic tears, dripping off his face and pattering onto the grass. He slapped himself. 'Get it together! Finish this. Finish it.'

Seth took the shotgun, and loaded two shells. He slid it into the bag, making doubly sure the safety catch was still on.

He carted the body into the woods, glancing at the low

moon in the clouds. Still a long time till dawn. He didn't dare get the flames going in the dark. For one thing it would be suspicious in itself – maybe too much so for his neighbours, who after all had had the knowledge that a murder-suicide took place, right here, before the old place burned down. So, no – he'd have to wait till daylight, come what may.

It might take until then, anyway.

Murder-suicide... that plagued him, as he wheeled the barrow along the steps, sweating freely. Which tree had Grainger's second son dangled from? Maybe his shade still swung there, a slow, creaking revolution on one of the longer, sturdier branches, eyes wide open to glare at Seth as he passed. Perhaps it would point at him, slowly, accusingly. Or the hands could creep around his throat, right now, as he had to duck his head to avoid the trailing fingers of a lower branch.

'Shup up with that shit!' He said it loud enough to startle some birds. He stopped, wiped his forehead, and took a moment. He took out a bottle of water – then paused as he unscrewed the cap. *I had a dead guy by the armpits with these hands*, he thought.

Seth tilted the bottle over his face, letting it soak him, cooling his forehead and the back of his neck, despite the cold. Then he drank the rest.

The Devil was more troublesome to load into the pyre. *Big bastard, this*, Seth thought. *Juicer, surely. A heap of trouble. But I killed him.* Acknowledging this, several paradoxical things occurred to him. A repellent burst of pride, like a kid winning a schoolyard fight; and then shame. Really, they'd beaten him up. For all Seth's bulk and his rediscovered bar-stool-swinging prowess, it had been a simple matter for the masked men. He'd barely landed a glove on either of them. Hit the floor, went down twice. In front of Vonny. He'd cheated. 'I brought a knife to fistfight,' he said, with no acknowledgement of his own joke, for once. 'Or was it a gun to a knife fight? Christ.'

No. He'd taken action. Two guys had held blades to their throats. Threatened to kill him and Vonny. But they'd failed – fatally. They underestimated him. Seth had outsmarted them. And now they were over. 'And things are going to get worse for you, too, lads.'

Once he'd piled the last of the timber over the Devil's face, he stood back, letting the torch beam play over the surfaces. There was no sign that there were bodies in there, now – but he couldn't be sure of that until daylight. *Pray to God no dogwalker comes through, no one from nearby wanders off the pathway...*

Then he heard twigs snapping regularly, somewhere up ahead. Seth's head snapped up, and his jaw clenched shut. Panic flooded him, then rage. 'Hey!' he yelled, instinctively.

There was someone moving through the trees. He could just make out progress being checked, a course being reversed, then a flight through the parallel lines.

'You fucker!' Seth bellowed, snatching up the shotgun. Then he gave chase.

# 31

Quick and spindly – a spider darting across a bookshelf. That's what Seth thought as he pursued the third man through the forest. He cradled the long barrel of the shotgun across his chest, careful that the barrel was pointing away from his face. *That'd be just perfect. Trip on a rock, pull the trigger, that's the end. They'll say it was murder-suicide. Maybe this place is cursed.*

'You – wait there!' Seth bellowed, the only words that made sense amid a spewing geyser of abuse. 'I have a gun. Don't fucking move!'

For a horrifying moment, Seth lost sight of the pinwheeling arms and legs. *He knows this place, whoever it is.* All was still and dark. As if his quarry had vanished into thin air. Then the absconder's luck ran out. Seth discerned a flicker in the branches of an oak.

In any other circumstances he'd have dismissed it as a startled bird, but something took over in him then. A rekindling of the relationship between predator and prey.

Seth wasn't particularly light on his feet, but they knew what to do. He made barely a sound as he crept up on the crackling-skinned oak with the twisted bough, beneath a tangle of roots emerging from the ground like a creature spilling its guts. The tree had been warped over time, bent almost back on itself to compete with the corona of spruce trees round about it. If you were nimble – and this fucker was nimble – you could scamper right up there and hide in the branches.

Seth got close, then said: 'Come down out of there. Right now.'

*What am I going to do? Shoot him? Shoot* another *person?* The last two had been simple matters. Them or us. Vonny's life had been in danger. He'd acted instinctively, but he'd done the right thing. They would have killed Seth and Vonny. Perhaps they'd killed Dan Grainger.

There was no sound from the tree. Seth raised the shotgun to his shoulder and braced his feet, like Clive from across the way had shown him. He aimed at the centre of a tangle of branches where it was just possible to make out the shape of a head and shoulders.

At the last moment, he dragged the barrel to the side, then fired.

The sound exploded in the night air, the barrel jerking high, the rifle flying out of his hands. Pine needles exploded in one of the trees to the right of the oak.

Aside from the creaking cry of a bird, there was no response. Then the figure in the tree dropped to the ground.

It was a kid – a gangler, wearing an anorak. He had a flask in his hands, which he dropped to the ground with a tinny rattle. The moonlight on his face was probably unnecessary. He had a pair of binoculars dangling from his neck.

'Please don't shoot,' he squeaked. 'I'm sorry about your wife. I didn't mean to frighten her.'

'What? Who the fuck are you?' Seth lowered the gun.

He hadn't reloaded; but even so, something in him relaxed. There's no chance this kid was with Skull Face and the Devil.

'I'm Crispin. Like the snack. Please don't shoot me. I'm here for Sadie. Sadie's an owl.'

'You're *birdwatching*? You're a bird*watcher*?'

'I'm a birder, definitely. Look, I'll show you. I got pictures of her. She's a barn owl.'

The boy swung round a very large, very expensive-looking long-lens camera from the back of his neck. The display came on. 'I got a great shot of her over the tops of the trees. I don't know where the nest is. She's a great hunter, the best I've seen...' As if he was a child wandering out to the teacher's desk with homework he wasn't quite sure about, he stumbled forwards, his face never leaving the camera.

'Stop where you are,' Seth said, catching his breath. He grabbed the camera and lifted it from around the boy's neck. The youngster's dark eyes flared wide; he looked on the verge of tears.

'That cost hundreds of pounds. My dad won't buy me another one! He told me!'

'How do you work this? I want to see your pictures. Calm down.'

'Just the buttons, marked left and right. Are you out hunting?'

'Yes.' Seth flicked the images back and forth. 'Don't worry, I only shoot rats. This the owl?'

'Yes – that's a great shot. I'm proud of that one.' The image Seth presented to the boy was an admittedly beautiful shot. It wasn't obvious that the bird with its wings spread wide in silhouette was an owl; the pine trees it swooped over in the night were garlanded with silver. The entire cache on the camera was shot after shot of birds. There was one image of the owl on top of the bonfire; Seth zoomed in on it.

'That one's quite blurry – it could have been better,' the boy said. The hope in his eyes as he looked up at Seth was pathetic.

'Sure. Not your best.' Seth flicked through dozens of shots, all of this bird in flight, until he reached daylight. Nothing else; just that one shot. 'Do you mind if I go back and delete that one?'

'What for?'

'Look, I'll level with you.' Seth looked one way, then another, a conspiratorial gesture from a cartoon show. 'You know this bonfire? I'm not sure it's legal. I'm going to put a light to it soon, and I don't want anyone getting too nosy about it.'

'Don't you live here? I mean, the new house – it's yours, isn't it?'

'It is, but… regulations, you know? They're a pain in the arse at the best of times. I can't be completely sure whether or not I'll get sued. Bloody councillors, mate, you know?'

The boy nodded, sagaciously. 'That's what my dad said when he was building his extension.'

'Extensions! Don't tell me about extensions.' Seth flicked the viewing screen onto the bonfire shot. He hit delete. He was given the option: Delete? Y/N? Very much Y, he thought, hitting the central button.

Seth smiled and handed back the camera. 'You not got school tomorrow? I thought you had another week of term before Christmas.'

'Yes. My dad said it was OK. Well, he would. He doesn't know I'm out. Don't tell him.' The boy snatched the camera and placed the strap around his neck. It rested awkwardly against the binoculars.

'Hey, it's a deal – you don't tell anyone about the bonfire; I won't tell your dad about sneaking out. Now, you'd best get home and get some sleep. Because you know this is my land, right?'

The boy nodded.

'That's good. So, you know you're not allowed?'

'Your wife said it was all right.'

'What did she say?'

'That it was all right to come and take photos of the birds. She said – just the other day.'

'Yeah, that sounds like her. Well, between you and me… It's not really all right to sneak over here in the middle of the night. Even if you're just being a birder. Some people might get the wrong idea.'

'I didn't see anything really,' the boy stammered.

'What do you mean, "see anything"?'

'She had on an overcoat… It was a total accident. I wasn't spying on her…'

'What?' Seth frowned. 'I think you'd better fuck off, son. And the next time you want to see some birds, you come to my front door, and you ask – politely.'

'Sure. Thank you.' Then Crispin ran – again, that weird gait, and that uncanny way of threading himself through the trees. Then he was lost to the night.

Seth sagged, breathing heavily. He had travelled beyond stress, nerves, shaking and anxiety. He wasn't exactly numb, just completely burned out, all adrenaline gone. He was empty. *Good God, I might have shot a kid for absolutely nothing. Would I have done it?*

There was no answer to that. He drank in the silence. He was tired, now. The night was still pitch-black, and icy cold. There was frost on the grass, and filigreed across the tree bark.

He would go back to the house and check Vonny. Then he'd get the petrol for the ride-along lawnmower. Then he'd get scrubbing.

Miles to go before I sleep, he thought, trudging back through the forest with the wheelbarrow.

He gave the combination knock. Vonny didn't answer.

'You asleep in there? Come on, it's me!'

Still no answer. He knocked again, tiredness and stress combining to inflame his temper. 'Open the door, for God's sake!'

There was a click, and the door slid open. Her eyes were puffy from crying. Instinctively he reached out for her, but she drew back, shaking her head.

'Our life is over,' she said. 'It's finished. Everything we planned... everything we ever dreamed... It's finished. Stained.' Her lips trembled. 'We can't ever go back.'

'We've had... an obstacle placed in our way. An obstacle we're going to remove.'

'An obstacle? You lied to me, Seth. Or you held back the truth. You sat in this house, with that secret between us. A pile of drugs, on our estate. And two men are dead because of it, Seth. What have you done with them? Have you dug a grave?'

'No… Not yet, anyway.'

'Then what are you going to do? Set them up as bloody scarecrows?'

'Actually, that's not the worst idea,' he said. He might have smiled, ordinarily, but a look from Vonny fit to ignite the very air around them stopped him. 'I've got a better idea.'

'What?' She folded her arms.

'I'm burning them this morning, at first light. Now, in fact.'

'Burning them?' Vonny began to weep again, shaking her head and turning away from him.

'It's the best way. Then I'll have the new shed replaced and burn that too. Say someone broke in and trashed it. Hire the same company. They made a good job.'

'They're not coming back, remember?'

'Another company then,' he said, tersely.

'And what about the drugs? Where have you hidden them?'

'Never mind the stuff. It'll disappear into thin banknotes in a couple of days. I'm on it. We'll walk away. No one will come near us. And we'll be rich. Do you understand? Set. For. Life.'

'Not in this house,' Vonny said.

'No. Probably not.'

'We should have phoned the police.'

'The decision's made.'

'Just like that. "The decision's made". God help you.'

'What's that supposed to mean?'

'The big I am. The gangster.'

He slapped his forehead. 'Might be a big revelation here, but they were going to kill us.'

Vonny shook her head. Now she was detached, distracted. 'I don't think so. You could have led them to the stuff and let them walk away with it. Instead, you tricked them and called their bluff. Then you got lucky.'

'Yeah, that's a good idea. Let two maniacs who'd already gotten around our security system lead us into the woods at the end of a fucking sword. Perfect. Why not go along with that? Hey, as a deposit, maybe I could have let them take you away, too, as a nice insurance policy. Just so they could make sure they got all the gear they were looking for. That was next, you know. That would have been their next trick. That'd be fun for us all. I could just act the big peacemaker instead of the big I am. "Sure, take her away. No problem, you seem like a pair of stand-up fellows! I can trust you, right?"'

'And you lied. You lied to me. You knew there were drugs. You found them and you didn't fucking tell me. What else have you lied about? What else do I not know?'

'Vonny...' He couldn't answer. He'd known, right away... the instant he knew, the second he was sure what he was dealing with, when he heaved that stone away... Treachery in his heart. Planning and plotting. Things that killed marriages. 'Please... Please understand. I had to solve a problem.'

'If those two hadn't appeared, you were going to keep it to yourself, weren't you? And what then?'

'And then nothing. I would have done it for us. Please believe me.'

The door slid shut. The lock clicked.

Seth sighed, clutching his back. More to do. But not far to travel, now.

First light wasn't till late. It was only when the sun began to appear that he realised how long he'd taken. And how close he might be coming to discovery.

At the pyre, he spread petrol over the top, and distributed chunks of barbecue firelighter they'd ported over among the stuff from the old flat. He dropped several extra-long matches into the pile, watching small, idle flames dance at various spots, before they reached the petrol on the other side of the pyre, igniting the fumes in between.

The bodies were still in there, he knew. He'd made sure of it.

The petrol ignited with a whoosh, bright white flames stretching up above the timber like an outstretched hand. Seth sat down and watched it take, the flames growing along with the sound. With the birds agitated all around him, and the sun's multiple eyes blinking awake through the branches, Seth wondered if it was going to be a beautiful day.

# 32

Susie McCracken opened the office door handle with her pinkie, somehow keeping four bags of bacon sandwiches clamped shut in the other four digits. She also kept three coffees wedged between her chin and her left hand as she opened the door with her backside.

As she entered the office, she saw that the other three were still there. Neither of them made a move to help her, though they did notice her. Or at least, Whelan noticed her, because he said, as he always did when she appeared: 'Three.'

At this, Struth and Brown also spotted her. They all broke out into applause as she deposited the drinks and the sandwiches onto a spare desk in the office, then came forward to feast.

'You're a legend,' Whelan said. Like the other two he was around twenty-four years old, with short black hair that he must have taken an absurd amount of time with each morning, slathered with wax or gel. He was the boss, Susie supposed, which is one of several reasons why she didn't raise any complaint when he peered into each greasy paper bag before choosing one for himself. Following suit on the pecking order were Struth and Brown. The latter was so much like one of Whelan's lesser siblings that Susie could not count out the possibility that he was one. Brown was the youngest of the three, having graduated the previous summer. Susie went out of the way to be nice to him, overcompensating because she had loathed him on sight. He was prematurely aged, a fifty-year-old man squeezed into the doughy, ill-defined features of a boy, and he irrationally reminded her of a loathed schoolmate.

'Aw cheers, Susie,' Brown said, tearing open the bag.

'Three's the charm,' Struth said, uncapping his coffee and taking a deep breath.

'Think you might be forgetting something, lads,' Susie said, leaning against the desk and folding her arms.

Whelan tutted. 'We were going to get you lunch.'

'I've heard that one before. I would like the money, please. Fiver each.'

'Bloody taskmaster.' Whelan nonetheless had a fiver ready, and tossed it onto the desk. The other two paid up as well. As they shuffled back to their desks, she wondered if this was how it would always be with them; always at these desks, into their middle age, the waistlines growing bigger, no wedding bands decorating their hands. Surely the marketplace would outmode them, if it hadn't already. Despite the cleaner's best efforts, their corner was always grubby; evidence of their games – this month it was 'get the scrunchie into the top bin' – were festooned all over the place. They were a throwback, a reminder of a drunken uncle at a wedding, or a rock star past his sell-by date who was tragically unaware of the fact. On good days, Susie would join in with their games. Most days, she kept out of their way.

'Oh, someone called for you,' Struth said, through a mouthful of bacon roll.

Susie waited until the silence grew unbearable. 'Who, exactly?'

'Coppers. Didn't leave a name. I'm not sure. Or maybe he did. Inspector something? Anyway, he said he was going to meet you at the front door.'

'Inspector something. Didn't you think to ask?'

'No, not really.'

'You're a journalist, aren't you?'

All three men said: 'Whooo,' and mimed holding a handbag.

'I'm a sports journalist,' Struth said, grinning.

Susie shook her head. Taking her breakfast and coffee with her – there were no guarantees in that office on a Saturday morning that it would still be there if she got back; in fact, if it was, that would be suspicious – she moved her shoulder with its security card underneath the sensor, then walked out to the front desk. Dee was on that day – perhaps the most bored person in the world, sat manning the phones for the whole of the industrial unit where the paper was based. She had probably been to her bed the night before, Susie was sure, but she was definitely on her way back out once her twelve-hour shift had finished at 6pm. Dee was pretty but could be severe-looking, with pale blue eyes that reminded Susie of a Siberian husky, captivating but hard – however, she was always warm and kind with Susie.

'All right, Dee? The three amigos tell me there was a message earlier. Don't suppose you've got a number saved on your call list?'

'Oh yeah, that was when you were out. Came through the

main switchboard. Let me check…' Dee frowned. 'Came in as a blocked number. It was Inspector Bell. Lovely accent. I think he said he was coming through to meet you.'

'Thanks. That's more than my colleagues could tell me.'

'They're not the world's brightest, Susie.'

Susie hesitated, then said: 'Does the name Three mean anything to you?'

'Three? No, not really.' Dee frowned. 'Mind you… They called me One the other day, now that you mention it.' Then she thought about it for a second. Then she blushed.

'Well, never mind,' Susie said. 'Won't waste my time talking about those clowns. And to think I felt guilty about dropping Whelan's bacon roll outside the shop.'

While they were both laughing, the buzzer sounded. Dee hit the intercom. 'Yes, Elmouth Park switchboard, how can I help you?'

'I was wondering if Susie McCracken was around?' came a mellifluous Scottish accent.

# 33

He insisted on seeing her outside, in a public square garlanded with beautiful Christmas wreaths, spoiled somewhat by haphazard fairy light placement. Although it was a dull day, bees were buzzing around the flowers, and the town's elderly population had come out. By night the memorial square could get a little lively for Susie's tastes, and the long-dried fountain at the centre was a plentiful supply of moral outrage stories whenever it was used as a bin, or a latrine.

Even from his seated position, with a broadsheet newspaper across his lap, she could tell Inspector Bell fit her template for a police officer in terms of height, he was well over six feet and skinny. He could have been about forty, with a pointy chin and long nose and grey eyes that surveyed Susie with amused detachment as she approached the wooden bench. The only incongruity was long, wavy sandy hair. Susie couldn't decide if it was a late flowering attempt to appear trendy, or just poor grooming.

He rose to greet her, folding the newspaper into the pocket of his overcoat and extending a hand. 'Susie, isn't it?' he said, in a pleasingly mellow Scottish accent.

'Hi there. You're Inspector…?'

'Bell. I'm from the Met – somewhat out of my jurisdiction.'

'A long way off your jurisdiction,' she said. 'What is that accent – Glaswegian?'

Bell's brow darkened with the speed of a thundercloud rolling over a meadow. Just as quickly, it smoothed out as he smiled. 'Ah, you're messing with me! You know I'm a highlander.'

'Big *Outlander* fan.' She smiled. 'Sorry, that sounds patronising.'

'Not at all. Take a seat, I just want to ask you a couple of questions. Nothing you've done, I should stress.'

'Um, before I do that with a strange man…?' Susie stood her ground, and raised her eyebrows.

'Oh. Oh!' He fished into his pocket. 'Almost forgot. Force of habit; I was at my desk the past couple of days. You forget how to interact with real people.'

Susie studied his warrant card, and nodded. There he was, with the long floppy blondish fringe, parted to one side. 'OK. Just making sure.'

'Not a problem. My bad, for not following protocol.'

The frozen bench bit into her as she sat down beside him, keeping a decent distance in between his buttocks and hers. She was discomfited by his relaxed pose once she did so, one hand stretching across the back of the bench, but not enough to get close to touching her shoulder. He crossed one crane's leg over the other. His suit did look expensive, though Susie's short time in journalism had been sufficient to foster a mistrust of pinstripes. 'It's regarding the job you covered the other day for your paper – last week's edition.'

'I cover lots of stories. Yesterday I was writing about a woman complaining about online music videos. I took a picture of her pointing at a computer screen. I'm sorry, you'll need to be specific.'

'The car – the Datsun. It was splashed across a couple of pages. That model's of interest to me. As are the people you spoke to.'

'How's that?'

'Well, I don't know if you know the history of Brenwood Green – forgive me, you look very young. I'd be surprised if you weren't at school when all this stuff happened, and I don't think you're local, going by the charming accent.'

Little sting at the end there, she thought. 'That's fair enough. I do think I know what you're talking about. Vonny and Seth – the couple who won the old Ryefields estate on the raffle?'

'That's the couple, yes. I've spoken to Vonny. She seems very nice?'

'I liked her. Quite warm. Genuine. Seth's a laugh. Wouldn't short-change him if I was the paperboy, though.'

'Haven't met him. He looks like Rupert the Bear in the photoshoot you did, mind you.'

'Is Rupert the Bear a wrestler?'

That delayed-drop grin again. 'Ah, you're still messing with me. I hope I never have to bust you for anything.'

'Me too.' She laughed nervously.

'No, I'm more talking about Ryefields' history as a place where bad things happened.'

'You mean Dan Grainger's death? His two sons? The murder-suicide?'

'That's the one. Horrible business, horrible.' He let the Rs roll around on his tongue. 'Whole building was razed to the ground... paddock and stables all destroyed. There's some suspicion the horses were killed as well. Seems old man Grainger went mad… But I have a doubt.'

'What about?'

'Well, those horses were very, very expensive. And there's no suggestion they were killed. Which makes me think they were stolen.'

'Interesting. That would mean it's not murder-suicide.'

'You could be right about that. You could be right.' He tapped the upper edge of the bench, close to Susie's shoulder. 'Now, the estate has been of interest to us for a while. Nothing was discovered on the site, which I find quite odd. How much do you know about Dan Grainger?'

'I don't know – everyone seems to kind of whistle and roll their eyes whenever he's mentioned, without going into details. I get the impression he was a…' she didn't want to say it '…gangster?'

Bell laughed aloud, slapping his thigh. She jumped when he did this. 'Gangster is right! Actually, he was one of the worst gangsters you ever met. Or… never met, I should say.'

'But you met him?'

'Yeah, I had a few, um, tedious dealings. You have to talk to these people, sometimes. He was a grass, of course. Police informer – they all are. They use what they know as leverage, to stay out of jail, and they do it to wipe out competitors. Becomes a bit like an old spy novel at times, never mind a gangster movie. Knowing which strings you can and can't pull. Give with this hand, smack you one with the other. But yes, you'd call him a gangster. He was that generation, you know… baby boomer, felt he had to be at the front of the class. Bit of a tart. Had to have the attention. People had to know he was a gangster, combatants and non-combatants alike. You tend to find that people like that aren't too clever. Plenty of muscle, they'll do you terrible damage. But they aren't criminal masterminds. Type of guy who enjoys being recognised at the golf club, or the spa resort, or a day out at the seaside. Enjoys the quiet at the pub when he walks in. That type of guy… won't be the winner, ultimately. Well, Christ, he wasn't. No. The winner's the guy you don't know. The guy who gets things done. The guy who doesn't feel the need to hear the music stop.'

Bell had disappeared somewhere while he said all this, staring off into the bottom of Brenwood Green main street, dominated by a convenience-store-sized supermarket and a hardware shop clinging on to life.

'You mentioned the car?' Susie asked.

'Yeah. The Datsun. You were there when they pulled it out the ground?'

'I was. Big shock. Except they didn't pull it out of the ground, exactly. I think a sub-editor put "unearthed" in my copy. That was misleading. Hate it when that happens.'

'You didn't mention where it was hidden in the story?'

Susie shook her head. 'I couldn't pinpoint the exact location. But it was hidden under canvas in this massive thicket – brambles, nettles. Had it been summertime, it might have been completely covered with vegetation. But they had co-ordinates, otherwise they'd never have looked in there. No one would have.'

'And the car was intact? In good nick?'

'Yes, I would say so. God knows how long it was out there for. Hardly any rust.'

'You saw it close up?'

She nodded.

'And was it opened?'

'Yeah, there was a set of keys to go with it... They found this map, in the old shed. Behind a dartboard.'

Bell squeezed his eyes shut. 'The dartboard. Fuck.' He chuckled. 'The number of times I looked through that place. No one thought to look behind the dartboard.'

'Is the car significant in some way?'

'Yes. There was approximately seven million pounds' worth of heroin in there. Street value could be a lot higher. More than double, to listen to some estimates. Pick a number, really. It was pharmaceutical grade. It's the stuff of legend – the Holy Grail batch. People still go on about it. A lot of junkies would have died with a smile on their face because of that. The gear was hidden in the back of an old Datsun Cherry. We knew it had come into the possession of Mr Daniel Grainger. I suspect that other people knew about it, too. That's the sort of value people will happily kill for. Bad, bad people. Not benevolent baddies, like Dan Grainger. Thinks he's a local hero. One of the Krays. No, really awful people wanted a cut of that. All your usual people with funny accents and names... No, not Scots, before you ask.'

He laughed, gruffly. 'People from all over Europe knew about it. There's a rumour about twenty people have died because of it, up and down the chain. Double-crosses, heists, ambushes. Lot of blood in the mix. The shipment was very, very valuable at all levels of the chain. I'm not sure how Grainger got it, but he did. And its last known resting place was in that Datsun. Since then...' Bell snapped his fingers. 'No sign of it. The car, as well as the drugs. Until it turned up in your paper.'

'That's a shock to me,' Susie said. 'There wasn't any sign of drugs when it was opened up.'

'You sure about that? How did Vonny and Seth react?'

'Well they were surprised about the car. They were quite keen to get it in the paper. Good selling point, for their careers. I got the impression they wanted the story to get picked up by the nationals.'

'They tell you what they're doing with the house?'

'Uh... living in it?' she said, in puzzlement.

'Not putting it up for sale and getting out? Cashing in?'

Susie shook her head. 'Not according to them. It's their dream place. Their forever house.'

'Interesting that they should take out a glorified ad in the paper, then. No offence.'

'None taken. That's what I assumed at first, too. But they were more looking to market themselves. She wants to showcase her designs. I think he's a DJ – had a number-one hit, too.'

Bell waved this comment away. 'I couldn't tell you any number-one since about 2002. I'll look him up, though... Anyway. It's an awesome house, that's for sure.'

'You've been there?'

'Oh yeah. I took a good look around. As I said, I spoke to Vonny yesterday.'

'Lovely lady.'

'That's right. So, I just want to ask – nothing was found in the car, to your knowledge?'

Susie shook her head slowly, as if trawling through files in her memory. 'No, I didn't see anything unusual.'

'Who opened up the car? Was it Seth or Vonny?'

'I can't remember.'

He frowned a little. 'You're a reporter, aren't you? I know some reporters in London. I've got a bet on with one or two – that a copper would always notice more than a hack. And I always win. But you look like you could be different. You look like you're a details person. Are you sure you can't remember?'

'It may have been Seth.'

Bell nodded. 'I get you. Sounds like I need to talk to Seth. He's a hard man to pin down.'

'I could send over some photos to you, if you like? Of the place we found the car, that type of thing?'

'Won't be necessary. I'm sure the car's clean as a whistle. I took a few boys over to check it out a few days ago. Guy who bought, this classic car dealer, was very helpful. Not a speck of drugs in there, that's for sure. The drugs will be buried somewhere, probably at the bottom of that artificial lake. Mice and badgers will have been into it. They'll have the time of their lives. Anyway – Susie, thanks for taking the time to talk to me.' They shook hands, awkwardly. 'I'll leave you a number to put in your phone, if you want to talk to me.'

She agreed to this, then that was the end of the interview.

It wasn't quite a nagging suspicion. There was no eureka moment, no time when Susie understood that something untoward had happened. Something seemed to pick at her psyche the way a cat will worry a torn patch in upholstery, until the hole is too big to ignore.

She turned towards the three men in the office. They were

surrounded by greasy wrappers, the second takeaway of the day. 'Hey, Wheels. Is it true your cousin's in the police?'

Whelan snorted. 'Yeah, sadly I can confirm. Based at Holmouth Street cop shop. An embarrassment to the family. And to the police as well, probably.'

'He on duty today?'

'How should I know?'

Susie googled 'warrant cards'. She googled 'Inspector Bell, Met Police.' She drummed her fingers. 'I think I'll go down there and see if he's on,' she said, shutting down her computer.

'You that desperate for a date?' Struth said.

'Not at all, twenty-eighty-five.'

There was silence for a second. 'Twenty-what?'

'Twenty-eighty-five. That's the number I've assigned you. Who's your number two, incidentally – that cleaner from Poland who comes in on a Tuesday? Looks like an athlete? Forgets her bra?'

She smiled at the silence as she put on her coat.


PC Whelan looked hilariously like his older cousin – as if the former had been put on a medieval rack, and had all the bad manners twisted out of him. He was very tall, with the same jet-black hair cut very short, very stiff in the shoulder, and as green as they came.

'How can I help you?' he said, guardedly, despite being behind the front desk of the police station. Susie thought of a meanie in an old cowboy movie, with his hand on his pistol under the card table.

'Just a quick question or two about a police officer I spoke to... Is your beat Brenwood Green?'

'Well, yes, that's our patch.'

'Did you speak to an Inspector Bell from the Met, in the past couple of days?'

'No... No one from the Met. Why?'

'That's weird. Can you show me your warrant card?'

'My what? Warrant card? What for?'

'I just want to know what the Real McCoy looks like.'

Glancing over his shoulder at a chorus of jackals sniggering at his back in the main office block, PC Whelan pulled out his card. 'Can I ask what this is all about?'

'I think someone might be impersonating a police officer.'

'Right.' Whelan raised his eyebrows, then began to make a note. He wrote out 'IMPERSANATING' in all caps. 'Tell me all about it, miss...?'

'McCracken. Call me Susie, please.'


Susie finished up at 7.30, exhausted. It was too close to the end of her wages, and she had a driving lesson the next morning; there would be no Saturday night, other than a catch-up on the telly and trawling social media. The three amigos had cleared up for the night, and Susie was on her own, typing up a report about the next month's council meetings. After twenty minutes looking for jobs – there weren't any – she logged off, switched off the lights, said goodbye to Brian on the front desk overnight shift, and went to catch the bus.

She was scrolling through Twitter when she saw

something about a property renovation show – *score one for the algorithm, at least it pays attention to my work* – when she had that faint alarm bell, the one that rang earlier on in the day when she'd noticed the photo on the warrant card Bell had shown her. She scrolled through her phone to Vonny Kouassi's number.

'Yes?' Vonny sounded like a startled rabbit.

'Ah, hi, it's me – Susie McCracken from the paper?'

'What is it?'

'Eh… it's a strange one. Have you had any policemen contact you in the past couple of days?'

'Yes, someone came over.'

'Tall guy? Quite gawky? Scottish accent?'

'That sounds like him. Inspector Bell?'

'This is hard to explain, but I met him today and… I don't think he's a policeman. If he shows up again, tell him you're going to call Brenwood police station, and see how he reacts.'

'That sounds weird.' Vonny sounded distracted. It was odd; as if her personality had undergone some sort of change. Or maybe she was drunk. Previously, Susie hadn't been able to get her off the phone, when she was setting up the feature about the house. She'd wondered who was interviewing whom.

'Yeah. I'm having a look into it, but just to warn you. There's something fishy going on.'

'Probably nothing,' Vonny said. 'I wouldn't bother. I'm really busy at the moment – can I call you back, maybe next week?'

'Sure.'

Vonny hung up.

Sat at the back of the bus, Susie stared at the dead screen for a second or two, hearing the distant bells chiming, a little bit louder this time. Then she opened up her Notes file, and began to write.

# 34

'Thing is, I can't sleep,' Vonny whispered.

Seth jerked awake like a sprung bear trap; his back sang, and he grunted in harmony. The room was a nest of phantoms, undulating like smoke, until he flicked on the bedside lamp. Nothing. No one there; just an after-image. 'What? Christ.' He was out of breath. He checked his phone: 2.34a.m. 'God's sake, Von. Do you have to wake me up as well?'

'I don't know how you can sleep.' She was turned on her side, facing him in bed. She might have been in a trance, her eyes wide. 'After what you did. After what we did.'

'I don't want to go over this again, Vonny. I've got a long day ahead of me. So do you. It's best to sleep. Please. Let me sleep.'

'What if the reporter is telling the truth? What if that guy wasn't a policeman? Seth, we've got to leave.'

'That's what we're going to do. I have one or two things to take care of, first. Then we're out of here.'

'What do you mean?'

'I mean, it's best we take a break. Get on a plane. Christmas in the Caribbean. Or the Maldives. Or Benidorm. Anywhere. Then… Then maybe we think about selling up.'

Her pulse quickened. She said nothing. The idea sliced into her. 'You did this,' she said. 'This house was all I wanted... This house...'

He sighed, but made no response.

A tear spilled out of the corner of Vonny's eye, but she didn't weep. It was the tears that came from not blinking for too long. Seth saw a drop hit the pale blue sheet she lay on. 'Things aren't the same. They never will be... I don't know if I can go on. Knowing this. Having seen that.'

'You need to speak to someone. You need to get this out.' Seth took her gently by the shoulder. 'But you can't talk to the police. We'll both go to jail, for a long time. Especially as we've concealed it, now.'

'You've concealed it.' She drew back from him. 'You concealed the crime.'

Seth took a breath and sat up. He was calm – almost eerily so. 'It's done, now. There's no point going over it. We could be a couple of days away from our problems being over.'

'Even if we get through it... Drugs, Seth.'

He said nothing.

'Drugs. You know what happens better than me, but I know enough. Mules... Prostitution... Corruption... Protection rackets. And the people who take the stuff. The ones at the bottom. The ones who die.'

'That's right,' Seth said, abruptly. 'All of those things. And yet, here we are, sitting in our pleasure dome. If we ever sell up, we could treble our money... quadruple it. The property market's full of crooks, Vonny, and dirty money... Where do you start? There's a reason gangsters and oligarchs invest in London.'

'We aren't talking about high rents or dodgy landlords, here – we are talking murder!'

'We didn't murder anyone. Those two would have stopped at nothing to get what they wanted. Their next move was probably to torture you, and worse, to make me talk. And if we'd given them what they wanted… If they knew that we had their gear… They'd have killed us. They would not have left us alive. And they'd have burned the place down. So that was out. I'm tired of going over this. The situation is what it is, and I'm dealing with it.'

'I have to know about the bodies.'

'Oh, for God's sake.' His head sank into his hands.

'I need to know how you did it. Did you bury them? Chop them up? I can't see it. I don't know if I can deal with the fact that I'm sleeping next to the person who did that.'

'If you must know I burned them,' he said, without raising his head. 'In the woodpile. The ruins of the old shed. I burned them, burned our clothes. Then I added the floorboards of the new garden shed, some of the panelling– then I'll have to burn down the rest of it, once I get the chance to knock it down. It took light easily. I don't have any gory details. I kept on piling wood, charcoal, shavings, fuel… Once or twice I might have seen an outline… but I don't know if it was my imagination. After it… the bodies didn't burn as well as I'd thought they would. It's hard to burn bones. So I broke up what was left. There were shards, fragments. I smashed them with the garden tools, shovels. I scattered what was left, buried it in places. There's nothing of them now. Then I did the same to the shotgun. I buried the shells in the forest.'

She was choking, her face covered. She could see him doing it. She could see the rigid, hard face, the one he'd kept hidden from her. The unsmiling one. She remembered the smell of smoke. And she choked. His hand touched her shoulder, and she flinched.

'There wasn't a trace of our clothes – not so much as a zip or an eyelet on the boots. I battered it all into ash, there was nothing traceable there. I dumped it into the stream with the wheelbarrow. I took all day to do it. Then I dug around the pit and piled in the rest of the ashes. There's not a trace of them left, nothing. I didn't chop anyone up. I didn't bury any bodies. They had to be destroyed, and I destroyed them. They'd have done the same to us, don't doubt it. They knew about our security system, and they neutralised it. That's professionals. That's serious people. They'd have killed us in a minute. When it comes to that amount of gear, people will get killed. And as for sleeping beside me... I'm sleeping beside someone who was prepared to blow a guy's head off. It was only luck... I'm not sure if it was good or bad luck... that you didn't.'

'I know!' she screamed, at the top of her lungs. She grabbed his shoulder, and he flinched, alarmed. 'You don't have to tell me!'

He waited until she let go of him and shrank back, appalled. 'This is awful, for everyone,' he said, controlling his own temper, facing her with an effort. 'Neither of us asked for this situation. We did what we thought was right, and we survived. We can do well out of it. I've got friends who are looking into things. I've got a deal set up where we can get the money nice and clean, into a bank account abroad. Just one or two details need to be sorted out, then we can move the gear.'

'You sound like a businessman,' she said, snuffling. 'Just like a real businessman.' Then she turned away from him. He stared at her back for a while, then clicked off the light.

'Try to sleep,' he said. 'If you can't do that, relax.'

'Blow it out your arse, Seth.'

He chuckled, only once.

'Where did you hide it?' she said, after a long silence.

'I won't tell you. It's safe – I'll tell you that.'

'In this house?'

'Good God, no. That'd tie us directly to it, should we get raided. No, it's safe. I can't tell you where, and I'm not giving you any hints. So don't ask.'

'I want out of here.'

'You can leave if you want. But if you do, you might get kidnapped. People might be watching out for you.'

'And what's the plan if they come back? Another shootout? Maybe we should order a tank. Will Prime do free delivery?'

'I don't think that'll be a problem just yet. We're the only people who know what happened here, the other night. It could just be two guys, and no one else. We don't know what's going on. If there's a gang of them, they'll assume we called the police. Home invasion? Machetes, samurai swords? This'll be the last place they'll want to mess with. They'll assume it's crawling with cops. And they don't know what happened to the other two.'

'This is too much of a gamble. I want out of this nightmare. I'm expecting the door to get kicked in, any minute.'

'Well, with the new locks, no one's getting in without making a lot of noise. That gives us all the opportunity we need. Once I make the swap, I propose never coming back here. We leave, and let the estate agents sort it out.'

'What are we going to do? Long term?'

'Live our lives. Take it one day at a time, until I get it sorted out. There's nothing to worry about.'

The idea would have been laughable. If it had happened to other people, in a different place.

She didn't believe him, of course, but it was still a shock to be faced with the two policemen the next morning. They arrived before breakfast time, and perversely, just when she had begun to sink into a decent sleep. The security cameras were still completely offline, but the buzzer and intercom worked well enough.

'Hi – am I speaking to Vonny Kouassi?'

'That's right. Who's this?'

'Detective Inspector Leonard and PC Whelan.' The accent was London – upbeat and bright. Vonny knew terror, then – absolute panic. She saw blue lights, handcuffs.

She turned to Seth. 'I'm not here,' he said, his volume control one or two notches above mute. 'Deny everything.'

'But you are here!'

'Say I'm out in the woods somewhere. Gone for a walk. I'm not talking to the police. Be polite, but say absolutely nothing.'

'But why? Can't you at least come out with me?'

'I've been moving old branches and logs over the top of

the fire site.' He showed her his grimy hands. 'Plus I need to make a phone call in the next ten minutes. I don't want them asking questions. Reasonable enough for me to be not indoors. Remember, nobody will suspect us of anything. We're the only people who know what happened. We can keep it that way.'

'How do I know if it's actually the police? Remember what Susie McCracken said.'

'Say you're not sure of their credentials. And don't let them in. Talk to them outside, at the gate.'

'You're joking, aren't you?'

'Absolutely not. They've no right to come into a house without a warrant – their status is the same as anyone off the street, until then.'

'I don't believe this! Why are you making me do this?'

'Because you're a better liar than me,' he replied, simply. 'If they ask you about two guys appearing at the house, break-ins in the area, anything like that – you've seen and heard nothing.'

'What if they ask to come inside?'

'Say the place is an absolute bomb site, that we're still decorating and you'd rather they didn't.'

'I can't say that!' Vonny shrieked. 'They'll pick up on it right away! If I stand there and tell a pack of lies, they'll know!'

'Don't piss about,' Seth hissed. 'The longer you leave them hanging, the more suspicious they might get. Say you'll meet them at the gate in two minutes. Hey – it could be absolutely nothing.'

'I doubt it somehow,' she snapped. Then she composed

herself, pressed the button and said: 'Sorry about that – I'm up to my eyes trying to get things finished in here. I'll come down in a minute.'

'Don't trouble yourself,' came the reply. 'We can come up to the house, if you'll buzz open the gate.'

'I'll come down to see you in a minute,' Vonny said, and broke the connection. She slapped her forehead, repeatedly. Seth put his arms around her.

'Deep breaths,' he said. 'This could be nothing. A missing cat. A paperboy fiddling his change.'

'It isn't though. This is it. This is the end.'

'Say nothing. Plead complete and utter ignorance. I'll head out the back way before you go.'

Vonny composed herself before heading down the path towards the gate at the bottom of the drive. She could still smell smoke in the air as she opened the door, and cursed this. The winter sunshine was low but bright; otherwise it was a chilly day, and the bite in the breeze gave Vonny something to focus on as she approached the two men by the gate. The PC in uniform was comically tall, with a glum expression on very young features that might have been better fitted to a comedy sketch. The man in plainclothes was wiry, with a long, pointy face and a curiously benevolent cast to his eyes. He had grey hair with a few dark strands remaining, perhaps having gone that way prematurely. He was maybe forty, surely not much more than that.

'Ms Kouassi?'

'Hiya. Vonny will do,' she said, zipping her fleece top up to her neck.

'As I said on the intercom, I'm DI Leonard. Mind if we come in?'

'Can I see some identification, please?'

'Sure.' Leonard held out his warrant card; PC Whelan did the same. It didn't look too much different to DI Bell's from a few days before. After he replaced the card inside his pocket, the detective rubbed his hands. 'Jeez, it's windy enough to blow my wig off out here. Didn't expect it to be so blowy. There's a wind chill factor, for sure.'

'It is breezy. How can I help you?'

'Thing is, I'll level with you – PC Whelan here's earning his trade, and he was supposed to sort us both out with some tea before we met up. Only gone and forgotten, hasn't he? Couldn't trouble you with a cuppa tea, could I?'

'Do policemen usually make house calls so they can get a cup of tea?' Vonny asked. She tried to sound ironic, but inside her every alarm bell was clanging. The tone, the bright delivery, and above all the coercion to let them in… This was serious, and they knew something.

'Well. We wanted to talk to you about fake policemen. Specifically this one.' Leonard held his phone at the ready. On it was a picture of the man who'd come during the week to speak to Vonny – the one she'd invited in, before the break-in. The one Susie McCracken was sure had been a fraud. A younger picture, his longish blond hair a little brighter, still ludicrously styled.

He was the one who had surely been casing the house.

Vonny made a quick decision: the simplest, easiest solution. 'He was over the other day. One of your colleagues, I think?'

'I'm afraid he isn't one of our colleagues,' Leonard said.

'Really? Who was he?'

'We'd rather speak about this indoors, if you wouldn't mind.'

'I do mind, if a bogus policeman came to my door. I mind very much.'

'Shame.' Leonard squinted into the sky. 'I hear snow's on the way later. Just in time for Christmas.'

'That man gave me the creeps,' she said. 'So I'm very nervous about inviting people in.'

Leonard and Whelan shared a look. 'Did he take any liberties with you, Ms Kouassi?' the elder man asked, gently.

'I wouldn't say liberties, exactly. Just a manner. If you don't mind, we can talk out here.'

'Understandable,' Leonard said. 'We just wondered what he'd said when he came over to you.'

Vonny paused. 'He was warning us about people who'd been in the area, looking to break in. He was warning us about making sure our security was up to scratch.'

'And is it?'

'Still a work in progress. Secure enough.'

'Looks like a Tanner system you have,' Leonard mused, nodding towards a security camera at the top of the fence. 'Do you have any footage recorded of when this man came to the door, or inside the house?'

'The system isn't online yet. We're having it done in the next few days. The guy freaked us out, a bit. You're saying... he's not in the police? Meaning he's a fraudster?'

'That's right. Anyway... you invited him in, is that right?'

'Yes. He came in for a cup of tea, in fact.' Vonny held Leonard's gaze. At no point was he challenging or forceful. The PC hadn't said a word, but it was the silence of gormlessness, she felt, not inscrutability; there was nothing intimidating about it. In contrast, Leonard had a face you wanted to trust; and that, in a policeman, was unnerving.

'Look, Ms Kouassi, I totally understand why you'd be wary about people coming into the house. I'll give you a card – we'll talk on the phone, if you prefer.'

'That would be good. The house… We're trying to get it all finished before Christmas. We've got a lot on.'

'I totally understand. We'll talk later, yeah?'

'Sure.' She took the card he proffered through the gates. This one at least looked the part, with the force livery prominent and a landline number attached. 'I'll give you a call this afternoon. I should have half an hour to spare after three.'

'No problem. Just so I can be clear – was your husband around, when this man came to visit?'

'He wasn't in.'

'Is he in now?'

'He's out doing some clearance work in the woods. He might not even have his phone on him – he forgot it the other day.'

'Ah, that's no problem. We'll catch up eventually. You get yourself inside, Ms Kouassi – you'll end up with pneumonia out here! Take it easy, talk to you later.'

# 35

Seth walked away from the house, and away from the scene of the fire. He'd done his best to clean it up, and the site was dampened down, now. He'd kept the blaze going all day. He had to do it – and not just for the obvious reason of there being two bodies to obliterate. He had to maintain a presence, to keep nosy parkers or genuine wanderers away. He especially couldn't chance that fucking kid coming back, looking for Hedwig the barn owl or whatever. He especially couldn't have anyone going for a ramble and suddenly coming across something incriminating.

Like everything else in the previous twenty-four hours, utility had taken over. He'd heard people being criticised for compartmentalising things before – being able to switch off, to get on with a job. An ex-girlfriend had once made this observation about him when he was working on the album that had made his name, a Mercury-Prize-nominated early grime album that had sold well and given him a career, if not quite enough money to put him in the superstar class. He had applied the same focus and drive to obliterate two human beings, utterly. He thought about what had happened to the bodies under that intense heat. Whether the pops and hisses had been their body fat; whether the grotesque masks had fused with their skin, along with the clothes; at what point the consistency of the bones had charred and changed, before he smashed what was left to fragments, as a mountain might become a sand dune.

There had been little left of them. He had scattered the fragments with the same grim disdain as he would have had for changing a grate, or – now the thought properly nauseated him – dealing with the remnants on a barbecue.

He knew things would get bad later; had the awareness to know he was not a tough guy, like some of the people he'd grown up with – meaning he was not a psychopath. He was a big man, and had lifted his hands once or twice. Maybe a few times. Just enough to provide a little bit of a reputation; just enough, added to his huge frame and height, to make people wary of him. In truth the idea of violence disgusted him. But he had that temper, that quickness, when things got rough. There had been an expectation of him, in certain situations. A reputation that went before him. And then Vonny had arrived; someone he'd spoken to at a launch party for the jazz album he'd produced. He'd felt like a wallflower at that event, utterly out of place – and then he'd got talking to the front cover designer. Vonny was a friend of a friend of a friend, who'd felt the same.

She'd been ethereally beautiful, so much so that she intimidated people more than he did. But he'd felt no discomfort in talking to her, at that uncomfortable event, the pools of conversation he couldn't enter, the topic that felt closed off. Talking to her had been easy. He'd felt no sense of grift or opportunism in asking for her number, and she'd been happy to meet him for a drink somewhere quieter. They were both driven in their own fields – one pathway didn't cross the other. Their professional lives ran parallel, while their personal lives intertwined. And he'd had no sense of being part of a soap opera with Vonny, none of the conflicts that had doomed earlier relationships. That was the thing about Vonny; she was the first woman not to make any sort of demands on him. He could trust her implicitly. She didn't want to provoke competition, as one or two women he'd known in the past had. He had seen a future with her. He'd even seen – and he'd only mentioned this to his mother, once – the woman who might have his children.

And now, this. How they'd come out of this anyone's guess. Seth had had work to do, and it had helped him focus. Now he had to sort out another part of the problem. And he had to do it fast.

No need for a burner phone just yet. All he was doing was calling Simon, one of the sound engineers. A guy he'd worked with, a guy he knew well, and more importantly, a guy who knew People.

'You're late, Seth,' Simon said. He sounded as if he was eating something.

'I've been busy. So talk to me.'

'You bringing it down?'

'What? All of it?'

'Maybe just a little taste, so we can see what we're getting.'

'I'd rather not. I'd rather find somewhere off-piste, if you know what I mean.'

'I'll see if I can arrange that.'

'You get any more numbers to me?'

'The numbers are the easy bit, big guy. The hard bit might be staying alive.'

Seth stared around at the trees. He could see a silvery ribbon of running water through the gaps; he wasn't far from the lake. 'What are you talking about?'

'I mean, this stuff you've got is legendary. You know about King Arthur, right? It's legendary like that. People don't believe it's real, but it is. There's a big score that went missing a while ago... Vanished off the face of the earth. Some people reckon it ended up being dumped at sea. Some people think it's still there on the bottom. Treasure of the Sierra Madre.'

'The Grail. Yeah, I heard about that.'

'It was thought to have been blagged, then it mysteriously disappeared. Lots of people think they own it. Lots of people very agitated, my friend.'

'Best you just find the one buyer and stick to it then, eh?'

'All in hand, Seth. Don't you worry. Just don't be telling anyone else about it.'

Seth ground his teeth. 'Agreed. Don't you be letting slip where it is, will you? Not sure I want too much trouble at my door.'

'Try to relax, Seth. We'll arrange somewhere to take a little taste. Find out if it's legit. Once they do, we'll get everything sorted for you.'

Seth hung up, and paced around the trees, glad of the cover. He wanted to shout, now. He clenched his fists. Then he turned abruptly, up the path towards the western side of the estate. There was a five-bar gate at the end, that let out onto a crossroads through the Fultons' fields, on the north side of the road. He reached it, tugging hard at the rusted latch and kicking away brittle nettles and other detritus that had curled around the gate. He might walk to the pub, and cool off a little. Let Vonny cool off, as well.

He had no sooner let the gate clang shut, and turned to head towards the tractor-wheel-rutted track to the main road, when a man appeared in front of him.

'The fuck?' Seth said, staggering back against the gate.

'Easy, my friend,' came the other's voice – a high, cockney accent, different to Seth's. 'Christ almighty, son, you look like you're about to pop an aneurysm. Take it easy, there.'

'Who the fuck are you?' Seth placed a hand in his jacket, and the other's eyes widened, more in mirth than alarm.

'I hope you're not packing anything in there I won't bust you for,' he said, chuckling. 'I'm DI Leonard. Was talking to your missus about ten minutes ago, back at the house. She sent me packing. So I just thought I'd take a look around. Hope you don't mind.' He held up his warrant card. Seth squinted at it, warily.

'This is private land,' Seth said. 'So yes, I do mind people wandering around.'

'In fact, there's public paths around the back, and even one or two really old ones up the middle of the estate that you can only find on old maps. Including the one that runs parallel to your wall, here.' The policeman grinned as he replaced his warrant card. 'I know. I checked.'

'What do you want?'

'Just wanted to pass on a few security tips. Seems there's been a bad lot around. Pretending to be policemen and whatnot. Coming around and asking silly questions.

Probably using the community-spirited chat to take a look at security systems and figure out ways around them. Some clever bastards, out there. It's easier than you'd realise. Conning people, I mean. All it takes is flashing a bit of a card and having more front than Southend.'

'Hope that doesn't include you,' Seth said.

'Ah, the warrant card's real enough. I will give you some security chat, though. You've got a few exits round here that could do with tightening up. That gate you've just come out of, for example.'

'Well, we're in the process of fixing the place up. It's been a big job. We've got some landscaping to do out here.'

Leonard nodded. He smiled a lot; it was difficult to see his small eyes, when he did so, and even harder to read them. 'Big job, no doubt about that. You built a few bits 'n' pieces already?'

'Just the house, really.'

'How about that shed?'

'What shed?'

'The shed. You know. You've got a shed near the house, haven't you?'

'Yeah, I'm refitting that.'

'I don't follow. I mean your new shed. Built it from scratch, didn't you? Are we talking about the same shed?'

Seth blinked. 'Yeah. Just up at the house. It still needs flooring and decorating inside.'

'That's weird – I could have sworn I saw a few pictures of the inside of your special shed. In the local paper. DJ equipment and that kind of stuff. Decks, is that what you call it? Yeah, it looked fully floored and kitted out.'

'Nah, it's not finished, pal. Believe it.'

The policeman pulled at his bottom lip. 'Unless you meant another shed?'

'Nah, there's only one shed on this property. The other one – the one that was still standing? Previous owners? That's rubble now. I got the builders to pull it down.'

'Strange one, that shed. And the Datsun, too. Hidden under some bushes, wasn't it? Tied up under tarps? Clever bugger, Dan Grainger. Wonder why he went to the trouble to hide an old banger?'

'You tell me. I sold it, incidentally.'

'Yeah, I know. Seems like it was packed with drugs.'

'Drugs?' Seth sounded appropriately incredulous; he let a good tot of his natural shocked reaction escape. 'I had a look through that car. No drugs there, pal. I can tell you that.'

'Oh no, no drugs in the car. Only we tracked it down and checked it out, and at some point, it had drugs in it, all right. A lot of drugs.'

'All I found was a bit of mould,' Seth said.

'Who knows what happened?' the policeman said. 'Maybe some squirrels ate it?'

'Lucky squirrels,' Seth said, chuckling.

'Hey, maybe one squirrel said to the other – let's go nuts!'

'Yeah. I bet they were all bright-eyed and bushy-tailed.'

The policeman howled with laughter, warming to his theme. 'They were out of their tree!'

Seth laughed. It was more a release of tension than genuine mirth. It felt treacherous, coming out of his mouth. He felt more like himself, and he shouldn't. *Guard up, old son. Tuck your chin in.* 'Well, I'll keep an eye out for any stoned squirrels. I'll see if any of them get the munchies.'

'You do that, fella. I've left my card with your other half. But I'll leave you one, too. Keep it on you. If you do hear anything, let me know right away. And do get your camera system set up, won't you? Big properties like yours, out in the sticks… Sorry, that's patronising. Somewhere rural, I should say… That can be a target, sometimes. If you've got any quad bikes, anything like that, keep 'em under lock and key. And of course, if you find anything that looks like drugs…'

'I'll let you know.'

'Good-oh. Well. I'll leave you to it. Where are you heading to, in fact?'

'There's a pub a little way up the road.' Seth dropped his voice, and leaned forward. 'I told the missus I was out working in the woods. Here's the inside story; I'm not. I'm off for a lunchtime pint and a bit of peace.'

'A man after my own heart! If I wasn't on duty, I do believe I'd join you. Now do give me a bell, Seth, if you find out anything about drugs, won't you? They say possession's nine-tenths of the law. You might have won a car, but don't be thinking there's any star prize behind Bully's Board, will you?'

The string of coincidences in his final words sent a jolt through Seth, but he only smiled. 'Mate, I wouldn't be gambling with something like that.'

'Good. If you do, you'll be in prison for a very long time, Seth.'

'Duly noted. Take care now.'

The copper moved aside to let Seth pass. Seth did not look back, but knew instinctively that he was being studied.

When he had gone half a mile down the twisty road, he called Vonny.

'I think we're being watched,' he said. 'The copper caught up with me. He was covering the way out through the five-bar gate. Maybe he knew I was around already. I might have to rethink this.'

'Rethink what?'

'Our plan.'

A note of panic crept into her voice. 'Seth, this is too big for us now.'

'I'm working on it. I'll need to think, damn it.'

'What do you mean? There's nothing to think about. You've got to get rid of the stuff, Seth. I'm scared. And where are you? I don't want to be here on my own!'

'The minute I move this stuff, I am going to get pulled. I guarantee it. Was the copper called Leonard? Cockney?'

'Yes.'

'He knows something.' He ground his teeth again. 'He fucking *knows* something.'

After hanging up, Seth trudged down an overgrown tractor track, still bearing the twin depressions of immense wheels. Dead pines were piled up here, as if a graveyard for Christmas trees. Shivering a little, Seth stepped over some sodden trunks, half fearing that the hem of his trousers would be pinched between two knuckled branches. He reached the mouth of the road.

A uniformed officer was stood in a lay-by just off the road. He had a twisted and somewhat gormless expression, his mouth cinched tight, as he crouched to inspect something at the side of the road – something Seth had not expected to see. The officer blanched when he saw Seth, and straightened up.

'Hi, sir,' he said diffidently. 'Are you the owner of the house?'

'Yeah,' Seth said. Fear made his knees weak; they might buckle at any moment like a new-born calf. He could not tear his eyes off what was parked in the lay-by.

'Just wondering, sir – do you know anything about these?'

He pointed towards the two motorbikes, parked underneath the spectral fingers of a yew tree overhanging the outer drystone wall like a drunk with no chance of reaching home.

# 36

The tall Scottish man with the blond hair was incongruous among the men in high-vis jackets and hard hats inside the portable cabin; he was taller than them by far, and his head almost touched the compact corrugated roof.

When the men inside noticed him, they put down their papers, rinsed and replaced their mugs on the draining rack by the sink, and quickly filed out.

The tall man with the longish blond hair sat down and rested his head in his hands. He was joined by the heavily built man who had been with him on the visit to the classic car dealership. He was wearing a suit that, despite being well cut against his frame, still looked too small for him going by the shoulder and neck muscles. This man sat down and waited for the Scottish man to straighten up. 'Anything, gaffer?' he asked.

The Scottish man, whose name was Cramond, shook his head. 'No one's seen or heard about them. Rob's girlfriend says everything's as he left it. She's beside herself. And Owen was apparently due to play poker tonight. Cars still parked in the drive. And here's the thing... The bikes were found. Parked up on a lay-by. Next to the new house.'

'You reckon someone's done them?'

'Hard to say. Those two bikes were stolen, so they're no problem – won't be traceable. Or shouldn't be, if they've done what they should have done.'

The big man grew very still at this last statement. 'What you saying? They've skipped out on us?'

'It's not out the question.'

The big man prodded the table hard enough to rattle the fixtures. 'I'm saying it is out of the question.'

'Use your loaf,' Cramond said, levelly. 'Count nothing out. I shouldn't have sent the brothers over to do it. Leaves doubt. And I don't like doubt.'

'They'd never have ripped us off.'

'The amount of gear we are talking about, it's worth skipping out on folk. Even family.'

'You saying you would skip out, boss? Is that what you mean?'

Cramond gave a lopsided grin. 'For the record, no, I wouldn't skip out on anyone. This is the Grail score. Only thing making me scratch my head is, why does it show up now? Place must have got torn apart. Us, then the cops. Now we find out it was on that plot of land all along. It's a bit mysterious, isn't it?'

Jay shrugged, and relaxed a little. 'I think the whole thing's mysterious, gaffer. Like we've been chasing something that doesn't exist.'

'You were there when Grainger tapped out. It's there, all right. Or it exists, anyway. Cops never seized it. We'd know about that. But we know he'd farmed it out for testing. Got very good results. Where it came from's a mystery. Someone said it was a perfect job. All the way from Afghanistan. Loaded onto a boat, all planned out, nodded through at every stage. Smooth as you like. Big money paid for people to turn a blind eye. Big money meant less of a risk, same as everywhere else. It just showed up, papers got signed, it got put on a truck. Money doesn't buy you integrity, though. A few folk found out about it. Grainger ripped it off first.'

'You're more fussed about the gear than you are about Rob and Owen,' the big man said, quietly.

'Not true. Rob and Owen and yourself... we don't have an operation without them. Just got to be open-minded. Someone might have taken them out. Grainger doesn't have close connections, but the distant ones might still be around. One or two idiots promised to kill us, but then you would, if you wanted to save face.' Cramond almost looked amused. 'Or – they might have run out on us. Those are the top answers. And the truth is, I need the Shandley brothers. And I don't do promotions at this time. But we need to have someone reliable on board, now.' Cramond's gaze lifted as the light changed, outside the cabin window.

A shadow crossed the frosted glass, and then the door opened. An older man came in, quite short, but lean. He wore a navy blue sailor's cap and a heavy coat the same colour. Neatly shorn white hair protruded beneath the cap, shaved into the faintest wisp of sideburns, thin fingers running down the ears. He had a craggy face, but not an unpleasant one, and a big smile. To put him at seventy would have been about right, but he might have been about a decade younger.

He unbuttoned the blue coat and sat down, revealing a Breton shirt. Cramond realised the older man had done this deliberately – a nautical ensemble, the type of thing a well-to-do retiree would allow his wife to buy him. And,

Cramond supposed, Lukas Vinnicombe was a well-to-do retiree.

'Nice little set-up here, Cramond,' the newcomer said, in a diluted Liverpudlian accent you might have heard on a newsreader or a front-bench politician. 'Building game, is it?'

'Got my fingers in a few pies. All business is legit, these days. This is Jay.'

'I know,' the older man said, looking right into Jay's eyes. Jay looked back, face unreadable.

'And this, Jay, is Lukas Vinnicombe. He's an old family friend, you could say. I'm bringing him on board to try and sort this out.'

'You know me. Am I supposed to know you?' Jay asked.

'No, you definitely don't know me, son,' Vinnicombe said, agreeably. Then he turned towards Cramond, his nimble fingers seeking out the salt and vinegar cellars on the table, brushing aside some of the salt crystals that seeded the tabletop. Turning the crystal containers with mesmerising speed in his fingers, the older man said: 'I take it you know this boy well?'

'He's with me,' Cramond said, shortly. 'Long term.'

Vinnicombe shrugged. 'Good enough. Now let's get to the base of the problem.' He sniffed the vinegar container, winced a little, then set both it and the salt cellar on the table. Linking his hands together, he said: 'You have good reason to suspect that the Holy Grail stash is somewhere on this couple's estate.'

'It's a strong suspicion,' Cramond said. 'Every bit of information we got at the time was that Grainger had it hidden on his property somewhere. Two different women told us that him and Grainger Jr had stashed it in an ancient Datsun Cherry. I did ask both of them, eighteen months ago. Their answers tallied up. But neither Grainger was amenable to telling me where the car was. I think we were very persuasive.'

Vinnicombe nodded. 'That's the car that turned up in the local paper. Yes?'

Cramond nodded.

'Give it up,' Vinnicombe said, sincerely.

'I'm sorry?' Cramond frowned.

'I said, give it up. This is a wild goose chase. This couple don't know where the stuff is. Even if they did... If they found the stuff in the Datsun Cherry... why in God's name would you put it in the paper? They can't be that naïve.'

'According to Vonny – that's the woman of the house – she was a bit annoyed that the car took up so much space in the paper. As if she regretted that.'

Vinnicombe raised his eyes. He looked almost interested. 'Now that's curious.'

'You follow my thinking. Now, we shook up the guy who bought the Cherry – nothing happening there. Pulled it apart – same result. But we managed to get hold of a drugs unit dog and the thing went off its head. So the stuff was in there, all right. At some point.'

'OK.' Vinnicombe began to fiddle with the salt and vinegar again, which annoyed Cramond. 'You may have a case.'

'Gut instinct tells me that the man of the house may know exactly where the stuff is. Seth Miller. Record producer. No real rep to speak of on the street. Might have bust a couple of heads, and you'd think he was Al Capone from the records he makes. Bloody racket. Well known among the young yins – I've got nieces who know who he is. He had hit records maybe eight, nine years ago. Nominated for prizes. One got to number one. Works behind the scenes. He's got the connections, though. Worked with one or two villains.'

'Doesn't prove anything,' Vinnicombe said. 'But I'll go with it. Let's say they've got the gear. And you send the two brothers over, to shake them up a bit?'

'Exactly right. Not so long ago.'

'And they've vanished?'

'Only sign of them was their bikes. They left them parked in a lay-by. Cops picked them up.'

'Now that's very interesting.' Vinnicombe sat back a little. 'Going back to this couple… the big guy, mainly… he going to be a problem?'

Cramond shook his head. 'No. He's got associates, but he's no hard case. Local boy made good, you could say. I wouldn't have guessed there was anything untoward, to speak to the lassie… So, far, so middle class. Except I was sure the woman was lying. Uneasy. One or two little spots and tells.'

'Maybe she was nervous?'

'Maybe she was. Taken in tandem with two of my top boys going missing, it's strange.'

'They might have topped them,' Vinnicombe said. 'The pair in the house. It's possible. Maybe unlikely. But it could have happened. Even if you get the drop on someone, you don't know what's in their house. So the guy pulls out a kitchen knife from his bedside table, and the game's over. Maybe the lass can swing a baseball bat.'

'Possible, but unlikely. She looks like she could be on the front cover of a lifestyle magazine. Polite as they come. Something about her shrieks "history graduate". Bakes quite a lot, maybe. Doubt she would swat a fly.'

'The other possibility is that the Shandley brothers found the stuff, it was a straightforward transaction, and they did a runner with it.'

'What about the two bikes?'

'Smokescreen. Creates a bit of doubt. It's done its job on you, if so. The thing about the Shandley brothers – and I had heard of them – is that they're a bit too clever to be someone's number two and three. The younger one, Robbie... He should have gone into politics, that one. Or the law. But in our game, he's one of the worst of the lot. I knew his father. Nasty piece of work. You knew to keep him off the tools. Not the sort of guy you want as site foreman. Clever. Too clever by half. You should have split them up. Sent one of them with this lad, here. The less clever one – not Robbie.' He indicated Jay.

Jay bristled. 'What you mean by that, old fella?'

Vinnicombe ignored him. 'They won't sell each other out, that's the thing. So if they've made it look as if they're dead, and left the bikes... That's exactly what someone who ran with the gear would make it look like. 'Cos make no mistake, if that gear is worth half as much as they say, it's still worth skipping out on someone.'

Cramond drummed his fingers. 'It was worth the risk. I had to find out what they knew, if they knew anything. I had to know if they'd found the gear in the car.'

'It's an interesting predicament. Maybe you should have gone yourself?'

Before Cramond could answer, Jay pointed at Vinnicombe. 'You've had your say. And I don't like what you've said.'

'All right. Duly noted. You got any other ideas or suggestions about what happened?'

'I don't know what happened,' Jay said. 'All I've been hearing since I sat down here is theories about what might have happened. I'm more interested in what we're going to do, old son.'

'Go on then,' Vinnicombe said. 'Fill us in. What's your plan?'

'We go back, and this time we go mob-handed. If there's any nasty surprises, there's enough of us to pull together and deal with them. We get the truth out of them – and we wait till their stories match up. Then at least we know what we're dealing with. And if they've got the gear on site, then we make sure we don't leave without it.' Then he glowered at Vinnicombe. 'And I'll tell you – I've run with the Shandleys since we were at school. There's no way they'd have skipped out with the stuff.' He turned to Cramond, a little discomfited by the older man's steady gaze in response. 'What did they have to get out of it? We were all quids in, however it gets split. They might have made a good chunk more on their own, but what's the cost? They're dead men if we spot them again.'

'Or maybe you two are the dead men?' Vinnicombe smiled.

'Is this guy coming on board with us?' Jay said. 'Can we sack him, gaffer? I don't like his attitude.'

'What you like and don't like is up to you. What you get with me is planning. And to be fair, I reckon that our big friend here is right, Cramond.' Vinnicombe cleared his throat. 'No faulting his reasoning.'

'That's it? We go back to the house?' Cramond snorted. 'No. We've already tried that. What is it they say about the definition of madness? Doing the same thing, and expecting a different result?'

'Except, we won't be doing exactly the same thing. We adjust what we do, to a better plan. No disrespect, but it wasn't great. If we get the stuff, fantastic. If we don't, we at least know who we're looking for. My money's on the latter.'

'Let's get ourselves together and move in on them, then.'

Vinnicombe nodded. 'I accept. If you're offering.'

Cramond nodded. 'We'll need your expertise.'

'Then you can have it. For twenty per cent.'

'We'll do the horse trading later,' Cramond said, laughing. 'But you know you're not getting twenty per cent.'

'Lot of football to be played, as they say. I may have one or two ideas up my sleeve before we do the old commando raid, though.'

'Be glad to hear them,' Cramond said. The two shook hands.

'I'm not happy about this,' Jay said. 'I've no idea who this guy is.'

'Ask around, son,' Vinnicombe said.

'I will. And I'll tell you, I don't care who you know, or what you did, during the fucking war, or whenever. Keep your mouth shut about the Shandley brothers. I don't know how, but someone's put them out of commission. And I'll find out who.'

'Brave of you,' Vinnicombe said, dripping sarcasm. He applauded, touching only his fingertips together. 'Commendable loyalty. Commendable.'

Jay exploded, without warning. He got up, scattering the chair, and laid a hand on Vinnicombe's arm. 'That's it.'

Before he could pull the older man out of his seat, Vinnicombe grabbed the vinegar cellar. The top – which he had unscrewed, without anyone noticing – spun like a top on the table. Cramond could taste the tang on his tongue as the vinegar splashed across Jay's face. Jay staggered back, rubbing the back of one hand against his face, and swiping wildly with the other.

Amused, Vinnicombe stayed out of his way, buttoning up his coat.

'That wasn't clever,' Cramond said.

'Have a word with him, will you, Cramond? When he's calmed down, that is.'

'I'll kill him! Stop him!' Jay had blundered over to the sink, and was pouring water into his hands, then throwing it into his eyes.

'I'm in charge,' Cramond told Vinnicombe. 'Get that right, from the start. I don't want any of this shit on the job. You step out of line, and I'll make sure it's your last job. Tell anyone about what we're doing, and the same applies.'

'I'll be in touch,' Vinnicombe said, turning towards the door. 'Think it over. Give me an offer.'

'And one last thing – you're taking your life in your hands, you behave like this.'

'No, I'm not,' Vinnicombe said, just before the door swung shut behind him.

# 37

Vonny's heart had taken on absurd beats and unusual rhythms. It was out of time again, as Seth laid out, with a terrible clarity and calm, what could and could not be done, stood in the kitchen doorway of the cold, alien house.

'There is absolutely no way I can move the stuff. That's a definite.' Seth stood at the head of the kitchen, hands by his sides, his expression blank. He had become an automaton in a matter of days – it could even be measured by hours – and Vonny feared what might happen if she had to break that uncanny composure.

'Then destroy it,' Vonny said. 'That's the only way out of this.'

'I can't. I've already told people that I have it. Serious people. We might bring them down on our heads, as well as whoever the other mob are. We have to follow it through. I'm just not sure how.'

'You're not thinking straight. We've already gotten ourselves into a nightmare, an absolute disaster... Say it's been stolen. Say anything. Put a light to the whole thing. Scatter it into the pond. Anything but this. I've already spoken to a solicitor. We can get this place put up for sale soon. Break-even money is fine – so long as we get out of this place and never, ever have to think about it again.'

'You're forgetting about my brother,' Seth said. 'He's looking at being murdered even if he manages to pay off his debts.'

'Then take out a credit card. Get him to take out a loan. Go to a loan shark, if he has to.' Her voice grew loud, and brittle. 'This was never your problem.'

'It's my brother, Vonny. I can take care of it. I can sort out the problem.'

'Fuck your brother!' she shrieked.

That almost did it. 'Don't ever say that about him. Ever. If he's in trouble, I sort it out. That's the way it goes. That's how family works. Surely I don't have to actually explain that?'

Vonny tried to master her words, although she couldn't quite do the same with her voice. 'Seth, we are talking about murder, drugs… This could put us away for a long time. On top of that, we are now messing with people who will kill us. I'm going to say it one more time, then I'm going to have to take action.'

'What do you mean?'

'I mean, destroy the stuff, or turn it into the police.'

'And then what – hope they don't find what's left of the two people I burned?'

'I think you mean the two people *we* burned Seth. I'd be going to prison, too, whether you lit the match or I did.'

The statement seemed to reverberate around the surfaces of the room, the shiny marble effect of the tabletop.

'Destroy it, Seth. You know this is the only possible way out.'

'No. The way out is to go on with what we said. The way out is to get rid of the gear, take the cash, leave this place, put it up for sale, and forget it ever happened.'

Vonny slid off the chair and walked towards him. 'You're dreaming, Seth. I don't know what this is... You want to be a hard case, or something? You want to dabble in that world? You produce records, Seth. That's as far as it goes. This is absolutely insane. I am sorry your brother is in trouble, but we can't make this mess any worse than it is. For pity's sake, destroy the stuff – or I will.'

'I can't. It's too late. The only problem is getting it off this property. For the time being, anyway.' The blank expression had come back; his downcast eyes, the burgeoning laugh lines in his face smoothed out. 'I'm sorry, Vonny. It's the only way. We were landed with this, remember. It's an accident. A problem we're taking care of in a way that doesn't put us in jail. As for the two guys...' He shivered, in spite of himself. She saw tears forming in his eyes. Before she could reach out to him, he turned away. He closed the front door quietly.

Heading to the windows looking towards the front of the house and the woods beyond, she saw him moving down the garden path, the clang of the gate swaddled in the double glazing. She saw him shimmer and dissolve into the woods through her tears.

Then the intercom sounded, an inch or two away from Vonny's ear. She flinched; hesitated, and then left it. It buzzed again, and she said, timidly: 'Yeah?'

'What do you mean, yeah?' a familiar voice said. 'Get the door open, lass, and show me this bloody castle of yours!'

\*

Chloe Bayley had barely changed her look since university days, and Vonny, who usually felt like an overstuffed sausage no matter what she wore, usually envied this. Her ensemble was generally a short dress with some boots underneath. She was short but she had amazing legs – seemingly chunky from a distance, until you saw the muscle move. Seth once mentioned that he could see her yanking heifers out of a shed somewhere green and remote with those thighs – and the boots usually accentuated them. This time, as she tottered up Vonny's driveway with a bottle of wine in each hand, she was sporting wellies rather than boots, with a short but very furry coat seemingly pilfered from the set of a cavemen versus dinosaurs movie on top.

'You look great,' Vonny said. 'Especially in wellies. That is so annoying.'

'C'mon then, it's icy up here, you silly mare,' Chloe said. 'Let's get these opened. Jesus Christ, is that a house, or the mother ship? I knew your gaff was big, but holy Jesus...'

'What are you doing here?' Vonny spluttered. 'I didn't even tell you when the move-in date was!'

'Saw it online. The report. Great car! I thought I'd come along and help you get settled... By that I mean, I thought I'd come along and have a really good nosy and poke around in your cupboards.' Then she noticed. 'Hey... What's going on? Are you all right?'

The bottles of wine were deposited on the driveway. Then she stole forward and wrapped her arms around Vonny. Vonny let her head sink onto the faux-fur coat, and took a breath of the same perfume Chloe had worn since the day they'd first met as freshers. 'I'm fine,' she said, after allowing a sob to escape. 'The stress of getting the house ready... It's amazing, but it's been hard.'

'Sure? No problems with Seth?' Chloe drew back and locked eyes with Vonny.

'No. Not really. Hard to say.'

'C'mon. Into your fortress of penitence, or whatever the hell you call it. That – that is your dream house?' She chuckled. 'It looks like it's begging for someone to throw stones at it.'

Vonny felt marooned in the centre of her kitchen while Chloe padded around the gleaming tiles in her bare feet. 'You remember that time we were temping and we both got a gig in this old manor house? And we played desk polo with office chairs on castors?'

'I know what you're thinking,' Vonny said, sipping her wine. 'Don't think that. The floor's brand new. And the castors squeak.'

'Aw come on. You must have a couple of office chairs up here, Mrs Stationery Fetish. Let's roll up some old bills and get a game going.'

'Not today,' Vonny said, sighing.

'Surely you've got some croquet mallets, at least?' Chloe pirouetted – she could be disarmingly nimble when the occasion called for it. 'Perhaps you have one in the study? Or in the annexe? Just above the dinette?'

'I've missed your absolute mockery,' Vonny said, sincerely.

'I'm not joking, though. Look at this place! You've built

a moon base in the middle of the forest. And you say this is your ideal home?'

'Pretty much just how I imagined it. I built it in my head, years ago. I think I saw something on a property show on the telly. Tall windows, trees outside. It blew my mind.'

'It's gonna go for a fortune.'

'We're not selling.'

'Guess you basically won the lottery. Building it must have cost you, though?'

'We got the land for nothing, the plot... But the building took all our savings. Everything we had. But if we play our cards right, and we both land new projects, things can work out nicely.'

'Personally, I'd have put up a little brick house a kid would design. You know, tile roof, chimney, four windows and a door. A little bubble cat in the garden with a flick of a tail. Then skedaddle with the cash.'

'They say that's what you should do. Don't put in anything fancy. Keep it simple. I got carried away, I admit it. But it does look good.'

'And a pool!' Chloe banged both hands against the tall windows, and pressed her forehead against the glass, like a child awaiting the postman on her birthday. 'Let's get naked and jump in!'

'In December? Please, love.'

'You did it Windermere. That time with the cold shock, I think it was...'

Vonny shuddered, then smiled. 'If you do, you'll only find leaves and maybe a dead badger. We're not putting the water in just yet.'

Chloe came back to the table and hopped onto the seat.

'Not sure I like these chairs, all the same. It's OK for you, you're above five feet one. And in my case, the "one" is an addition. Like when guys say they are five feet ten on their dating profile. I think I'll bring mountaineering equipment next time, never mind wellies.' She sank her round little face onto the palms of her hands. 'All right, enough chat. Talk. What's going on with himself?'

'Nothing,' Vonny said. 'Nothing with him, exactly.'

'What, then? Exactly?'

Vonny sipped at her wine. 'It's kind of complicated.'

'If it's not to do with him, then it's to do with something else. And as you're obviously not working... Then it's to do with this house. How much are you in for, really? You in debt?'

'It isn't that, either.' Vonny wanted to spill it. If she had a best friend any more – the concept had become laughable after she'd turned thirty, before it became perverse – then she supposed it was Chloe. 'It's difficult to explain.'

'Whereabouts is he, anyway?'

'Out in the grounds.'

'Mighty regal! Surveying the scene? Hunting with dogs?'

'Not quite. He's just checking out fallen trees. Water drainage. Something. I left all that to him.'

'If you're not wanting to talk... mind if I ask you something?'

'Sure?'

Chloe grinned. 'Can I have a little look at your woods?'


Vonny had downed half a glass of Chablis in double-quick time, and its warmth had spread its treacherous fingers through her belly. She was somewhat annoyed to leave the glasses behind – and she noticed Chloe hadn't drank any of hers, yet. But she indulged her visitor, and donned heavy boots while the other put her wellies back on.

'Bought these buggers at the farm shop up the road,' Chloe said. 'Expensive, too. Might as well get the use out of them.'

'Are you driving?' Vonny asked, as her friend stamped her feet down into the green rubber.

'Don't worry. I'm only having half a glass when I get back. It's still allowed. I think.'

Vonny placed a hand on her arm. 'C'mon. You're joking. Surely.'

'Wish I was.' Chloe patted her tummy. 'Not showing yet. I kind of want it to, though. I want people to open doors for me and offer seats. Then I'll say, "I'm not up the pole, I'm just fat."'

'My God! Congratulations!' She hugged Chloe close, burying the little face in her Gore-Tex.

'Easy! I'm a respectable woman!' Chloe giggled.

'That's awesome! Scott chuffed?'

'Over the moon. Always wanted kids.' Here Chloe grew serious, and teared up. 'He was up-front. Never hesitated to talk about it. No matter how many times I laughed in his face. And I guess… I felt the same way. That's the truth. Now! That's the news out of the way. Let's have a walk around the moat and flirt with your guards.'

The inspector had been right – snow had arrived, though only enough to dust the pathway and lawn. The trees looked the part, for a change – the pines and spruces in their absolute element, she supposed, the perfect weather, the perfect time.

As they crunched down the path, Chloe pointed towards the shed – which Seth had ripped apart, even having dragged the wooden panelling inside away. 'What's going on with that?'

'Still a bit to go on that one,' Vonny said. 'We're having it finished off soon.'

'Funny – it looks like someone's broken in,' Chloe said, peering at the dark, open doorway. 'As if it was finished already, and it got trashed.'

'Nah, 'fraid not. Another project to tick off. Feels like it's never-ending.'

'I'm not sure I'd like sleeping there, with the door open like that. I'd imagine all sorts hiding in there.'

'It'll be finished soon.' Vonny guided her friend towards the woods. 'It's a fair old walk, this, I have to warn you.'

'Just a little peek at the trees would be good. I can't believe you own your own woods! And in the snow and frost, as well... Isn't it scary?'

'I wouldn't say so. You get used to it.'

'I've seen too many scary films. I'd imagine all kinds of people hiding out here.' Chloe shivered and drew the collar of her heavy coat tighter. 'Or things.'

'Too cold for stalkers, I think,' Vonny said – although she kept a close eye out, all right. The snow on the branches gave the forest path a picture-perfect look, as did the red berries on the holly bushes. But every branch seemed to quiver with tension, wherever Vonny looked. She had to stop herself, suddenly sure that every naked tree bough hid an assailant. It was like swimming over deep water at night. The minute you started imagining something stalking you from below, it was a big step towards losing your mind.

'Still, bet you'll be glad to sell up. Anyone ever kill themselves here?'

'Why in Christ's name would you say that?' Vonny said, alarmed. 'That's a terrible thing to say.'

'Ease up, Vonny.' Chloe laid a warm little hand on her arm. 'I was just being Mrs Flippant. That's my role in life. I didn't mean to freak you out...' Then she grinned. 'So someone did kill themselves, here?'

'Apparently. I'm not sure where, exactly. They wouldn't tell me. Just as well.'

'Look at that thicket, over there... I've never seen nettles that high and that thick. Even this time of year. Are they still alive? They're like a giant eyebrow creeping after you. Whereabouts was it you found the car?'

'Just beyond that treeline... It was hidden under a tarp.' Vonny frowned. 'How did you know about that?'

'Oh, I cyber-stalked your ass,' Chloe said, offhandedly. 'Every single frame of it on online maps. Every scrap of detail on property websites. Had you been sunbathing I'd have zoomed in close enough to count the fleas in your armpits, sweetie. The classic car was quite high on the search list. Beefy-looking number. A Datsun, was it?'

'That's got a lot to do with...' Vonny lowered her voice, and checked around for Seth. Worried about Seth, now. Her life partner. She was anxious about bumping into her husband in the woods. 'It's got a lot to do with my problems just now.'

Chloe shook her head, perplexed. 'I don't follow. That

rusty old bucket caused you a problem – how? Let me guess, Seth wanted to keep it and fix it up. I didn't think he was a boy racer, but you never can tell – until you catch him watching *Top Gear* on a laptop at two in the morning.'

'No, it's more to do with things that came with the property.'

'What?' Chloe whispered, theatrically. 'Dodgy things? Creepy things? Sexy things? Is this a dogging hotspot? Wouldn't surprise me, love. The things that go on in places like this at night... Public parks, you name it...'

'It's complicated.' Vonny sighed. She so badly wanted to share it; to share something. This afternoon, Chloe had gone from being a deadly interruption to salvation. It was a slice of normality; and Vonny hadn't had that for a while.

'Did you find something? A body, or something like that?'

Vonny's mouth twitched, alarmingly. 'No, nothing like that.'

'Was it drugs? Because if it was drugs, you know, I could help you with that.'

Vonny stopped. 'What do you mean?'

'Just making conversation,' Chloe said, brightly. 'I can help you if you found something like that. Like drugs.'

'I didn't find anything like that. I think we should forget it.'

'Like if you found drugs in the car. The old car. I could help you with those.'

Vonny's voice creaked as she spoke – the creak of an ancient door swinging open, the creak of an old lady trying to speak from her deathbed. 'Chloe... Have you spoken to someone? About this house? And the land?'

'Not really. Just offering my services. If you had to get rid of something quickly. Like right now.'

'Chloe... I need you to leave. Right now.'

Then, something happened to Chloe's composure. A ripple seemed to cross her features, and her focus hardened into fury for a second. 'Vonny, they spoke to me two nights ago. Tracked me down through social media. They came to my house, they... Vonny, for God's sake, you've got to give them what they want! They're going to come back here and they're going to hurt me, hurt the baby. I told them about the baby, and they said they would... I had to come. And if you don't do what they say, they're going to kill you.'

'I don't know what you're talking about.' Vonny struggled to breathe. She wanted to run; simply take off into the woods, let the branches whip her if they must. 'Chloe, you've got to go home.'

'Call me. Please, Vonny. They came into my flat. They waited till Scott had gone to work... The things they threatened me with. You can't imagine. They can get in any time they like, anywhere... You're dead if you don't give it to them, Vonny, you're dead! They're coming, and when they do, you have to give them what they want. Have it ready. That's what they said. Be ready!'

'Get out! Get out of here!' Vonny shrieked. Then, like a child, she covered her eyes. When she opened them, Chloe had just about disappeared on the path leading to the security gate and the driveway.

# 38

*Two roads in or out. Can't use those. How am I going to move it?*

'You think laterally, my man,' Seth told himself, as he approached the stream. He had two holdalls, heavy and full, with the straps looped around either shoulder. 'That's what you do. Think outside the box.'

It had grown cold and dark quickly. Seth had seen lights on in the upper levels of the house; he was sure he saw Vonny pass, several times. The homely glow comforted him. Once, he was sure he heard voices somewhere in the woods, heading back towards the house, but these had quickly faded. His imagination, surely.

*They come for me, they won't be chatting when they do it*, Seth reasoned. *Whoever they might be.*

Another phone call to his connection down at the studio had turned distinctly frosty. Simon had a note of panic in his voice when Seth broke the bad news – and Simon was a man who never panicked. 'You've got to come up trumps, here, Seth. You can't keep these boys waiting on hold, you know? You have to give me something to work with.'

'I'll level with you, Simon – I am a little bit worried that this thing's attracting attention.'

'What do you mean, attention – fuzzy attention?'

'Not exactly. It's hard to explain.' The strain between them seemed to crackle in the very air. Seth felt and heard Simon's vocal tremor harmonise with his own voice. *I'd have asked for one more take on the vocals*, he thought, ruefully.

'Look, man, whatever issue you have here, you've got to sort it out by Thursday, all right? You're spooking the horses.'

'Thursday. I can do Thursday. No problems here.'

'Glad to hear it.' Simon did not sound glad. 'Don't miss it, Seth. This isn't amateur hour. You've got to do what you say. If you don't, you'll embarrass me in front of my friends. You'll get a time and a place. And you have to be there. Stay tuned.' He hung up.

Surely he couldn't do Thursday, though. The minute he drove out of the estate, he'd either be stopped or followed.

'What a mess,' Seth said, into the lengthening shadows, casting the bare branches as claws. 'God, what a mess.'

Huddling into his coat, and wondering if it might snow again, Seth went through his options. He couldn't drag Vonny into it. Whatever part she'd played in the other night, she wanted nothing to do with the gear, and he owed her that, at least.

Get Fulton, the farmer, involved? He had some involvement, having provided the gun, but... the drugs were too big. Involve him in it, it made it more likely that he'd call the police, or something. Or rather his meddlesome wife would, no question.

Sneak out over the farmers' fields? People walked through them all the time. At worst, he might get a bite in the bum off a springer spaniel, but he'd live. Play dumb with the other farmer, in the other direction. He snorted at the idea. Ludicrous. Might as well tunnel underneath... There had to be a way to sneak it out, though. Wasn't there a road cutting through the farmland opposite? It was always worth a look... Seth flipped open his phone, fingers quivering. A snowflake landed on the flat surface of the phone screen, a perfect crystallisation, and promptly died. He looked up to see more and more flakes falling – one tickling the edge of his nose. The ground at his feet was bone dry. 'And there we have it. The icing on the cake. Snow in time for Christmas.' He laughed, bitterly.

Yes, in fact, there was a route through – he could walk over the field, drag the suitcases, fob off any awkward questions, maybe have a taxi or even Vonny's car parked, waiting for him at the far end... Get it all the way to London, make the drop... It could be done...

But until then, Seth was left with ancient holdalls with millions of pounds' worth of heroin. There was no question of burying it; all he had to do was find a place to stash it. Somewhere obscure, but not somewhere he'd be likely to forget about. *Imagine losing enough gear to get you killed in your own forest... in fact, no, Seth, don't imagine that at all.*

Were they watching him now, in fact? It wasn't a nice thing to consider. Maybe there was a drone, tracing his every move from above. Could they do that? If so, then at least they couldn't follow him from above into the trees.

Seth laughed, with no mirth in it. It was ludicrous, but the fact remained... His every paranoia might be vindicated. He hoisted the bags onto his shoulders. It was a perversion of the feeling Seth got on the rare occasions he had the chance to hold a baby – the feeling of dread that something so fragile and delicate had been entrusted into his hands. Now, he felt like he was handling a bomb; a dead weight sagged against him, its mass collapsing in on itself, twin black holes.

Silly, he thought. Surveillance. Spies. Next it would be a frogman in the pond. A strangely stiff-necked woodpigeon that never flew anywhere but craned its neck to follow him. They couldn't do it on his property, could they? There had to be some legal problem with that.

Then a white face appeared in front of him, with deep black eyes. There was a suggestion of mellow *tapetum lucidum*, then a flurried bating of white wings, like a set of long johns untwirling on a washing line.

As the barn owl swooped over the trees, a thunderbolt lit up the scene.

Stressed, stupefied, static, Seth could only blink for a moment or two.

'That could be it. That could be it,' he muttered to himself, once he realised what he had seen. An idea didn't so much percolate as boil over. He dropped the bags and ran, stumbling over the hard-packed frozen path, already mottled with fresh snow.

'Hey,' he called out – whispering at first, then realising how ridiculous this was. He raised the volume but modulated the tone. 'Hey, Crispin, was it? You there, mate?'

*Of course, it might not be Crispin. It might be a police photographer, with a—*

The lanky shadow dropped down from a tree. He waved at Seth, uncertainly.

'Sorry, Seth,' he said, 'just getting a few shots while I can at night, before the snow comes in. Did you see it?' The boy was nervous as ever, but his eyes shone. 'That was the perfect take-off, an absolute cracker. She is absolutely huge! I think she got something, too.'

'I need to talk to you about something,' Seth said. 'Well, it's more of a business proposition.'

The boy looked up, biting his lip. He had been scanning the photos he'd taken on the DSLR camera, but he lowered it, and frowned slightly. 'What do you mean?'

'Well, you know how you know this woodland really well?'

'Yeah?'

'Well, how would you like to own your own path through these woods, all in your own name? I'd have the rights drawn up for you tomorrow if you like.'

'Why would you do that?'

'I'd need you to do me a really, really big favour. But first, I want to pick your brains about something.'


Seth was close to jogging as he headed back to the house, with the snow coming down thick, landing on his jacket in pillowy clods. There was a route, now; there was a road map.

His phone buzzed when he approached the gate leading to the front lawn and the path towards the high glass house. Every light seemed to burn inside.

'What's up?' he asked, tensely.

'Get inside – now!' It was Vonny, and her voice was on the edge of panic.

Seth felt a terrible sinking sensation in his guts. 'What's wrong?'

'You have to get inside! We need to lock the doors! They're coming for us!'

# 39

Seth hadn't taken his jacket off yet, and the shoulders were still pattered with fresh snow. He held his hands out, trying to placate Vonny, but his own fear was obvious in the tone of his voice. All it did was make her feel worse.

'Slow down,' he said. 'Chloe? You mean that lass who goes everywhere with her Doc Martens – that one? Punched someone at your mate Eddie's wedding?'

Vonny could only point to the two wine glasses, one of which – on her side of the table – was still mostly full. 'She showed up, out of the blue. I had no idea why – I didn't think I'd even given her our new address. She plonked down a couple of bottles of wine, asked to be shown around. She asks to be taken on a walk round the forest. Before we'd gotten to the bottom of the gate, she starts asking about the car. Claimed she saw it online, then stalked us, then decided to show up.'

'What? Doesn't she live in Hastings, somewhere like that? She can't just "pop round"?'

'I know!' There was a hysterical tone to Vonny's response, a high note that cracked near the top. 'I told you it was weird! I didn't think there was anything wrong at first. Or if I did, I didn't really pay any attention to it. I thought she was on the level.'

The horror grew in Seth's face. 'Please tell me you didn't tell her anything.'

'I didn't have to! She fucking knew!'

'How?'

'They must have tracked her down... Whoever's after the stuff. Searched her out online, social media... Christ, everyone's traceable these days! They got to her. She didn't say what they'd threatened her with, but out of the blue, she starts jabbering about drugs, then she lost her head and said we had to hand the stuff over.'

'When? Did they give a time frame? Twenty-four hours? What?'

'I don't know! She freaked out and ran.'

Seth paced the floor, head in his hands, bare feet furrowing the carpeted area as if they were tracks in the snow. 'Dear God. How did she know? Did you tell her anything? Anything at all?

'No!'

'Did you admit anything? Did you even agree with her?'

'I said, no! She freaked out and took off. Dear God, they could have killed her. She could be wrapped in a carpet in a ditch by now!'

'Forget about her – we've got our own stuff to worry about now. I'm sorry – but forget about her. It's her problem now.'

'How can I forget about her!' Vonny sank to the floor, her hands creeping towards her own throat. 'Who's next? Your mum and dad? Mine? Jesus Christ, I can't have that! Whatever they want, give it to them!'

'I can't.' Seth's jaw muscles bunched, and relaxed. 'If I don't deliver, my brother gets killed… then we get killed. The deals I'm making… These people aren't very understanding if you pull the plug at the last minute.'

'Then we're dead!' Vonny sobbed, still on her knees. 'We're dead! I can't believe this happened to us! Why did this have to happen to us?'

He got down beside her; he tried to pull her towards him in an embrace, but she resisted. 'Listen – we didn't ask for any of this to happen.'

She shook her head. 'You found the drugs. Without telling me. You saw them. You made a decision. You tried to play it cute. You tried to be the smart-arse. Mr fucking big. Listen to you! "The deals I'm making". This is not a game! Two people are dead already, on top of the people who died here before we came along! This place is cursed. *Cursed*. We can't live here now.'

Seth ignored all this. 'Did Chloe give a phone number, or say anything about a contact, something like that?'

'No… she just said they're on their way. No details. Oh God, they're probably here already.'

'Right.' Seth swallowed, and got to his feet. 'First of all, we get everything locked down – then we get you safe. I'll lead them off into the forest. In the meantime, you get the word out that we've got intruders.'

'Why not just call the police now?' Tears were rolling off her face. Her expression was ghastly, borrowed from an artwork. 'End it – call the police right now.'

'Because we killed two people the other night, that's why! It's got to be a last resort. There's a way out of this. Trust me. Now – I locked the front door. I'm presuming the back door's locked down tight… So now, we'll sort out the balcony.'

'Seth, please – just give up,' Vonny got to her feet. 'Forget about the drugs. Forget about the two guys from the other night. Just give ourselves up. You know it's the right thing to do. Give up, or I'll do it for you.'

Seth took a deep breath. 'I'm sorry. Too much is at stake. And we've come this far. We have to see this through. My plan is, as I said, to get you safe.'

She ran at him, but didn't have the rage in her to strike him. She bunched her fists; they quivered in front of his face, two knotted dumplings. This might have been comic, but for the deadly seriousness, and her earth-tremor rage. 'Get me safe? You don't control anything, here! It's down to you that we're in this mess – your fault!'

Seth turned away from her. His voice was absurdly upbeat, as if he was reading out a surprisingly pleasant weather forecast. 'First, we check these patio doors are locked…' He tugged at one. Then he frowned, gazing out onto the balcony. Snow dotted the frame in lazy clumps; the furniture outside was already dusted with a good half an inch or so. Beyond the chair and table right in front of him, it was difficult to make out any other details. This was partly due to the slow-falling grey curtain, and partly due to the glare of the lights, shining on the window and showing only reflections.

Seth tried the door, then cupped his hands around his eyes, placing them against the glass, shutting out the light.

There was a face directly in front of him. It wasn't a reflection.

'What the fuck?' He staggered back.

And then the lights went out.

# 40

The chair outside on the balcony was iron, an indulgence, expensive. It and its identical twin had been christened the iron thrones, even as they were ported upstairs by the delivery men. Seth had barked his shin against it when he first moved it onto the balcony. 'Wouldn't like to get that over my head,' he had hissed through his teeth, as he rubbed his leg where it hurt.

Now, he staggered back as one of the iron thrones disintegrated the tall window. A cascade of glass, shards, hexagons, diamonds. Vonny felt the sparkling shower sting her scalp as she backed off, screaming.

A man kicked out two or three longer shards of glass with a ruthless, terrible efficiency. Vonny saw the soles of thick boots; he wore no comedy mask, but his face was contorted in quivering rage, above a pair of bunched shoulders like too much mortar slabbed on top of a brick wall. The big man moved in with a deceptively sinuous grace. He had a curved blade that Vonny recognised as a Gurkha kukri, with that weird angle to it that suggested lopped-off limbs and heads rather than scars and lacerations. 'Nobody move!' he screamed. The tip of the blade pointed towards Vonny. 'You – up on your feet and get in the corner, by the wall!'

Numbly, she obeyed. Seth moved to close the gap between the intruder and Vonny. The man defiling her home was shorter than Seth but more powerfully built, with the muscle and the ball face of someone who took steroids. Corded sinew on his neck looked fit to explode from his flesh like a sci-fi creature; his pale blue eyes were glistening with an intransigent rage. He was quite the ugliest man Vonny had ever seen.

'No,' she screamed, raising her hand, disliking the angle Seth was travelling at, but far too late.

The intruder swiped at Seth, teeth compressed into an ugly crescent. It was close; the blow wasn't meant to hit him, but it was near enough. Seth would have felt it on the tip of his nose. He checked his run, stopped and raised his hands. He stood between Vonny and the newcomer. 'Take it easy,' he said. 'You don't need that.'

'I'll give the fucking orders. Let's get downstairs, into the kitchen. Now.'

Numbly, they obeyed. At knifepoint they were guided downstairs, where they wanted to cover their eyes from the brutal overhead lights. Then they were both stood at the far wall. The kitchen table and chairs were in the middle; the intruder backed away to the side, moving towards the door. 'Simple question for you two: where's the stuff?'

'What stuff?' Seth said.

'Enough of this,' Vonny blurted out. 'Enough!'

'Shut up,' Seth growled, anger spilling over.

'We've had enough! Just leave us alone!'

'I said, shut up!' Seth darted forward and grabbed her by the shoulder.

'Looks like the lady wants to say something,' the

newcomer said. His bottom lip trembled; his frame shook with adrenaline. 'I think we should let her say what she wants, no? So get your hands off her, big man.'

Seth let her go; pain throbbed through her shoulders. That would leave a bruise, she realised. Other pain came to her; a set of prickles tingled across her scalp. She wondered if she was bleeding; she put a hand to her hair, but there was only a spot or two of red there.

'The stuff is gone,' Seth said. 'You mean the stuff under the car? It's gone.'

'Where?' the man with the blade said.

Seth swallowed. 'Two guys came over. A few nights ago. They did the same shit you did. I took them to the stuff. They've gone with it.'

'That a fact? What did they look like?'

'I don't know. They were clever enough to wear masks.'

'And you were clever enough to stay in this house after it, big mouth. I don't believe you. I think you know what happened to them. And you've still got the gear, here. Know how I know?'

Seth shrugged.

'Don't say anything stupid!' Vonny hissed. 'For God's sake!'

'I know,' the intruder continued, 'because their bikes were found round the back of your house. No one's seen anything of them. Their phones are dead. No contact, nothing. No signs they were going to do a runner. One of them had a kid. I knew them like my own brothers. You think they're going to dump us for some gear? When they were going to get paid anyway? It doesn't make sense. Plus, word reaches my ears that someone's looking to make a deal. Sounds very like the gear that belongs to us. So why don't you tell us where it is? And while you're at it, tell us what happened to the two guys who came here a few nights ago?'

'I've no idea. It happened like I said,' Seth said. 'I don't have anything else to tell you. They came here, they put blades to our necks, I took them to the gear. I'm not going to take a chance with my wife being here, and I'm not going to do it now. They've got it. There was piles of it. I wasn't even sure what it was.'

The man with the blade laughed out loud. The sound made Vonny flinch. Something in it told her that the awful ending they'd been spared a few nights ago had only been stayed. *He doesn't just want the drugs. He wants revenge. He knows. Or he suspects.* 'You knew exactly what it was, twerp! Why didn't you just give it to the cops? Or ask someone, maybe? I think it's because you were trying to cut a deal. And it's going to cost you.'

Seth licked his lips. There was a tone of panic in his voice. 'Look, we can sort this out. I kept some of it back. I just need to...'

He moved faster than she'd have thought possible. He leapt for the bottle Chloe had left on the kitchen table. A rill of wine spewed out as he spun the bottle round, leaving a slick trail on the white tiles below. It splattered the newcomer as well, as the bottle rebounded off his face. The bottle did not break, at least until it hit the tiling.

The brawny man with the kukri sank to one knee, a cut oozing beneath one eye, the other gazing into space, wavering like a pale blue gas flame.

With scarcely believable strength, Seth heaved the table,

too, then thrashed out with the chair. 'Run!' he screamed. 'Out the front door, now!'

Vonny did it; she was crying, or shouting, or sobbing, an incoherent garble as her own feet threatened to hurl her onto her face, the flooring rumbling beneath her like the percussion blasts at horse racing, Seth behind her, yelling: 'Run, run, for God's sake, run!'

Then the front door wide open, and a scrunched-up older man standing there, picture-perfect in the porch light, with a pair of pristine false teeth reflecting the light back onto them. He had a shotgun in his hand. 'Where you two going, now?' he asked, affably. 'Carol singing?'

Vonny turned tail, rebounding off Seth as he charged out at her back. She caught a glimpse of the man with the kukri, teeth bared, a scene from a nightmare, blood trailing down one side of his face like a bad fringe. Seth ran for the basement door, fishing the keys from his pocket. 'Only chance,' he wheezed, 'get in, go on... stay in...'

Disaster; the keys slithered from his fingers and tumbled across the carpeting that led to the staircase. Seth and Vonny both groped for them; collided, and fell.

Just in time to see the basement staircase door open.

The slim, fair-haired man strolled up the short flight of stairs. He wore the same dark coat he'd worn when he posed as a policeman.

'You know,' he said, 'your basement studio is bigger and tidier than some flats I've lived in. Cosier, too.' He grinned, as the two other men appeared at their backs. 'Did I crack that joke already? Well, never mind. Don't be lying around there all day, you two. We've got business to attend to.'

# 41

PC Whelan was in his running gear, tying his shoelaces, crouched on one knee in the police station car park. Susie McCracken thought of a pylon bending down suddenly on the horizon. When she clocked the policeman's face, she decided he looked more like a boy who had forgotten his kit, and had to make do from the spares box in the PE teacher's cupboard. Protruding from a pair of petrol blue shorts, he had the skinniest thighs she'd ever seen on anyone, male or female, and she wondered as she approached him if he was still taller than her from that position.

He started when she approached and straightened up. He was sweating, clearly at the end of his exercise. 'Oh. It's you.'

'I called at the front desk – they said you were on a run.'

Whelan might have been blushing, rather than tired out; he palmed sweat off his brow. 'What can I do for you?'

'Just had a brainwave about Brenwood Green.'

'Oh yeah?'

'Yeah. I'm wondering if there's maybe something on the property that might be of interest to our mystery impersonator.'

'Oh, him... Scottish guy with the blond hair? Yeah, the DI I work with, he's on the case.'

'Who's the DI?'

'Leonard. A real DI, before you ask.'

'Any leads?'

'Curious one, in fact.' Whelan sniffed, and looked around casually before answering. 'No sign of the guy on any database. Came up completely blank. So Leonard said, anyway.'

'He based in your office?'

Whelan shook his head. 'Nah, London. Maybe we should head somewhere else for this?'

'For what?' McCracken smiled.

'For an off-the-record briefing.'

Showered, he had changed back into a white shirt, open at the collar, which gave him the look of a slightly harried-looking waiter. His cheeks were still flushed pink as he ordered a mineral water at the café, which he didn't drink – he only revolved the bottle in his hands, which irritated Susie, although she didn't say so.

She had her lined notebook out in front of her, the pages pressed flat. 'So you were actually over there at the house?'

'Yeah. Saw Seth Miller. He was trying to sneak out a side gate – that's what it looked like, anyway. He'd already spoken to the gaffer. Looked nervous when he saw me.'

'Learn anything from him?'

'Not in what he said. Gaffer thinks he's lying. This is the bit I shouldn't tell you...'

Controlling a mounting sense of excitement, Susie kept

her voice and expression neutral. 'It's OK – you don't have to tell me anything you don't want to.'

To her horror, he nodded in acquiescence, then let his head fall.

'But if you did,' she continued quickly, 'I think you could help that couple.'

'What makes you say that?'

'Last time I spoke to her, she was scared. She could have just had an argument with her husband, and I called at a bad time. But I think something's happened there. Added to a fake copper coming over to our office and asking all kinds of questions, then I think we might have to go over and see if they're all right.'

'OK.' Whelan took a deep breath. 'There's something else. Two motorbikes were found at the property. I found them, actually. They'd been driven along a path into the new estate, then hidden at the side of a drystone wall, in a lay-by. Near the side gate I was talking about. When we ran a trace, it turned out they'd been stolen. My gaffer was suspicious but wouldn't tell me why. He reckoned that someone might have been on the property and maybe set up shop there, or...'

Susie blinked. 'Or what?'

'Or they were taken out of play.'

'What? Murdered?'

He nodded. 'He reckons it's serious. Made all kinds of phone calls after we went to the house. But you know what really got me?' Whelan leaned forward. 'When Seth Miller saw me, in uniform, he just kind of turned tail and went back into the house.'

'Something's dodgy. No doubt about it.'

Whelan frowned. 'What do you know? Spill it.'

'I don't know. I only suspect, but... Well, for my money, there was something ropey about that car. Why would you go to that effort to hide an old Datsun? It's not that valuable. A Lamborghini or a Ferrari or something, sure. But not that type of car. So there had to be something strange about it.'

'I don't get it – if there was something dodgy, then why did they agree to have the pictures run in the paper?'

'It was only later that I thought there was something weird about it. I was helping them out, or so I thought. It was a great story for a local paper. It got picked up nationally, too – was on the *Daily Mail* website the other day. We got a few bob out of it. Doesn't always happen when a national picks up your story.'

Whelan's expression completely changed – a little mirth around the eyes, which reminded her of his lunk-headed cousin in her office. 'So I guess all of this is your fault?'

'You what? No, of course not. I just took a few pictures for the paper. Christ, I didn't know anything. I'm only speculating... Look, maybe we'd better find out a thing or two before we go off on weird tangents.'

'What have you got in mind?'

'What I'm proposing is we head over there and speak to them. Talk over our fears, tell them what we know.'

'Absolutely not. My gaffer says we're not supposed to approach them. He says he has a watching brief, for now. He reckons the house is probably being watched by other people as well as the cops.'

'How about if I took you over there privately? You're off duty, aren't you?'

'Well, yeah...'

'And Vonny and Seth haven't committed any crimes, have they? That we know of?'

'I guess not.'

'All right then – we can go over personally. I'll say I was in the area... in fact, I can say I want to get pictures of the house in the snow.'

'Seems a bit thin, to me. But sure, I can do that. I don't think there's a law against me going there, privately.'

'They don't need to know you're in the police. They might not recognise you out of uniform. Hey, this could be your big break. And – if they don't buy our excuse, they might fall for an inducement.' Susie tapped her bag, where the gold foil wrapper of a bottle of prosecco protruded.

'Sure. Now, what if they tell us to bugger off?'

Susie shrugged. 'Then I guess you've still got half a bottle of prosecco.'

# 42

Vonny wasn't tied to the kitchen chair, but she might as well have been. She gripped the bottom of the wooden seat as tightly as she might have clung to the edge of a sinkhole.

'Hey,' Jay said, stabbing a finger at her – she'd heard them address each other, on the other side of the door. 'Keep your hands where we can see them.'

She did as she was told, but her hands shook, an appalling tremor she wouldn't have believed had she seen it on a TV drama. She clasped them tight, to keep them from quivering out of control. She couldn't quite do the same for her jaws, and her teeth chattered.

*They're going to kill us. We're going to die.*

Vonny and Seth were sat at either side of their huge to-die-for kitchen table – remarkably unscathed after its earlier gymnastics. Vonny wondered how perverse things could get; how they might both meet their ends, sat here, their foreheads pressed against solid oak, eyes forever staring. Death might come through the back of the head, over in a single sharp pang, an exclamation mark of shock, then nothing. It might slip between her ribs, with drawn-out moments of fear and agony as she drained away. It could be heralded by a sharp slap across her neck.

She didn't remember them beating Seth, but his nose bled, anyway. He sniffed it back, tilting his head like you would have been told to at school. The short, wiry older man with the close-cropped white hair and the lined, pugnacious face that made him look curiously continental had found a packet of cloths in the cupboard without asking, and had offered one to Seth, who had pressed it to his nose without a word of gratitude, or defiance, or anything.

Then – and this had particularly chilled Vonny – the little man had used another of the cloths to quite fastidiously wipe away a few spots of blood on the table, before rinsing the cloth thoroughly at the sink.

'Fancy taps, these,' Vinnicombe said, as he dabbed up the spare drops that silvered the chrome worktop. 'You mind if I steal them?'

Jay glowered at Vonny, ignoring Seth. 'You know why we're here,' he said. 'You know what we want. Talk as if your lives depend on it. Because they do. We want the gear that was stashed in the car. Then we want you to tell us exactly what happened to the two boys who were here the other night.'

'We don't know,' Seth said. 'There's no point repeating myself. I gave them all the stuff, and they left.'

Cramond, who had stood with his back to the worktop at the far corner of the kitchen, his back to the cabinets with his arms folded, had said nothing for the past while. He only watched, with a faintly amused air. Finally, he

said: 'That's your story, mate. Fine. All good. Now you.' He
nodded at Vonny.

'I don't know,' she said. 'Seth took the two men outside.
He said he gave them the stuff. That was all.'

'Both stories match,' Cramond mused, with a kind of
oily, sixth-form irony. 'But I don't think that's the case.
Here's the part you might not have known: the two boys
who appeared at this house were meant to find out what
happened to the drugs that were in the old Datsun. Once
they got the answers they were looking for, the plan was
to kill you both, and put your bodies into the pond. Water,
you see. Wipes away a lot of traces. So, if they split with the
gear – and I admit this is a possibility – then why did they
leave you alive?'

'You'll have to ask them that,' Seth said, laying down the
cloth. 'They're long gone.'

'I wasn't asking you.' Cramond unfolded his arms and
stood up straight, then turned to Vonny. 'I was asking *you*,
darling. Does it seem likely they'd have broken in here,
taken your security system offline... And I have to say, they
made a superb job of that... Escaped with the gear... and
then *not* killed you, as per their own plan?'

'They gave us their word,' Vonny said, the words
tumbling out, in a higher and higher tone of voice. It might
keep rising through the octaves until it disappeared with a
tiny squeak. 'They told us they wouldn't hurt us if we told
them where the stuff was, and they kept their word. They
just left.'

'They didn't take your phones, either,' said Vinnicombe. 'I
mean, think about it – you break into someone's house, roust
them out of bed in the middle of the night, then you *don't*

take their phones? Just leave them behind, like? Schoolboy error, that one. Even if they were being nice. They'd have turned your phones into confetti. SIMs, the lot.'

'So, we're not buying it,' Jay said. The muscles around his frog-like jaw appeared to have a life of their own, quivering and roiling back and forth. Perhaps he was chewing a rock. 'So, let's have another go. The truth, now.'

'That's it,' Seth said. 'That's all to tell. There's nothing else.'

Jay came forward. Vonny shrank back, raising her arms to ward him off; Seth got to his feet, but Vinnicombe darted forward with his sawn-off shotgun.

Jay grabbed her by the hair and yanked her out of her seat. Even allowing for the fact she offered no resistance, it was preposterously easy to do, as if he had pulled a doll off a shelf. She was on her feet in an instant, and pain seared across her scalp as some of her hair detached.

Seth started forward, but Vinnicombe jabbed him in the chest with the shotgun, and he sat down. A gleam of ugly, sadistic amusement illuminated Vinnicombe's tiny rodent's eyes; Seth's own eyes glistened, molten black.

'Don't hurt her. Please,' Seth said.

Cramond tutted – at Jay, not at Seth. 'No, that's not it,' he said.

'Wrong option,' Vinnicombe said. Never taking his eyes off Seth, he explained, in a stage whisper: 'Bit of a rookie, our lad, here.'

'Shut your mouth,' Jay snarled to Vinnicombe. He shook Vonny by the hair, as if in retaliation over the other man's comment.

She screamed; by instinct she grabbed him by the

shoulder. He shoved her, and she rebounded off the seat and crashed to the floor, the side of her face glancing off the table leg. Sobbing, she curled into a ball.

Vonny was helped to her feet by Cramond, who said gently: 'I am so very sorry about that. The big guy's just a bit nervous. There's quite a lot at stake. I'm sure you get that?' Cramond stooped to pick up the chair, and guided Vonny into it.

Seth, who still had the shotgun pointed at his chest, said to her: 'Take it easy, pet. It'll be all right.'

'It won't,' Cramond said. He walked towards the cutlery drawer, and opened it with his back to them. They heard the silvery chime and rustle of the knives and forks.

Vonny imagined the biggest butcher knife she had; one from a previous house, too big for the fancy knife block her father had bought them as a moving-in present.

But when Cramond turned around, he had a rolling pin in his hand. He grinned. 'You know, I never actually used one of these to make food? Never baked, never made a pie, anything... I mean, I love to make something fancy, but pastry's just like too much hard work.'

He tossed the pin in the air, twice, catching it expertly as he strode across the kitchen floor. Upon catching it the second time, he took a firm grip, then swung it hard at Seth's face.

Seth managed to block it with his upper arm, twisting his features away. The second blow took him across the shoulder blades, and he cried out; the next blow fell mostly on the backs of his hands as he covered his face.

'Nah, this is how you do it,' Cramond said, teeth bared.

'Tell us where the stuff is! No more fucking around! Where is it?'

He raised the rolling pin again.

'We've got it! It's all right!' Vonny cried out desperately. 'Don't do anything. Just promise to let us go. We've got it. We've got the stuff.'

'Where?' Cramond roared. Jay and Vinnicombe peered at her, both completely still, as a tiger behind glass at the zoo might assess a child.

'I don't know,' Vonny gasped. 'But it's here. We can take you to it.'

Seth's teeth were bared. Blood made a sharp contrast with the enamel of his teeth. 'She's lying,' he hissed.

'Shut up! It's over! It's done!' Vonny said. 'Seth knows where the stuff is. He can take you to it. You get it, you let us go.'

'See?' Cramond said, hurling the rolling pin into the sink. 'That's all it took. You don't hurt her – you hurt *him*, and let her do the talking. Leave the weak point to spill the secret. The hard nut wants a beating, so give him one. It all works out. Appliance of science.' He winked at Vinnicombe, who nodded. 'And now for the second part of the burning question – and please don't waste our time by telling any lies. What happened to our two mates?'

# 43

'That part was true,' Seth said. He was still obviously shocked by Vonny's outburst. 'They did get some of the stuff, and then they left.'

Cramond sighed. 'More details, big guy. Don't hold back. Quick recap: the stuff is still here, but the two men who came to house before... Left with some of it? A wee taster session? You're not making sense.'

'It makes perfect sense.' Seth licked his lips. 'I split the deal into two separate parts. Seemed safer, if it was found, or someone came looking for it. Then I'd only lose one half. The other half would be plenty. I gave them one, and let them think that was the full amount. They didn't ask any questions. It was a lot, but obviously not as much as they were expecting. They seemed as if they came to a decision. Then they left. I don't know anything about bikes, where they went, what they had planned, anything like that, and they didn't say. That's all I know.'

'So they just left the bikes lying here? Just like that?'

'I don't know why they did what they did,' Seth said, angrily. 'I didn't know there were any bikes left behind. If I did, I'd have called the cops, or gotten rid of them.

I wouldn't have just left them lying for anyone to find, would I?'

A silence followed this, and Vonny allowed it to continue. She could almost divine the three men's thought processes from the glances they shared. It had the ring of truth, particularly the part about the bikes.

*The last thing they will suspect is that we killed them.*

Then Vonny thought about what they had mentioned about the two men who came to the house that night – the casual bombshell that the two men had indeed intended to kill them both. And what that meant about tonight – particularly as the three intruders were unmasked. *They will never leave us alive to identify them. They know there's no security system any more. This is just a transaction, now. A chore to be gotten out of the way.*

'OK,' Cramond said at last, turning to Seth. 'Here's what's going to happen now. I'm going to stay here with the lady of the house. You and my two associates here are going out to find the stuff. Where did you say you'd hidden it?'

'I didn't.'

Jay lunged, stopping with his nose a couple of millimetres from Seth's. 'Don't get smart,' the heavy-set man snapped.

To be fair to Seth, he didn't move, though his Adam's apple bobbed once or twice. 'It's out in the woods,' he said. 'Hidden out among the trees.'

'You got a map?' Cramond asked.

'No. But it's well stashed. You'll need a guide.'

'Good job you're here,' Vinnicombe said brightly. He stepped in front of Cramond, somewhat peremptorily. 'Now, let's head off. My big friend here's going to be standing very close to you, and I think it's fair to say he is a very stressed, high-tension individual. So, nice and calm, nice and organised. All right?' He nodded to Jay. 'You two in front. As we walk, Seth, you'll talk us through it. I'll be listening and watching very carefully.'

Jay produced the kukri again, and Vonny gasped as he pressed it into Seth's side. Seth winced, though not from the proximity of the blade – more to do with an injury he'd suffered earlier. He tried to ignore this. 'Don't hurt her,' Seth said, gazing levelly at Cramond.

The three intruders laughed at him, heartily and openly. Vonny shrank from the sound, hearing in its callous mirth a herald of their doom. Still laughing, Cramond said: 'Just take us to the stuff. Don't try anything comical… And that's all I can say, really. It's not even an offer, or a promise, or anything. Just do it and come back here and then we'll have a conversation.' He showed his big teeth in a gruesome smile. 'Off you go, then.'

The two men led Seth outside. Vonny shared a moment's eye contact with him, but there was no communication, no shared moment, no tenderness. Vonny stared down at the table after the door closed behind them, wondering if that was the last she'd seen of her husband.

She heard Cramond's boots squeak across the floor as he walked slowly to the other end of the table, where Seth had been sat. Cramond sat down, his hands flat on the table, staring at her. Vonny threw her shoulders back and met his gaze.

He smiled. 'Well, this is nice. What shall we chat about?'

Vonny said nothing.

'Ah, don't be so shy,' Cramond said. 'Why don't you make yourself at home?'

She cleared her throat. 'Listen... I know that you're probably here to kill us.'

Cramond exhaled, slowly, the mocking expression smoothing out on his face.

'So, I'm going to beg you for our lives.' Vonny's voice cracked. She gripped the table till the muscles on her forearms ached. 'Please, don't kill us. We aren't bad people. Seth made a mistake, that's all. I told him he should have told the police first thing, or dumped the stuff in the lake...'

Cramond snorted at that. 'That'd have been a fine way to finish it! Dump it in the lake! There'd have been some mellowed-out old fishies in there, that's for sure. Any angler catches something for his tea in there, he's in for a shock!'

Vonny seized on his levity. 'Just as well he didn't listen!'

Cramond sighed. 'All we want is the stuff. Turn it over to us; there's nothing to worry about.'

'Just don't kill us, please. We wouldn't call the police... We'd be crazy to, wouldn't we?'

'Yes, you would,' Cramond said, sincerely. 'That's the truth.'

'Take anything you want from the house. Anything.'

'At this point I have to remind you – it's not up to you to hand control of anything to us. You don't have control. We could burn the place down. We could strip it down to the bare wiring. Anything.'

Vonny's voice had been stolen; her throat was parched. There was nothing more to say.

Cramond decided to break the silence. 'You say you're

innocent, and you don't know anything. But your boyfriend isn't totally innocent. Is he?'

'He's not involved in your world. I know that for a fact.'

'Yeah, he's not involved, but he's not totally separated from it, either. A wee birdie told me something a few days ago – that he's trying to get rid of a big shipment that somehow fell off the back of a lorry. It's one we've been looking for ever since Dan Grainger ripped me off, after we did all the hard work by working it past Border Force. Those guys can be really hard to bribe, but we did manage to get a couple who were sympathetic. So you can guess, we're really keen to get our hands back on it. And yes, it is an amount worth killing for. Care to have a stab at guessing how much it's worth? Have a go.'

'I wouldn't know where to start. I wouldn't even know a ballpark figure.'

'You could buy this house… the woods… the place where Dan had his paddock… the pond… the stream… all of it, about eleven times over. And still have change. That's how much we're talking about. Retirement money, you might call it. Fuck You Very Much money.'

'Then have it. Have all of it.'

'Oh, I will, that's not in doubt.' Cramond leaned forward in his seat. 'What I want you to understand is that your man out there wanted all of it, too. I get that. You could say I'm a businessman. That's the nature of it. Go from a penthouse down to the gutter, we're all the same. But he had enough connections to try and make things happen. He took a chance. I get that.'

'It's for his brother,' Vonny said. 'His brother owes

money. He's already been slashed for it... It's to help pay people off.'

Cramond laughed. 'What did the brother do, bring down a bank? How much does he need, exactly? "For his brother". Makes no material difference to me. That's the nature of greed. I get it. But what I don't get is the missing link.'

'I don't follow you.'

'The missing link between my two missing men and this house. Because I've got a funny feeling that the two boys I sent over here came to some harm. Clever boys, I'll give you that. If anyone could come up with a plan to rip me off and fake their own disappearances, it's them. But I've got a massive doubt. And if my doubt is on the right lines, then that leaves one last possibility.'

Vonny made no sign of acknowledgement.

'The possibility that you somehow killed them,' Cramond continued. 'Far-fetched, but it's not impossible, if you know the terrain. Get the drop on them somehow. It happens. Maybe you even pulled the trigger. Not the first time I'd have heard about a woman going haywire to protect her man. I've seen some stuff, let me tell you. Massive, big beefy blokes on the ground, having their eyes scratched out. You've got to watch out for anyone. You never can tell. I wouldn't have expected you to do that... And neither would those two boys. Maybe that's the answer.'

His expression had gone smooth, like a store mannequin's. All he did was look closely, right into her eyes. Vonny looked away. 'I don't know what you're talking about,' she said. 'They took the stuff, and they left. We don't know anything else.'

'That's good,' Cramond said gently. 'Because if there's ever any sign that you harmed my two boys, you're going to die in agony. Every personal hell you can imagine, that's what you'll experience before you die. Then I'll feed you to some pigs. And I'll watch it.'

The intercom buzzed, startling them both.

# 44

Cramond recovered his composure fastest. 'Expecting someone?'

Vonny shook her head. The house itself seemed on edge, waiting for the buzzer to sound again. When it did, Vonny's shoulders leapt. Then she laughed, a high sound that she recognised as hysteria. The last time she had made that noise, she'd been about to have root canal surgery.

'Something funny?'

She shook her head, stifling the laughter with her hand. 'Maybe it's your missing boys. Maybe they've come back?'

'Or maybe the two I brought with me tonight have already got the stuff and killed Seth?' That stopped her laughing, at least. But Cramond said: 'No, don't think so. Hardly think they'd bother with the intercom, do you?'

As if in response, it burred again.

'So now what?' Vonny whispered – as if the person on the other end of the line could hear.

Cramond kept his voice low, a terse growl, from a dog you already guessed wasn't friendly. 'What's going to happen is, we're going to sit here, very quietly, and not make a sound.' He glanced at the back window. 'Can we be seen from the main driveway from this window?'

Vonny shook her head. Then, remembering something her neighbours had said, she added: 'The lights can be seen, but I'm not sure if you can make out any details.'

'If you're not expecting someone, who could it possibly be?'

'No idea. We don't know anyone out here.' She did have an idea, though. *Hopefully it's the policeman who came round earlier.*

The intercom buzzed again. And again.

'Could be a parcel?' Vonny said, in earnest.

'At this time? Don't be fucking smart.'

It buzzed again.

'Can you check who it is without answering?' Cramond asked.

'I could have done – except the two guys who broke in the other night cut the camera links and the sensors to this intercom. Expertly, that's the word I think you used. There's an audio connection and nothing else.'

She had allowed a little acid drip into her tone; Cramond ignored it. 'Go over to the intercom and find out who it is. Then send them away. I'm hoping you're going to be sensible, because I make it a rule not to hurt women. So, no slip-ups, eh? No sudden moves, no running your mouth, and don't think about dropping any smarty-pants hints that I'm here.'

Vonny did as she was told, walking slowly over to the second unit. It would have had a picture – available in night vision – now sadly offline. The intercom buzzed yet again, just as Vonny reached out for the button.

'Christ, they're persistent, whoever they are,' Cramond said. 'Answer it, but don't say anything.'

Vonny pressed the button.

A woman's voice. 'Oh, hello – is someone there?'

Cramond indicated she should let go of the button. When she did so, he asked: 'Who is that?'

'Prill. It's my very nosy neighbour.'

The implication was not lost on Cramond. 'Right. She won't be daft, if she's like half the nosy old middens I grew up with. Here's what you're going to say…'

After the intercom buzzed again, Vonny answered. 'Hello?'

'Thank goodness!' Prill said. 'I hope you don't mind, I just came round to see if you're all right. I saw all sorts of lights over here, and I know the police were over the other day… Is everything all right?'

'We're OK, Prill. You've managed to wake me up out of a sleep, in fact. Isn't it a bit late for you to be coming round?'

'Well, I was just worried. You know. With what happened here before. I do worry, Vonny.' Prill sounded somewhat hurt, at this final statement.

'You're not to worry yourself, Prill. Get yourself home, pour a brandy. There's nothing to worry about, here.' Then, remembering Cramond's injunction, she added: 'We had a bit more building work done earlier on – if you saw some lights, that's probably it. Just some last-minute snagging.'

'Well, quite. If you're sure you're all right?'

'Never been better, Prill. Goodnight. Thanks for asking after us.'

'You're very welcome.'

Vonny let go of the button and sighed. 'That should be that.'

'On a scale of one to ten, how nosy would you say this Prill was?'

'Ten being the highest? Ten. She probably knows me better than I know myself.'

'So would you say she's probably had a look round the house and garden tonight, already?'

'It's possible, but she'd have to have gotten over the fence at the back to see us here. It's not overlooked, unless she wants to climb some trees.'

*Unless... Unless she got in through the side gate. Like she did before, to keep an eye on the builders.*

'OK,' Cramond said, his shoulders relaxing. He glanced at his watch. 'You did well. I wish half the people I kidnap were as nice as you. You're a model pupil. Let's sit tight. The others will be checking in soon. As before, slowly turn around and walk back to the kitchen table.'

Vonny heard something behind her that put her nerves on edge. She paused; Cramond had heard it too. He reached into his jacket; she saw a pistol appear in his hand.

The voice at the front door carried through the house, loud and clear; loud enough to play a chord on the glassware in her cupboard; a voice fit for a choir or an afternoon recital.

'Vonny? It's me, Prill. Your door was unlocked. Are you up there? Or in the kitchen? I hope you don't mind me intruding, but there's all kinds of commotion going on in your woods tonight.'

'Prill, what are you doing in here?' Vonny yelled, in utter consternation. 'It's late, you need to go home! You can't come barging in here when you feel like it!'

Cramond darted behind her and mouthed: *Get rid of her. Now.* He brandished a handgun, right in front of her face.

For a second all Vonny could focus on was the dark circle at the end of the barrel. Cramond snarled, and she flinched, expecting him to drive the barrel into her face.

She turned to the door out in the hallway. As she did so, Prill flicked on the light.

The older woman was dressed in a Wimbledon-green pullover with plaid shirt collars protruding from the neckline. She looked as if she'd been horse riding, perhaps. She had on boots over dark leggings, and she brought in a faint smell of fresh earth.

'Ah! There you are. I do hope you don't mind. I just don't want you to be taken advantage of. The property being, you know, what it is.'

'Never mind my property,' Vonny hissed. 'What in God's name are you doing here, prowling around my house?'

'It's only me,' she said, waving her hands in a frustrated gesture. 'I heard there were those, you know, traveller people about in this weather, and you know what they can do. God knows, you know me, I don't judge, but a fact is a fact, Vonny. My goodness... is that blood on the counter?'

Vonny took her by the shoulder and turned her towards the open doorway. 'You were right to get in touch, Prill. You're a star for checking things out. But it's time to go now, OK? Thanks for coming. In future, please don't just wander into my house. I could be up to anything.'

'I just... Look, I'll level with you.' Prill folded her arms and stayed put in the doorway. 'I saw your Seth, out on the path. He was with two other men. They didn't look friendly, to me. And Seth didn't look happy to be with them. It looked like they were... steering him, you know? Like he didn't want to be there.'

Cramond stepped from the kitchen. Prill looked up, startled, as the newcomer closed the distance between them.

'I believe I can offer an explanation,' Cramond said. He held out a hand and grinned. 'I'm Detective Inspector Bell. The two men you saw with Seth were two of my detectives. We have reason to believe criminal gangs are operating in the area. And you are...?'

'You should know who I am, if you've been doing your job properly. Can I see your warrant card, please?' Prill didn't waver, her voice and gaze steady, her arms still folded across her body warmer.

Vonny bulged her eyes and she tilted her head slightly towards that big open doorway that beckoned, so agonisingly close, hoping that Prill would pick up on this not-so-subtle cue. But the older woman didn't; she was too focused on trying to stare out Cramond. He reached past her and smartly shut the front door. 'Of course, I'll show you my warrant card.'

He reached into his coat and pulled out the pistol. He then reversed the gun expertly in his hands, and smashed it against the side of Prill's head.

She collapsed, simply and without fuss, into a pile of limbs and polyester on the floor, a dead weight seemingly dropped from some height, arms and legs splayed out.

Cramond chuckled and shook his head. 'All the times I've wanted to do that to nosy neighbours, man, I tell you...' He bent down and took her by the shoulders. 'Best we see if she's still alive, first. I'll grab the arms; you get her legs.'

There was a sharp click. Cramond looked up; his chin dropped. Prill was dropped, too, her head striking the floor.

'What the fuck?'

Where Vonny had been standing a second or two before, there was no one. She'd gone. She'd disappeared.

Cramond touched the door, seized by the insane suggestion she'd somehow squeezed past him, opened the door and run in the second or two his attention had been diverted. But no; it was shut fast, and even a conjuror couldn't have diverted his attention for long enough; nor could a contortionist have gotten out without him seeing it.

The answer was directly ahead of him, at a section of wall just to the right of the kitchen, where the stairs began their spiral up to the balcony level and the bedrooms. A delineation that bulged for a moment, then settled with the click as a lock engaged.

Cramond ran up to the wall, kicked it, battered it, and snarled his worst threats, his most dire warnings. It was to no avail. He stood back and surveyed it, still astonished.

'A fucking panic room!'

# 45

They stopped shoving Seth long enough to laugh at the caravan, parked at the top of the slope.

'Fuck is that?' Vinnicombe said, nodding towards the glowing paintwork. 'Apache? Jesus, they don't half come up with some ridiculous names for these things. "Warrior Spirit". Your nan's sitting in front of it, reading the paper on Skegness seafront.'

'I think it suits the big guy here,' snarled Jay. Seth felt his breath tickle one of his ears: 'You fancy being buried in it?'

Seth didn't answer him. His mind was about one hundred yards behind him, where the lights burned at his back. He couldn't see any silhouettes moving, the last time he'd looked back. That had been when Jay had slapped him – hard, from behind, right in the ear. He hadn't looked back again after that.

'Mind if we take a look inside, big chap?' Vinnicombe nodded towards the caravan. 'Just in case you've got any nasty surprises in there.'

Seth shrugged. 'Be my guest. Take it away with you, if you like. It was going to be a pain in the arse towing it back to the showroom.'

He reached for his pocket; Jay's fingers tried to punch

through the flesh of his arm; Vinnicombe's shotgun appeared, Spaghetti-Western quick, from within the folds of his blue duffel coat.

'Oh, come on now,' Vinnicombe said, laughing. 'Slowly. Throw the keys onto the deck, beside me. And for goodness' sake, don't give our boy here an excuse to zap you one. I think he's itching to do it.'

'For once, Captain Pugwash here is right,' Jay said. 'Now do what he says. Nice and easy.'

Despite the hardware pointed right at him, Seth considered hurling the keys at Vinnicombe, and taking his chance on his heels. The moment he got to the woods, he surely had an advantage.

*Not yet. Not yet...*

He did as he was told. Vinnicombe stooped to collect the keys, never once taking the pistol off Seth. Then he disappeared up the short incline to where the caravan was berthed. 'Can I say something to you, as a professional? Not sure about the positioning of your caravan here, pal. Hope it's secure. This ends up going down the hill, the momentum will probably take it through your wall.'

'You a builder?' Seth asked. 'Seriously, if you are, I might have a job for you when all this is over.'

'He's funny.' Vinnicombe snickered, without apparent mirth. 'He thinks if we like him he'll be all right. Just go on believing that, big guy. Be safe in the fantasy.'

Vinnicombe unlocked the caravan and went in, clicking on the light and rooting around.

While he was gone, Jay whispered: 'You know, you don't have to worry. I'm not going to shoot you.'

Seth said nothing. Through the window, he saw

Vinnicombe opening drawers and festooning surfaces with a handful of clothes Vonny had left behind. He recognised what he called her 'comfort bra', an off-white warhorse that she'd had for as long as Seth had known her. He clenched his teeth.

'No,' Jay went on, 'what I'll do is, cut you with the blade. Remember? The kukri? Family heirloom. Grandad traded it, back in the day. Know how many people I've cut with it?'

'They say you have to draw blood every time you draw it.'

'That's absolutely right,' Jay said. 'And it's going to be yours – if you don't give us what we want.' The voice was closer again. 'You're running out of room. You're running out of tricks. And you're running out of time. Your mind will be racing, just now. You'll be making plans. You might even think you can run for it. So here's your first and last warning – don't be doing anything we don't like. I won't hesitate.'

Seth didn't reply. Vinnicombe came out of the caravan, grinning. 'Nothing in there that I could see. Course, if it's under a panel or it's stuffed somewhere underneath, we'll find it, one way or another.'

'Lead the way,' Jay said. 'But first, tell us where we're going.'

'If we're going in the dark, we'll have to follow a strange route – if you want to go straight, you have to go through the woods, and I wouldn't trust my judgement in the dark. We'll follow a path to the left, heading up towards the drystone wall. Then we cut around it, back towards the pond in the middle of the estate. That's how we get to the hanging tree.'

Jay chuckled. 'Sounds familiar.'

'You been there before?'

'Couldn't draw you a map. But I can see it, in my mind's eye. That's where you left the gear?'

'That's where we're going.'

Vinnicombe's face darted forward; even in the gloom, it came into sharp enough focus to discern the stiff white spines of stubble on the end of his boxer's chin. 'Don't get smart. The man asked you a direct question: is that where it is?'

'Yes,' Seth said.

They followed the slushy path, the air becoming slightly less frigid. As they passed the treeline, slow, fine flakes began to fall again.

'Why couldn't they have done this in the summer?' Jay whinged.

Vinnicombe kept step beside Seth, with the gun held towards his ribs, while Jay was somewhere behind. Seth's breath steamed up in the chill air, and he cinched his coat tighter.

'Where did you hide the other half of the deal?' Vinnicombe asked. 'Out of interest?'

'In the bole of a tree, on the other side of the pond.'

'Might take a look, after we're done,' Vinnicombe said, menacingly. 'You'll point it out to us, won't you? Just to make sure you're not telling lies about our two friends having done a runner with the gear.'

'Be my guest.' Then Seth stumbled, and fell flat on his face.

Jay chuckled, as Seth got back up. 'I thought you were about to plead, then,' he said. 'I thought you were going to go on your knees and beg.'

Vinnicombe frowned, his eyes pooled in shadow. 'What've you got in your hand there?' he asked.

'Nothing,' Seth said. 'Slipped on the snow. Greasy surface, here.'

'Greasy surface, my plums,' Vinnicombe said. He shoved the pistol in Seth's face, then grabbed Seth's wrist. He twisted, quickly, expertly, and a rock about the size and shape of a slice of sponge cake fell out of Seth's hand.

'Hey,' Jay said, all traces of mirth gone.

Vinnicombe scooped up the rock in one fluid move. 'Sly bastard. Was that for me, maybe?' Before Seth could answer, Vinnicombe wrapped his fingers around the rock and swept it round, hard, into Seth's face.

This time he fell genuinely, and in all seriousness. The cold bit into his backside as his mouth filled with blood where his cheek met his teeth, and he couldn't feel the pain yet across his cheekbone, but he could feel his pulse throbbing along the place where the rock had hit him. He touched it; his fingertips were stained blackish with blood in the silvery light.

Vinnicombe hurled the rock deep into the woods. 'Now, you won't be doing that again, will you?'

Seth said nothing. Vinnicombe kicked him.

'Get up. Keep going. I'm watching you.'

They walked on for a little while, the line of trees closing in to the right. Falling snow penetrating the black bundling of branches gave an impression of a constantly shifting landscape; Seth and his two captors' eyes were drawn to the movements, unconsciously.

One white flare was bigger and brighter than the others.

'What in the name of Christ was that?' Jay exclaimed.

They all watched the ghostly arc gliding through the treeline before disappearing somewhere in the forest.

'Barn owl,' Vinnicombe said. 'Big bugger as well. Must have spotted a mouse.'

'That'd have your eye out, man,' Jay said.

They approached the five-bar gate. Seth strained his ear, listening out for the sound of someone in the lane. Would the police have kept a lookout for him, this long into the night? Bound to have, he thought.

If there was a raid of some kind, he could argue his way out of it. Say the intruders asked him to guide them through the estate, to where they'd hidden the stuff... It was as good an argument as he could manage. And they had the guns.

'It's along here, now. We head up the path, then turn right again, through a clearing in the trees. The gap should be harder to spot if there's been fresh snow.'

They left the gate behind; there was no sign of the other police officer, now, and no sign of the lanky PC who'd been waiting at the top of the road where the lane opened out. They soon came to a gap between two ancient oak trees whose growth had taken a weird turn, with the branches spread out like the legs of a dead crab – oddly arresting in any kind of sunlight, but simply sinister in the treacherous dark.

'This is it.'

'We got far to go?' Vinnicombe asked. 'This has taken too long for my liking.'

'Almost there. Two minutes, tops.'

The temperature wasn't low enough to freeze over the stream, and its trickling told Seth that the hanging tree was nearby. Sword-quick flashes of light showed through the trees as they picked their way over the path, barely affected by the snowfall, the winter-bare trees providing enough cover. There was no wind to stir them; they only creaked.

'Oh, I remember now,' Jay said. 'That's where Dan's other boy took his last gasp.'

It looked strangely lonely in this ghastly night, Seth thought; with its tousled head and thin, slightly kinked bough, it could have been a maid in mourning for a husband who never arrived.

'If someone had asked you to point out which one someone was hanged from, that's the one you would pick,' Vinnicombe said. He stabbed a finger towards the hanging tree. 'Am I right?'

'That's it,' Seth said.

'Dan Jr died yellow, you know,' Jay added, almost casually. 'Once he knew Daddy and the tough brother were out of the game. I thought he would. You know the type.'

Vinnicombe spat on the ground. 'Dirty job, that,' he remarked. 'It's one thing putting them out the game, but it's another thing to make a mockery. Wouldn't have wanted anything to do with it.'

'Well, you didn't have anything to do with it,' Jay returned. 'And no one's interested in what you think about it, either.'

'Just telling you, son. Not much class involved, there.'

'Class?' Jay snorted. 'Yeah, tell us about the war, Grandad. Don't give me "class". You and "class" don't match.'

'Maybe. But I know it when I see it,' Vinnicombe said. 'And I'm not seeing much of it here. Big guy – you saying it's at the hanging tree? Explain. Whereabouts?'

'You see the hanging tree? Now look to the left. There's an ash tree up there. Now look at one of the thicker branches, stretching out towards the hanging tree.'

'What's that?' Vinnicombe's attention was fixed on the tree, the gun held loosely at his side. Now was the time!

Then a pistol barrel nestled into the small of his back.

'I know what you're thinking,' Jay whispered. 'I was in your position, I'd think about it, too. Just don't.'

'There's a box, in among the branches. Is that a bird feeder, or something? A hide, or a nest?' Vinnicombe squinted hard.

'A nesting box. Or, it used to be. Vonny got it in; it was meant to go on top of a bird table, but I made it into something else. I sealed it tight so nothing could get in. That's where the stuff is. That's it.'

The structure was bulky, about two foot square, and precariously balanced, maybe eight or nine feet off the ground. There were no obvious ways to get to it.

'Wait here,' Vinnicombe said, cautiously, and stepped closer to the tree.

Seth waited until he was out of earshot, then said to Jay, quietly: 'You going to let him talk to you like that?'

'What you say?' He heard Jay step forward.

'Jean Paul Gaultier's black sheep cousin, there. He talks to you like you're an idiot. If I was you, I'd smack that little prick.'

'I see your thinking,' Jay said. 'If you were me, yeah, you might smack the little prick. I might even applaud you. But you're you, and I'm me. And I've got the gun. So shut up.'

'You're getting angry at me – you should be getting angry at him. Guy doesn't rate you. It's obvious.'

'I said, shut up.'

'And, begging your pardon,' Vinnicombe called out. 'How do you propose going up there?'

'That's the tricky bit. You see the stumps, on the bark of the tree? Places where the branches were removed, right? You have to climb up.'

Vinnicombe burst out laughing. 'No, *you* have to climb up. Go on. Show us your skills. Become the Human Fly!'

'Whatever you have to do, do it slow and careful,' Jay said, shoving him forward.

Seth remembered how easy it was to clamber up the branches, but the darkness and the melted snowflakes added considerations. He called out like a startled pigeon when his foot slipped off the lowermost stump, and he had to cling hard to the bark, feeling it pinch his swollen cheekbone. Soon, he reached the box, bracing his feet against the stumps. He was relieved to see the catches were still intact on the wooden lid – his greatest fear had been that his forest friends both furred and feathered might have found a way in, and spoiled what was inside. He tried the lid once, for luck; it was shut tight. Then he flicked open the catches, and opened the box.

There was silence for a moment.

'Whatever's in there, throw it down,' Vinnicombe said. 'Bit by bit. Toss it down. Just let it drop beside you. Don't lift your hands, and don't turn around.'

'I can't,' Seth said. His voice squeaked with tension and panic.

'What do you mean, you can't?' Jay snarled. 'What's the problem?'

'It's gone,' Seth said, panting, his head seeming to expand and contract with every convulsion of his heart valves. He clung onto the tree bark tighter, the better to stop himself falling. 'There's nothing there. The stuff is gone!'

# 46

'I'm going to shoot him.' Jay pocketed the kukri, raised his pistol and took aim. Seth flinched, throwing his arm up, tucking his head into his armpit like the bird in the nursery rhyme.

He had nowhere to go but down. He prepared to drop from his ungainly perch, trying to second-guess when the explosion would come. Perhaps the slicing agony would come before the report; a white-hot meteor tearing through him; the sense of being unseamed.

'Not yet,' Vinnicombe growled. Seth heard, but did not see, a brief struggle.

'Just one in the leg. Just one to motivate him. Bastard.'

'Put it down, I said!'

Seth dropped his arm and chanced a look. The two men were wrestling, legs braced like two jujitsu fighters.

He let go, forgetting to put his legs together but remembering to roll. His back still sang upon impact, a terrible agony that bent his frame the wrong way. Seth wondered for a terrifying moment if his back had broken; but his legs moved, and he got to his feet, only to find that his actions had ended the scuffle, and both men were pointing their guns at him.

'Stay where you are,' Jay said, backing away from the older man. They were both breathing hard; Vinnicombe had a scratch down the side of his face, stark and black in this light. It was the first time Seth had seen him discomfited in any way. He wondered if Jay had taken his advice.

'Do not shoot him. Understand?' Vinnicombe turned to Seth. 'Not to say we *won't* shoot you, if you don't explain yourself.'

'I can't explain it.' Seth could barely stand. He wondered if he might fall to his knees, just as they'd said when he tried to pocket the rock. He wondered if he might plead for his life. He couldn't plead for Vonny's.

Vonny. Alone in the house with that grinning used-car salesman twerp. It sickened him, agonised him. The thought gave him what was required to stand up straight. That gave him the nerve.

'You say there's nothing up there?' Vinnicombe said, pointing to the box. 'You say that's where you left the stuff?'

'Yes.'

'Prove it,' Jay said. 'Go up there and bring it down. Slowly.'

Seth did as he was told. His joints ached as he climbed up once more. 'I nailed it in. It's attached to a bracket... Hold on.'

'I don't give a shit what it's attached to,' Jay said, in more of a gurgle than a statement. 'Get it down here and open it up.'

His fingers stung by the frozen metal, Seth dislodged the box from its bracket. He tried to tuck it under his arm, but struggled to keep his balance. 'It's too big to carry.'

'Then throw it down, genius,' Vinnicombe snapped. 'I don't care what happens to your birdie box.'

Seth let the box go. It landed hard and rolled over, but kept its shape and stayed shut.

'Go get it,' Vinnicombe said, and for once Jay didn't argue or prevaricate. Jay found the seam and opened the box.

'Absolutely fuck all in there,' Jay said, horrified, revealing the box.

Seth came down, and faced both of them.

No one said anything. The two intruders didn't consult each other. They didn't even share a glance. They started in on him. Punches snapped Seth's head back and forth; he was buffeted across the ground, tumbling end over end, and taking blows at all points. It seemed to go on beyond the snapping point of rage; it became measured, considered violence. At one stage, they fought each other to be first in the queue. One nasty kick hit Seth in the ribs – pointed toes; the smaller, older man, surely – and he cried out. A knee exploded against the side of his head, and he went down, curling up into a ball.

'Where is it? Where?' Seth wasn't sure which one had said it. He caught a glimpse of Jay, or a creature wearing a mask that looked like Jay, literally drooling. 'Find that fucking stuff or we'll rip you apart!'

A noise broke in on the dull eruptions on every exposed part of Seth. A phone.

Jay was out of breath. 'Thought this was a no-phones job?'

'Quiet,' Vinnicombe said – also breathing hard but horribly self-assured, after the storm had passed. 'Adults talking.'

Seth slowly uncurled; his right arm was shaking beyond

control. He wasn't sure if his fingers were broken; he could barely extend them. He uncovered his face. He could taste blood; he was not sure where he was bleeding from.

A kick in the balls from Jay returned him to the ground, flat out. Seth had been knocked sick by such a blow before, but he hadn't realised you could be knocked out by one. Lights scored lines across his vision like fingernails down a blackboard. He lay silent for a moment, listening to Vinnicombe's conversation.

'Yeah, I hear you... Is there another way out of the house?'

A clear Scottish accent, compressed and highly strung, could be heard in the response.

Vinnicombe responded: 'Best you get checking. Make sure. And don't worry. It's only a problem. I can sort it out. I've brought tools. That's why you hired me, kiddo.' After hanging up, he said to Jay, 'Keep that bastard right here. Watch him closely. Ask him questions, but don't hurt him any more. You awake over there, big fella?' A prod with pointed toes in his side; Seth struggled to a sitting position. 'That's good. Still compos mentis. Great. You up for telling us what happened to the stuff?'

'I don't know,' Seth managed to say.

'I believe you!' the little man said. 'I truly do. You might want to start speculating. You can speculate *wildly*, in fact. Because you're not just a dead man if that stuff has gone missing. You're going to die in agony. But not before your beanpole *Good Housekeeping* cover girl wife dies, in a horrible, horrible way. I'll leave it to your imagination. I'll leave it for you to ponder. Same question, said a different way. *Where – is – our stuff?* Seek the truth. Find an answer.'

Vinnicombe didn't wait for a reply. Nor did he acknowledge Jay as he strode off back down the path.

Seth listened to the blood roaring in his ears. He curled and uncurled his fingers. Still working. Not broken. That was something.

'I hope it's permanent,' Jay said, balefully. He tossed a stick of gum into his mouth, and stared down at Seth, unblinkingly, as his jaws worked. 'Your hands. Your face. Everything. That's if you get out of here alive. Which I am starting to doubt.'

'Why don't you shut your mouth?' Seth said, after he was sure the little white-haired gargoyle had scuttled off far enough out of hearing range.

'That's a big statement considering I just kicked you all over the place on your own manor,' Jay said, chewing the gum hard. 'Quite bold, in fact.'

'Yeah? There's only one of you now,' Seth said. 'Not to mention you're holding a gun. Not fucking yellow, are you, son?'

Jay laughed, but only after a pause. 'You just do what the man said, and tell us where you think the stuff's gone.'

'The truth is, I don't know. I'm the only one who knows where the stuff was. I was alone when I planted it.'

But this was not true. Someone had been with him when he had planted the stuff.

It was the same person who he could see now, positioned over Jay's shoulder, both eyes peering out of a tangle of branches at the top of a tree.

# 47

The door was locked from the inside, tight, secure. Cramond had no way of getting through it, but Vonny still clung to it, even as he pounded and kicked it from the other side. They only made a faint impression on the door's integrity – the faintest vibrations, such as you might discern in the air if you stood next to a powerful speaker system. His words carried through the intercom, triggered when Vonny had put on the lights.

The video screen had been cut, here, too; Vonny could imagine how his face might have looked, distorted through the fish-eye effect of the video screen, bulging in and out of good order as he peered in at the lens fixed in the wall.

'Open this fucking door, or I swear to God, I'll...' He seemed to think his response through, though he didn't stop his hammering. 'Your husband. I'll bring him back here. You can sit in there and listen to the sound he makes when I slit his throat.'

Inside the panic room, Vonny had been like a plane passenger clinging to the armrests of their seat and deluding themselves that doing so kept the aircraft steady. She made herself let go of the door, and took a step back.

The hammering continued, but the door was firm.

She'd designed this room especially. It hadn't been in her mind until she'd come to submit the final plans to the architect. *If I'm going to live in a palace*, she'd said to her, *then I might as well have the kind of protection a queen might have.*

*You do hear about it all the time*, the architect had replied. *In a lot of ways it's easier to break into a remote place as opposed to a semi-detached two-bedroom house in a suburb, surrounded by nosy old buggers.*

She'd even had fun planning it out. It reminded her of plans she'd drawn up in felt tip for a secret base as a girl, after she'd read an Enid Blyton novel about spies and junior detectives. Zip line. Tunnel. Launchpad. Gun tower.

The room was roughly the size of a box room that most people would use for books and old CDs, and a single camp bed for the friend most likely to vomit after a night's drinking. It was perfectly square, with a single bulb burning overhead, a fridge with bottled water and snacks inside, an office chair in the other corner, and, of course, vertical against the whitewashed wall in bright red and more reminiscent of a defibrillator, was a landline telephone.

Vonny tried it, stabbed at the receiver, then slammed it back down. Dead, of course.

'Shit! Dinosaur technology, anyway. Dodo Enterprises Inc.' She slapped herself, for no good reason, then she began to laugh. If she could have seen herself right then, she wouldn't have recognised herself; utterly on edge, face demoniacal, eyes glassy. She was on the verge of collapse; she did collapse, into the seat, as her giggling became sobs.

'Open the door and don't be silly,' said the voice in the speaker. More conciliatory, edging towards importunate, now. This sounded more sinister than the roaring and shouting, after he'd collided with the door what seemed like milliseconds after the automatic lock had engaged. She could not have cut it any finer. She could picture him, forehead pressed against the door, eyes blank, even as he modulated the tone of his voice into something less threatening. 'Come on, now. There's no need to be silly about any of this. We'll get the stuff, and be on our way. That's all we've ever wanted. I'm sorry about the rough stuff. But we had to let you know we were serious. We weren't really going to kill you. So, let's have no more of these games. Just come on out. I promise I won't hurt you. I'll even stay in another room, if you like. You can just sit quietly until it's all sorted out. You won't even know we've been in.'

Vonny had had a boyfriend like that. He'd sounded just like this, one time after she'd locked him out, when he'd grown angry and paranoid after she'd spoken to someone male who wasn't him, on a night out. *Come on, now*, he'd said. *Let's not be silly. Just let me back in.*

This memory provided Vonny with an impetus she might not have had otherwise. She got up and stabbed the button that activated her mic. 'The police are on their way. I'd say you have ten minutes for you and the other two to get out of here before they arrive. If you're very lucky.'

'The police? How have you managed that?'

'There's an alarm,' Vonny said. 'A panic button. Connects to 999.'

In a hint of his former tone, Cramond said: 'An alarm? Or a panic button?'

'Call it what you want. You're not getting in here. It's best you leave. Soon as you can.'

'Thing is, there's not a panic button in there. If there is, it would have been disabled, along with your phone line and your internet connection. Is there a phone in there? You tried it yet?' He began to laugh.

'You'll never get in here,' Vonny said, keeping her voice steady. 'You'll need a tank. Or a missile. Steel bars across the doors. You'll never get through.'

'That's where you're wrong, sweetheart,' came a separate, cockney voice. 'I don't have a tank or a missile. But I've got the next best thing. The appliance of science, you might say.'

Vonny's sense of security emptied out into dread. She took her hand off the intercom and sprang back, collapsing into the chair. The momentum pushed it on its coasters into the wall, and she leaned back against it, after the impact. The paintwork was cool against her forehead. Tiredness struck, implausibly – something beyond exhaustion, not unlike jet lag. She wanted to shut down. There was an option, but the builders had warned her about it... And then...

*And then of course, they'd left the site early without completing it. Screws loose all over the house. Thanks to these fuckers.*

Another voice carried over the intercom: Vinnicombe's. Their conversation was indistinct for a moment or two. Then they both broke up laughing, a ridiculous sound, a mockery.

*The appliance of science...* that had been one phrase Vonny had picked up. She pictured someone connecting a computer terminal to the console outside... A simple balancing act of zeroes and ones, the code cracked... The door sliding open to reveal the faces of slavering jackals.

Instead, there was the sound of industry – clanking,

something being clamped, screws being turned. A moment of complete silence.

'Thing is, I've gotten into bank vaults, dear,' Vinnicombe said, in his breezy taxi-driver manner. 'It was my speciality. Some took a long time. Some didn't take long at all. They all had one thing in common, though. They were all much harder to crack than this. And I've brought everything I need with me. Just in case. That's why they pay me the big bucks, don't you know?'

The drill might have begun to turn in Vonny's forehead, never mind the wall outside. Its electric bark sat her bolt upright, her fatigue gone at the flick of a switch. She covered her ears and cowered for a moment. Then she made a decision. No decision at all, really.

Vonny turned to the wall she had previously rested against. At the bottom right-hand side was a panel. Just big enough for a person her size to crouch in.

She took a bottle of water out of the fridge, but her hands shook so badly that she dropped it, then abandoned the idea. Water could wait.

Vonny punched in a code in the console next to the panel. It slid open.

A draught chilled the sweat at her forehead, and her breath steamed up immediately as she crouched before the pitch-dark tunnel. There was no light anywhere, nothing that promised salvation other than that frozen air.

The tone of the drill changed, as if it had broached something. Close, now. Perhaps close enough to splinter the plasterwork and poke its silvery nose right through.

All or nothing.

Vonny clambered inside the tunnel.

# 48

The crawlspace was in near-total darkness, and the concrete sides were clammy to the touch. She gasped as a spider's web caressed her cheek, and something seemed to pop underneath her thumb as she inched forward. It was only a matter of a few feet, but Vonny could see nothing. A design flaw, she told herself.

Behind her, the drilling had stopped. A door slammed against a wall, and heavy footsteps vibrated the building, frighteningly close. She imagined a hand clamping on her shoulder, even though it was impossible.

'Where did she go?' Cramond cried, the strain in his voice clear despite the new doorway.

'Look closely, Aladdin,' said Vinnicombe. 'Down there, bottom left. Open sesame.'

'Hell is that? An escape tunnel?'

'Yep, that exactly. I'll bring the stuff.' A matter of inches behind her, the door rattled. 'Yeah, this one shouldn't take me twenty seconds. Stand by.'

Vonny hurried forward, and almost pitched forward into empty space. This was the slope. The one the architect had tried to talk her out of. *It isn't a playpark.* A slide, taking her into a channel, which would reach the outside, at the back, near the swimming pool. But she hadn't reckoned on actually having to use it. She had included the entire panic room and escape tunnel as a joke, almost.

*Some joke.*

Behind her, the voices, way too close now. The Scottish accent, reverberating off the tight angled surfaces like a pebble in a pipe. 'She launched an escape pod or something?'

'Don't think so,' Vinnicombe said. He grunted; he was crouching, slithering into the crawlspace. He was right behind her. Then light flooded the space, bluish and cold, from a powerful torch. It cast a Vonny-shaped shadow into the dip, where the chute angled down into darkness, her hair coiled like Medusa's. 'Wherever you're going, you can't be far away... Ah! I think I can see her. Almost there...'

There was no time to think about it now. Vonny twisted her legs around, so that she was sat forward, and launched herself down the slide.

'Here!' Vinnicombe was astonished. 'Where'd she go?'

The surface was slightly abrasive, so she didn't quite fly down the chute. This was fortunate, because when she reached the short distance at the bottom, she was soon in freezing water up to her shoulders.

Her whole body convulsed, and she twisted and clawed some way back up the chute, like a house cat taking an unexpected dip in a birdbath. Vonny emitted a grating whine and her insides seemed to contract to a dense, thudding core. The water was freezing, and it was almost up to the top of the tunnel she had to crawl down. It seemed incredible this could happen. Again, she remembered the conversation with the builder: *There are pieces of snagging you'll have to look at. Your special room... it's not secure at the outside.*

*That'll flood.* It had flooded. During the snowfall, water had seeped in.

Vinnicombe's torch bobbled two or three feet above her head, as he inched forward.

Hands clutched tight against her chest, Vonny looked at the tunnel. There was an inch or two's clearance at the top of the pipe; as she moved, the displaced dark water slapped at the top. Eight to ten feet in length; that was all.

*They're going to kill me. No choice.*

Vinnicombe's head appeared at the top of the chute. He had a head torch; its blue light blazed directly into Vonny's eyes. He chuckled. 'Did you actually build a water slide in your own house, love? What's going on here? If you'd come to me first, I could've sorted the house out for you. What a mess!'

Vonny crouched into the water, shivering. The cold was beyond imagining, her shoulders convulsing with the effort.

Vinnicombe's beam moved past her head and lit up the waterlogged tunnel. 'Now... Where's that going? And more to the point, where are you going?'

Vonny moved forward. The tunnel floor was treacherous, and she slipped forward. Swim. She would have to swim. Ten feet, tops, then out. *Couple of kicks, really. That's all. Nothing to it.*

Vinnicombe's voice was gentler, now. 'Think about it, sweetheart. Think about the water. Whatever's at the end of that tunnel, isn't worth the effort. Imagine it's blocked? Imagine you can't open the hatch? You go down there, you're not going to come out. You'll be stuck. In the dark. Under the water. Now see some sense, please. I'll help you back up.'

Adrenaline kicked in, at long last. Vonny glared at him over her shoulder. 'Come on down, Popeye, and let's find out what's at the end of the tunnel?'

'No kidding, now,' Vinnicombe said. 'You'll drown. There's no space to get a breath. You won't come out of there alive. You aren't gambling, you're losing. Think about it. Come on up here, and at least you're taking a chance.'

'Take a running jump!' she screamed, and dived forwards.

# 49

All around was darkness and terrible, awesome cold with the sudden immersion. Vonny felt bubbles tickle her cheeks and nose. The soft explosion was all around her head and her ears. She knew the roaring of her blood, her pulse wild. She stretched full out, kicking towards the end of the tunnel.

Ten feet. No more.

As she moved through the water, she envisaged a rapidly reducing distance. At the end, she knew, was a hatch she had to turn, which let out into a small box that resembled a cover for an electricity meter. Once she was in there, she was free, in the sprawling garden space.

She propelled herself along the concrete tunnel, scraping her fingers and tearing a nail. This was not painful; it barely registered in the dark and cold. Her chest burning, she expected the hatchway to touch her fingers at any time.

It didn't. She kicked on, pulling at the walls. Nothing... Still nothing.

A bubble burst from her mouth. Instinctively, she headed for the surface – but there was no surface, only the upper edge of the pipe, and it was concrete, and she bashed the top of her skull on it. A sudden, biting pain. Blood might well have curled into the water in tapered red threads, had there been any light to see it. But there was no light, and no air, and seemingly no end to the tunnel.

*Focus! Push forward, it's there, it must be there!*

But there was no end to the tunnel. Surely she had gone beyond ten feet? Twelve feet? How long had they made the tunnel?

Another bubble burst from her mouth. Panic reared, full, untrammelled, and she thrashed in the water. It had to be there! She was going to drown!

She pulled herself through the tunnel, faster now, her fingers and palms glancing off the fine-grained texture of the new tunnel. Something that might have been a fallen leaf prickled at her forearm. Tucking her arms in at her chest, she surged forward. Then, suddenly, the end of the tunnel was there. She crashed into it, her forehead and nose taking the brunt of the blow.

More air escaped as she screamed, a horrified gurgle that could scarcely have been worse if she had met a crocodile. Her hands found the wheel that locked the hatch, the metal like ice on her fingers, a measure below the numbing cold of the water.

*It won't turn!*

Now out of control, beyond the realms of rational thought, she gripped the wheel hard and planted her feet, knees bent, keeping herself anchored as far as possible, and heaved...

It gave a quarter inch. Then more.

Now the lights were streaking across her vision, purple and white comets. *This is it. This is the end.*

The wheel gave another inch, two, more, definitely

moving, just as Vonny felt herself sinking into a light-speared pit that she knew she would never emerge from, and then the water was rushing past her. She had opened the hatch and was carried through as the water gushed out. A gap that felt like air, a different kind of frigid knife blade stropping her neck and shoulders compared to the water, and she inhaled, at last, plenty of water there now, full dark but the water was escaping. She was bundled into a new structure, the fake electric meter cover, and she nudged it forward and then she tumbled out into snow rendered into slush, head, shoulders, sodden clothes flailing, into clean, cold air with the thick motes of snow still falling onto her face.

Vonny got to her feet instantly. She was in the garden, the pool covered in leaves and filled with snow, the loungers glazed with the stuff, glittering frost on the surfaces. Her breath was making great spuming ever-changing sculptures in the air, and she sobbed and gasped for breath. She was alive; all that was required now was an escape over the back wall using the loungers, then into the trees, and from there it was the road.

Cramond appeared from nowhere. His hands clamped over her neck and shoulders, and she was thrown to the ground, ruthlessly, efficiently, easily. A boot clamped on Vonny's chest as she tried to get up. She didn't. She was in a state of stupefaction, frozen, exhausted, defeated. She might have been dead, lying there, flat on her back, hands formed into claws, jaw gaping, eyes wide open.

Cramond smirked. 'Had a quick look at the blueprint. We stole that, you know. When we were casing the house. You left the panic room off, which was clever. But all I had to do was draw a line. And I had a decent employee on contract. Bad luck. C'mon into the house. You look like you could use a towel.'

He extended a hand, and the pressure of the boot was eased on her chest. She took the hand, and got to her feet.

Then Vonny clawed at his face, snarling at him. He threw up a hand and turned away, utterly shocked. Vonny turned and ran, her trainers slapping wetly against the snow. She slipped and stumbled forward. Cramond grabbed her, caught her really, before she fell full on her face. His scratches oozed blood. And he was laughing. 'You can't do it, love. Forget it. Time you realised…'

She elbowed him, hard, and he let go long enough for her to turn away, and strike out blindly. She tripped full into the snow, clearing the edge of the pool, and plunged into that vast, dirty white square.

# 50

There was no need for Susie and Whelan to creep along the drystone wall at the edge of the plot, but they did. There was something in the trellis of shadows cast against the edifice by the orange sodium lights, straggled along the main road. The thick snow and the unsmudged white path at their feet gave everything a curious mellow light.

Susie resisted the urge to crouch as they skirted the wall. She lowered her scarf in order to speak. 'Where did you say the two motorbikes were found?'

'Just up there, near where that big Christmas tree thing is.'

'You mean the fir tree?' Susie was glad of the cover for her smirk.

'Whatever,' the policeman said, defensively. 'It's just over there.'

'Ah yeah, just by that passing place. And they were just abandoned?'

Whelan shrugged. 'Looked that way. No sign of the two guys they belonged to. My gaffer said they belonged to two dangerous characters, but according to the database they were stolen ages ago.'

'Interesting. Where are the bikes now?'

'We had them lifted. Maybe still on the back of the flatbed truck, I'm not sure. Might be returned, but more likely they'll end up at an auction.'

'Why would you just abandon some bikes? Surely you should have a word with Vonny or Seth about it?'

'My gaffer did.'

'That's DI Leonard.'

'Yeah. Guy from the Met.'

'You know him well?'

'He's not bad,' Whelan said, dipping his head as a particularly harsh blast of snow sliced across him. 'Quite fair as far as it goes. Good laugh, like. For a DI.'

'And what does he reckon?'

'To what?'

'To Vonny and Seth. Does he think they're involved?'

'He thinks that the DJ guy, Seth, might be involved in something. Apparently he knows some dodgy sorts. Doesn't have a record or anything.'

'You checked?'

'I do my research,' he said, tersely. 'How far have we got to go before we get to the house?'

'I reckon we should take a shortcut.' Susie nodded towards the gap in the wall, leading onto the lane. 'I think there's an old track here, cuts into the property, and leads onto a gate at the bottom. We get down there, we're into the property itself.'

'What for?'

'Because, it's a shortcut.'

'Yeah, it's a shortcut on someone else's property. Why not just go to the front door? It isn't that much further, surely?'

'Well... I'll level with you. Before we knock their door, there are one or two things I want to take a look at. You could say I'm curious.'

'You were at the house the other day, yeah?'

'Yeah. And I want to take a look at the old shed. The one they found the stuff in. The place where they found the car. I just want to check one or two things, make sure I'm remembering everything right. And to see if anyone's burned it down since then, say.'

'Well... That's trespassing. Technically you're breaking the law. Technically you could get arrested. By, eh, me.'

Susie smiled as best she could, and turned her wrists in front of his face. 'You can cuff me, if you like.'

Bless him, he might have been blushing. It was difficult to tell. 'I mean it, I don't want to wander onto these people's property and get a mouthful of shotgun pellets. Or have to crowbar a guard dog off my backside.'

'We'd only be trespassing for about fifty yards. Besides – you're a copper. You can say you were investigating something untoward. You can say it was me. You can say you caught me.'

She nudged him, then. He looked harassed, but followed her into the cut. 'OK. Let's get down here quickly. I don't like this spot at all.'

'That makes two of us. It's got that sort of crime scene look to it. Sorry,' she added hurriedly, 'I guess you've seen a couple of those.'

'Once or twice,' Whelan replied. His face took on something of a Clint Eastwood cast as he slightly turned his head. The illusion was broken as Susie's footing slipped on the uneven ground, covered in thick snow. He grabbed her as she fell.

'Sorry,' Susie said, straightening up. 'I should have packed my snowshoes.'

'I hope you've packed an excuse,' came a new voice.

Susie and Whelan stopped. In the eerie light, a figure moved forward from the edge of the five-bar gate that marked the entrance to the woodland path. It wore a bulky parka jacket with the hood up, but the face, pinched as it was in the cold, was easily discernible to Whelan.

'Who are you?' Susie said, drawing back.

'I'm DI Leonard, PC Whelan's boss,' returned the newcomer. 'Who might you be?'

'Susie McCracken. I'm with the *Brenwood Green Advertiser and Chronicle*.'

'I thought it was the *Chronicle and Advertiser*? Anyway, ah... Miss Scoop! I heard all about you.' In the ever-thickening snowfall, the cheery voice was incongruous. Everything about his posture and positioning radiated threat. 'Now, you first, love, before I speak to your boyfriend: why are you here?'

'He's not my boyfriend,' she said, carefully and calmly. 'And actually, I came here to apologise. They wanted me to showcase their interior design skills; I wrote a silly story about a Datsun Cherry.' She patted the bottle of prosecco – mercifully untouched in her bag. 'It had already gone to the printers. I'm hoping to come back for another photoshoot when the house is completely finished, so...'

DI Leonard cocked his head. 'You old enough to have a bottle of prosecco in your bag, Miss?'

'Yes I am. I'm eighteen years old.'

'I'm only pulling your leg. Try to smile a little.' Leonard's demeanour barely changed. He turned to Whelan. 'And what's your excuse, Officer Lighthouse – he is awfully tall, isn't he? Why are you here with Miss McCracken?'

'I bumped into her earlier. I'm escorting her onto the premises. Given that we know there's been some unusual activity on this road, lately.'

'Very gallant and civil of you. Don't blame you, son.' He chuckled. 'Well, the bad news is that you can't come onto the property. The place is locked down.'

'You what? Sir?' Whelan bit at his fingernail. 'I wasn't aware…'

'You wouldn't be, would you?' Leonard returned, still smiling. 'It's an operation for the bigger kids. Full secondary school boys. Have you got a car?'

'We parked a bit further up.' Whelan nodded back up the road. Susie could have kicked him for this.

Leonard asked the question that Susie would have done, had she been in the detective's shoes. 'Why did you park all the way up there? There's a driveway you could have parked on, next to the security gate.'

'I thought it was blocked off,' Susie said. 'Or they were having work done on it, the other day. Pretty sure Vonny told me it was blocked off.'

'When did you speak to her?'

'Just the other day.'

Leonard nodded. 'Anyway… best you both get back to it. I've got a long night out here. Just out for a cigarette break.'

'Didn't know you smoked,' Whelan said.

'I might go for a big steamy piss against the wall while I'm at it,' Leonard thundered. 'Now get your arse up that path, Officer Whelan, quick as you like – and take your girlfriend with you. I'll talk you through the dangers of cosying up the press at the station. Now, goodnight.'

'Sir,' Whelan said. He actually strong-armed Susie back up the path. She fought free, utterly furious, but kept in step with Whelan as they retraced their steps in the shin-deep snow.

'Don't put your hands on me again,' Susie said, through clenched teeth, 'unless I give you permission – which isn't likely, for the record.'

'Sorry. Leonard… I heard that about him. That his bite is worse than his bark. He can go from nought to ninety. Hard case, they say.'

'Yeah, whatever. And did you notice something about DI Leonard?'

Whelan shook his head. 'Apart from the dodgy jacket, like?'

'He had a gun in his hand when he stepped out.'

'Bollocks he did,' Whelan snorted. 'A gun?'

'Yep. Guarantee you. He had a handgun on him. Put it in his pocket when he made out who we were.'

'Rubbish,' Whelan scoffed. 'He's not licensed to carry a gun. This isn't America.'

'Yes. You're getting the picture. He has a gun. That's unusual. So come on.'

They had reached the cut in the wall. To the right was the road they'd come down; to the left was the path that led to the main driveway towards the house. 'Where are you going?'

'Where I said we were going. To take a look around in the house.'

'I could get sacked for this.'

'Then stay here, if you want,' Susie said, simply.

She heard him trudging along behind her, and she smiled.

## 51

'If it was up to me,' Jay said, taking careful aim, 'I'd just finish you and have done with it.'

'Then I guess you don't get your precious stuff,' Seth said. He lurched towards a tree, with the aim of leaning against it. His breath came in starts and stops, thick and mucosal like a stuttering chainsaw, and he still bled from his mouth, and possibly his nose. Drips of it infused the snow at his feet. One tree was coated in snow, and he wanted to press it against his lips.

'Don't touch the tree,' Jay said. 'Seriously, anything appears in your hands that looks like a weapon, you're done. Stand back.' The gun moved to cover him. Seth stopped where he was.

Separate to stopping himself falling to the ground, the other aim had been to divert the squat, muscular man from what Seth had seen over his shoulder; he'd changed Jay's line of sight so that the two eyes he'd seen peering from the branches were staring into the back of the shaven skull.

'See, the thing is, I don't think you've got the stuff any more,' Jay mused. 'If you still had the stuff, and you actually meant to drag us out here then pull your magic trick by showing us an empty box, then you would have to be insane. Either that or you'd need a really, really good plan. And I don't think you've got a plan, have you?'

'Wonder what's happening up at the house?' Seth said absently. 'With the phone call.'

'Yeah, I wonder?' Jay grinned. 'Whatever it was, the little guy out here seemed upset.'

'Maybe my missus has escaped?'

'She could have done, very true. But you see the little guy out here? He's a bit of an expert, you know. Safe cracker. But he's known for other things, too. Mass murderer. A real one. Not a sex killer or anything, but he's put a lot of people in their graves. Nice quiet graves. Maybe the same kind of quiet grave you're heading for?'

Seth said nothing. He only fought for breath, plumes of it steaming in the ethereal light.

'So just imagine what he could be up to right now, with your missus,' Jay leered. His tongue protruded through his teeth. 'She could be in all sorts of trouble. Beautiful lady. Wouldn't mind interrogating her myself. Looks like Iman. You know, David Bowie's wife? A real stunner. Just imagine what's going on right now.'

Seth ground his teeth.

'I mean right at this very second. And you could stop it. Just tell us where the stuff really is. That's all you need to do. Put your mind at ease.' Jay nodded, eyes bulging. He was like a desperate strip-club tout in a city too handsome to be selling itself so cheaply.

'I think she'll do just fine, pal. I wouldn't get yourself worked up about it.'

'No, that's true, I need to stay calm and think through

what I'm going to do to her. Are you absolutely sure there's nothing you want to tell me about the stuff?'

'I think it's probably been moved off site.'

'By *who*?'

'That I don't know,' Seth said, helplessly. 'The guys I talked to... honestly, I don't know.'

'It's going to cost you your life,' Jay said. 'Let that go through your head.'

'Yeah. Or through your head. Right now,' Seth said.

Jay twigged that something was going on, and turned quickly, but not quickly enough.

He flinched, and wheezed like an old man with a morning cough.

He grew a branch, it seemed – from the centre of his chest. It protruded outwards, having punched through the material of his top and torn the zip of his jacket open. The tip of the new appendage appeared wet.

The shaft had flown true, and gone right through Jay's back, a perfect shot.

Jay squawked, not unlike a bird, and pitched forward onto his face. The bolt that had pierced him stopped him from landing fully face-first, anchoring him at a slight angle. His arms waved; he made a snow angel, a final obscenity. Then he was still. The back of the bolt protruded from the centre of his back. It was thin and shiny grey, a bit like graphite. The white-feathered end of the arrow quivered, once, twice, then no more.

Behind him, Crispin's gangling shadow dropped to the ground. Seth saw that he had on what appeared to be army fatigues, and... dear God, camouflage make-up?

Crispin's eyes peered out through a dark wave arcing across his forehead. He had a crossbow, with a long stock and a broad string. The kind of thing that might be used to kill a bison, by someone who fancied a challenge.

Seth snatched the handgun up, inches from his fingertips in the snow. He put it in his pocket, and watched the teenager approach.

'I killed him,' the boy said.

'Yes. You probably saved my life.'

'I've actually killed a man.'

'You going to be sick?' Seth said, uselessly. The boy peered at the crossbow he held in his hands, then pointed it towards the ground.

'Nope. He's definitely dead?'

'As the proverbial doornail, son. That was a shot in a million.'

Crispin grinned. 'Awesome!'

## 52

Seth practised flicking the safety catch on and off on the handgun. A few feet away, Crispin peered closely at the body. 'I'll go to prison for this,' he said, his back turned to Seth.

'Not necessarily. I've got a question for you, though. What have you seen?'

Pretty much everything. I saw what happened the other night; I heard the commotion at your house. I stayed out of the way. Then I heard gunshots...'

'And you never told me?'

'I didn't know what happened. But I could guess.'

'Question two – you moved the stuff out of the box. So, where is it?'

'Yes. I came out and moved it away when I saw you had company. I guessed that's what they were after.'

'I don't have to ask you the third question, do I?'

Crispin struggled a little with this, but eventually he got it. 'It's safe. It's out in one of my hides, on the east side. You'd struggle to find it. I thought about moving it off site for you and hiding it near my dad's... But I also thought you'd need some help when I saw the three guys creeping around the woods.'

The boy had stashed his crossbow in a backpack. He slid his arms through the straps, then cinched them tight.

Seth was a long way from laughing, but there was some mirth in his exclamation: 'I thought you were a birdwatcher! What's with the Rambo gear?'

'I hunt as well. Be a hypocrite if I didn't. Barn owls have to eat. They have to kill to do it. Way I see it, you can't be a nature lover and not also be a bit of a predator.'

'What do you hunt, exactly?'

'Squirrels make a very satisfying shot. Not too bad barbecued, either.'

'All this time I thought you were a shy kid with harmless hobbies. But it turns out you're a weirdo, after all! Thank God.'

'I think you meant to say: "Thank you".'

'Thank you very much, Crispin. Good God. You saved my life, there. And for what it's worth, you have bagged yourself a prize arsehole.'

'He didn't seem the nicest.' The kid's eyes had changed in the night. Now they seemed to shine among the falling snow and the effulgence of moonlight. Seth felt a curious twinge of fear. *Kid just shot a man dead with a crossbow, and... he seems chuffed about it? Is there a psychopath out here with me?*

'Where are we going now?' the boy asked. 'Only... we can get off this property and away without anyone seeing us. Now, I've war-gamed this scenario quite a lot over the years. There's a path...'

'No, we're going home,' Seth said. 'Come with me, if you like. Bring your crossbow, please.'

## 53

Vonny crashed into the bottom of the pool. The snow cushioned her, but it held her there, too. Just the right consistency to sink clean into. Cold shock; the white slap in the face, snow in her mouth and ears, so cold it burned. Handfuls of it, all collapsing, no traction. Her feet treadmilled uselessly, snow piling upon snow... How could it be so deep?

Finally her head broke through, and before she even thought to look over her shoulder or haul herself out of the pool, a hand clamped on her shoulder and plucked her from the pool.

The other hand closed around her throat, and then she was dangled over the dirty white space in the pool, with Cramond's nose close to hers. She gripped the wrists that held her; there was nothing else she could do, but choke.

Cramond's suave façade had completely cracked. There was an awesome, feral leer on his face, eyes wide, teeth bared. 'Game's over! Isn't it? It's over!'

*Please*, she tried to say. *Please don't...*

With a cry of disgust, Cramond threw her. She collided with a sunlounger and tumbled over the top, clothes sodden, hair clinging to her face, utterly frozen. She hunkered down, shivering, arms wrapped around herself.

Cramond's gun bit into the back of her skull. Vonny closed her eyes. 'We're going to go for a walk in the woods, now,' he said. 'Up you get.'

'Coat... Please, can I have my coat.'

'Nope, you can freeze.' The sardonic element had returned, though he still looked furious, and was out of breath. *Angry enough to kill me. Just one squeeze of the trigger away.* 'Up you get. Through the house. Come on.'

Even the shelter from the snow was a boon, as Vonny shivered, leaving slushy footprints over the carpet. 'There is no way you'll get away with this, now,' she said, her lips struggling to form the words, breath hitching in the back of her throat. 'The police will surely be on their way. They'll be here any minute. Any minute...'

'I'm sure you said that before. Did you think I was coming here for a jolly? A walk in the woods?' His face darted forward, the tip of his long nose punching Vonny's cheek.

'Killing me won't help you.'

'No – but threatening to kill you might light a fire under your clown of a husband. Let's go. Maybe some torture. I'd rather not torture you. I don't like that bit of the business. That's for the perverts. But I'll do it if it gets a result. Got it? That's where we're at now. So get moving!'

He shoved her through the kitchen. There was no sign of Vinnicombe anywhere, though his handiwork was apparent; dust and chunks of plaster from where he'd drilled through the wall in a neat rectangle, then curls and slivers of steel where he'd made his way through the physical lock itself.

It appeared he'd swept up – there were no footprints on the carpet in the dust. Already Vonny's house was violated, utterly changed – its grid patterns and perfect curves switched one way, blackened another. It was like a pristine Rubik's cube twisted at random. Even though Vinnicombe's intrusion into her wall had a symmetry and precision to it, something in this rearrangement made Vonny sob.

Then she noticed the cupboard door, ajar. Cramond saw it too. His face was a picture of horror.

'Forget something?' Vonny said, before she could stop herself.

The door, where Prill had been shoved, was crudely, blatantly open. It seemed unlike the woman, Vonny thought, not to close a door over behind her. Maybe she was sending a message, in her own way.

The front door was closed, however.

'I'd say you've got a big problem, now.'

Cramond shook his head. 'This changes nothing. We're leaving here with the stuff. And it is here, somewhere.'

'Please, please let me take a jacket. I'm freezing.'

'Yeah. Wait there.' Cramond crossed over to the coat hooks next to the front door, and snatched up a fleece. He checked the pockets, feeling along the seams and pockets, and hurled it over to Vonny. She could not catch the coat; her fingers still wouldn't work properly. She got to her knees and pulled the fleece up. She pulled it over her head. As she did so, she nudged the wall console with her elbow.

As she popped her head through the neck of the fleece, the console flared blue. The legend stared her in the face: *MOTÖRHEAD, THE ACE OF SPADES, Track 01, The Ace Of Spades.*

'Get the fuck back!' Cramond screamed. 'What is that?'

'So sorry,' Vonny said, 'it's our stereo. Just our stereo.'

Cramond stole forward, peering at the pale blue light and the LCD lettering. At that point, Vonny raised both her hands... and in so doing, triggered the sensor.

The sound of the bassline was colossal to begin with. Vonny swept her hand to the right, and put it as high as it would go.

*Turn this off!* Cramond yelled, his words utterly lost in the noise. *Now!*

Vonny shook her head and mouthed, *I can't!*

Cramond stood back and raised the gun. Vonny screamed, threw herself to the floor, and covered her head.

One sharp thunderclap somehow rose above Lemmy's grated sandstone howl and the particle-accelerator bassline. It did not stop it, however. Vonny felt glass and plastic sprinkled on her scalp. She chanced a look through her fingertips: the console was spiderwebbed, the blue light extinguished, the ichor of the LCD display bleeding out through the shards of glass. But the music didn't stop.

Vonny saw the gun turn towards her; she braced to run, but Cramond kicked her thigh, and she dropped to the floor. *Get up!* She just about made it out. He must have been screaming. *Up!*

He took her by the scruff of the neck, pulling her to her feet again. He bundled her towards the front door, and opened it, the gun hard against her skull, just behind her right ear. She smelled her hair frying against the hot metal.

Then she screamed, silently. At the front door were two figures. Susie McCracken and PC Whelan.

# 54

'Keep watch,' Seth told Crispin. 'You see someone sneaking up behind me, shout.'

Crispin nodded, and vanished into the treeline.

Seth crept along the edge of the forest until he could see the top floor of the house, clear of obstructions.

The snow still fell, but it was easy enough to make out the lights burning on the top floor. Like a cruise ship, he thought. There was no activity there whatsoever, illuminations aside. Seth glanced across at the front yard. Nothing. Over the top of the fence, he could just see the footprints leading through the snow down the pathway to the back gate.

Dead men's shoes, Seth thought, and shivered.

He had killed men, now – and while his mind couldn't quite process the fact, his body did. Maybe it was the cold; maybe it was the pain; or maybe it was his nerves that caused his hands to tremble. He clutched the handgun, to make the tremor stop. It worked up to a point. Cold hands, cold air, cold metal.

Seth had never fired a handgun in his life. Crispin, who professed to some knowledge in these matters – naturally – told him that his supposition over the safety catch deployment had been correct.

His stomach lurched as he moved; everywhere hurt, every piece of muscle, every gap between his ribs; then he thought of Vonny, and stole forward. It hurt to crouch; his knee had crossed beyond the turnstile of pain and into a worrying numbness. He couldn't put much weight on it. Seth had seen enough five-a-side football injuries to know that this could be a big problem.

*Save it for later.*

Wincing slightly, he glanced over the fence. The front gate was about thirty yards away, wide open, inviting, big enough to get a bus through, and almost certainly some kind of trap. That was why he'd left Crispin keeping watch, though God knew where he was, now. He stared at his knee, sighed, and doubled back along to the outside corner of the fence, then trailed along to where the dividing wall separated out the front yard from the back garden, swimming pool and patio. The fence was six feet tall. It hadn't been constructed with climbing in mind. Specifically, it hadn't been designed with Seth's damaged knee in mind. Nonetheless, he made sure the pistol's safety catch was on, then scaled the wall.

By Seth's admittedly unOlympian standards, it was a ridiculous effort. He actually cried out, as he tried to gain a foothold, his fingers at the top of the fence, arms straining to take his own weight. *Never much good at pull-ups. Never much of a fan of the gym, either.*

He got up and over, then considered a drop onto his better leg. He considered what weight ratios might do to his other knee upon impact; then something took the decision out of his hands, and he dropped, quickly, to the other side.

That something was the sound of Motörhead. As loud

as it could go – louder, maybe. The entire house seemed to distort or blur in the sonic detonation. For a moment, he saw some movement at the front door.

There were two people at the front door of the house. One tall, one short. They were cast in silhouette by the full brightness of the main lights in the hallway, but Seth thought he recognised Susie McCracken. He crept closer, when he was aware of some change in the light; or perhaps it was an interruption in the patter of the slanting snow, a flaw in the weave cast from behind him. Whatever it was that alerted Seth, he paid attention to it, spun around, and saw Vinnicombe emerging from the caravan at his back.

*That bloody Tin Coffin. The death of me.*

The older man held a shotgun that seemed all too familiar; truncated at an almost identical point, similar stock visible through Vinnicombe's gloved hands. Pointed right at him; and braced perfectly well. Seth's neighbour might have been pleased.

Vinnicombe's lopsided grin threatened to slide off his face. He yelled loud enough to be heard over the music: 'What's that you've got there, pardner?' he said, in a faux accent from a 1950s western. 'That a shootin' iron there? Don't move a muscle, incidentally. Or it's over. Throw it on the deck. Right in front of me. Do it now.'

Seth stared at the gun in his hands, then tossed it into the snow. All of a sudden he felt tired, rather than frightened, or sick, or adrenalised. He had simply had enough. He missed the relative peace of the forest. *When I get out of this, I'll do some forest bathing. A nice, quiet stretch with the foliage for a mattress. Springy moss. Bliss.*

Seth raised his hands, but held his ground.

'Over here, I said,' Vinnicombe yelled. 'Scoot on over, son.'

Seth limped forward. Vinnicombe kept Seth covered, then kicked the handgun far away into the snow. 'I'm going to assume you took care of Jay,' he said, nodding towards the gun. 'I hope you did him properly. Never liked the boy. Thuggish, you know?'

Before Seth could open his mouth to reply, Vinnicombe's arms blurred, ending in a terrific crack on the jaw.

Seth's lower face seemed to bisect, flexing and straining fit to break at the corners. The snow tried to kiss it better on the side of the head as he fell. He'd been hit with the shotgun, or the stock of it. Seth had barely seen the older man move.

'Yeah,' Vinnicombe went on, casually, as if nothing had happened, 'I thought I would have to take care of him. Plan was to take him out the play, and grab the stuff for myself. Or at least, my share. I never made much of Jay, and as for our man in the house... he promises, but he doesn't deliver. Lot of talk. Tough guy. But doesn't have the nous, you know?' Vinnicombe actually tapped his own temple with the barrel of the shotgun, as he might have tapped it with his finger. 'Didn't have the *knowledge*. Typical gaffer, you know? All plans, no practice.'

Seth sat up. Vinnicombe delivered a sharp, ugly kick into his side, right in the centre of a waystation for his nervous system. It might have been luck, or it might have been some unspeakable expertise, but Seth's entire body seized up as if struck by a lightning bolt; he jerked in the snow, and screamed out, along with Lemmy in the background.

'Yeah,' Vinnicombe went on, breezily. 'I'll say this to you, because I think it really is your last chance. It's a good offer. I'm good for it, you know? The only chance you and your missus in there have of still breathing after tonight is if you tell me, right now, where you have stashed the gear. Me personally. As a token of goodwill, I won't shoot you. If you give the stuff to me, then I will kill the boss in there, and be on my way. You can spin it to the cops however you want, but it'll be as if I was never here. You can claim the win, if you like. Say you were the hero. Now you can't say fairer than that, my friend. Given your current predicament. And believe me, son, when I say: I won't make any idle threats. I'll just kill you if you refuse. So what do you say?'

Seth got onto one knee; a trail of drool stretched out towards the snow. His body was coming to a decision, whether or not to retch, and then the stubby shotgun barrel was brought down onto his knee – his good knee, as an extra insult.

'Come on! Make a decision, big man. Make it a good one. Because I'll level with you, I reckon I've had enough of this gig. And it's cold.'

'Let me consider that a minute,' Seth wheezed. He began to crawl, heading away from Vinnicombe, moving over to the western side of the lawn. He moved as fast as he could, arm over arm.

Vinnicombe laughed aloud, a reedy, unpleasant sound, even as 'The Ace Of Spades' moved onto the second song, 'Love Me Like A Reptile'. Seth glanced towards the house; there was no sign of Susie or the tall, gangly man he'd seen at the front door. The door itself was closed.

'Where you going, pal?' Vinnicombe said. 'Escaping? Sunbathing?'

'Just needed to stretch my legs,' Seth said, wheezing. 'Got to keep supple. Key to good joints.'

'Mate, I'll shoot you. I'll pop you from here. Stop. Don't waste your time.'

'It's OK,' Seth said, turning around and sitting up. 'I'm done. And so are you.'

The light changed. The flow of the snowfall was diverted. And the noise of the wheels had finally overridden the sound of Motörhead.

Vinnicombe spun around, in time to see the raised silver lettering spell out APACHE before the caravan smashed him to the ground and rolled over the top of him.

It hit him head-on, and threw him into the snow. The caravan barely slowed as it crushed him underneath; there was a jaunty flip, such as a loosened colt might perform, before the caravan continued onwards. Seth had an impression of Vinnicombe's craggy face, eyes wide, mouth open in utter, fatal astonishment; then he went under.

Seth gazed at the caravan as it careered past him, its momentum proving Vinnicombe correct in his earlier assessment. Seth might have been looking at a flying saucer making a pass over the top of the house, or a brontosaurus lumbering past him in somewhat stately fashion.

It gained a little more speed before hitting the house. The metal struts halted its progress, but at least two of the immense ground-floor windows were gone in a near-phosphorescent shower of diamond shards in the snow.

Seth got to his feet, slowly. Both knees, now.

'Bastard,' he said, spitting into the snow. He approached the tufted material that denoted the body in the snow, directly underneath the furrows ploughed in the snow by the wheels. He gazed at Vinnicombe's face, turned slightly towards him. The man was dead, hands curled into claws, his throat and chest cavity horribly flattened out, like pounded dough.

Crispin trotted down the ski-trail progress of the wheels down the driveway into the snow.

The boy looked like he wanted to burst into tears, and Seth felt the need to comfort him, calm him down. Just a kid.

'You uncouple the caravan from its berth?' Seth asked. 'You did that?'

The boy nodded. 'I am so, so, sorry about your windows. I didn't mean for that to happen...'

'Never mind that, son,' Seth said. 'We've got to get in that house. There's one left.'

Then the music, and the lights, cut out in the house. The sudden silence was shocking. Seth cringed, completely exposed in the front of the house. The glare might have prevented anyone from seeing him inside; now, he would have been obvious to anyone watching.

'Grab that clown's shotgun,' he hissed. 'And help me find Jay's gun – the one I threw over there.'

'Don't bother,' came a new voice. 'Both of you, stay where you are, and keep your hands where I can see them.'

Wherever Leonard, the police officer, had chosen for a hiding place, it had been a good one. Now he strode across the lawn, padding confidently through the snow. His progress wasn't the steadiest, but his aim with the pistol was. He moved it between Seth and Crispin, picking them out expertly in darting, lizard-like movements. 'You, Junior Commando – get over there beside him. Right now. And how about you tell me what's going on here, Seth?'

# 55

Cramond yanked Vonny to the side; she rebounded against a wall, crying out. It was lost in the thudding music.

He pointed the gun at Susie and Whelan. Their expressions matched.

'Get inside,' Cramond yelled. 'Now!'

They complied, hands up. Whelan seemed to have difficulty walking; he stumbled forward like a new-born foal.

Cramond stepped back, the better to keep the three of them covered. He gestured to Susie to shut the front door, which she did.

'Now you, beanpole – you see that fuse box? Turn everything off.'

Still on the floor, Vonny saw the look of utter fear on Whelan's face. Pity for the young officer gave her a new, strange impetus. Poor boy, she thought. Utterly terrified.

'This one?' Whelan had flipped over the fuse box, on the wall opposite the front door.

'All of them!' Cramond shrieked. 'Right now!'

Whelan did as he was bid, and the house was silenced; and plunged into darkness.

Vonny thought to make a dash for one of the spare rooms; Cramond anticipated this, and the gun barrel stabbed into her shoulder. 'Now that the noise is over... Let's head into the kitchen. I think I recognise you, young lady,' Cramond said, returning to his previous condescending manner, a middle manager at a company barbecue. 'Yes, we've spoken, haven't we?'

Susie cleared her throat, and composed herself before saying: 'Whatever's going on here... It's over. You must see that. There's the front door – get out. Leave. Just split. The cops are *here*.'

'I don't see any cops,' Cramond said. 'Unless he's one. Which I doubt. I think I can see piss running down his leg.' Whelan actually whimpered, as Cramond turned to him and Susie. 'Here's what will happen. You two – get down on the floor. Face down, hands over the backs of your heads.'

Whelan followed the instructions to the letter, burying his face in the carpet. 'Do what he says,' he said, voice trembling on the top note. 'Follow his instructions.'

'Shut up,' Susie grumbled. But she followed suit. Her eyes locked with Vonny's. Did she have a plan? Something up her sleeve?

But all Vonny could think to do was shake her head. They were helpless.

'Starting with the girl, I'm going to shoot bits off them. I'll give my man a call. He's out there with your man. You can tell him what's happening. Let's make it a live broadcast. That might help jog his memory. Apparently he's having trouble finding my gear.'

Cramond pulled out a mobile and dialled, still keeping the gun on Vonny. They all heard the dialling tone. No response. Cramond frowned. Then there was a flickering outside the front door; a change in the light, nothing more.

Then, concussion; the windows along the east side exploded; the house shook.

Cramond hesitated for a second, in as much shock as the rest of them. Vonny frowned...

He had dropped his gun.

As he darted forward to retrieve it, Vonny saw her chance, running for the staircase. 'Pick a room! Split up! He can't follow us all!' she screamed.

Following the curve of the staircase, clothes still sodden and clinging to her, sudden uplift in cold, everything electric; and she had to be quick because he actually fired at her. She heard the thunderclap, saw the stairs spit at her; realised the expectoration had splinters and shards in it, red pepper mist across her arm, shrapnel from the gunshot.

She did not stop. Cramond fired again – a close thing this time, something patting the outside of her right thigh and poking a hole in the wall. Once more around the curve, and she was on the balcony. His footsteps, right behind her. Below, Susie's face, stricken, calling out to her, even as the tall lad dragged her away out of the door. Long drop. Designed that way. Vonny would take her chances. She placed her hand on the balcony. Felt something; remembered something; then stopped.

Cramond had her covered as he reached the top. He was angry now. He pointed a gun at her but looked as if he would keep on going, piling right over the top of her. She set her jaw; she stayed standing. She did not raise her hands.

Cramond jammed the gun underneath her chin. 'Any last requests?'

'You've lost. You're going to jail. That's if you don't get shot. Leave me in peace. I had nothing to do with it. Nothing.'

He removed the gun from her throat. 'You're probably right. I knew I should have gone with your lump of a man. He'll break, all right. No question.'

'He won't break,' Vonny said. 'But you're about to.'

Then she launched herself at him.

He managed to throw up a hand to ward her off; the one with the gun in it. He did not fire. Vonny threw her arms around Cramond's neck, planted one foot on the balcony floor, then arched backwards, using her weight, using the element of surprise.

Seeing the balcony approaching, Cramond used his spare hand to brace himself against it, and shifted his weight onto the standing leg. Assuming the metalwork rushing towards him was fixed in place. Braced for an impact that never came.

The balcony simply fell away, just as Seth had feared it would. A tinkle of screws fell alongside them as they plunged towards the stone bench by the water feature. Just over three metres to fall, head-first, not even long enough to scream, but long enough. They both fell, Vonny's limbs entwined with his.

Then impact. Then silence.

# 56

Whelan dragged Susie outside. When he turned around, he shrieked. There were three people stood in front of them in the snow. Whelan recognised one of them.

'Sir,' he said, 'that's gunfire – there's a suspect in the house. We think he's...'

'Settle down,' Leonard said, and that's when Susie and Whelan noticed the gun.

Whelan saw the significance now in Susie's earlier observation. He raised his hands. Susie misread it; misread Seth's tense expression, despite the wreckage of his face, and that of the bulging-eyed boy who appeared to have smeared himself with army camouflage make-up. 'The guy you want's in there!' Susie cried. 'He's got Vonny!'

'Get out of the way,' Seth said. When he hobbled forward through the snow, his face compressed into tight lines and sharp angles, and he hissed through his teeth, clearly in pain.

'Stop where you are,' Leonard said.

'Shoot me if you have to, dickhead,' Seth said, and tore open the door.

It was dark and silent inside. The water feature was stilled thanks to the electricity being off. On the black marble slabs in front of the fountain, two bodies were entwined.

'Oh no, no, no, no!' Seth lurched forward; he fell before he reached them.

Behind them, Whelan flipped open the fuse box and pulled the switch. The lights came back on. Perhaps mercifully, Motörhead did not.

The two bodies sprawled across the black marble were those of Cramond and Vonny. They were frozen in a dance, arms and legs splayed, heads lolling. Vonny's head rested on the edge of the slab, her cheek against Cramond's bent knee. Water pooled under her chin.

As Seth sank to his knees, she blinked.

Seth scooped her up. She sobbed and wailed when she saw him; they held each other tight.

Behind them, Susie, Whelan, Crispin and Leonard came forward, Leonard with the gun in his hand. Crispin looked back for a moment. Leonard said: 'Good Lord, is that a crossbow?'

Crispin nodded. 'I know how to use them. They're legit.'

'I'll decide what's legit, Robin of Loxley,' Leonard said, as a grin carved open his face. The gun he held on the boy was, however, deadly serious. 'Put it down on the floor, and get up against that back wall. On the double. Whelan, and his blushing bride-to-be – join him. Make friends. Link hands if you like.'

Whelan said: 'Sir, we believe there was a kidnapping situation here. Miss McCracken and I came over, and...'

'Shut your trap or I'll put some holes in it,' Leonard said tersely.

Whelan did as he was told, gazing helplessly at Susie.

Leonard, keeping the gun low but maintaining a

convenient angle to turn the gun on anyone in front of him, came close to Vonny and Seth.

'He had a gun on me,' Vonny babbled, against Seth's chest. 'He had lost the plot. He wanted drugs. He was going to kill us, whether he got them or not. Him and the other men. There are two others out there...'

Seth hugged her closer still – a gesture of warmth and tenderness, ostensibly, but Vonny instantly understood what he meant. *Keep schtum.*

Leonard cocked his head and stared at Cramond's – perhaps in mock imitation of the angle of the latter's own posture. Cramond's neck was twisted like an action figure's, and his sightless eyes and wide-open jaw were all the proof required that he was dead. He had landed on his head, and Vonny's weight on his back, added to the impact on the black marble, had finished matters. Conveniently for Vonny, his body had absorbed most of the shock of the fall. Vonny was dazed, frightened, freezing cold and wet to the skin, but alive and unharmed.

'You did a number on old Cramond,' Leonard said. 'No doubt about that. Well.'

'There were two others,' Vonny said, 'a stocky, heavily built one, and a little guy who looks like, I don't know, a pleasure boater or something, older guy...'

'The older guy's name is Vinnicombe, and he's stone dead, love. Had a disagreement with a caravan, of all the things. Had his guts squeezed out. Nasty. And I think I saw Jay's body bobbing around in the lake, just at the back of the woods. Clever move to put a body in water. That what you did with the other two boys, Seth?'

'We don't know what you're talking about,' Seth said.

'Our house was invaded. We've defended ourselves. There are witnesses.' He nodded towards Crispin, Whelan and Susie. 'They've seen and heard everything. Then there's you.'

Leonard tutted. 'That's true. Absolutely right. That's the problem, isn't it? I'll have to figure something out, here.'

Then Leonard felt the shotgun touch his back. He flinched – then stopped.

'Drop that gun,' said a polite, but firm voice.

Fulton, the farmer, had crept in at his back through the front door. None of them had made a sound as he had crept in behind them, a finger to his lips, the long-barrelled shotgun slowly brought down to bear. They hadn't even moved their eyes.

'Do it quickly. If I stick both barrels into you, then your best outcome is being a hemiplegic. And I don't think that's your preferred option, is it, sir?'

'I'm a police officer,' Leonard stammered, trying to turn his head to get a good look at the newcomer.

'Armed police?' Fulton asked. 'That's a very strange-looking weapon to have, even if you are an armed police officer. Which you aren't. Drop it. Throw it across the floor. Now.'

Leonard let it fall out of his hands. Fulton stepped forward, using the gun barrel to push Leonard forward, then kicked the gun into a corner. 'You're making a big mistake,' Leonard said.

'Am I?' Fulton said. 'In what way?'

'We have a very odd situation here, and you're making it ten times harder.' The tension was clear in Leonard's voice. There was anger in it, as well as fear, and this gave it a rough edge. 'Throw your own gun down and let's talk about what's happening here.'

'Call the police,' Susie said. She turned to Whelan. 'Put a call in, now. That'll get to the bottom of it.'

'Don't,' Leonard said. 'Nobody do anything. Whelan, take your phone out and throw it on the floor. You too, lass. And Action Man over there. If you've got one, drop the phones.'

'Sir?' Whelan looked from one face to the other – seeing conspirators, all of a sudden.

'You should do what he says,' Fulton said, with the tone of a games teacher who might have seen someone with athletic talent. 'This is fascinating. A little strange that I'm responding to your orders, when I've got the gun. All the same, it gives me an idea.' Fulton's gaze fell upon Vonny and Seth, particularly the latter. 'Good Lord, old man... What's happened to you? You look like something I snagged in my combine harvester.'

'Long story,' Seth said. 'I'll live.'

'You just might. And you, my treasure... Please tell me no one's hurt you.'

'I'm fine,' Vonny said. 'Now please, for the love of God, get the police round here. I want this nightmare over with, now.'

'Of course,' Fulton said. 'Now, our senior police officer, you pick up the phone. The one closest to you. Doesn't matter which. Come on – your move, old bean. Pick it up. That's right.'

Looking uncertain, Leonard picked up Whelan's phone.

'Now, it'll have an emergency function on it, although I'm

sure the tall poppy here won't mind giving us his security code, if there's a problem.'

'I can't see one,' Leonard said.

'It's the big red button on the right-hand side,' Whelan said, helpfully. 'Just press it and it'll make the call.'

Leonard smiled. Then he let the phone drop to the floor.

'He's not going to call for back-up,' Susie McCracken said. 'He could have done it half an hour ago, but he didn't do it then, either. That tells me one thing. He's in on it. He's on the force, but he's dirty. I don't think Whelan is – he deliberately recruited the dumbest policeman I've ever met as his sidekick on this job. And maybe that was the point.' She turned to Whelan, and whispered: 'Sorry.'

Returning to Leonard, Susie said: 'You're in on this, whatever it is.' She addressed Seth. 'What was it – drugs in the car? The one you found?'

'I don't know what you're talking about,' Seth said – in a listless tone that implied the exact opposite.

'Your bollocks,' Susie said. 'Sorry, you're a nice guy, but you're an awful liar. I heard gunshots, here. Then I saw this guy here carrying a gun out of an action movie. Detectives don't carry guns. So why don't you talk us through it?'

Leonard pressed his hands together as if in prayer, and looked towards the atrium, foamed over completely with snow. 'Now, look, folks. We can all very calmly work something out.'

'Oh, I think I've done that for you,' Fulton said. He levelled the gun at Leonard. Everyone held their breath; Fulton had the satisfaction of fear in the other's eyes, and a mumbled entreaty that sputtered out. 'Over there, with the other two,' he said. 'Stand just apart from them. Thank you. Everyone, keep their hands in the air.'

'We can come out of this smiling,' Leonard said. 'Everyone.'

Fulton nodded absently. Backing up and turning slightly, he asked Vonny, gently: 'Is that the man who hit my wife?'

Vonny nodded, as he gestured towards Cramond's broken body.

'Pity.' He sighed. 'I should have enjoyed killing him. I should thank you for doing the job. Prill's awfully upset, back at the house. Not badly hurt. All the same, it's upsetting.'

'He was a psycho. They all were. I regret nothing. I regret…' She choked on the last word. She did regret. She regretted it already. She would hear Cramond's last scream, and the awful crack that silenced it, for the rest of her life.

'Quite,' Fulton said, as he picked his way over the remains of the balcony. 'I have to say – that bannister was a bad job, Seth.'

'Sorry. Didn't get round to fixing it,' Seth said, his face blank. 'I've been awful busy.'

'This his gun?' Fulton asked, deftly scooping up the weapon no one had noticed.

'Yeah,' Vonny said. 'He let a few rounds off… He missed me. I think he missed me…' She began to tear at her sleeve and the leg of her trousers, frantically searching for a wound. 'I mean it was close, but he didn't hit me. I think.'

'You're fine.' Fulton weighed up the gun in his free hand. Vonny noticed he had thick green gardener's gloves on. 'If he'd hit you with this, you'd know it, all right. They do a lot of damage, these things.'

'Make sure the safety's on,' Leonard said.

'I can't be sure it is,' Fulton said. 'Let's find out.' Then he fired the pistol.

Everyone ducked; Vonny, and possibly Whelan screamed.

But Leonard screamed harder. He was on the floor, holding what was left of one foot. A red explosion below it had detonated across the carpet, a scarlet star gone supernova. Blood seeped out from between his fingers. Vonny covered her face, and turned away. Seth stood in front of her, hands raised. Leonard remembered to scream.

'It appears the safety was off,' Fulton said, with an expression of mild surprise showing through a fine veil of smoke. 'Awfully loud, those things. Louder than you'd expect from the television. You can hear them for miles. Do pipe down, inspector. You're not going to die. Unless you go into shock. Try not to go into shock – it'll ruin things if you die.'

'What's going on here?' Seth said.

'I think Leonard, here, is after the same thing I've been after. The thing that was promised to me by Dan Grainger, for safekeeping. The Grail haul. Heroin, isn't it? Lots of heroin. At least eight figures' worth. We were quite close, Dan Grainger and I. Had our disputes – what neighbours don't? – but we trusted each other and got very friendly. He asked me a favour, and I was prepared to grant him it. He wanted to hide his drugs in a pile of dung. Might throw the dogs off the scent, you see. In return he guaranteed me a percentage. Now I won't lie, I'm not poor, but farming is a fragile game. I'm sure you see my predicament. You have to diversify these days. So I did. I was prepared to help.

'But then he had a better idea. Except he didn't tell me

what it was, which is a shame, because Inspector Leonard here, and the other lads we see strewn around this estate, in one state or another, got to Dan and his son and killed him. But they didn't find out where the stuff was. I assumed it was off-site. He did mention a car – a classic car. Datsun Cherry. My brother-in-law had one, you know. Anyway, when that car was found, and Seth here became all evasive, I knew there was a chance to make good on what I was promised. Now, here we all are. Where's the stuff? Crispin – you know where, don't you?'

Crispin slowly nodded. In the light, his camouflage make-up was somewhat terrifying, stark under the lights. 'Yes, I do.'

'That's good. Crispin is a good lad, you see. Amenable to reason. Bit strange, but who isn't, these days? Crispin, you're going to get it for us in a bit.'

Leonard had gone bone-white; he seemed faint; Susie McCracken ran to him and tore off her jacket, wrapping it around his foot. Her hand and the jacket were instantly sodden with blood.

'He needs to go to hospital, now,' Susie said.

'Not yet. He'll live, as I said. Just support his head, there. He looks a little faint. First, we'll talk deals. Then we'll get our stories straight about who fired what gun, and where. Who wants to start with the bidding?'

'Me,' Seth said, numbly. 'I've got a little brother. That's priority one.'

'Now we're showing sense,' Fulton said, grinning.

Vonny began to sob.

# Epilogue

## RAFFLE HOUSE SOLD
### By Susie McCracken

The fairy-tale story continues for Vonny and Seth.

Pictured here in the parlour of their completely refurbished house, Britain's luckiest couple popped the bubbly as they celebrated selling the pile they won in a raffle – to their next door neighbours. Clive and Prill Fulton (pictured inset) stepped in to buy the plot of land from the lucky couple. And Clive said: 'In a way it's a shame – we'd formed a close bond in a short space of time. But the plot is one we've always admired and it was a delightful opportunity to expand the farm – with luxury accommodation for visitors thrown in.'

'We're gutted to be going,' Vonny admitted, 'but if anyone can make this plot work for them, it's Clive and Prill, and we were delighted to give them the opportunity to buy the land.'

Although everyone is tight-lipped about the value of the private deal between the two parties, it is understood that Vonny and Seth are now millionaires.

The house at Brenwood Green is familiar from a series of tragedies and notorious incidents, including the murder-suicide of well-known businessman Dan Grainger and his two sons, and then the shootout that saw hero cop Noel Leonard disarm and kill an entire drugs gang single-handedly, a feat for which he is rumoured to be in line for the George Cross.

'Some not so nice memories,' Seth admitted, 'but we'll always be glad that we had our dream house, however long.'

This story also marks the last of this reporter's career with this newspaper. I will now spend some time travelling, but I'd like to place on record my thanks to Detective Inspector Leonard for saving my life, and also my admiration for Vonny and Seth's fortitude in the wake of a terrible event, as they head off for a new life in the sun.

'I'm building a new dream house,' Vonny said. 'I'll start from scratch. We'll do it all over again.'

In other news, it has emerged that a quantity of drugs was what the two rival gangs who clashed in Brenwood Green were looking for. This was recovered by Noel Leonard shortly before he was shot and wounded in the face-off at the house. It is understood to have an estimated street value of around £25,000.

# Acknowledgements

Thanks to old friends and new friends - Robbie and Justin, and Holly and Greg. A tip of the hat once more to Helena and the rest of the editorial team at HoZ for picking up on my errors and helping to turn out a smoother dram. And special thanks to the bloggers – too many to mention – who do it for the love of books.

# About the Author

P.R. BLACK lives in Yorkshire with his wife and children. He is the author of five thrillers for Head of Zeus, including *The Beach House*, *The Family*, *The Long Dark Road* and *The Runner*.